Hell, Inc.

At the end of this book get a sneak peek at Book 2

Hell to Pay

Novels by DICK WYBROW

THE HELL INC SERIES

Hell inc.

Hell to Pay

Hell Raisers

The InBetween

The Night Vanishing

Past Life

Copyright © Dick Wybrow 2018

www.dickwybrow.com

Edited by Crystal Watanabe www.pikkoshouse.com

For my wife, Tiffany.

You always ask, so here's your answer.

This.

This is how much.

Hell, Inc.

a novel by

Dick Wybrow

Prologue

In the beginning, God cheated.

Looking at it objectively, to be fair, it'd be hard not to see that Satan got a raw deal. Not that he knew it.

At least, not at first.

Sure, there were several hundred million worlds in the universe where, over thirteen billion plus years, the Devil had begun to exert his supreme dark powers.

One example: He'd held final sway on the planet of Nal'tan, commanding and controlling its inhabitants. But the most advanced life form on that water planet was, by all accounts, a species of bitter starfish.

Where was the fun in that?

And, in fact, they'd been rather moody even before the Dark Lord picked up that planet, so what was the point?

And the gas giant, Phutatu-lit?

God had pretty much given up that planet without a fight, and Satan begrudgingly welcomed a microscopic, translucent amoeba to his evil ranks. And while, granted, these single-celled organisms could be categorized as "predatory," in a good ol' head-to-head Good versus Evil battle, they basically did fuck all but stain the shag carpet.

Now, on the other end of the scale, the hyper-advanced civilizations were also of little help to either God or the Devil because most of them had long since discovered the existence of the domains of Heaven and Hell through a combination of quantum physics, federally mandated employer holiday allotments, and budget travel websites.

On the whole, both chief magistrates of Good and Evil require belief and not, actually, outright knowledge of their existences. Belief fuels both Hope and Fear equally—they are the unique and powerful currency for the worlds above and below.

Surety, on the other hand, collapses Hope and Fear into Complacency and Resignation. Mere scraps to gods of all sorts.

As the Devil once expressed it at a quarterly board meeting, "Turning truly advanced minds to evil seemed to have so much promise. Like an old woman with Parkinson's giving you a hand job. But in the end, it was disappointingly unsatisfying and just left little red welts from the cheap costume jewelry."

But there was a zone, a "Goldilocks" intelligence/advancement zone—not too dumb and not too bright.

And laying smack dab in the middle of it was Earth.

Earth!

What a prize!

Not too civilized to dismiss (or possibly litigate itself out of) the influence of God or Devil and just advanced enough be the charging infantry of either side.

What fun!

Now, the same rules apply for gods, angels, demons, and so on as they do for the natural-born creatures that live in the universe: relativity and all its little inbred country cousins.

That's where the trick lied.

That's where the secret was buried.

And that's how God got one over the Devil, right from the start—taking ownership of the Earth, quietly knowing it could never truly fall into Satan's hands.

This is the story of Raz Frewer and how he inadvertently screwed all that up.

However, he had a very good excuse.

Chapter One

The wind gust hit me like a drunk stepfather, and I fell forward.

On all fours and exhausted, I struggled to keep from collapsing into the pools of rain in the long, shallow trenches time had clawed out of the dirt road beneath me.

The hidden beasts beyond the clouds were still tossing their electric balls to one another like some threat. I knew somewhere in my head it was just lightning, however, they now seemed content to limit their play to the part of the sky behind the dark man.

Naturally I couldn't see his face, which was probably the point. Asshole probably thought it made him look cool or something, all backlit and spooky.

And I dunno... it kinda did.

Craning my neck up to look at him, I tried to pull his face, an expression, out of the darkness but didn't try too hard. His was a face you weren't supposed to see unless everything went real bad. Thankfully, when the sky flashed, all I could make out was the brim of his hat.

He may have spoken by that point. I don't remember.

"Either way," I answered. "I don't..." I collapsed into a coughing fit. He waited until I was done, mainly because it seemed like he enjoyed watching me experience this very basic discomfort.

Maybe it reminded him of old times or early days. The simple pleasures.

Because it doesn't seem like the Devil on Day One was all about burning souls for all eternity and all that. First morning on the job, he probably drummed up a couple hay-fever attacks, maybe someone got popcorn stuck in their teeth with no floss handy, a couple of light bruisings.

I lifted myself back off the road.

The only things that moved were his hands as they slowly manipulated the top of his walking stick. Where the stick met the road, there was some meshing or a bumper that stopped it from digging too deep into the Mississippi mud.

Then, I tried again: "I don't know how it... works."

Pitiful as it was, this made him laugh—an awful sound that trailed off into the sky, folding itself into a roll of thunder. This made the damp, dead grass tremble, and for a brief moment individual blades shed fat drops of rain; the ground on either side of the road appeared to burst with starlight.

Then, dark again.

"Seriously, man—" I said.

"Of course, you *know* how it works," he said. "That's why you came." Silent for a moment, I could feel his eyes on me, taking me in. "What's your name, boy?"

"I dunno... I thought you'd know that."

With a twitch of his hand, he lifted his walking stick, and through the torrent of rain, I felt a dull throb of pain where my neck met my skull. It rose like a fever and then washed over me.

"Don't fuck with me," he said flatly, as if he'd just ordered a cheese sandwich or something. "Me, I know your real name. The names you had before you were born to this shithole, that is. Hell, y'all don't even know that much. What do they call you 'round here, is what I was asking. What is your name?"

"Raz," I said. "My mother called me Rasputin. Named after some—"

"Shut up. Don't care."

"Got it."

"Raz," he said, a smile in his voice. "Ha! That is one fucked-up name you got. Goes well with your fucked-up life, I suppose. And your fucked-up wife."

My fists turned to balls, and this time I looked up at him, caught his eyes. I wanted to hit him. But I knew better. At least, I knew now was not the time. Not when I needed something from the prick.

That aside, who throws a punch at the Devil?

That seemed like a lose-lose scenario to me, so I kept my knuckles buried deep into the Mississippi muck.

The dark man let out a big breath of air, like he'd been holding it for a long while. It stank like he'd been licking a dog's ass half the day, then ate a corndog found in the back of a refrigerator three months past its sell-by date and washed it down with some warm Clamato.

Couldn't hit the guy, but I could at least rag on him. If only in my mind.

"Okay, so, me I'm not an accountant or anything," he said, his words tumbling down onto my head, "but… I don't have to be. Got a *fuckload* of accountants. Christ, we're up to our collective assholes in accountants, truth be told. And lawyers. And more recently, corporate 'brand ambassadors.'"

By the way, no joke, the Dark Lord of the Underworld, Satan himself, *actually* used air quotes with his long fingers when he said that last bit.

"Whatever," I said. "Like I care about your overcrowding issues. Just tell me: What do I have to do?"

The stick went up again, but he didn't strike me. Instead he said: "If you'd just— Damn it, your kind does not listen! That's your big problem. Everything's about you, you, and you."

My arms were weakening, so I locked them to prevent myself from collapsing, but I couldn't hold my head up any longer. Dropping it, my chin hit my chest, and I closed my eyes and listened as the rain poured down my face.

"Gotta check what it's worth," he said. "What you're puttin' up here—barter, right? That's the plan?"

He stood up to leave, and I snapped my head to where he'd been sitting earlier. He was gone from the stump.

"Right," I said. "Yes, that's the plan."

"You'll know," he said, standing next to me now. "We'll have one of our people reach out."

I nodded, then nodded harder so he was sure. "Yes, yes. Whatever, *yes!*"

He chuckled, the laugh dry and heartless. "You don't even know the deal yet, but you're already saying yes to some accord?"

"Yes, yes," I said, spitting out water and snot. Raising my head, I still couldn't see his face. My eyes wide, I said again: "Yes."

He took a few steps, but I couldn't tell which direction.

"Don't work that way, Raz. Wish it did, but there are rules," he said. "But let's say you and me, we've got a tentative agreement. You gotta sign off on the final still."

My chest began heaving. I was sobbing. "Yes! Christ, yes! I'll do it."

For the first time, I saw a part of his face. Just his mouth, really. He smiled wide. "Not yet. But real, real soon. It will all come together real soon."

I yelled with what little strength I had left. "You... but you promise to do *your part*? That's how it works, right?"

"Sure, of course. As long as you meet the terms. Need to run the numbers, and then—"

"Just save her," I screamed at the smug prick. "It's eating her up from the inside, and you fucking probably put it there in the first place."

"You lookin' to blame someone for your wife dying, you gotta look up, not down, little brother. Not my thing, Raz."

Leaning on an elbow, I cocked my finger and pointed at him. "This is *exactly* your thing!"

"There are concentric circles, sure, but... nah. I don't get into that line of work. Me, I'm more of a global mover."

He was gone again, slipping away from my sight, my outstretched hand just hanging out there in the rain. A moment later, I felt his breath on my neck.

"Listen, you know what they say about pointing fingers?" he said, grabbing mine with a hand that was both ice cold and warm. His other hand, bone white, appeared in front of my face.

With that hand he merely pointed at my forehead as if it were a gun, then pulled back his thumb, cocking the hammer. "When you point a finger at somethin', you got three pointing back… and one at God."

The rain stopped as if a spigot had been twisted shut. There was a final low rumble off in the sky somewhere, but the lightning was gone.

Then everything turned black as a deep, deep hole in every direction.

Finally collapsing, wet gravel dug into my cheek but before I passed out, his voice drifting toward me one last time.

"My people… they'll reach out sometime tomorrow. Then the clock will be ticking, Raz. You better get your rest."

And with that, I was seconds away from passing out in the middle of a lonely, rain-soaked dirt highway in bumfuck Mississippi.

Some "Crossroads."

Not that it mattered. I had already proven them wrong! They said she couldn't be saved.

They said "say goodbye to her" and things like "it's just her time."

They said there was nothing that could be done, and they were wrong.

Wrong!

At least… shit.

I damn well hope they were wrong.

Upon brief reflection, as I passed out shivering and coughing, it occurred to me that I may not have thoroughly considered the totality of my actions before green-lighting my plan.

I had just made a deal with the Devil to save my dying wife. Me.

Damn.

Chapter Two

The next morning, I woke up slowly, frying under the Mississippi sun and caked with Mississippi dirt.

Given the circumstances—that is, if evolutionary forces had been aligned in my favor—one might have guessed that, sensing imminent danger, I'd have instantly sprung up, crouching like a tiger dragon, ready to test my fight-or-flight instincts.

But no.

I'd fallen asleep, lying facedown on a muddy highway in rural Mississippi, and my mind was slowly drifting back into my skull as if I had no cares in the world.

As if there was nothing that should concern me. Nothing at all.

Like the fact that I was lying facedown on a muddy highway in rural Mississippi.

Ultimately, it wasn't the sun beating down hard that finally woke me. A deplorably early riser, the sun had already been up for hours.

I wasn't even stirred by the binaural hum in my left ear, which turned out to be two small black flies that had found a dark place to express their forbidden love.

And it wasn't the choking dust, which had risen up again after the sun had burnt away last night's rain. That put the humidity somewhere around what you might expect to find if you tested the gap between the plastic seat and the taint of a 350-pound NASCAR fan during the final lap of the Daytona 500.

No, what actually pulled me from sleep's embrace was the sensation that my balls were being jiggled.

And it seemed, for the first time in months, I wasn't the jiggler.

It took me a full ten seconds to finally process all this, but when I did, my body instinctively flipped over.

"What the fu—?"

Then I was on my feet, unsteady and momentarily blinded by the sun.

I ached everywhere but managed to swing my arms in the air, hoping whoever had been digging in the front pockets of my shorts would feel the wrath of my fists.

They did not, in fact, feel my fists' wrath.

I stood there, eyes like slits, swinging my arms like an angry drunken orchestra conductor.

A gravelly voice tumbled toward me. "Aww, you ain't dead."

"What?" I said. "No!"

"Shit, I thought you was dead."

Cracking one eye a little farther open and shielding my vision with a dirty hand, I saw an old woman, heavy and sweating, baking in the sun where she stood. Thick, bulky clothes despite the punishing heat.

She looked disappointed.

"Gross," I said. "Weirdo. You normally go around jiggling the balls of seemingly dead men?"

She didn't answer.

Stumbling a few steps out of the road, I found the stump the Dark Man had been sitting on the night before.

"I know this is a bit of a flash judgment on my part," I said to her as she continued staring at me, "but if that's your thing—ball-jiggling dead guys—you've got some deep-seated, emotional fucked-upness that you should probably address with a trained professional."

She didn't answer.

I plunked down onto the stump, and my sore legs briefly loved me as if for the first time. For a man of thirty-two, it didn't seem like I should feel this old yet.

Could be that the previous night's accommodations had been rather lacking.

Could be that many of my thirty-two were "hard-livin' years" as George Jones had once put it. Or maybe that was George Thorogood. Possibly George Michael.

"I thought you was dead," she said again. She started walking away, slowly and wobbly, in a way only old women can.

"You already established that little fun fact, ma'am."

"Was looking to see if you had anything… worth having."

"Wait," I said, letting out a deep breath. "You were robbing me?"

Nice. That'd make it the second time in twenty-four hours.

"I thought you was dead."

"That… you know, every time you say those particular words, my thoughts turn a little more violent. I'm not normally, but… you know—"

"You don't got nothing anyhow worth taking," she said, still wobbling away, but she hadn't yet traveled more than a few feet. It must have taken her weeks to make it down the road to get to my balls.

"But you thought digging through my pockets, stealing from me, would be a good way to kick off your morning, huh?"

"Well, I thought you wa—" She cleared her throat. I stood up from the stump to follow her. She was slow, but my best guess was she at least knew the way back toward town. She continued: "You seemed like you wouldn't miss whatever somebody else might find."

The old woman ambled down the middle of the dirt highway. The sun at our backs, I matched her pace but still clung toward the edge of the road.

"I'm just trying to get a feel for the locals," I said, my voice frayed at the edges. "So when you find a guy facedown, instead of, I don't know, calling the police or a doctor… you fine folks jiggle the man's balls."

The buzzing in my ear had suddenly reached a crescendo, and realizing there were two insects having sex in my skull, I violently shook my head back and forth, trying to forcibly evict them from their love nest.

Not the wisest choice. This became clear when I found myself flat on my back, down on the dirt highway again.

Thankfully, in the torrent, the bug lovers had quickly checked out. For a brief moment, I felt a little cheap and used.

I made it back up to my feet, slower this time. The old woman was now about thirty yards ahead of me.

Crazy old bat can move when she wants to, damn.

When I finally caught back up to her, the effort it took drained any last bit of anger from me. We walked silently for a few minutes.

I thought about the previous night. As much as I could say that it seemed like a dream, I knew it was real enough. Having exhausted every effort to save my Carissa, as she'd saved me time and time again, I found I'd had no options left.

In fact, that very scenario had been explained to me in detailed medical terms. But still, when it came to my wife, that wasn't good enough. So I'd ended up at *the* famed Crossroads to make a deal with the Devil.

And it seemed a deal had been struck.

Or a tentative deal.

My part, which was easily established, was wagering my soul. Whatever. Frankly, without Carissa, it didn't seem worth very much anyhow.

The deal—or "accord" as he'd called it, all fancy-like—still wasn't clear. He'd said something about his people getting back to me. Odd.

So in essence, I was only *vaguely* sure that I'd put my everlasting soul on the line, hoping to save my wife from her deadly disease.

Sure, it was selfish, in part. I just didn't see the point of being here if she wasn't around. As I said, she'd saved my life countless times—nearly every precious day we'd had together.

And she was—if you pardon the mushiness and potential irony, given my present circumstances—my soul mate.

If she were gone, I was essentially dead anyhow. It had taken me years to finally realize a humiliating fact about myself: I'm no good on my own.

Seriously.

If it had been me on that deserted island instead of Tom Hanks, I would have died within twenty-four hours. And fuck Wilson because a) he didn't have any hands or anything, so he was no help at all, and b) he was a critical and bitchy little leather asshole. Total downer.

I freely admit the shortcoming, but at least realize my own Achilles heel. Most people never do.

And now the only partner I wanted in the whole world was dying in a hospital bed as I trudged along, frying in the late morning sun, next to an old woman who moments earlier was trying to rob my not-dead body.

Things were not going terribly well.

"How far is it back to town?"

The old woman sighed. "What town you trying to get to?"

"I don't know… any town."

Then she stopped and slowly turned toward me. Staring intently for a moment, she then twisted her head back to where I'd been lying, where she'd found me not dead. She looked back at me. "What the hell was you doin' out here, then? You fall out your car?"

"I don't own a goddamn car, haven't for… It doesn't matter."

Walking again, she said, "And you say I got the deep-seated, emotional fucked-upness. I ain't the one who falls asleep on dirt highways."

"That's not… those aren't my usual accommodations. I passed out," I said. "It was… You wouldn't understand."

"Oh, nah, dumb ol' woman like me wouldn't get you and yo'r big thinkin' ways," she said, all syrup and sass.

"I don't mean it like that. It's just… it's kind of unbelievable."

The old woman chuckled, deep and throaty. "Oh, I understand all right. Didn't realize it at first. Don't get so many out here no mo'," she said and pointed a thumb back over her shoulder. "You thought you was at the Crossroads down here to make a deal with Lucifer hisself, right?"

My mouth opened, and my jaw hung there for a moment, then I closed it and said nothing.

"Boy, they ain't no Crossroads," she said in a manner better suited if she were rocking in an old chair on an old, dilapidated porch. And maybe smoking a pipe. Or whittling. Maybe whittling a pipe. Or smoking a whittle. She added: "That's just a dumb ol' legend some record company made up to sell blues records."

"Okay, whatever."

"Fine, believe whatchu want."

She hadn't been *there* the night before. This woman was someone who attempted to rob not-dead bodies for chrissake! What did she know?

Ahead, through the dust and haze coming off the hot road, I saw the first signs of several buildings. Shops.

Still, my fists were banging off my thighs at how quickly she'd dismissed my incredible, mind-boggling metaphysical experience from the night before.

"So, I *talked* to the guy," I said. "Not that you'd buy that."

"Talked to who?"

"The guy. The Dark Man. I came out here, damn right, to the Crossroads. And he was there, had this wide-brimmed hat. Waiting right there for me."

She was quiet for a moment. "That was probably Randall."

"*No*, it wasn't a guy named Randall!"

"Fine. What'd he look like?"

"What? It was dark. And he's, you know, *the guy*… so you can't see his face. I think."

"You didn't see the man's face?"

"No… 'cause, you can't, right? It's just black."

She shot me a look.

"I mean, it's dark. No light. You can't see."

She nodded slowly. "Sound like Randall."

"*No, no, and NO!* Of all the things that could possibly be anyone called Randall, this guy was none of those things!"

"Uh-huh. So I'm guessin' you came up on a guy in the middle of the highway you didn't know, a face you couldn't see, and you went and said you'd sell him your soul."

"It… it's way, way more complicated than that."

"Yeah?"

"Yes!" I said. "He had this… stick."

"A stick."

"A walking stick. Very powerful. One tap, it sent these… bolts of pain right through me!"

"Right. A stick."

"With… uh, I think it may have, sort of, had a tennis ball on the end of it. For the mud."

"Uh-huh," she said, looking toward me with a mocking, wide-eyed expression. "You right. Stick with a tennis ball on it? That sounds like some *serious* Old Testament shit right there."

"Whatever."

"So spooky!" She put her hands to either side of her mouth very theatrically, and I asked myself if I could live with having punched an old lady. "Boy, sounds like you met the Devil hisself!"

And all signs were pointing to yes.

"Stop talking," I said. "Now. Okay? Please?"

Kicking up little swirls of dirt as we walked in silence, I watched the buildings form before us. One looked to be a diner, and the thought made my stomach growl.

I was hungry and so thirsty it was hard to swallow. Curling the toes of my right foot, I could feel my ID and credit card were still there. Hopefully the card hadn't gotten too wet from last night's storm.

"That there's Wardoff. Sort of, uh, in between spots out here. Not a big place," she said, nodding ahead. "Got a Kmart, though. Hardware store. Diner."

"Great," I said. Then: "Thank you."

She nodded, and with that, we'd made some sort of unspoken peace.

I offered to buy her lunch at the diner—after all, she'd led me back to town— but she said she'd just stick to the road, whatever that meant.

With about ten minutes left of walking before we'd reach town, she coughed something up and spit it out. Cleared her throat.

"So, why would you come all the way out here, risk expirin' in this heat? You obviously ain't used to it. Just to offer up your soul to Randall?"

"It wasn't any guy named Randall."

A small smile bent her lips, and she raised her hands as if surrendering.

"Fine, not Randall," she said, then paused and stopped. Her breathing was a little labored. I guess nobody really gets used to that kind of heat. "Well, hold on, now. You really wanted to make a deal with the Devil, din't you?"

I nodded, eyes closed.

"Boy, why would you even consider that? You talking about your everlasting soul, now, ya hear? For what? For a chance to be a better guitar player or to discover the unified theory or something?"

"No, nothing like th— Wait, what was that last thing?"

"I read the science magazines at the dentist's office. Not much else to do out in these parts."

"Except rob dead guys," I muttered.

She shrugged. "Certainly better than jigglin' their balls."

I laughed, and she gave me a smile. As we walked the final few minutes into town, I explained to her why I was willing to risk my eternal soul.

Chapter Three

The hoses in Alvin Stoddard's '52 Ford pickup seemed older than the truck itself. He stood hunched on the dirt highway, the lower half of his body baking in the Mississippi sun. The top half, while shaded by the rusty hood of his vehicle, was enduring the last gasps of a steam bath.

He waited.

Alvin did a lot of waiting these days.

In a moment, he'd be able to see where the leak had sprung. As he waited, his eyes drifted toward the bent metal rod that propped up the heavy iron hood. A small, tired voice deep in his head whispered. It was a voice that used to be, years ago, more insistent, pleading, but now he knew better. A thick pair of calloused fingers gently stroked the hood prop, then fell away.

Too late for any of that now.

Finally, the steam cleared enough where he could at last see the engine block. As he got to work, the plaintive voice in his head dimmed, shrunk, and drifted back into the darkness.

When he'd been a boy, his uncle taught him things Alvin's father hadn't been around to. At least he did when that skinny, bent-up old man wasn't putting out belly fires with rot-gut whiskey.

"What's that s'posed to do?" Alvin asked once when he was eight.

"Al, tha' there's real special. That is tar tape. Fix everything an' anything," his uncle had explained to Alvin as he fiddled under the hood of his old red truck. "When your mama says she's done with her dressin' for the town ladies, you ask if she got some strips of cloth for ya."

"What do I want cloth for?"

"Well, I'm fixin' to tell you, if you close your trap," his uncle said, grunting as he twisted whatever he was holding. Below them, something *clink-clanked* to the ground. Alvin moved to grab it. "Leave it!"

"Okay."

"Get the cloths from your mama. Then, take ya cloth, and you head to'rd town. When you come across one of them black roads—not dirt, now, like we got 'round here—at the end, where it meets the dirt, you'll find a pile of black stuff."

"That's tar."

Uncle shot him a hard look. "Now, if'n the sun's hot enough, you can push ya cloth down in there and get it good and covered, so's the cloth is black and oily. Like your grandma."

Young Alvin laughed, then put his hand to his mouth.

"Uh, don't tell her I said that," his uncle said. "Now, you got tar tape. Keep it up in a old coffee can, ready for when ya need it. Good for all sorts of stuff." The older man showed young Alvin how, wrapping some ink-black cloth around an old crumbling hose. "Quick fix, see?"

Young boys and young girls needed older folks like family members or neighbors to give them the important life lessons they wouldn't get in school—not that Alvin went to much school back then. With age, wisdom is often imbued upon our elders.

But not always.

You see, Alvin's uncle was an idiot. Alvin realized that years later after the third time the man's moronic tar tape idea burst into flames under the hood of his own car.

Sure, one could argue his uncle had been beta testing for what would become duct tape. A million uses for the stuff.

That kinda tape is a great quick fix for leaky hoses on a vehicle.

What's not good for leaky hoses on a roasting engine block? Tar tape.

It's messy, sticky, and—and this is the important bit—*petroleum* based. In an environment so hot that it will burst into a merit-badge-worthy bonfire under the hood.

But, family is family, and family comes first, although it wasn't entirely clear what that means, unless maybe you're prone to fits of occasional axe-murdering.

Now, under the scorching Mississippi sun, a broken, old body having long ago replaced the boy's, Alvin wrapped the strip of tar tape around the leaky hose and moments later, put the hood back down and climbed inside the truck.

Firing the vehicle back up, he sighed as the numbers instantly started again, tumbling out of the old radio's only working speaker. He didn't bother twisting the dial. All the other stations—at least all the stations he listened to, everywhere and all the time—would be repeating strings of numbers, too.

The volume knob had been snapped off long ago, but it hadn't worked anyhow.

Alvin put it out of his mind as best he could and squinted toward the west through the haze and dust.

He drove slowly, hoping the truck wouldn't kick up so much dirt, trying to catch a glimpse of the two people he'd seen from his porch a half hour earlier. A twinge hit his chest. He quickly rubbed it away with his thick black fingers.

A mixture of sadness and relief washed over him; he saw no one.

"Best jus' get to it then," he mumbled, and the old dog sleeping in the passenger seat stirred for a moment, passed gas, rolled over, and squeezed out another one, this one smaller albeit exponentially more foul.

Passing by the stump, he looked and saw that, sure enough, the dirt looked all stirred up despite the rain. Someone had been there. He was sure of it.

Another fool had come down to the Crossroads.

But his job wasn't to read patterns in the ground like some tracker in the movies.

He just had to get the video recording, and if there was someone on there doing what people do at the Crossroads, then he was to get it to the General Manager.

Alvin was a recon man for Hell's new blood—a faction growing stronger by the day, looking to take control of the underworld from the Devil. Alvin's job was to keep an eye on who might be offering themselves as a new recruit for the Old

Man. As he understood it, from there, some minion down the line would be tasked with handling or eliminating that potential new piece from the chessboard.

Moving at a good speed as he came up to the long-dead tree a couple dozen yards down from the stump, he punched hard on the brake pedal, flipping the old dog next to him onto the floorboard in front of the passenger seat.

The subsequent satisfying thud pulled the smallest of smiles to his lips—it may have been the only joy he had left in his day-to-day—but it quickly faded as the nasty little creature eased out another long release of vile gas from the floor.

Out in the sun again, it was hot.

Each stride was a little shorter than the last.

When Alvin reached the tree, he ambled around back and lifted an odd type of key from his overalls pocket. It was a key without any teeth, so dark in color it looked like a hole in time and space. He pressed it into a slight divot in the bark.

A small black-and-white monitor jutted out the side, and Alvin twisted the key counterclockwise, rewinding the video.

Quickly, it played through the events of the last twelve hours.

On the small screen, thorough an incredible torrent of rain, it was hard to see anything. But with the flashes of lightning, halfway through the tape, he saw that someone had indeed come to talk with the Dark Man.

Alvin sighed, turned the key hard to the right. There was a whirring sound, then a flash drive stuck itself out of the tree like a small, petulant tongue. He grabbed it, yanked the black key back out, and returned it to his pocket.

He then headed back to the truck.

He hadn't seen the face of the man on the highway, but it didn't matter. Alvin knew all the General Manager needed was the quickest of looks at somebody, and she'd know who it was. That was all it took. That's how she'd found Alvin, all those years ago.

Back in the truck, he did a three-point turn in an extra four or five points and headed back to the house as the radio crackled with a new set of numbers, a woman's timeless voice dispassionately reading them one by one.

He just had to put the tiny thumb drive into the prestamped envelope and drop it in the overnight mail box. All he had to do. That was his job. Had been for a long time now. No use even thinking about the poor soul on the video.

"Brought it on hisself anyhow," Alvin said. The only reply was a low, lazy gurgling sound from the seat next to him.

"There's something about coffee in country diners," I said to the waitress, who looked like a cross between Flo from *Alice* and Methuselah.

"Tha's yesterday's coffee," she said with a smile that would have made even the most steeled orthodontist weep in great, heaving sobs. "We done heated it up."

"Just the thing," I said and grinned at her.

The name of this particular country diner was Kenny's.

It looked like it had been a bar at one time. This being a dry county now, it likely had been converted after the liquor stopped flowing.

Sitting at the counter, I looked into the one-time bar's mirror, caught my own reflection, and could tell my alternate other didn't like the look of me. I decided there would have to be a bath and soft bed in my near future.

Then what?

We'll have one of our people reach out.

Seemed like an odd sort of expression to exist within the lexicon of Prince of Darkness. Like he was prepping to hit me with some hell-born meeting maker.

But either way, it meant I had to wait for... what?

A phone call? An email? A screeching owl carrying a message in its talons?

My hope, actually, would have been on the owl.

The town didn't look like it would have much in the way of Internet access. I certainly knew better than to ask the ancient waitress about Wi-Fi, lest I be dismissed with a quick and inevitable "She don't work here no more" type of response.

And receiving a phone call was out of the question. My cell phone had been stolen during a terrifying two-minute rough-and-tumble mugging in the bus station's bathroom thirty-six hours earlier.

At the time, I'd been happy to give up the phone due to the paranoid visions instilled into me after the long-distance bus driver, a miserable man, had decided the appropriate entertainment for a trip into the Deep South was to fill the overhead TVs with the movie *Deliverance*.

So, when less than ten minutes after we arrived in the Jackson terminal, two sweaty skinny white boys burst into the bus station bathroom, their eyes hollowed out by years of meth use, I was actually relieved to *just* lose a crappy phone.

Thankfully, after getting pickpocketed in a train years earlier outside Paris, I'd decided to forgo the traditional wallet route and put any cash, cards, and ID into my shoe.

It kept the cards safe and left the cash in a particular state often rejected by the finer retailers. A money saver, when you consider it.

Awesome tip there. See if you get good shit like that from Suze Orman.

"Do you have a menu?" I asked.

"Not really. Whatchu want?" She clicked her gum.

"Uh, what do you have?"

"Don't know til you order," she said, and I realized she wasn't chewing gum. Ick. "I go back, and Cook tells me if he can do it or can't."

"How about, I don't know... Do you have soup?"

"I think so, yeah."

After a moment of silence, fruitlessly anticipating maybe a little more info, I prodded her. "Do you have any idea what kind you have?"

She sighed with annoyance. "Brown. I think."

"Brown soup?"

"Yeah," she said, then shrugged. "Could be the gravy."

"Gravy."

"Or the tomato soup from our Tuesday special."

I was marginally sure it was Sunday. "No soup," I said. "How about a sandwich, then."

"Well, you gotta tell me what kind, so I can go back and ask—"

"No, no. It's fine."

"Cook is known for his sandwiches."

"Oh? Which ones?"

"All of them."

This time, I sighed. "Just… how about toast, then. Just toast."

"We're out of toast."

"Your diner doesn't have any *bread*?"

"No, we got bread," she said, jabbing her fingernail at something in her mouth. "No toast."

"No toast? How..?" I said. "It's toast! What? Did you misplace the secret recipe?"

"Out of toast."

"You said that."

She dropped her pad in front of me. "When you want something, write it down."

"Okay. Helpful."

"I'm going on a smoke break," she said. Before she left, I noticed her eyes flickered toward some corner of the room behind me. Looking in the mirror, I saw a table with three local yokels. One of the men nodded toward her.

Briefly, an odd expression passed over her face, then she shooed it way, forced a ragged smile, and was gone.

It was a few hours before I needed to call Carissa. Of course, before leaving, I hadn't told her what my plans were—if she awoke, she'd likely only know that her husband wasn't by her bedside as he had been every day the last four months.

In truth, as I sat there in Kenny's Toastless Diner, the entire idea seemed unreal. Irrational. But after trying everything rational, irrational was all that was left. It's a thought which, I think, is some bastardization of the Sherlock Holmes quote about eliminating all the possible impossibles to find the truth.

Which in itself was some bastardization of some monk's Big Thinking that eventually got him a big, papal frowny face from the Pope—not a good idea in the 14th century. Or any century, probably.

That's what I was going on: irrational was all I had.

I remember those first signs, nearly a year ago now. At first, she'd just been tired. Working too hard. Allergies. Putting up with me. All those things can sap the life-energy right out of you.

But then the headaches began. It took a full five months before we had a clue what was wrong.

And by that time, it was too late. At that point, the American medical community set the countdown clock on my wife and moved on to other matters.

Like some adolescent, I felt sorry for myself as I could only watch as the most full-of-life person I'd ever known was slowly bled of her nineties, her eighties, her seventies, her sixties, her fifties, her forties…

My Carissa had, again and again, been there for me, in big ways and small. And here she was, dying before me. It was my turn to at last repay a small portion of that eternal debt owed to her.

Turns out, although all my efforts were sincere, I wasn't really any good at helping anyone.

Over the years, I'd done really well convincing others to help me with whatever goal I was trying to attain. It hadn't been malicious or even Machiavellian. I got what I needed, but usually others did too. All boats rise, that sort of thing.

However, *me* help someone else? Hell, I could barely help myself sometimes. I wanted to, but that just wasn't a muscle I'd ever spent much time developing.

So to help my wife… I looked for help.

Even divine help.

The last time I prayed (clumsily, sure) was at her hospital bedside after she'd once again drifted off due to exhaustion. I could only watch as the blood drained from her face.

Panic gripped my chest. Was this the end? At that point, the doctor had said she had a few weeks. Maybe a week. She'd looked so frail then. This woman who'd been bursting with life—enough to sustain both of us—was now a shell.

It's something I did… She's perfect, I thought. *Somehow being with me did this to her.*

Before slipping into sleep moments earlier, she'd asked me, "Are you okay?"

But how could I tell her my thoughts? That maybe she was being punished for hooking up with a barnacle like me? She deserved better. She deserved every last bit of me and more, whatever I could do.

As trite as it sounds, as she lay unconscious in front of me, I did the whole "Help me, God. Gimme something here, I'll do anything…" spiel.

Nothing.

Praying harder, I got nothing again.

Despite being sober for a few years, I found myself wishing the hospital had a pub. Instead I settled for coffee, and it was a moment that changed everything.

Or might.

Or won't.

I don't know.

But that was how I ended up in Mississippi looking to sell my soul to the Devil in exchange for a chance to save my wife.

In the hospital canteen, I'd spilt my freshly purchased coffee on the guy in front of me in line for the cashier. In an odd twist of fate, it turned out to be the actor, Ralph Macchio.

Feeling foolish, I jumped back and begged him not to hit me with the "wax on/wax off" move and insisted I pay for his food, despite his objections.

We sat down together, and he assured me, clearly tired of having had the same conversation over and over again, that he'd actually done other movies and not just *The Karate Kid*. He even pulled up his IMDb page on an iPad, detailing each of them, despite my objections.

That chat inspired The Plan. The idea that put me in my current situation: In the hazy aftermath of gambling my soul with Satan (or possibly Randall), sipping really shitty coffee in the worst diner ever.

"You new in town, buddy?"

I'd seen them stand up from their table at the Toastless Diner, slowly and in unison, then watched them in the reflection in front of me as they traded quick, fevered words with each other. Arguing, it seemed, as they approached me.

The shortest one was just off my left shoulder; the other two stood behind him with arms crossed. Each of them wore faded concert T-shirts, which seemed odd at the time.

Not for long.

"Sorry, pal," I said, sipping my terrible coffee, watching him in the mirror. "I'm married. But the two guys next to you look like they're available. Permanently."

All three once again traded soundless, angry words with each other, their fists curled into tight balls.

He forced a smile, then finally saw me watching him in the mirror, actually *waved*, and started up again:

"What's your name, friend?"

"Nope. It is, in fact, not."

"Huh?"

"How about you first," I said. "What do the old ladies at the local American Legion call you?"

He frowned for a moment, then shrugged. "You can call me Dr. Love," he said, as if he'd practiced it in the mirror at home time and time again. "As in a purveyor of God's divine love, prescribing only goodness and light. And joy."

"Sounds like a tough accreditation to pick up," I said.

"The gentleman next to me is Love Gun, and the other man is Deuce. We are representatives of a brotherhood. An army, of sorts."

Nodding, I recognized each of those "names" as titles from an iconic rock band.

"KISS Army, then?"

Dr. Love, the talker of the group, started saying something, then changed course and smiled.

"Well, former KISS Army, actually," he said. "Semi-retired and now an arm of God's Undamned Army—Wardoff Chapter. We keep an eye on those who might be up to any sort of… malfeasance in this particular area. Some believe these parts to be the Devil's playground."

Uh oh.

"However, I do have to tip my hat to you," he continued. "Many around these parts would not have identified those as KISS songs. So… you're from out of town?"

In the back of my head, I took a mental note to never return to the town of Wardoff. In fact, if there was time, I'd make an annotation on Google Maps to avoid it at all costs.

Still, it didn't matter how odd these guys were, or that their army was not any sort of real army, you still had to watch out for idiots in groups. Individual idiots are usually easier to deal with, but idiots are pack animals.

With a group of them, you had to be far more careful. Dark chapters of human history were written by idiot herds taking society's toboggan down Holy Shit Mountain.

"Uh, I used to be a jock," I told him. "Deejay, you know, on the radio."

"Oh, how fun."

"Sometimes," I said. "That was a while back. Long time now."

The guy called Deuce was apparently tired of the happy happy talk. "As semi-retired members of the KISS Army," he chimed in, "each of us was inspired by the spiritual leadership of drummer Peter Criss."

"He walked the Path, and we followed," said Love Gun, adding his two cents.

"We've now committed, *devoted,* ourselves to good and are Watchers of the Crossroads."

Dr. Love seemed to be irked about losing the mic. "Thank you, Deuce," he cut in. "I was jus—"

"You were just chatting up what could be one of the servants of darkness, Dr. Love! We're not here to make friends with those who dance with the Devil!"

"Oh my god," I said, my gaze slightly unfocused. "Is that a KISS Your Face Makeup Kit under the counter?"

"WHAT?" Dr. Love froze.

"It's from Remco." Love Gun added.

"Yeah, one time on Halloween, I went, full makeup, as all four of them. It was confusing and strange," Deuce said. "I was twelve and went missing for three days. I don't remember what happened. But ever since then, I had the tiniest tattoo of a bat on my—"

As the other two stared at him, that was my cue, and I spun the barstool and slammed into Dr. Love with my knees, sending him crashing into Deuce and Love Gun.

God's Undamned Army—Wardoff Chapter in toto collapsed to the diner's floor in a panic of pasty white limbs and faded black concert T-shirts.

Pumping my legs, I was at the door quickly, but when my hand went out to grab its handle, sparks flew, and something clanked to the floor next to me.

There on the brown-gray linoleum, a circular, jagged piece of metal bore the KISS Army logo.

"What the hell, man?" I said and shot a look over my shoulder. "You whipped a throwing star at me? Who *does* that?"

The only one standing at the moment was Deuce, and he was digging in his fanny pack, presumably for more throwing stars. Or maybe a tampon. Seriously, what douche bag still wears a fanny pack?

"You know that deuce is another word for 'shit,' don't you?" I asked. "Right?"

Not waiting for an answer (or potentially a KISS Army-issued lawn jart), I hit the door's handle and was quickly out in the Mississippi sun.

There weren't many places to go. A couple shops to my left looked closed. To my right...

"Need a ride?"

Appearing right there in front of me, gleaming brightly in the dirty street, was a black stretch Lincoln Town Car.

"Where the hell'd you come from?"

Behind me, on the other side of the thick wooden door of the diner, the shouting was getting closer, so I jumped at the car, pulled the door open, and got in.

Before I'd closed it, we were already moving.

"Hello, Rasputin."

Chapter Four

I faced the rear, the driver somewhere behind me. Two men faced me.

Sitting directly across from me was a man in an expensive suit. For someone as heavy as he was—he took up nearly half of the rear passenger space—it had been artfully tailored to his body.

As the large man lounged on a padded half-bench, a smaller man next to him was regulated to a flip-down seat. His suit likely off the rack. His tie had most likely been a gift from an older relative who didn't like him very much.

These, it would seem, were the Dark Man's people I'd been told to expect.

A quick glance at the door told me there was no handle to get out. I may have been much safer back with God's Undamned Army—Wardoff Chapter than in the slick black Town Car. That thought was affirmed when I looked out the windows and saw only long, thin streaks of light quivering against a deep black sky.

It was quiet for a moment as the heavy man looked through some paperwork clipped to the interior of a file folder.

The smaller man shifted on his seat and looked at me briefly, then looked back to what his boss was reading. He pointed to something on one of the pages I couldn't see.

"We can do a revision and have him initial. It'll be fine," the big man mumbled, then looked up at me.

Again, it was quiet.

"What do we do now?" I asked.

It was a full minute before he answered me. Then: "Well, I'm going to go through some of the details of the contract, and Mr. Pendleton here, among his many talents, is a global notary and will help us finalize the paperwork."

"The Devil has a notary?"

He laughed and beamed at me unpleasantly. "I am not the Old Man. I am one of his attorneys. *Chief* counsel, in fact. A top role."

The large man slipped a blood-red silk kerchief from his pocket, patted his upper lip, then returned it. He continued.

"First, are you in a position to enter a contract with another party? That is, are you legally or eternally bound to any other group, entity, or individual in such a manner that would prevent you from entering into a contract with my employer?"

"What? No, I… I'm not… no."

He offered me a smile. "Splendid, then!"

The smaller man looked at the file as it was handed to him, and he began to run down the details.

"The initial term of the contract will be four days, which begins when the contracted party awakens the day after said document is signed by both parties. You are to procure the item as detailed in Addendum ii to this contract. Both the contract and its associated documentation cannot be modified in any way without both parties' consent. If there are any amendments, the time frame, unless explicitly stated, does not change or reset…"

The smaller man droned on like that for at least another ten minutes, and despite the stakes, I was getting a serious case of the sleepies and considered taking a nap on the Town Car's upholstered seat.

Finally, he stopped talking. I snapped fully awake.

Pendleton handed the documents back to the large man, who produced a pen from the same pocket as his kerchief. The Advocate signed in three different places, initialed in two, and then handed the entire packet to me.

"Wait," I said. "Hold on. So, I'm risking my, uh, soul so that my wife can live. I just wanted to confirm that."

"If the terms of the agreement are met."

"And what… so when I sign that, does that mean she's cured?"

The two men in suits frowned.

"I'm sure you detailed all of that explicitly, but can you give me a quick rundown again? Just a thumbnail sketch."

The smaller man grabbed the files and began again: "The initial term of the contract will be four days—"

"Mr. Pendleton, that'll be enough," the boss said and put his large meaty hand on the file. "Rasputin, within the details of your contract, you'll see that you have been given a task."

"A task? Okay, sure."

"Yes, if you complete that task, your wife's life will be spared. She will be cured, and as a bonus, you will not be further indebted to my employer. Two happy little monkeys."

"Oh, okay. That seems good."

His eyes darkened, and he smiled. "If you fail, she dies all the same, and we get you for eternity."

"Oh."

"Simple, really."

"Okay," I said. "And what was that… what am I supposed to do? The task?"

Mr. Pendleton held up several sheets of paper, his voice scraping along the edges of his throat. "All of that is detailed—"

The large man turned his hand slightly, a flick of the wrist, and the smaller man lost his words entirely.

He looked toward me, his brow knitted. "You're stupid," said the lawyer, "and you don't have the gift of a photographic memory like me, so I'll explain it slowly."

"I got a photographic memory," I said. "It's just outta film."

"That passes for humor in your world, I suppose," he said and shifted his weight. "Your wife's illness is in its last stages, and it would seem the only tool that could possibly snatch her from death's grip is a rather old one. Ancient."

"And I have to get it."

"Ah, not entirely stupid. Good for you!" the Advocate said. "It's called the Lamp of Life by some. That's not just some euphemistic dogma, by the way. It is a lamp. A very old lamp."

"Where is it?"

Exasperated, the smaller man looked to his boss but was silenced again with a look.

"Ah," the fat man said. "That part's a bit tricky."

"How tricky?"

He twisted for a moment in his expensive suit then said, "If Houdini fucked David Copperfield, the resulting offspring wouldn't be *this* tricky."

Wow.

"Uh, they're..." I said, "I mean, not to get nitpicky here, but they're both dudes, so—"

"Which adds to the tricky bit of that particular analogy."

"Ah, I see. Well played, sir."

He then laid out what I was supposed to do.

Centuries earlier, as he explained to me, there was a woman born in misery, and it seemed, destined to stay there. She lived in a hopeless existence and nothing looked to change that.

So a little like North Dakota, then.

"But as it happens," the Devil's Advocate said in the sing-song voice of a practiced story teller, "through some evolutionary cross-wiring, this woman was born with a voice that sounded as if it had drifted down from Heaven itself."

"Uh, you know that's, like, the mother of all mixed metaphors, right?"

He smiled unpleasantly. "I'm a lieutenant of the Devil, Raz. When I go bad, I go big."

"Gotcha."

With a hand that looked like a boiled ham left in the sun all afternoon, he brushed my interruption aside and got back to his tale of yore.

So this woman then goes from town to town with her brass pot, literally singing for her supper. But more than just making cash as some primogenital Lily Allen, she was actually making people happier and healthier. Better.

Not just people. Entire *towns* of people.

"In fact," the fat man continued, "it was really buggering up the MX something awful just when we were making headway."

I fell silent, and he simply waited, staring, his eyes gradually turning to slits. It began to creep me the hell out.

"Fine, fine," I said, giving in. "Please, do tell me. What is the MX?"

"Ah, in very basic terms, it's how our side gauges how well we're doing. We can track the global misery index, the MX, to see how close we might be to tipping the balance in our favor."

"Got it. I was in radio; it's like ratings."

"A dreadful, anemic, and fundamentally incorrect analogy, but sure, go with that."

"Gotcha."

This next part he blazed through a bit. She happens upon some old guy, like a leper, who shows up thinking that she can heal him, and when he touches the girl, she ends up with a wicked-bad case of the leper cooties.

Her health quickly declines, but before she expires, a lamp—a very special lamp—is brought to her would-be deathbed, and when its light shines upon her, she heals and continues wandering the globe, singing and making folks happy.

"Huh," I said.

"So it's a powerful, powerful device, this... Lamp of Life."

"Huh," I said again. "So, lucky that lamp was around, then. Where'd it come from?"

"All your terrible little questions. They never really end do they?" he said and shifted his weight from leg to leg. The car's suspension complained beneath us.

"I think you may have rocketed over some parts pretty quick."

"Well, you are low on time, aren't you?"

"Sure. But where'd it come from? It's not like a magic genie sort of lamp, right?"

He frowned. "And for a moment I thought you might go a full minute without sounding like an idiot."

"Right," I said. "A lamp genie with a knapsack of wishes is a *crazy* suggestion... Says Satan's lawyer to me right before he sends me to look for an ancient miracle flashlight that, when it shines on my wife, will cure her incurable disease."

"Ah, well," he said, clearing his throat. "That again is the tricky part I'd alluded to… after the poor little songbird, now healed and ready to do more good in parts unknown, after she left the town, the lamp was deemed too powerful to be lying about, so it was thereafter broken into separate parts and sent to the far corners of the Earth." He sighed and rapped his thumbs on his stomach. "Or so I'm told."

"Of course it was."

Pendleton finally regained his voice, saying: "You'll be able to determine the location of each piece, as described in the contract's Addendum ii. You'll have exactly four days to collect the four parts and assemble the lamp."

"Four days."

"Yes, and once you shine its light upon your bride, she'll be cured," The Advocate said with a flourish. "The Grim Reaper himself will spin on a heel at her doorstep and walk away."

Looking at the contract, I flipped through the listing of parts I was to retrieve.

"So, wait, I can assume these are all over the place, right? Different countries, likely different *continents*…"

"Yes," he said. "Tricky, as I believe I mentioned."

"Just four days?"

He shrugged. "Ninety-six hours from when you wakey-wakey tomorrow, or as the contract states, the moment of your wife's death. Whichever comes first."

"Her death?"

"Yes, if she dies, the contract is up. We can't bring her back from the dead, Rasputin. Ghoulish business all around."

The buzzing in my mind grew louder and as I sat and considered the task.

It seemed impossible. But as crazy as it was, it was my only shot.

I signed the documents, reading what I could as tears filled my eyes. Finally, I asked him, "Can I have anyone help me?"

Mr. Pendleton pointed at the paperwork and said, this time in a far more measured tone: "It's all detailed in the contract you just signed."

"Yes, yes," the large man said. "You can be assisted by three others. They are not bound by the contract, but you can… compel them to help you."

"Compel?"

"Force."

"I can *force* people to help me? What does that mean?"

"You have entered into a contract with Satan, Rasputin," he said, his smile showing more teeth now. "You'll find your Facebook friends won't exactly be clamoring to join in."

"We can *force* them? That doesn't—"

"It's a bit of a loophole. We discovered it during a weekend offsite in the Poconos a few years back. Within reason, they have to assist you."

"Just three."

"Well, two, actually," the smaller man said, glaring at me. "The third has to be random."

"Random? *Random*? Jeez… I feel like I got on some hell-spun merry-go-round and the fuckin' thing just goes round and round and round…"

"Yes, *random*… sort of," the large man said, rolling his eyes. "It's an EOE thing—Equal Employment Opportunity. We're bound to it, since you're likely to seek out only the wealthiest or most powerful people to assist you."

"It evens the playing field for other potential candidates," Pendleton added.

"Sure. And increases the odds I'll fail."

"Actually, after you leave this vehicle, it will be the thirteenth person you set eyes on. The other two, you have an entire planet to pick from."

"Jesus."

"No, they have to be living."

I shook my head, but before I could say another word, the door was opened, and I was flung onto the street.

When I stood up, the car was gone. And I was nowhere near Wardoff, Mississippi.

Chapter Five

"Good morning, this is Shelly, your personal digital assistant, courtesy of the Grand Metro Hotel in Atlanta, Georgia. It's seven a.m., and you asked me to call so ha—"
Click.

So it may seem a bit odd that I'd get a hotel in my own city, but going back to our house in Marietta, an Atlanta suburb, was out of the question. Carissa's parents, her sister and her fat husband, and some weird aunt who smelled like cleaning liquid were camping out at the house.

On the day I left for Mississippi, I'd spent six hours sitting and talking with my wife. She was pretty wiped out, so she nodded off a fair bit during that time. When she did, I just sat nearby waiting and reading on my tablet until she woke again.

This had been our pattern for nearly four months.

The evening I left on my trek, catching the Greyhound bus downtown at Forsyth and Brotherton, I hadn't actually told her family I wouldn't be coming home.

For me, it was a relief. In part because her family travels with the expectation of the best service and most accommodating accommodations, even when staying with other family.

When I'd returned home each night the previous week, it felt like swooping in as some mother bird, with various pink faces and mouths turned up to the sky, looking for a nice meal.

That and I didn't want to have to explain where I'd been. Or where I was going.

After being deposited in Atlanta by The Advocate (four hundred miles in about twenty minutes is not a bad way to go), I got a room at the Grand Metro. Before going to bed, I did three things.

First, I set the deadline on a cheap watch I'd purchased in the hotel gift shop. There was no "days" entry, so it would have to count back from ninety-six hours. I set it but didn't hit start yet.

The second thing I did was call my wife at the hospital, but it had been too late in the evening by then. She was sleeping, and I had to just leave a gushy message for her on the hospital voicemail hoping she could listen to it when she awoke.

Finally, I pulled out the contract, Addendum ii, and a black-and-red notebook I'd picked up in the gift shop the night before.

In fact, you are reading from that very notebook.

At this point in my story, as I write this down, I don't know if I'll pull it off. Don't assume that because I tell this story now it's because I'm sitting back in a comfy chair with a roaring fire in the hearth as I dictate my story of victory to some publishing company's intern.

By now, I could very well be dead. Chattering away like the creepy dead girl from *The Lovely Bones*.

Or worse.

So that morning, I started taking these notes. My task was to acquire four parts of an old lamp within four days. The pieces would likely be scattered all over the world. But it wasn't like their coordinates had been written down, and I could just shanghai Richard Branson and *compel* him to hop me around the globe on his private Virgin Galactic Airbus.

Me, I don't run in those circles.

You=shocked?

No, I didn't think so.

So the lamp. It was what's called a paraffin lamp. A quick Google search on the hotel's computer told me it was like some old camping lamp, a kerosene lamp.

Here were its inner workings:

Part One: The Wick Manifold. A metal clutch that grips the wick and is part of the mechanism that separates the fuel from the glass globe.

Part Two: The Font. The lamp's base and its fuel container.

Part Three: The Globe. My contract described it as a "glass chimney." This is the area protecting the flame.

Part Four: The Spindle. The smallest and simplest piece. Like the pin that winds a watch, it had a long thin bar with a circular cap. The cap would be ridged.

Okay, so that left me with my first problem: fuel. Could I use lamp oil or gasoline or what? Would it have to be paraffin?

Maybe whiskey? Whiskey would be good, but it'd have to be a single malt, surely, beca—

There was a knock at my door.

Unsure if I'd actually heard a knock, I kept perfectly still and just watched the door. Not a muscle twitched.

Another knock.

"Yes?"

Two words came back at me: "Room service."

Damn. Damn, damn, damn!

In these scenarios, if you know your contemporary horror fiction, anyone saying they're "Room Service" are not simply liars but homicidal maniacs or government agents with similar vocational aptitudes.

This thought was center stage for me. There was something dangerous on the other side of the door. Mainly because I'd not ordered room service.

"You must have the wrong room," I said, walking slowly to the door. "I'm leaving shortly. And I didn't ord—"

The voice on the other side of the door said, "It's complimentary, sir. No charge."

That totally made it even worse.

No charge? Hotels were just airlines that couldn't flap their arms fast enough—they nickel and dime you to death. *Nothing* was "no charge."

"No, thank you," I said, nearly pressing my eyeball flat against the peephole. All I saw was the top of some guy's head. "I'm not… terribly hungry."

After a moment's hesitation, the man said: "You're missing out, sir."

"Listen," I started to say but then was suddenly tossed back toward the wall as the door burst open.

From my well-honed Preparing for Danger posture, I waited for the inevitable physical assault. When it didn't come over the next couple of moments, I cracked an eye open from the near-fetal position on the floor.

A short, squat man in dingy white polyester was wheeling in a breakfast cart.

I jumped up. "There it is!" Rubbing my eye and holding my index finger out, I said, "Just… was down there looking for my, uh, dignity."

Over his shoulder, the man dressed smartly in the hotel's uniform, grinned (I think) as he pushed the cart deeper into my room.

The food instantly made my stomach growl. I hadn't eaten very well since I'd left. And all I'd had at Kenny's Toastless Diner was a half cup of day-old coffee and a handful of KISS lyrics.

And the food was absolutely beautiful, presented on spotless bone-white plates.

Not beautiful, was the bellman. In fact, he was terrifyingly freaky looking.

His eyes were shriveled and black like olives; his skin gray and dried out to the point of actually *flaking*. When he smiled, his breath smelled like something a wild animal might have pulled out of the dumpster of some long-shuttered restaurant, then discarded.

The man stood, palm out. I gave him a fiver, paying for him to just leave.

Once the door clicked shut, I put my middle finger in my ear and cupped my hand around my cheek.

Which, according to the contract:

If [agreeing party] needs to contact the Advocate (for emergency, counsel or clarification [please check subsets and addendums as, depending on agreement, these may be billable hours, rounded up to the whole]), the [agreeing party] may employ what is colloquially known as FU Mobility: Simply put

the middle finger of the left hand in the ear, cup this same hand
downward toward the mouth....

The explanation seemed a little odd, even silly. Still, the gruesome bellman needed an explanation.

"Yes, hello. Billable hours begin now depending on your individual contract," the Advocate said. "Who's this?"

"FU Mobility doesn't have caller ID?"

"Please answer the question." The Advocate's voice sounded pinched. "This may be a matter of billing, for Hell's sake."

"Rasputin. We talked yesterday. In your Lincoln."

"Ah, yes," he said, then spoke to someone else in the room, his voice muffled. "Give me a moment, will you? Non-revenue call. You can rape the receptionist if you like; he won't mind. Masochist, you see. Unfortunate... rather takes the fun out of it, my apologies."

I cringed, cursing under my breath, and said, "If you're busy, sir—"

"Hellfires, no. Why would the chief counsel of all Hell be busy? What's on your tiny mind, Rasputin?"

"Ah, well, I've been trying to wrap my head around some of the contract here, you know, the ins and outs of what I'm after."

"Good. Seems a little late in the game, but whatever. What's the reason for your call?"

"Uh, the... well, I just got a breakfast delivered—"

"Yes, compliments of the home office here. It's sort of a welcome-and-good-luck gesture. Empty calories, to be honest, but there it is."

Catching myself in the hotel mirror, it momentarily reminded me of my brief stop at Kenny's the day before. I quickly turned away.

"So, I had a quick question about the man who delivered the home office complimentary breakfast. It seems he was sort of... *ruined* or something."

"Sure, yes."

"Is he dead?"

"No, he is in our service," he said, then briefly spoke to someone in the room on his end. Then he was back. "It's... some years back now, there was a restructuring of the Dark World, nothing that concerns you, believe me. However, in that shuffle we acquired a number of interests. Entities."

"Entities? Like formless mythical beings or something? Winged demons with razor-sharp talons that—"

"*Corporate* entities."

"Oh, okay, sure."

"So we have those in our employ who are the worker bees, yes, and very important, crucial, I could even say, to tipping the MX in our favor."

"Yes, yes, the MX."

"Misery Index, as I've explained" he said and sighed. "We cannot have direct contact while here at the home office. Only a very few can travel there so, more efficiently, we have agents like your nasty little friend there. But don't worry. Nothing to concern you with. He's no threat to you."

"But, wait, so he's an ordinary hotel bellman who is contracted to the Devil? Why is it he looks all messed up, then? Don't people notice?"

"Oh, ho! You are an inquisitive little bunny, aren't you? And all of this non-revenue time." The Advocate sounded like he was grinding his teeth slightly. "Oh, yes, yes. Well... right, while you are under our employ—an independent contractor of sorts—you will see those who work directly for the Dark Lord as they are represented in Hell. To others, he's probably some middle-aged, half-fat, half-balding hotel employee. But because *you* work for the Old Man, the usual feints are inert."

"So I can expect to see a lot of people like that?"

"Some. The idea is that, well, you won't get caught off guard."

"Meaning what?"

"It... there really isn't the time—"

"Make the time."

"For now, all I can say is… it's not exactly, um, one for all and all for one down here. My employer is no longer the only player here. Not anymore. A dreadful man, a former human, if you can believe it, has this little start-up, which has changed the whole culture. Sad, really. All this corporate structure is so dreadful. Alas, our side has had to adopt some of those machinations for our very survival."

"Weird."

"So, to answer your question, there *may* be others that approach you from, let's say, the competition. A wee bit of a power struggle at the moment for control of the underworld. Nothing to be concerned about."

"Right. Two devils fighting it out for control of Hell."

"Hardly," he said and chuffed.

"Actually, considering where our world is right now… that explains a lot."

"I'm off," he said. "Anything else you may need, please, hesitate to call."

He hung up.

Slowly, I walked over to the breakfast cart and lifted up one of the silver tray lids.

Scrambled eggs, bacon, ham. Biscuits and gravy. I wondered briefly if one of the "entities" Hell had acquired was a manufacturer of cholesterol medicine. The bill was taped to the tray, and when I lifted it, I saw it was indeed charged to a Big Pharma corp. I couldn't help but laugh.

"I'll be damned," I said to my reflection in the shiny, silver tray lid.

Scooping up some gravy with a biscuit, I smashed two pieces of bacon into it and capped it with another biscuit.

Looking out the window, it was clear there was a long, long day ahead of me. Likely the longest day of my life.

Or one of four.

But before embarking on the day—and I would say in any other circumstance that I'd been prompted by a devil on my shoulder, but in this case, I was just being a bit of an asshole—I put my finger back in my ear.

"Christ, I'm like a Time Life operator today!" The Advocate barked when I'd called him back on FU Mobility. "Yes, hello? Billable hours begin now depending on your individual contract. Who is this?"

"So if you're not allowed to have direct contact from there to here, why is it I can talk to you right now?"

"*Rasputin? Again?*"

"I mean, that's direct influence, right?"

Only silence came back. I wiggled the finger in my ear to be sure I hadn't lost the connection.

"Don't you have better things to do, Raz?"

"Yes," I said. "Just, you know, my inner inquisitive little bunny." I blinked in such a way that I'd hoped he could hear it.

He let out a huge breath and said, "Loophole."

"What?"

"Loop-fucking-hole. Are you deaf?"

"No," I said, "but it is kind of hard to hear you. I've got a finger stuffed in my ear."

"And to think you're no longer employed as an entertainer," the Advocate said drily. "Such wit."

"What loophole?"

"Jingle bells Jesus… To get around the restriction of no direct line here to there, when we use this little trick, we take advantage of a little quantum physics super-position—don't bother asking, you won't understand it because you're stupid, and I'm not going to explain it—but basically it means that I am neither here nor there. Which can be damn inconvenient while driving because I can slip right through the car."

I didn't care about the explanation. For some reason, I just got a real kick out of bugging the guy. He was, after all, a demon or something.

Then a thought: If I worked for the guy… was I one, too?

Finished with the prick, I simply said, "That's cheating, you know."

"Loophole, Rasputin," he said, sing-songing the word. "You'd prefer everyone play by the rules?"

"I prefer everyone play by the *same* goddamn rules. What's so wrong with that?"

"Well, that's why you lose. Eventually, Rasputin, you always lose. Every time." With that, Mr. Peptalk was gone.

I threw the bit of gravy-soaked biscuit I hadn't eaten at the hotel room's mirror. The gross, wet *thwop!* was pleasing but not pleasing enough.

Then I quickly cleaned it up, because it kinda wasn't fair for some housekeeper to have to clean up my biscuit tantrum.

Chapter Six

"Hey man, we're here. Wake up."

For a moment, I was disoriented. *How'd I get into a cab?*

For most of us, waking up anywhere that's not firmly established as part of our daily routine briefly drops our brain into a hot iron saucepan to fry up some low-boil bewilderment/panic/fear/incontinence.

For the second time in less than twenty-four hours, I'd been pulled out of the blissful world of dreams by someone I didn't know. At least this time no one was jiggling my balls.

As I've said, being roused from sleep by a complete stranger, at least for yours truly, doesn't actually elicit "fight or flight" but an unfortunate combination of both.

"Hey... *man*," the cabby said, fending off my sleep-weak, spasmodic, wide-gecko-style-fingered palm thrusts as I scuttled backward across the seat in a panic-blinking retreat, utilizing only my butt cheeks for locomotion.

"*Muhnnnrpt*," I said, though I'd planned on saying something else entirely.

From outside the door, somewhere in that blaze of sunshine, I heard a familiar voice: "Raz! Jesus, man, what are you doing?"

Adam was my best friend from high school, and we'd kept up since then, usually hanging out every other month or so. He'd worked for a while in a warehouse and used to be a bit of a drunk on the forklift but cleaned himself up. He was now, of all things, teaching third grade. Given that vocational departure, I'd always believed giving up drinking had been a bit shortsighted on his part.

He's now got a far more positive attitude; he's taking care of his health and even started to learn how to play guitar so that he can bring it to class as a learning tool for his kids.

Ugh.

I sort of missed the drunk.

There are few people you can really, really trust in the world. The kind of friend that if you showed up on his porch at three in the morning, wild eyed and exasperated, toting a bloody dish rag wrapped around a severed hand, saying you need them to bury it in their backyard and to not ask any questions... they'd go, "Lemme get my garden trowel."

Adam was that kind of friend for me. I had his back, always. He had mine, always.

"No fucking way, dude."

"What?" I said, my mouth hanging open a little.

Adam stood up so fast from his rickety little kitchen table that the motion sent the chair about a third the length of the floor. In silence, Adam wrung the fingers of one hand, then the next.

Without a word, he snatched a coffee mug from the collection of mismatched ones in his cupboard and thrust it under the faucet. Twisting the spigot, he filled the cup, took a sip, and spit it back out.

"Shit," he said. "I put warm water in there."

"Gross."

"Yeah, tasted a little like dog spit."

"You know that *how*?"

Damn. That quip didn't even earn a small smile from my friend. I'd really thrown him for a loop.

He'd been mostly quiet for the full ten minutes it took me to tell him the story of the past forty-eight hours. Initially incredulous, there'd been a lot of confused smiles, split momentarily by utterances like "What?" and "This is a joke, right?"

When he was younger, Adam's family had been pretty religious. No R movies, no MTV, no rock concerts. So naturally, once he got out of the home, he'd lost his damn mind.

Lost.

His.

Damn.

Mind.

Like Newton's third law of motion, and I'm paraphrasing: If you keep the totality of this world's weirdness away from your kid, your kid will eventually go *find* it and compress eighteen years of sheltered youth into a subsequent two or three years of oh-my-fuggin'-god crazy that even Dr. Phil would take a glimpse at and go, "Oh my, that is just not appropriate for daytime television…"

For a time, Adam had been on the so-called "raggedy edge."

A lot of drinking, a lot of weird drugs—the kind you can easily find at music festivals where the attendees are given free water so no one dies; or at least, not on the concert grounds—and many bleary-eyed mornings waking up in very unfamiliar places with very soiled pants, and not always because he'd been the one who'd soiled them.

But now, as he trembled slightly while listening about my contract work with the Devil, I began to wonder if he was still in the grip of some of those old-timey religious teachings.

"Listen, Raz, it's… n-not that I'm religious or anything…"

Well, okay then…

"… but, are you serious? I can't even wrap my head around it." He sat back down, his eyes never leaving me, never blinking. His voice was thin now. "You *actually* made a deal with the Devil? THE Devil?"

"Yes," I said and shrugged.

"I-I'm not even sure I believe in the Devil," he said with a hollow laugh.

"Well," I said, "he believes in you."

Fwoop. All the color drained from Adam's face. It seemed some of those old-timey beliefs had stuck with him after all.

Still whispering, he said, "Did he… did he say that?"

"We didn't chat a whole lot."

"No?"

"No, the main dealings were with more of a worker-bee kinda dude," I said. "One of the top guys. He's a lawyer."

"And that guy you're working for… *he's* from Hell?"

"Well, yeah," I said. "You heard the part where I said he was a lawyer, right?"

We talked a few more minutes, but I couldn't break him. At one point, I caught sight of the clock on his kitchen wall.

I'd already lost more precious time and hadn't even begun to search for the lamp.

The breath caught in my chest. Watching Adam freak out, I began to come to grips with the realization of what I'd committed myself to. It was messed up, sure, but what choice did I have if there was any hope of saving Carissa?

I cut bait, because it was clear this was too much. Adam loved me like a brother, I knew that, but working for the Prince of Darkness was a line he couldn't cross.

I stopped pushing.

"I'm sorry, man," he said, staring at the calluses that had developed on his fingertips from playing guitar.

Behind me, I heard a familiar tired and phlegmy voice. "Sorry for what? What'd you do, Razzie?"

Spinning around, I was a bit stunned to see Adam's uncle. It had been years since I'd laid eyes on the guy.

Smiling, because he was the sort of guy that could elicit a smile just walking into a room, I said, "Nothing, Uncle Jer'. What's up?"

Now, I wouldn't swear on a Bible (if I *had* been compelled to swear on a Bible, given my recent short-term contract employment arrangement, the book would likely have burst into flames the moment my fingertips touched its cover), but it seemed like Jerry was actually wearing the same maroon sweatpants and gray hoodie I'd seen him the first time we'd met.

That had been at least fifteen years earlier.

Jerry said, "Just getting some agua, mi amigo."

As he slid past me, gliding across the floor (impressive for a guy carrying an extra forty pounds), the familiar waft of pot emanated from the man. In the right light, I was sure you could actually see smoke rings puffing from his pores.

Adam blankly watched his uncle reach into the fridge. "Uncle Jerry's between jobs, so he's been crashing here for a while."

Then Adam's posture changed, now sitting more upright. Like he'd had his battery changed out.

"You know…" he said, "Jerry's a *pilot*."

"Huh?"

My friend lowered his voice, determined now, his eyes cutting toward Jerry. "A pilot! If you're going to pull this off, I mean, you're not going to drive, are you?"

"Well, sure, no, of course not, but—"

Adam held up one hand, the other pointed toward Jerry, and he mouthed: *Pi-lot.*

In less than four days, I had to gather four pieces of an ancient lamp, scattered across the globe, and use it to cure my terminally sick wife.

A fat, fiftysomething, stoned Jerry was not my first choice to be on Team Raz. In fact, nearly every human being on the planet and a rather large contingent of domesticated pets would top the potential candidates list far, far ahead of Uncle Jerry.

My eyes narrowed, I was talking through my teeth, trying not to move my lips while voicing a wee bit of concern—if not outright opposition—to my childhood best friend's suggestion.

"Man, *seriously*, I don't think…"

However, I think Adam was just happy to, at least temporarily, have the attention drawn away from his pussified cowardice.

I could feel the eyes of the frumpy man in the dirty sweats boring into me. Finally, I looked up.

"Yeah, I'm a pilot," he said and took a swig of water. Some of the liquid instantly drizzled down the lower part of his goatee, while some droplets held on to his scraggly mustache, clutching for dear life until they also fell and were soaked up by his dirty hoodie.

It occurred to me, off-handedly, that might be how he passively cleaned the garment over time.

Adam nodded hard and then smiled at me way too crazily.

"Pilot. Cool," I said.

"What of it?" Uncle Jerry said.

"What of... what?"

"Why do you need a pilot?"

I shook my head. "No, no. I don't *need* a pil—"

"Rasputin made a deal with the Devil," Adam said, his words coming out like machine-gun fire. "He's got about a half a week to collect these pieces of some ancient magical lamp that's the only way to save his wife, who's sick and dying. The pieces are spread all over the world, which means, of course, he'll have to fly, sooo he needs a pilot."

My eyes fell to the table. Damn. As Adam said it all out loud, it really sounded totally batshit crazy.

What am I doing?

Uncle Jerry said, "Okay."

Adam and I were silent for a moment, neither of us even taking a breath. Finally, my friend prompted Jerry. "*Okay, what?*"

The man closed the fridge and leaned against its cold metal door. He looked out the window, blinked a few times, then looked back at us. He shrugged.

"I'll do it."

And just like that, my childhood best friend's Uncle Jerry was now a part of my deal with the Devil.

"You can sit on the bed if you like. Just be a sec," Uncle Jerry said, digging through a gap in the wall that was, best guess, the closet.

His arms churned through an unbelievable mound of clothes and books and ancient electronics and cardboard and lobster bibs (WTF?) and whatever else was in there. Every so often, he'd shift his head left or right to avoid whatever was tumbling from the very top as it rained down.

At the threshold of Jerry's bedroom, I stood in a bit of a helpless stupor, reeling a little from the thought that *this* guy was going to be one of my Warriors of Good in my lunatic quest to save Carissa.

"How long we gonna be gone?" he asked, voice muffled as a T-shirt, its faded and flaking iron-on sprinkling bits onto his shoulders, briefly clamped itself across his face like a lethargic, tie-dyed jellyfish.

Jerry thrashed his head side to side for a moment, and it set him free.

Every few seconds, he'd extract something of some apparent value and toss it into a leather duffel he'd pulled out from under his unmade bed.

"Uh," I said, "it's… you know, man, it's more than half a week. I feel awful about taking you away from…"

The room fell silent save for the sounds of some way-too-short cascading gym shorts, spiral notebooks, and broken pencil sharpeners.

"Huh? No, I'm cool. No plans."

From behind, he looked like some heavyweight boxer. And by heavyweight, I mean he was fat. Fatter than yours truly. Not that hard fat like some mid-twentieth-century Navy dad but the spongy kind one earns from a strict, consistent routine of cheap beer and Funyuns.

In surreal slow-mo, Uncle Jerry the boxer would jab one arm at his bulky opponent, rip something out from it, toss it in the duffel, then jab in the other.

The glass-jawed closet monster just took the blows, defeated, as it had likely done time and time before, simply waiting for the flabby-armed beating to end.

Frankly, it was kind of difficult to watch.

I was sure this massive, dirty heap represented the totality of all the efforts ever made by the man, accumulated over all his years, and it was just a big gross pile of rubbish.

I turned to the opposite wall. There was a large black poster, its corners secured by thumbtacks, but its edges were still curled while the white backing underneath had yellowed unevenly.

The poster was the *2112* album cover from the Canadian rock band Rush. In the background, a red five-pointed star—which at that moment, looked more like a pentagram—was housed in a red circle. In the foreground, a naked man faced toward the star with arms outstretched, as if holding it off.

I'd seen this cover before, but the naked guy looked a little different.

Well... different and familiar. I couldn't quite place it, but...

I glanced back to my left. Jerry was still working the closet. Left jab, right hook.

I realized just then that Uncle Jerry's hair had been styled (or completely neglected) into some sort of Leif Garret oh-my-what's-happened-to-you-Tiger-Beat? sort of thing.

I looked back to the other wall, at the poster, at the naked guy who braced himself in front of the circle-star thing.

Ugh. It looked like Uncle Jerry. A *naked* Uncle Jerry. I would be unable to ever listen to Rush again. This was a bad idea.

"Hey, is this going to be..." Uncle Jerry said. "You know, dangerous?"

"Huh?"

Jerry turned only his head while his arms held the massive torrent of junk at bay.

"Dangerous," he said, his eyes going unfocused momentarily. "Is this... going, uh, to be?"

This was *such* a bad idea.

"Uh, yes, actually. Likely *very* dangerous," I said, almost chipper, in an attempt to sound as if I were downplaying the actual danger with a light tone in my voice. Uncle Jerry would infer this as some obvious deception, surmise that this would be far more dangerous than I was letting on, and instantly reconsid—

"Okay. Cool. I'll bring my fanny pack."

"Right," I said. "We'll totally be safe now."

I walked away. Who knows, he might have some throwing stars in that shithole closet. They seemed to be making a bit of a comeback.

Standing in my childhood friend's small living room a few moments later, I just stared out the bay window as the sun beat down on the browning grass outside.

My eyes began to water, and my breath hitched. Only a few miles away, my wife was dying in a hospital bed without me. And where was I? Running errands for Satan, waiting on some fifty-year-old burnout?

This was a joke.

Another folly of mine… probably to avoid being there when she needed me most. Was I just a coward?

No, I can't think like that. I can make this work.

I became aware of something just then: the beauty of nature displayed outside the window.

A light breeze toyed with the branches of a maple tree, its leaves quivering and catching the sun, as if they were passing bursts of warm light between themselves in some lazy game.

The brown grass now looked a little more golden than brown.

I let that vision fill my eyes and my heart.

I can make this work!

"This is why I'm doing it," I whispered, clearing my throat. "I want to share *this* beautiful world with my Carissa. We have a whole world to explore together. It'd be so empty to do this… alone."

Several tiny birds landed on the home's mailbox. A squirrel jumped from a telephone line to a rooftop, stumbled, regained its footing and ran toward a prize in the distance only it could see.

I smiled again.

Yes, *yes…* this did feel right. I could do this.

Tall flowers across the road, maybe inspired by the fun the maple leaves were having, began to sway in the wind.

There was music, soft and subtle. I couldn't place it, but looking in its direction I saw a TV news van ambling down the road, shiny and glinting in the sun.

"Ready to roll, brother," Uncle Jerry said from behind me.

When I turned, it looked as though he was steaming.

"Wha—" I started, then caught a whiff of the guy. *Oh, Jesus.* "Uh, before we go, I should... Where's Adam?"

"Dunno. Probably floating in the tub naked on his back and pretending Jennifer Connolly was in a shipwreck and is using him as a raft."

"Ugh, *what?*"

"Or possibly Paul Bettany," he said and lugged his duffel up onto his shoulder. At his waist, he was indeed wearing an oversized fanny pack. You know, where other people, everybody, could see it clearly.

"Jesus, man!"

"Or both Paul and Jennifer. Probably Jennifer up on his face for simplicity sake, but—"

My hands flew up to the sides of my head. "Dude, I don't want to know about that kind of stuff about Adam." I walked toward the door. "How can you talk like that about your nephew, Uncle Jerry?"

"We're not actually related, Rasputin," he said. "I'm just a really good friend of the family. 'Uncle' is a colloquial and familiar, if inaccurate, designation."

He smiled at me.

Huh.

I pulled the front door open, and the Atlanta humidity smacked both of us in the chest like a double-barrel drive-by shooting. Another puff of residue smoke lifted off Jerry.

Walking outside, something suddenly came to mind. "Wait," I said. "I don't have... Do you have a car?"

Uncle Jerry turned to me with a grin way, way too large for his face. "Do I got a car?"

He breezed past me and glided toward the garage.

Still coming off my nature high—and possibly a little bit of whatever came off Uncle Jerry—I drew in a deep breath but found my lungs wouldn't hold as much as I wanted them to. Atlanta can be a beautiful city with all the blooms and foliage, but even if you don't have allergies, in Atlanta, you got allergies. Usually in exchange for all the stunning colors and breathtaking flowers. It seemed like a fair trade-off.

At the garage to my left, Jerry punched a few numbers into an ancient keypad and the door creaked and shook, slowly slipping away from the concrete driveway's embrace. Just before he slipped into the dark of the garage, he turned toward the street, catching sight of something.

In my comfortable daze, I heard him say something like, "Wonder what they're here for?" Then he disappeared into the dark garage.

It took me a moment, but I finally turned and saw that the news van I'd noticed a moment earlier had, in fact, stopped outside Adam's house.

Right where we were.

Fear gripped my chest.

Not because I'd believed our bizarre quest had been made public.

Not because the reporter, joined by a cameraman lifting expensive camera equipment above his head, was one famously known to embrace hyperbole like hungry babies clutch mama's titties.

No.

My fear came from this: The reporter was a light-skinned African American, and given his vocation, *usually* a handsome man with a lovely café-au-lait complexion.

Not this time.

Both he and his camera guy were, in fact, ghoulish as fuck.

Shit, shit, shit!

The network newsman smiled—he still had perfect teeth, mind you—and said: "Happening now, me killing Rasputin!"

Oh, damn.

"Heard you're working for the Old Man," he said, sneering through thin yet supple lips. "Man, looks like everybody's getting picked for Hell's kickball... and you got fingered by the wrong captain!"

"What?" My stomach knotted. "That's nasty."

Both men looked like they'd been dead for ten days and left to rot.

In a car.

With the windows up.

At the equator.

These, it would seem, were some of the folks the devil's advocate warned me about. Part of the "new blood" down below looking to take control of Hell from Satan.

Minions from the so-called Hell, Inc. moved in on me quickly.

I stumbled and yelped. "Hey, *wait!*" Then I reversed direction too quickly and again had to catch my footing.

My eyes locked on the reporter, and a flash to my right, a glint of sun on metal, caught me off guard.

"Die, fucker!"

Ducking, the German cameraman (yes, German was just a guess... snap judgment), I nearly fell to the ground and heard the whistle of thirty pounds of electronics swinging past my skull.

"Jeez, wait!" I shouted.

The cameraman let out a grunt, then another as the reporter inadvertently plowed through him trying to get to me.

I'm moving way too slow, thinking way too slow. Christ, I'm going to die on my friend's lawn!

Terrified, I turned to call for Jerry, but my jaw was slammed shut, hard, so hard I heard a crunch and tasted blood, as the reporter rammed the tip of his left Mercanti Fiorentini Wingtip Oxford into a soft spot under my jaw.

My head filled with stars, bursts of light, and an electric crackling sound, but I managed to roll away from my two attackers, who were both hell-bent on gutting me themselves and struggling to get past one another.

Back on my feet and steadying myself, I turned to run but took another blow to the head, this time in the temple, and there was an encore of the electric light show that nearly knocked me out.

A thin black snake wrapped around my shoulder, and I screamed.

No, not a snake. A microphone cord.

The reporter had whipped the mic at me like some sort of bola and was now retracting it to take another shot at me.

Holding the side of my throbbing face, I yelled at him: "Preening hack!"

Bearing those great teeth again, although nowhere near smiling, his pupils went to pinpricks, and an animal sound erupted from his mouth.

The two men leapt toward me, and I tried to step back, but I'd run out of room.

Behind me, the neighbor's rusty fence gripped my body, wrapping around me, and held me steady as they pounced.

Wham!

Reddish-black glasslike shards of sun filled my eyes, and an incredible, spine-splintering roar like I'd never heard was nearly on top of me, ringing my ears and rattling my chest.

I crumpled to the ground, and it seemed the only thing keeping me conscious was the powerful smell of exhaust fumes that were inexplicably tinged with the familiar smell of pot.

"Hey, man," Uncle Jerry said as he wheeled back around, fishtailing and tearing up Adam's front yard. The passenger-side door of his car popped open just above my head, bouncing on its hinges while I tried to process it all.

Grabbing the long black door uneasily, I stood.

The growling of the limited issue 455-engine reverberated up and down my spine and spread to my limbs.

"Jesus," I said and spit out enamel, grit, and blood.

"Nope. It's just Jerry."

"Don't... whatever happens, okay? Just *don't* say dad-joke level shit like that over the next couple days."

Dizzy and weak, I fell into the car, my sore body cupped by the car's leather bucket seat. Out the back window, the Hell, Inc. reporter and cameraman writhed on the ground—two tire marks cut through the grass and over their bodies like something out of a Roadrunner cartoon.

"Where to?"

"Just get us the hell out of here."

"Gotcha," Uncle Jerry said and gunned the engine, doing a doughnut in the front yard, splattering grass and sod onto the living room window I'd been staring out of just minutes earlier.

As the tires bit into the dirt below us, I felt my brain slide backward inside my own skull.

There was a brief rimshot-like *budda-buh-dump* sound as we ran over something (or I guess two somethings) in the yard, and then we hit the street.

My driver gunned it, and the muscle car flexed itself, then launched us down the road.

Gingerly, I raised my hand and tugged at the seatbelt, which simply fell into my lap.

"Broken," said Jerry.

I nodded slowly, arched up in my deep bucket seat to get a good look at the creature emblazoned upon the black hood of the roaring black car.

It was a huge depiction of an eagle. Or a phoenix. Or more correctly, a firebird.

"Of course," I said, flicking the radio to something to match the pounding in my head. "*Of course* you drive a Trans Am."

As an affirmation (I didn't even need to see the man's huge grin to know it was there) he punched the accelerator, and the world outside was left behind in a blur.

Chapter Seven

An hour earlier, a red-faced man in a tight suit had waited until he'd had the full attention of the manager on duty, then theatrically spat a piece of shrimp toward the Styrofoam container he'd laid on the fingerprint-dappled metal fast-food counter.

He missed.

"It's fricken cold," he said.

The tall, graying woman forced a smile. Actually, it wasn't entirely forced—there was the smallest bit of joy there.

Because she knew it wasn't really shrimp.

As the sweaty man prattled on, she reached up slowly, and her fingernails dug mindlessly at a spot where the paper hat met her hairline. Still smiling, she then snatched the container from the man and started toward an ancient hulking microwave oven.

"My most humble apologies, sir. I'll just heat it—"

"Well, don't nuke it for chrissake," he said. Sweat trickled down his cheek. "You can't microwave Styrofoam! It… the chemicals in there leak into, you know, into the food."

In a swooping motion, she arched the container into the air, and it landed perfectly atop an overflowing trash can.

The man took a half step back. "Well, listen, you didn't hav—"

"What was it you ordered, sir?" Her teeth looked like little gray blades as she spoke.

There was a moment of quiet, the edges of which were lined with the tinny sound of some poppy eighties tune dribbling out of an unseen speaker. The disheveled customer couldn't quite place the song but remembered disliking it immensely.

Wiping his lip, he said, "Uh, I had the Hong Kong Suey."

"Right."

She grabbed a fresh container (well, not *fresh*. She'd lifted it from the trash then sloppily wiped it out an hour earlier) and filled it with a collection of noodles and chunks of "food," all resembling colors you would most likely find in a baby's used diaper. That is, if said baby had some troubling eating disorder.

Watching her load the container up, he unpopped the top button of his collared shirt, licking his lower lip with the tip of his tongue.

When she finally turned back around, he had a replacement portion of food. In one corner, segregated from his order by a small ineffective partition, was a yellowish dessert that looked like a despondent peach had taken its own life and bled out.

"Tossed in some DongPo Dessert for you, extra," the large woman said.

He took a half step toward the food, and while his eyes leered in a manner that would have made nearby women scuttle away small children, his mouth twitched and puckered, unsure.

Before she snapped the lid shut, he could see tendrils of DongPo groping at the suey.

"O-okay. Thank you," he said and cast his eyes downward. He reached out for the stained container with both hands.

The moment he turned and wobbled away with his food, the smile fell, and the permanent frown settled back onto the face of Hell, Inc.'s Southeastern US regional manager.

She watched the back of his head with dead eyes, wondering what sort of sound his skull would make if it was struck with a pitching wedge, until she was startled by a shuffling clatter at the far end of the counter.

Her jaw clenched for a moment. She didn't even have to turn to know it was one of *them*. From Hell's other side—the washed-up fuck-twits, as she called them—one of the old guard.

The day's mail, sliding ever so slowly, was just half on the counter, the rest having already toppled to the floor. The man in the Devil's service, dressed in a US postal uniform, gave her a half shrug, which may have seemed like a sincere wordless apology, but with his ashen face, skin sloughing off like scales, she knew it was all just part of the job.

And she knew she didn't look much better to him.

"Fuckin' pencil dick," she muttered, walking toward the mail, which was still slowly cascading off the counter. As she reached the end of the counter, timed so perfectly, the final yellowed letter fell onto the dirty floor. In truth, although she'd never admit it, she was mildly impressed by the man's professionalism, the level of skill.

"Greasy bitch," he grumbled back without any real malice. This was a ritual they'd played out for as long as either could remember. He turned, then slipped on something smeared across the tiled floor, and fell hard.

He stood slowly and nodded toward her. *Well played.* And he shuffled out the door.

The fast-food manager bent over with a grunt and came up with a stack of mail in her right hand, a brown paper package in her left fist.

She felt the package and easily recognized the small lump with hard edges: a flash drive.

On the front of the prepaid envelope, addressed to her, it read:

To: The General Manager
Panda Pit
Mobile, Alabama

From: A. Stoddard, Wardoff, Miss.

Seven minutes later, she looked from her small, private video monitor to the phone on the wall. She lifted the handset off its cradle and punched at its keypad like she was trying to break one of the nails she hadn't chewed to the quick (which was none of them).

Six digits.

There was no ring.

She looked to the front of the store; no one was coming in. Wouldn't matter if there were. This was too important.

The other end of the line crackled. "What?"

"We got someone to deal with," she said. She looked back to the grainy image on the small screen. Wind, rain, flashes of light. A thirtysomething man on the ground, hands clasped. He was making a deal. No question.

But it was much more than that, and she knew it. Something else. She could tell.

That ability to "see" was what had earned the General Manager a very unique position at Hell, Inc. Sure, she oversaw the day-to-day administration in the American Southeast but she was also tasked as one of the underworld corporation's very few counter-recruiters.

The job: vet would-be talent for the Old Man, through various means of spying, eavesdropping, and closed-circuit TV.

She'd been described as being something akin to the opposite of colorblind. She just saw more.

And with the guy on the tape? What she saw was real trouble. In a short time Hell, Inc. had already come so far, and they were so close, but there was something about this guy.

At first the voice on the phone was unimpressed.

"So deal with it."

"You think I'd be calling only for you to fucking say that to me?"

"Maybe you're lonely."

"If I got batteries, I ain't lonely."

"I think I may puke a little bit."

"Shut up," the fast-food manager said, scratching a spot at the back of her head with a plastic fork. "This goes way up the ladder. No time for games."

"What do you mean up? How far up d'you think this goes, then?"

She sighed, knowing that if she was wrong the CEO would never let her forget it. As in never. Like forever never.

Still, this one. She knew this recruit could be a problem for them.

After decades of planning, Earth's Misery Index had not just been climbing, but the bulk of it was now tipping, even surging, in Hell, Inc.'s favor.

They had the momentum. The Big Mo! Were they were poised to finally take control of Hell from the Satan himself? Time for the new blood!

But… this guy. She stole another glance at the tape as it played back, rubbing a spot on the front of her head hard with the heel of her thumb. She knew this one guy could destroy all of that.

She hit the nuclear option.

"Get me a kill squad," she said and held her breath, bottom teeth nipping into her upper lip.

There was a brief silence on the other end.

Then, a somewhat significant silence.

Then, actually, a rather long and disquieting silence.

"He-hello?" she finally said.

A moment later, "Sorry! Sorry, I clicked over. Call waiting. Damn thing, sorry!"

"Oh."

"You were saying?"

She steeled herself and repeated what she'd said, not quite as dramatic the second time: "Get me a kill squad!"

"Ha! You're not serious? Do you really think th—"

"Yes!" she shouted. "Not just one! This is going global. Anyone, *everyone* we can get up!"

"Listen, even if I did pull the trigger on something like that, we're a bit hamstrung on the whole world-wide, open-ended freelance contractor all call. Anti-trust issues are tying us up—"

"Just do it!"

"Europe might play ball, but other than that—"

"And you better move, move, move on this, or you'll end up with a pitchfork up your ass, fucktard!"

Another sigh. "Uh, we don't really do the whole pitchf—"

"I *know*. I was making a point," she said. "I got a guy that's gotta go. We need a kill squad on 'em, pronto."

The person on the other end of the line paused. "You know the rules about that! Attracts way too much attention. Besides, if this guy is so special, we should bring him over to our side."

"Nope," the General Manager said, and something in her chest tightened. "Don't... don't even bother. We need to put the guy down and be done with it."

"Fine, but it'll take time. We hafta find a patsy, we gotta set up a hist—"

"No time."

"You've got to be jok—"

"NO time!"

The voice on the other end of the line started to say something but stopped. When he spoke again, the bored edge in his voice had been replaced with something far less steady.

"Where?"

"One of our tech entities got a facial match. He's in Atlanta."

"Got a name?" the voice said.

"Rasputin Frewer."

"Shit." The man let out a fluttering sigh. "That don't sound scary at all. Sounds more like some feline neurological disorder."

The General Manger allowed herself a small smile and said, "Well, this kitty doesn't get nine lives." The smile faltered. "Kill 'im... um... dead of the one he's got."

"That..." A small cough. "You know, fine effort there, but that really didn't work—"

"I know, I know." She nodded quickly. "It sounded much better in my head before it came out."

"It would have had to."

Chapter Eight

I'd known "Sideshow" Dan Pinette for more than seven years. We'd met when I first started out in radio, back in Orlando, Florida. Alternative rock music was still a happening thing in Florida after much of the country had moved on.

But something in Florida that's considered "alternative"? If you've been there (or watch the news or read the tabloids), you'd know alternative, weird, incomprehensible... that *is* the norm. I think the Sunshine State is anxiety-riddled because it's never gotten over the fact that it essentially looks like a flaccid cock. It's like the place can hear nearby states snickering.

And listen, when you've got *Alabama* looking down on you, there's really no recovering from that.

Dan had come up to Atlanta to work nights at the same radio station I did. I loved the guy, and he was really, really good. Great, in fact.

But, it took a while to convince the station's program director to hire my buddy. I pushed and pushed and kept at it, telling him how good my friend was.

Finally, he came up for a tryout weekend, and ultimately management couldn't help but agree. I was let go about seven weeks later, and he took my primo gig in the afternoon drive time slot.

Not his fault. And he felt like shit for a long time about it. I'd brought it on myself. Up too late, drunk at gigs. He still worked at the radio station, and even though we only lived a few miles from each other, we hadn't seen one another for a couple months.

I stepped out of Atlanta's oppressive heat into his freezing house. Sideshow's mother was from Britain, so he'd inherited the intrinsic belief that one's climate should always be physically displeasing.

Adam and I had grown apart over the years, so I considered this man to be what I could call my best friend. Basically, that amounted to being able to tolerate hanging out with the guy for more than a half hour. Aside from my Carissa, no one other than Dan fit that bill.

My heart felt better when I saw him. Good friends have that effect, and I suddenly recalled that the last I'd heard, he'd brought his girlfriend up from Florida now that he'd settled in.

"Wife, actually."

"What? When wife?" I said as I sat down on the sofa of his home in Vinings, a semi-posh Atlanta suburb.

Uncle Jerry was waiting patiently outside in his Trans Am, motor running. That was for two reasons. One: a black car with black leather seats in Atlanta? What had the guy been thinking? He needed to keep the AC cranked. Two, given my terrifying run-in with Mr. Hellspawn Breaking News, it was obvious that the "other" faction of the underworld had put some quick bounty on my head. Or soul, I suppose. However that worked.

Things must be pretty tight if the two groups in Hell go toe to toe over each individual prospect.

If Jerry needed to get us out of there (or run any of them over, since that seemed to work surprisingly well), he was good to go.

Dan had been nursing a beer and offered me one a little hesitantly. I think he was relieved when I shook him off. He'd seen me at my worst. But his upbringing had been a bit more "old school" than mine, and he'd always felt—and had told me—a man makes his own choices.

"Who am I to say which ones are right or wrong?" he often said just before I did something mindblowingly stupid.

Now he was a Mr. to some Mrs.

"Yeah, we got married."

"Wha? No invite?"

"No invites. We kept it, uh, quiet, actually," he said, sitting down in his recliner.

"Oh, one of those. Can I meet Baby Dan?"

"No babies," he said and grinned. It had been too long since we'd seen each other.

"Oh?" I said. "Then this I gotta hear."

"Nah, nothing to it. Now she's up here, and we can get all her paperwork settled, and she can go back to teaching. She was a teacher in Mexico before I met her."

"Paperwork? She's trying to get her Georgia teaching certificate? That's cool."

"No," he said and took a long pull from his beer, which looked really, really good. "Her green card."

"So… she's here on a visa?"

Dan shrugged and gave me a sloppy grin. "She's got a Visa *card*. But, no. No visa." He laughed, then asked me what had prompted me to stop by.

On the drive over, the bucket seat kept dropping me low in the car like a kidnapping victim unable to see the world around me. It gave me a chance to herd my thoughts together.

I'd given Uncle Jerry basic directions to Dan's home, but in the silence, I'd simply felt time slipping away. Four days was so little time! And it was going by *so quickly*.

And I hadn't even taken the first damn steps to recover the pieces of the lamp.

If there was even a lamp to find. Who knew? Maybe the Devil made it all up. It seemed all so unreal.

I looked down at my wrist to check the time, sucked in a quick breath, and gave Dan the quick version. Thankfully, after my failure to convince Adam, I'd learned from that and was able to improve my pitch tremendously.

When I was done, he said, "You're fuckin' with me."

I should have given him the long version.

Explaining a little more, he listened to me as his eyes darted from me to the kitchen several times. I could hear someone—his green-cardless wife, probably—preparing lunch.

Christ, it's lunchtime already?

He seemed a little distracted, but strangely, a smile had begun to bend his face.

"I know how crazy it sounds, man, but you know I wouldn't make shit like this up."

"I thought you were an atheist," he said and smiled, his eyes never leaving me.

"Sure. I still don't think I believe in God. But from what I've seen in this world, it seems surefire that there's a Devil."

"Dark," he said and looked over at the kitchen, trying to get his wife's attention. She didn't see him. "That's dark, dude."

"Trust me, man," I said. "In the past thirty-six hours, I've already seen things that just ain't, you know, *normal*."

Briefly, I told him about my limo ride, the bellman in the hotel, my run-in with the network news guy and his German cameraman.

"How'd you know the guy's German?"

"I dunno. Screamed at me, sounded German."

And finally about my deal with the man on the stump.

Dan stood up and nodded me into the kitchen.

It was still sunny outside (which made it feel still early, thankfully) the view partially blocked by several glass-encased candles. Votives, I think they're called.

In the corner, there was a small television that caught my attention until Dan drew my gaze back and introduced me to Esperanza.

She looked tired for a woman so young, barely meeting my eyes as we were introduced, then looking away quickly.

At first I thought it was just shyness. Then I realized that she'd been watching the TV in the corner of the room as she was building sandwiches. Her gaze went back to her show.

"Anza's been bored out of her mind for nearly a year now."

"Daniel, don' say to him," his wife said, her accent surprisingly thick, not looking away from the television. The short, dark bangs that framed her pretty face parted in the middle, hanging a bit low. Like they were curtains, slowly closing and parting again.

"She was a teacher back in Chilpancingo. I met her when we did a vacation giveaway thing at a station in Florida."

I didn't know really what to say. "You guys look good together."

"Well, she'd be much happier with a job and, you know, legal status," he said to me as she put together lunch on the rollaway island in the kitchen. He then dropped his voice. "She spends most of her day around the house just watching TV and duckin' the neighbors."

"Why isn't she—"

"Legal? Paperwork. Takes forever. She's got a master's but can't get even a substitute teaching job until the residency paperwork comes through."

"That sucks."

"We've been waiting more than three years."

"Jesus," I said and got a scolding look from her.

Dan raised his hands and said something in Spanish. I didn't even know he knew Spanish.

"Yeah, about that sorta thing," he said quietly, leaning against the fridge. "She was raised pretty religious. Catholic. So she's not into that sort of, uh, *stuff* in the house."

"Sorry, dude."

"No, but that's…" Dan said and was quiet for a moment, staring off. "That's the point. It brings us to what I'm thinking."

His voice trailed away from me for a moment as something on the television caught my eye.

No, that wasn't right.

Not… not something happening on the TV. Something on the screen.

Or not on the screen? I couldn't put my finger on it.

"Raz, you listening? Did you even hear me?"

"Yes. Just repeat everything you said so I can check if I heard it right."

He blew out a long breath.

"She really needs to get out of the house," Dan said. "And as you describe your, uh, quest… I mean, there's historical and religious shit there, right? That she definitely knows a lot about. So, seriousl—"

"*Wait.* Hold on."

"What?"

I turned to face my friend. "Are you trying to pawn your illegal wife off on me because she's *bored*?"

"Naw, dude."

"Yeah, you are."

"No, no," he said and leaned toward me, thought for a moment, then leaned back again. "She's super smart."

"Still, she married you."

"Yeah, she's got some lapses in judgment on occasion," he said, smiling.

"So she seems *perfect* for a quest to rip my wife from the clutches of an incurable disease, while battling for my eternal soul."

"Right? Totally!"

Esperanza, eyes not leaving the television, barked something at him in her native tongue. He nodded.

"Her English is coming along, too."

"Oh, Jesu— I mean, *fuck*, dude."

He gripped me hard on the shoulders with both hands and laid on one of his huge Dan grins. He then turned and gave his wife a version of my story—in English, mind you—in a synopsis even shorter than I'd given him.

However, he began to use larger words when describing the bit about this being sort of a deal with the Prince of Darkness, Satan.

Still, she nodded along, her eyes actually clearer than when I'd first seen her.

But I wasn't sure if she completely underst—

"Sure," she said and looked to me, smiling. "Sure, I'll go."

"Uh, *what?*"

Stepping up beside her husband, she began to speak faster, which actually made her grip on English borderline arthritic.

"My mother is reading out of the Bible when we were on her nipple for years."

"Years on the nipple, huh?" I said. "That's beautiful."

"Also, there is more Spanish in much of the world than in English!"

Out of the corner of my eye, I noticed something strange on the TV screen again.

No, no… It's not something happening *on the screen. What* is *that?*

"Oh, and she's got a lot of miles saved up," Dan said proudly, his arm around his tiny wife's shoulders. "She goes back and forth to Mexico all the time to see family. That might even help you guys get around."

I nodded slowly, distantly. "Oh, Uncle Jerry's a pilot. He can fly. I'm not sure what—"

"Then it's settled," Dan said and clapped his two big meaty hands onto my shoulders again. "This is awesome. Anza, you're going to love Raz. I've wanted you two to get to know each—"

"Wait," I said, blinking away the fog. "Hold on, man."

"What?"

"You…" I said, trying to concentrate, but something was drawing my attention elsewhere. "You don't actually *believe* me, do you?"

"Raz…"

"No, seriously. Wait! You think this is some stupid, um, lark of mine or…" I lost my train of thought. Then I reset and slowly raised my hands, batting them around as if trying to catch a sound only I could hear. "What… *is* that?"

Dan and Esperanza followed my gaze, turning toward the television.

The show rolling across the screen wasn't one I normally watched.

His wife said it was some program about kings and queens and a lot of schtupping (she didn't use the word schtupping). Obviously it was pay cable because there were two, maybe three, people writhing around on the screen without clothes on.

It wasn't really clear where one person ended and the other began.

And where there wasn't naked flesh, it was all leather… and goblets… spotty British accents.

Some sort of period piece, then?

An actor's face appeared near the navel of some very skinny girl. I'd caught it earlier, but it now looked so odd on the screen.

Then it hit me. *Oh, Christ. Oh, shitburgers, what..?*

I said: "Oh, sweet Jesus."

In some sort of faraway distance, even though she was just standing a foot away from me, I barely heard: "Daniel, I don' like that talking with the house!"

In my mind, I could see the entire day quickly playing back like a segment on some late-night cable practical-joke show. Moments that I hadn't bothered to pay attention to.

And if this was what it was, then this was the reveal, all laid out for some audience who'd been in on the joke the entire time as they laughed louder and louder, *obscenely* even, while I had to sit through the sequence that was to undoubtedly end badly.

The ghoulish bellman who'd brought me my breakfast, he was the first.

Then, as I stumbled from my hotel room, down the elevator, squinting in the sun that poured into the lobby. I could see their faces: an old couple getting in the elevator as I exited. One person reading a *USA Today* as he sat in an overstuffed chair.

In this replay, each wore a little paper square, like a marathoner would. These people were labeled 2, 3, and 4.

A woman at the check-in desk. Number 5.

The deep voice of a man resonated in my head. "Shall I flag you a cab, sir?"

"Yes, thank you."

Old man at the door. The doorman. His cheap tux-and-tails getup hadn't originally been capped off with a fluttering bit of paper, tied with string and a 6 emblazoned upon it. I would have noticed that before.

But it was there now, in the playback.

The cab driver was 7.

Fast-forward to my friend Adam. It spun my childhood bestie through time-lapse anguish, then delight. 8.

Uncle Jerry, turning toward me as he fought off the closet monster: 9.

My second run-in with the ghoulies, this time the network news guy and his possibly German cameraman.

10 and 11.

Then Dan. 12.

His illegal wife, who'd just joined Team Raz with Uncle Jerry, she would have been thirteen.

But, no. That wasn't right. Glancing toward her as the last few minutes played out, I could see she wasn't wearing a number.

In an echo, as if it were done for comical effect for the show playing in my head, was a replay of my conversation with the Advocate about the people who would be allowed to help me:

"Just three?" I'd said.

"Well, two, actually," the smaller man said. "The third has to be random."

"Random?"

"Yes, random... sort of. Actually, after you leave this vehicle, it will be the thirteenth person you set eyes on."

But Esperanza, *she* had been the thirteenth.

Right?

No.

I realized, I'd caught sight of the television *before* seeing Dan's wife.

"It... that can't be," I said quietly, looking intently at the face on the TV screen.

Unbelievably, right there in front of me was a butt-ass naked actor wearing only a square of thin paper, which was lightly rippling against the forehead of a pretty young actress.

On the paper: 13.

At the front door, as if on cue, a knock. Dan looked past me toward the front of the house, then back at Anza. "You expecting anyone?"

"No, honey," she said, shrugging. "I here illegally. No guests."

He breezed right past me.

"Wait..."

He opened the door, but I had closed my eyes. Everything was spinning out of my control.

In that quiet moment, I was so ashamed. To save my beautiful Carissa, I needed to be strong for her! Stronger than I'd ever been. The man fuckin' IN CHARGE! Kickin' ass and takin' names!

But I wasn't in charge. No ass-kicking. And frankly, I'm terrible with names.

From behind me, Anza let out a delighted shriek.

"I can' believe it! *I can' believe* the tiny man is on my house!"

Opening my eyes, I saw it was indeed the actor from the goblets-and-schtupping television show.

He was in a fluffy red bathrobe, half the size of any I'd seen before. Because, he was… What do they call them now?

He was, uh, a little person.

"Holy shit, honey," Dan said. "Look! It's that dwarf guy you like from your show!"

"I think… I think it's little people," I called out. "Uh, little person."

His thick brown hair going in all directions, brow furrowed, and swaddled in his fluffy robe, he just stood at the open door.

Behind him, Uncle Jerry ran up, stopped about fifteen feet away, spun in a small circle, and put his hands out like he'd likely seen in some 1970's karate movie.

The actor crossed his arms, looked up at Dan, and said: "Who the fuck are you people? And how the *fuck* did I get to this shithole, assface?"

The Wick Manifold

29 November

Dearest Carissa,

Thank you for taking the time to find my finger.

I thought spending your birthday at the pop-up Cobb County Fair would be great but admittedly should have been aware of the news reports about the rise in prescription drug abuse by carnival workers.

Who knew the teacup ride could be so dangerous?

After the "safety" bar whacked my pinky into the darkness, it was nice of the haunted house staff to come over to help and look for it in the tiny fake cemetery with the all those tiny fake headstones.

However, despite the undead zombie racecar driver's promise to look again on his next smoke break and the sincere apology from "Brad the Impaler" that it happened at all (I think it was an apology. He'd refused to take the costume dental accessory out, so it was hard to tell... at least I think it was a costume dental appliance), I only felt better when you'd remarkably fished my tiny digit out of that angry lady's cotton candy.

Putting it in her snow cone was genius, and all while ducking the subsequent volley of fists she threw. It showed a particular athletic grace.

You're the total package, sweetheart.

In a few months, I'll be the proudest man on the planet to stand in front of all of our friends and family to take your hand in mine so that we can be wed forever.

So I guess it's a good thing you found my pinky.

Love, Your Rasputin

P.s. The nursing staff says my finger *may* be permanently "blue raspberry" stained, but it will always remind us of the nice time we had at the fair.

Chapter Nine

"Raz, we gotta skedaddle," Uncle Jerry said, looking at his wrist, tapping a small bone that slightly protruded at the joint. I wondered if he'd worn a watch at one point. "Burnin' daylight."

The moment the Actor walked in (*loudly* for a little dude, I'd like to note), Jerry had followed closely behind.

Standing in Dan's living room, the Actor's eyes darted around, and he shuffled his limbs, looking like a man who had one extra hand and one less pocket to put it in.

After the vehicular lookout station turned out to be a big fail, Uncle Jerry had come inside and switched into mob hideaway lookout mode. Or maybe more accurately: low-budget horror flick's terrified-camp-counselor mode.

He stood with his leather duffel draped over his shoulder at the living room window with the curtains drawn, except for the spot where he was peeking out. There he'd gripped either side of the heavy fabric, fashioning a sort of peephole just large enough for him to see out of.

There was very little question that, from outside, it would appear as though someone were trying to go unnoticed as they peeked out of a small gap in the curtains.

I looked at him for just a moment, and again, it was as if I was once more staring at the old rock album poster back in his bedroom. Thankfully, this time Uncle Jerry was fully clothed.

Occasionally his head would swivel casually from the window to a bowl of uncracked nuts on the living room table. He seemed to be mortally locked in some type of battle of wills with the contents of the bowl.

The nuts were winning.

Dan's wife, Esperanza, stood at the entryway by the kitchen with hands clasped at her chest, watching the Actor, who was working his mobile phone. He'd called both of his assistants, then his manager, a publicist, then a former assistant. He'd spoken to his agent in a low, angry tone. Then briefly rang his mother, I believe.

For a full minute, the Actor stared at the phone, finger poised over the keypad under the glass. He seemed to have been scrolling through a contact list but had run out of choices.

The man jumped slightly when his agent, who was apparently in Atlanta on business, finally called back and agreed to come get him.

The rest had chosen not to take his call. Including his mother.

Satisfied that life would soon return to normal, the dwarf actor ran his palms down the length of the red robe and cinched the waist a little tighter.

"I just want to know, " he said, "which one of you pricks had me drugged? Is this some stupid hidden-camera TV-prank thing? Bor-ring." Glancing at his reflection in a glass cabinet, he slipped his mobile phone back into the robe's pocket and then fingered his hair for a moment.

My good friend was now sitting on the couch, rubbing his temples hard enough to cause memory loss.

"Hello? You, the lanky fuck on the sofa. *Hell-lo?*" The Actor glared at Dan, who seemed not to hear him. "Seriously, I'm suing everyone here. After I get to a doctor to find out what… happened, they can test for whatever you kidnapping lunatics gave me. They've got kits for that sort of thing, you know. I'm fairly certain of that."

I was in a big chair facing my friend, who may I remind you went by "Sideshow" on the radio. A BarcaLounger with its footrest kicked out held me so comfortably that I never wanted to leave it.

But back to Dan. He wasn't doing too good.

See, at the time, when he'd committed his wife to my Devil's quest, he'd believed it to be one of those "Rasputin things." And, true, in the past, I had been occasionally in the grips of the occasional bizarre, tangential, and fruitless outing. Mostly harmless. It would all often end in a night of beers and some storytelling.

And possibly a bail bondsman. Occasionally, a free clinic. But all in all, harmless.

Mostly.

When the Actor had appeared upon his doorstep, and I'd explained where he'd come from (or more accurately, *why*), Dan shook with a jolt of realization. The sort of jolt usually reserved for those lying flat on their backs with someone hovering over them shouting *"Clear!"*

No, this wasn't just one of those "Rasputin things." And it no longer sounded remotely harmless. Not even a little bit.

Dan now had a beer in each hand and was drinking both.

"Sorry, man, I told—"

"You *didn't*, Raz," he said. *Sip, sip.* "You said this was some sort of Crossroads pact, a deal with the Devil…"

"Uh, well. It is, man."

"Right, yes, I know, but *you know* I didn't believe you, right?" he said—*sip, sip*—and a little bit of beer spilled from each bottle onto his pressed cargo shorts. "Obviously!"

"Hey, I'm sorr—"

"You think I would have agreed to something like that?"

"I told you, though. I wasn—"

"Excuse me!"

"You could have been more explicit, Raz!"

"Excuse me!"

"You mean more clearly expressed than 'Dan, I've made a deal with the Devil?' How the—"

"Ex-fucking-scuze me… dirty common little plebeians."

Our heads snapped toward the kitchen and we both caught sight of the Actor. He smiled at us unpleasantly, then said, "A car will be here in five minutes."

"That was fast," Dan said.

The Actor shrugged. "I'm important."

Flash!

The room lit up with a brief crackle of white light, and I braced for something horrible, but instead the next moment was filled with the childlike squeal of Dan's wife.

"I can' believe the little man is in my kitchen!" Despite one of her favorite actors being only five feet away at the kitchen table, she stared at the screen of her camera phone and the picture she'd just taken of the Actor, as if the photograph itself were right then the premier experience to be cherished.

"Oh, hmm," said the Actor. "Well…"

"Oh." She looked up, the joy draining from her face in an instant. "Is this okay that I make your picture?"

"Yes, yes." The Actor grinned, showing an impressive set of teeth. "Come here. We'll make one together."

Her joy was back like a slap, and she went to hand the phone to Dan.

"No, no," he said with an arm propped up on the kitchen table, waving her over. "I can do that. I'll hold it out. We'll take a selfie."

"It… what?"

"A selfie. Haven't you ever done a selfie?"

"No," she said, eyes dancing as she walked toward the dwarf. "I'm Catholic. But I caught Dan doing it one time in the bathroom—"

"Hey!" Dan said and half stood from the couch. "Come on, now, he's talking about taking *photos*, Anza! Is that really appr—"

She said, "I don' wanna see no photos of that."

"Anza!"

"Is bad enough to having wash the popcorn ceiling in the bathroom."

"*Anza!*"

I gave Dan a sideways look with hooded eyes and said evenly: "Ceiling? Bravo, my friend. Bravo."

The Actor took the phone handed to him and extended his arm. She nestled under it, crouching and smiling wide.

"You good?" he said, still grinning.

She smiled sweetly toward the smartphone in his hand. "*Si.*"

"Wonderful," he said and looked toward it too.

He then slapped his hand down sharply on the table. As the phone smashed, there was a crunch, and several pieces spit out from under his stubby fingers, jetting to opposite sides of the room.

He exhaled loudly and smiled once more. However, this seemed to be the first real smile I'd seen from him since he'd arrived.

"No pictures, then, okay?" the Actor said. "Okey dokey, all right."

Esperanza shrugged, looked toward Dan, and began chattering away in Spanish. She sounded angry, but her face did not betray that particular emotion. Still calmly *rat-a-tat-tat* muttering, we watched as she walked to a drawer, pulled out an identical phone, then went to the table and removed the SIM card from the entrails of the smashed phone, putting it in this new one.

Her stream of words didn't end, only dimmed, as she walked from the kitchen toward the bedroom.

"That was a prick thing to do, man," Uncle Jerry said from the window.

The Actor sighed. "Screw you, spongy smelly."

I stood. "You'll be paying for her phone, Mr. Important."

He exhaled again, scooted back toward a chair, and sat down. He pulled an invisible wallet from his bathrobe.

"Fine, fine," he said. "In fact, I'll pay double if none of you talk to me before my car gets here."

Dan waved me off before I could lay into Mr. Hollywood.

Me, I'm a genuinely jolly guy. Almost one hundred percent of the time.

Almost.

However, at least in my case, that means when I do get angry it's a bit disproportionate. On more than one occasion, Dan had talked me off the proverbial ledge before I potentially lost my mind on some bona fide asshole.

My friend stood, tugged at my elbow, and walked me into his dining room. Uncle Jerry went back to his curtain watch.

Passing by the table, I noticed several nuts were now missing from the bowl.

"Okay, okay," Dan said, leaning onto the back of a wooden chair. "Putting aside all the other horrific shit you've brought to my doorstep today and simply focusing on the here and now—"

"I appreciate that."

"—and ignoring the total existential reflective chaos that I'm barely able to hold at bay—"

"Probably best."

"I thought you said that little prick in my kitchen would be *compelled* to join you? Right?"

"Yeah, that's what they told me," I said and looked toward the couch while patting my rear pocket. My copy of the contract wasn't there. Had I left it in the car?

Dan rubbed his large face. "Well, okay, think about that, right? Maybe it's all bunk. If that's not true, if he's not *compelled* right now, then maybe none of it's true."

"Nah, then he wouldn't have shown up at your door from hundreds of miles away," I said. "You heard what he said. He'd been at some hotel in Seattle or San Francisco. Cincinnati?"

"Sydney," the Actor called from the other room. "*Thousands* of miles, which of course, you know already. Look at you trying to act surprised in front of a trained professional! You shitty little people are all in on this shitty little prank!"

My hand flew up, and I flipped the guy off through the kitchen wall.

"I heard that," he said.

Turning back to my friend, I sat down at the slightly dusty dining room table.

"Listen," he said. "I know Carissa's real sick and all, but did you really think the solution here for you was to become Satan's fluffer?"

What an image. "Uh, *not* his fluffer."

"You know that expression 'going from the frying pan and into the fire?'"

"Wouldn't want to be *that* guy's fluffer."

"I mean, you literally did that. You put yourself into the fire. Or... fires!"

"He probably has a massive, scaly devil cock," I said, nodding. "All thorny. They don't make rubber gloves thick enough—"

Dan pulled something grayish out of a bowl between us on the dining room table. He then tossed the sad, dried-out orange at me.

"Stop, stop! No more Satan cock talk," he said and tried to hide a grin. "You really screwed the pooch on this, man. Only Rasputin could take the worst possible moment of his life and make it exponentially worse."

"I'm glad you're getting such a kick out of it."

"No, man," my best friend said. "I love ya, but you know, you do this to yourself all the time. It's terrible, but you do."

At that moment, the Advocate's words again echoed in my head: "*Eventually, Rasputin, you always lose, every time.*"

What was I doing? No way could I *really* pull this off.

Then Dan's voice brought my attention back to the present. I asked him to repeat what he'd said. Looking toward him, I saw there was dampness in his eyes.

"I'm... sorry that you're going through this," he said and finally sat down across from me. "I know how much she means to you."

"More than you can imagine."

He nodded and cleared his throat. "But this... How is this an option? How did you even know this *was* an option?"

"Oh, that's funny. Remember the movie *Karate K—*"

He just kept talking, ignoring me. "This is so crazy, man. Even for you. Why, Raz?"

I looked at him like it was obvious. "She is my everything."

For a moment, his eyes lost focus, and then a smile crept to his lips. "Yeah. Yeah, I remember you before Cassie came along."

"At least one of us does."

He chuckled. "Man, it's probably best you *don't* remember those couple years before she showed up."

I laughed. "Well, see? That's what I've been saying!"

"Yeah, you're fucked without her."

"Right," I said and laughed. "I owe her. I'm doing everything I can to be a better man, you know, be someone who can step up and save her."

"You've got a messed-up way of doing it, man."

"I'm outta options."

"Deal with the Devil ain't really an option. Jesus."

From the hallway, his wife's voice split the heavy air: "I say before and now again: I don' want talk like that in my house."

"Sorry, baby."

She plopped onto the couch, flipping through some crumpled pages. Once I finally realized what she was reading, I opened my mouth, but she cut me off.

"Okay," she said. "We haf' to find five pieces for your lamp, but there is no directions or nothing."

"Hey, where did— Wait, it's four, not five."

"Four plus fuel," she said. "So, is sort of five."

"Where you'd get my contract from? I thought it was—"

Not looking up, she said, "I took it from out your pocket."

I turned to Dan. "She's a master thief. Did you know this before you married her?"

He stood. "Of course. It only took her an instant to steal my heart."

From his window lookout, Uncle Jerry glanced toward me, and we both made a sickened face. "Blech," said Jerry.

"Do you wan' me to read how to for finding your pieces, then?"

Dan stood from the table and sat next to his wife on the couch. He then looked up at me. "You don't *know* where to find this thing, Raz?"

"It's spread out all over," I said, shrugging. "And that… I was getting to that next. It'll tell us where we have to go."

Anza shook her head. "It does not tell us where we have to go."

"That'll make getting there more difficult, Raz," Uncle Jerry said, gripping his curtain hole, not looking back at us.

I dropped back into the BarcaLounger. If I were now condemned to burn for eternity, at least I could meet the fires of Hell in a comfy chair.

"This… this is very lawyery gobbledy-gook," Anza said.

My eyes drifted to the ceiling. "Is that your learned opinion, then?"

Shuffling between several pages, she said nothing for a full minute.

"Can I have my Hell contract back, Anza?"

"Can *you* read lawyery gobbledy-gook, Raz?" asked Dan.

"Not so much, but I doubt your wife—"

"Heez wife has a master's of education from University of Chihuahua, Mexico," she said, then shot me a look. "Rasputin, Daniel say you have a certificate from the Connecticut School of Broadcasting. And you never even been to Connecticut, I bet."

"Sure, but also never went to a fucking doggy school—"

Dan raised his hands between us. "No, give her a second. She's been acting as her own immigration lawyer. She spends half her time reading this sorta shit."

"But isn't she still here *illegally*, man?"

"Well, yeah, technically, sure."

Uncle Jerry spoke from his post, again not turning around. "We're all here illegally, man. If you think about the Indians— who really ain't Indians, right?—we're all illegals except them." He added: "Technically."

After a few moments, the middle-aged man turned toward us, probably because he could feel me and Dan staring at him.

He blinked a couple times. "Something I picked up at the prison."

"You were in p-prison?" I said, the words tripping up somewhere around my teeth. "You left that out earlier, man! When where you in prison?"

"Alcatraz."

Dan went a little white. "You were in Alcatraz? Dude, how old *are* you?"

Uncle Jerry turned back to the window. Instead of answering, he said, "Black Lincoln coming down the street."

Dan's face drained a little more.

The Actor said, "My ride. Prepare yourselves for my leaving."

"You weren't at Alcatraz, Uncle Jerry," I said.

"Yes, I was at Alcatraz," he said, still peeking through his hole. "They got a tour. And there's a side part where they got stuff about Indians, which you don't gotta pay extra for."

"Does anyone else feel like the world is spinning uncontrollably off its axis?" Dan said and slumped farther into the couch.

"Okay, Uncle Jerry, very helpful," I said, reaching for the contract, but Anza snatched it from my fingertips, holding it away from me.

"Listen to your Uncle Jerry," she said.

"He is *not* my Uncle Jerry. And I doubt any of tha—"

"Hush," Dan's wife said, interrupting me. "It say location of pieces is… 'app-parent.'"

"Oh, jeez."

"Don' *say* 'jeez' in my—"

"That doesn't count," I said. "It's only part of—"

"It counts. It counts. It's what you intend, what you mean to say, so it counts." I started to protest, but she talked over me, reading from my Hell contract: "Any necessary destination— one which is imperative to fulfilling this signed accord—will be apparent to either the contract holder or an agent of the same, depending upon which of those aforementioned is most aligned with the essence of the contracting party…"

Dan exhaled heavily. "Well, that's weird."

"Yep, Black Lincoln approaching," Uncle Jerry said again.

My head was spinning. "Okay, what? So what does it mean, then? Does it mean anything?"

"Yes," she said and looked toward me. "It means *you* will know the location. It's in your head. Because you are 'most aligned with the essence of the contracting party,' I am sorry to say."

The three of us fell silent and waited.

She added: "It means... I'm not sure how to say... since they are, you know, Hell peoples... whoever is the most not, uh, not the *goodest* one of us. Location of pieces is *app-parent* to that person. Which, is you, Rasputin."

"Me?" I said. "I'm the most not the goodest?"

Dan nodded. "You had a rough couple of years. Did some pretty bad shit, man."

Couldn't argue with that. "Okay, okay," I said. "Shit... uhh..."

My head spun again, this time in other direction. Still, I concentrated harder, trying to pull the app-parent destination out of the ether.

Nothing.

"I... What do I have to do?"

"It's in your head, Rasputin," Anza said. "Focus and *consecrate*."

"I've got a lot of stuff in there," I said, my voice a little shaky. "And a lot of it's fuzzy around the edges. A lot of stuff. But what I *don't* have is a goddamn—"

"Not in my hou—!"

Dan started shaking his head at me. "Raz, seriously, stop doing that, man."

Uncle Jerry chimed in: "Black Lincoln in the driveway, man. Stopping outside the house now. Just, you know... FYI."

"I don't have anyth—"

"Brussels," a voice behind Dan said.

Everything went quiet for a moment. Then we all turned toward the Actor, who was standing at door of the kitchen, spooning frozen vanilla ice cream into his mouth from a tub in his hand.

"Brussels," he said, then added: "That's in Belgium."

The Actor then turned to me, shrugged, and said, "Hey, they weren't all fat years in my illustrious career. Especially back in my starving-in-Brooklyn days. But you're looking to go to Brussels… app-parently."

"Ooo," said Anza. "What did you do so bad?"

Before he could answer—not that he was going to answer—but before he could, someone or something large and strong *kicked in the door* to my friend Dan's house.

Chapter Ten

Looking back over all of my life's experiences, on only two occasions had I seen someone actually kick down a door.

The first time? That's a story for another time.

The second time someone did it, they ended up standing in the middle of my friend Dan's living room, looking ghoulish and rageful.

"Which of you is Rasputin?" the door-kicking intruder growled.

I looked quickly toward Dan, but he'd grabbed Anza, and both were tearing off toward the master bedroom.

My man at the curtain? Gone.

I yelled, less in anger and more to push the fear in my stomach back down, "Nice lookout, Uncle Jerry!"

From behind me, I heard the Actor gasp. "*Stanley?* Jesus, is that you?"

A muffled voice came from the bedroom: "I don' want talk like that in my house!"

Stanley was a short and very round man with an immaculately trimmed jet-black beard. He did not look like the sort of man who could ever smash a door in. But a look at his face—with the new visual acuity imbued upon me by my contract with the Old Man—told me he was a demon possessed.

And it was clear he was working for Hell's new blood. Corporate turf wars come to the dark side.

Stanley the Fat Demon looked at me menacingly. "Ras-puuutin..."

Mocking him, I growled back: "Stan-leeee!"

The gruesome, heaving man turned toward the Actor, who wasn't quite on the same page as me and Stanley yet. "What the hell are you doing?" the Actor asked. "Why are you *here*? And what in all that is holy happened to your face, man?"

Stanley's eyes went to me, and he spoke with a mouth full of bloodied teeth. "In town, working out a deal for a Ron Howard interactive web series. Rom-com thing. Then I was alerted—"

"No!" The Actor stomped his small foot with surprising force. "No, I mean *here*! At this house. I thought you were sending a car to get me the hell out of here?"

I pointed at the fat man. "You're his agent?"

He laughed in an odd, phlegmy manner and began to creep toward me. "Rasputin, I want you to give the Old Man a message from my employer."

Trying to mask my fear, I again turned angry. "Do I look like fucking Western Union?"

The agent-demon faltered briefly, looking down, his Brillo Pad-like eyebrows knitted together. "Actually, that's not a very good analogy. Western Union has long since moved out of the message-slash-telegram space."

"Shit, I know, it was just a throwaway lin—"

"They're mainly for wire transfer of funds from one country to the next. Big business from the 'day labor' market in the U.S. to south of the border. Great points for that, if you've seen the breakdown."

"Seriously," I said. "For the love of…" I stopped, glanced toward the bedroom, and edited my words in deference to the woman of the house. "*Gandhi*, it was just *a line*, man… Never mind."

The agent/demon had an expression in his eyes that one might see moments before a prison-shower violation. "You want to get a message to the Old Man?" I said shakily, but still trying to sound cool. "Hit 'em on Twitter. We don't chat."

Stanley the Agent's flesh trilled with dark, disgusting ripples. Tendrils of electricity danced across his hands, whipping and snapping between his fingertips. When he smiled now, a muddied red glow bled from his mouth.

While I'm not quite ready to wholly admit it even now, at that moment, I think a little bit of poop came out of me.

The ghoulish electrified man pulsed with some otherworldly energy as he walked closer and closer to me. The air in the room began to choke with the smell of fried circuitry.

"Doesn't matter, Rasputin," he said as he raised his arms up. "You'll see him momentarily. I'll burn your flesh so deep, it'll scar your soul with a memo from Hell, Inc. to him: Your time is nearly up!"

I said: "Pithy."

The Actor muttered something, and I turned to him. He's a performer, sure, so I didn't take much from the utterance, which could be easily mistaken as some moment of kindness.

But his face was turned to me, and his expression had softened from before.

If you could discard his training, which you can't, I'd have almost believed he was pleading for my life.

The Actor had said, simply, "Don't."

Still, that one word froze me for an instant. The ever-present rage/fear/anxiety within me reflected back upon itself and for a brief moment, it quieted.

And in what could easily be determined as a wrong place/wrong time sort of personal reflection, the one thought now rolling around my mind was: *Why am I always so angry?*

My face must have softened, which told my demonic attacker that this was his moment to strike. His squat body lifted from the carpet with a crackle of static electricity. Stanley the Agent arched and flexed ready to strike.

With my back literally against the wall, there was nowhere left to run, so I let my shoulders fall and scowled at him.

"Seriously, when was the last time Ron Howard was actually relevant? They doing another *Cocoon* anytime soon?"

The Actor looked at me. "You don't get out a whole lot, do you?"

For his part, Stanley the agent's reply was a roar that split time and space, rattling both this world and the next. "Raaarrrnmmaaaahhh—!" *FUP-FUP-FUP-FUP!*

Now, to be clear: He did not actually say *"FUP-FUP-FUP-FUP."*

No.

The first bit, sure, that was all Mr. Demon Agent. Scary, phlegmy, death-chant style. Very scary.

The last bit was actually courtesy of Uncle Jerry, to which I asked, "What the hell was that?"

I spun and looked toward the dining room, and standing there was Jerry, a dried orange at his feet and some bizarre contraption in his hands, which was winding down from its full-on spin. As it slowed to a stop, I swear it looked like the large spindle of a .38 revolver. But this one was as big as a double boiler.

Staring at Uncle Jerry, I amended my question: "What the hell *is* that?"

Stanley the Agent's body sizzled and hissed, then it fell to the floor. A moment later, a smell that someone needed to instantly and profusely apologize for flooded the room.

I prodded the eldest companion of Team Raz: "Jerry? What is… that contraption you are holding?"

He looked to his hands, as if he'd momentarily forgotten what had just happened. "Oh? It's… well, you said back at the house this could be dangerous."

"Right… yes," I said slowly. I saw Dan come out of the bedroom and nodded to him that it was over. "Yes, I remember telling you that."

"So, hell… I thought, 'better bring my spear gun.' I, uh, had it modified a bit a little while ago."

"This I see."

"'Cause, *officially*, I'm no longer allowed to carry a firearm."

"Clearly, that's for the best for everyone," I said.

"But this'll do in a pinch," he said and propped the modified barrel onto his shoulder like he might a shotgun or rifle.

"Well," I said. "Good thought, then. Thanks for saving my life. Again."

Uncle Jerry looked down at the agent/demon, still smoldering and crackling with sparks, then back to me. "No problem, bossman," he said. "We gotta save your lady, right?"

Instantly, my eyes watered, and I smiled at him. A dark, hidden part of me was ashamed for so quickly dismissing him as I had earlier. Something told me that this was a judgment I'd have to make up for.

However, the time for judgments was coming despite my success or failure. Soon.

"Raz," Sideshow said to me in a voice that made me uneasy. "I'm wobbling here. Seriously, I'm pretty sure a freakout is coming."

"No, no," I said. "Everything's cool. This... whatever-guy is aligned with another faction in Hell."

My friend took a half step back. "Just... man, for a little bit, don't say that word. It makes it all too, you know, real."

"Sure, fine."

"I mean, there's a *dead guy in my house*. I can't even wrap my head around that, man. And, shit, my wife is going lose it when she sees that. I don't think—"

From behind Dan, we heard a long creaking sound, and we all stared with jaws hanging a little bit, half waiting for another creepy demonoid assault. Instead, Anza came into the living room, and her hands went to her mouth when she saw the dead man on the floor, still smoldering.

"Tha's Berber carpet! I do not think dead fat guy will be coming out of it, Daniel!"

"S'okay, baby," Dan said and breathed through his teeth. "I'm sure Raz will pay for the carpet later."

"Of course!"

Dan looked at the body, then to me, then to Anza. He closed his eyes for a second. "Any way I can pull her back out of this? I really didn—"

"You offered. She accepted," I said. "Somewhere that flips a lever that can't be unflipped."

"You never were very good at contracts."

Nodding, I said, "Wasn't good at much. But she'll be okay. I promise."

My friend stared at me for a long moment. Then, he softened. "If you guys are going to go, then you better go."

Anza ran from the room. "Quick packing!" she yelled.

I shouted back at her. "If you've got a revolving spear gun back there, leave it. We're good."

My other best friend in the world walked up to me and clamped his large hand on my shoulder. I didn't even have to look, I knew he was shaking his head, eyebrows arched, half smiling.

"So I guess I gotta get rid of *that* nasty thing on the floor?" he asked.

I patted his hand. "Be a dear, would you?"

Chapter Eleven

No one can exactly put a date on it, because it had begun without flourish and without announcement (Years later, Hell, Inc.'s marketing department rebranded that time as a "soft launch"), but a short time ago, relatively speaking, something changed.

Or as some in the dark, brooding underworld would have argued, *nothing* was changing.

So in response to this static nature, a smaller, albeit more organized, faction began to quietly grow within the dark, smoldering environs of Hell itself.

Initially, when the Old Man (aka the Devil, Satan, Beelzebub) got wind of this very small group of recently deceased corporate hacks, he watched them with glee as they struggled. This was his house, after all. He was the man with the plan. And the biggest horn, when it came down to it.

But from the beginning, in the struggle between dark and light, the former had always found itself second fiddle to the latter. Then there had a been that brief moment when it seemed like, yes! Finally they would claim their prize. Hell would finally rule the Earth!

But no… the Old Man had it but let it slip right through his pointy manied fingers. He had cocked it up. It was time for new leadership.

Now, when the Old Man and his lieutenants caught wind of this insurrection brought on by hell-sent corporate types, he'd jokingly labeled this new batch of fresh-faced young'uns Hell, Inc., a name that would spin them into laughing fits so intense, so joyful, that they'd all have to go out for a weekend-long soul-crushing bender through a number of impoverished countries to get back into the Hell "groove" of things.

In a bold, if derivative, marketing move (see: Big Bang), this new group actually adopted this apparent pejorative. They even had letterhead bearing the Hell, Inc. name.

So while Heaven and Hell had been at war since time began, the Battle for Down Below was now a more pressing struggle. And it was coming down to the wire.

For both fights.

So, *so,* close now.

Hell, Inc.'s chairman, Steve Janus, watched as the black Trans Am slowly pulled out of the driveway, paused at the curb—a man with slumped shoulders was at the door waving to them—then peeled away at an unnecessarily high speed.

The kill squad had failed at the initial location, but that hadn't been entirely a surprise when he'd seen who had been given the task.

"TV people," he muttered to his executive assistant. "Entirely useless."

The failure of the agent in the house he was looking at now was a surprise, though. As a talent representative, the man had caused far more misery and broken dreams than a vast majority of the chairman's other soldiers. He was a TopOne, a top-one-percent performer.

As the muscle car grew smaller and smaller down the road, he turned to his dog, which had deposited a pile impossibly larger than its own body.

"Maybe I'm thinking about this all wrong," he said and looked back up just as the car turned from sight. "We're heading back. I'm calling a meeting. We need a new action item."

The Actor frowned as he stepped from the car. "This is not the airport."

Uncle Jerry rubbed his face, probably in an attempt to look calm and casual. But, his sharp gaze, set beneath massive scrunched eyebrows, cut the air between him and the huge house we'd pulled up to.

Without a word, Uncle Jerry let the driver's side car door swing closed and walked up the path toward the expensive home.

Standing in the street, I held the seat forward for Anza.

"Uff, thees is like climbing out from a mouse's butt!"

We both stepped out of the passenger side, then closed the Trans Am's heavy steel door and followed Jerry.

"Uh, Uncle Jerry?" Anza said, flashing her eyes toward me, "there is not airport here. We haf' to get to Brussels, remember? Quick, quick!"

The eldest of our group looked back over his shoulder. "Yeah, nah, it's not the airport. But if we get that little bastard *near* an airport before we've secured our ride, he's going to bolt, and we'll never see him again."

"She asked the same thing I asked, but you'll answer her and not me," the Actor said.

"But the airport," I said slowly, walking next to Anza a little crablike, not entirely committed to where Jerry might be headed. "That's where all the airplanes are, right? We were going to get a plane, you said."

Uncle Jerry nodded, never changing his lumbering pace, then smiled in a way that didn't make me feel better. "I got an idea."

"What is idea?"

"Well… lemme just go ring the buzzer up there and see if I can get us in."

I looked at the house, then realized I hadn't *really* looked at it before that moment. In part because much of it was obscured by luscious sugar maples and a line of full, unkempt American holly trees that stood like the fat, slovenly door guards likely seen in the Actor's medieval sword-and-sex television show.

Obviously the tree line was less scenery and more screen. The mansion's owner was trying to keep his or her multi-million-dollar home on the down-low. A ten-thousand-square-foot house on the down-low.

Anza was less impressed.

"This is crazy ugly house."

"Well…"

"Uncle Jerry, you want to be inside of that?" she added. "Who lives inside there?"

Jerry turned toward us, walking backward now, and held his hands up. "Just gimme two minutes."

I looked at my best friend's wife and shook my head. "What are we supposed to do? Just wait here on the sidewalk?"

"Sure," Jerry said. He turned back around, then pointed over his shoulder with a stubby thumb. "Or you could stop the little bastard from taking off down the street."

We both turned and saw the straps of the Actor's tiny red robe flapping in the breeze as he ran toward a vacant cab skulking at the far end of the street in the fading light of the day.

Chapter Twelve

"How big is this damn house, anyhow?"

"It's big," Uncle Jerry said.

The old man who'd let us in was now in front of us, shuffling along, leading us through the ninth or tenth (I'd lost count) entryway.

"I have a place in Sicily probably twice as big as this," the Actor said, grimacing smugly. "But this place is... well, it's very special."

Uncle Jerry didn't bother to look at him and said, "What makes you say that?"

"Well, it's obvious that the owner's interior decorator battles with a serious case of self-loathing."

"Yeah," I said. "It's a little gaudy."

"Oh, no," said Anza, shaking her head disapprovingly. "I do not think even God would be feeling okay to come in here."

The Actor ignored her and continued his critical review. He was likely still a bit pissed after being caught in the street, lifted at arm's length like an escaped pug, and taken into the house. "It's like an old-school downtown Las Vegas casino crash landed into a soon-to-be condemned Thai restaurant in Jersey, and they force fed the wreckage to a reanimated Salvador Dali who vomited it all back out during a bad mushroom trip."

The three of us stopped and turned toward the Actor.

"Wow. That's actually kinda spot on," Uncle Jerry said.

When me and Anza smiled at him, he'd had enough Team Raz bonding, I guess, and slid past all of us, saying: "Let's go! If we lose the old geezer up there, we may never get out of this damned place."

Finally, about ten minutes later, we met our host.

"I am Enrique Chavez," he said with a huge smile topped with an amazing mustache. "Any friend of my friend is my friend... my friends."

Uncle Jerry turned and introduced each of us—lying about the Actor's name and instead calling him Steve, which earned him a scowl—then turned back to the owner of the huge home.

"Enrique, meet the guys. Guys, meet Enrique," he said, then added: "My drug dealer."

Enrique the drug dealer threw the French doors to his garden open with a flourish and stepped into the enclosed garden. The open, flowing sleeves of his silk kimono fluttered in the sudden burst of wind.

"Excuse me if I am lightly sweating. I was practicing tae kwon do down in my subterranean dojo."

I scanned the darkness, trying to make out any shapes I could. "You do have a somewhat musky dojo mojo about you."

With a huge smile twinkling in the moonlight above us, he bowed with his head. "*Muchas gracias*, my friend."

Darkness turned to light as he did—flood lights engaged by motion detectors.

"Come, my friends, and let me offer you the gift of *soledad*—the quiet and peaceful garden of my modest home," he said. "There is a sitting area in the middle, perfect for our chat time."

The moment we stepped into the garden, I felt the seed of a headache taking root. Looking up to the flood lights, I shielded my eyes, hoping to keep a potential migraine at bay.

I'd caught Anza's face and wondered if the light bothered her, too. She hadn't said anything since meeting Uncle Jerry's dealer, and her expression told me she did not approve. The lush—*very* lush—garden didn't do anything to change that.

"Garden," in fact, didn't seem appropriate. "Jungle" even struck me as a little too modest. Here was a man obviously trying to reverse the effects of global climate change from his backyard. And in truth, I think he had a shot.

Enrique beamed. "Beautiful, isn't it?"

"I love what you've done with the place, Enrique," Uncle Jerry said, politely agreeing.

"This is my serenity. *Mi centro*. My center," he took a deep, theatrical breath and despite himself, sneezed.

Walking slowly, I raised my arms perpendicular to my body because the foliage rose to my chest. My hope was we were heading to some sort of clearing.

I was anxious because light was fading (not in the garden, mind you), and if I had any chance of piecing together the Devil's lamp, we'd have to be en route to the first piece ASAP.

Leading the way for my best friend's wife, I glanced back and saw her sour expression had not changed. It would seem her religious upbringing made being anywhere near this guy a challenge. Still, she was quiet and braving it for the moment, and I silently thanked her.

Uncle Jerry had said he knew where to get a plane, and we'd need one to make the treks required to gather up the pieces of the lamp. He had not said the plane he had in mind belonged to a Honduran drug dealer living in the swanky Peachtree Battle neighborhood of Atlanta.

"Wait," I said and stopped walking. "Where's the Actor?"

"Rrrreeeccccccctttckkkktttt!"

"Ohmyfuggin'god, what was that?" Jerry yelled.

Above our heads, Anza and I caught sight of strange ribbons of brilliant color—deep swaths of red, yellow, and blue—that played between the white-hot light of the floods.

"Nnnrrraahhnnnttt!"

The light was then briefly eclipsed in front of me as those colors spread and unfurled before my eyes.

"Beautiful, no?" Enrique the drug dealer said in accented English. "They are *macao*. Macaw."

Ahead, some of the brush moved, and Jerry said, "Jeez, why'd ya paint your eagles?"

"No, no," our host said. "They are macaw. Like parrot. But don't shit as much, I think. These are the birds of my homeland. *Very* expensive to get here all the way from Honduras but worth every penny."

My eyes finally adjusted, and I again saw one of the birds swoop in a low arc and land on the low branch of a sweet gum tree. It was all very beautiful in a somewhat coke-fueled Charlie-Sheen-aimlessly-tramping-through-the-Vietnam-jungle sort of way. But still, beautiful.

Anza broke from her scowl spell momentarily. "Wait, where's our leetle man?"

"Right," I said. "I was just—"

"Here," a voice sprung up from an area of dense fronds to our left.

"What are you doing way over there?"

"Getting a reach-around from a ficus, I believe," the Actor said.

The scowl in Anza's voice was in her words. "What is—"

"You don't want to know."

"—ficus?"

My mouth hung open for a moment. I smiled. "It, uh, it's a plant. Or a tree," I said. "But right now, I'm going with plant."

"Huh," she said and started walking toward where Uncle Jerry and Enrique had headed. "If he's doing that with the plant, he's gonna get splinters right where you don' want no splinters."

"I think it was a joke."

"Good, 'cause I don' wanna have to put ointment on it."

"It was a joke, trust—"

"*And* I did not bring my glasses," she added.

She kept walking past as I just stood there. On her face was a tiny, barely perceptible smile. It was right then where I saw how my best friend had fallen in love with her.

And it was my duty, maybe above all else except for saving my own wife, to get her back to Dan safely.

A few moments later, we broke through the brush and found a small island of chaise longues and cement statues of either cherubs or naked babies, I wasn't sure which. There was also a series of stone fountains, each one larger than the next, lining the clearing's outside edges. Our host was already lounging in a chair.

"There they are! *Mi amigos!*"

With a huge, bleach-white smile beneath his thick black mustache, Enrique waved with one hand. In his other, he held a cocktail. Which was odd, because as far as I could remember, he hadn't brought one outside with us.

On the opposite side of the small clearing, the bushes gyrated and trembled. This stopped both Anza and me in our tracks. If some hairy, toothy creature was about to burst from the hedges, there was nowhere for us to run.

From the shuddering bushes came an animal-like sound. "*Rrrrrrr.*"

And again, now louder. "GggrrraaHHH!" Then: "*Fuck nature.*"

A moment later, the Actor stumbled out from the leaves and twigs with cuts across his forearms and hands.

"There he is! What a grand entrance!" Enrique cheered. "Would you like a drink, señor? Maybe a low ball?" He chuckled to himself, only stopping when no one else joined in.

Cinching his robe tighter, the Actor walked toward a chaise near the two other men. "Uh, I'll take Phrases You Never Have to Ask Someone Who's Worked for David Mamet for a thousand, Alex."

A moment later, we were all sitting in a semicircle around Enrique. While I'd turned down the offer of a cocktail—despite everything in my skull demanding the opposite—the others put their orders in with the old butler who'd casually skulked out from the bushes moments after we did.

When he returned, he'd gotten every one of the drinks wrong.

"Don't mind him. He's Portuguese," Enrique said, waving his hand dismissively as if that explained everything.

With a grunt, the Actor threw his drink in the bushes. "Mine had an umbrella in it!"

"Yes, very nice. They're imported."

"I'd ordered a vodka *martini.*"

Uncle Jerry sipped something brownish with whipped cream on top of it. He'd asked for a beer. "Why'd you import drink umbrellas? They don't got a drink-umbrella factory here in the States?"

Enrique beamed. "I have thousands of them in a climate-controlled storage area. Never run out!"

"And," I said, as the energy began to drain from me, "if there's a really bad rain storm, the mice will be terribly appreciative."

"Where do you having mice?" said Anza.

"No, Anza," I said, debating ordering something, if for no other reason than to see what I'd get instead. "It just—"

"Okay," our drug peddling host said, clasping his big hands together. "While you guys were playing in my luscious garden there, Uncle Jerry told me about your dilemma."

The Actor chuckled and crossed his bare legs as he laid back on his chaise. "I'm sure that went over splendidly."

Enrique's face dropped, his eyes softened. "It must have been so very hard all of these years, my friend," he said to the Actor. "The confusion…"

"What?"

"No, no," Enrique said, shrugging. "It's not any of my business. But it's great you can tell your friends about such a thing."

"Right, and as I'd said, Enrique, it'd be a special favor," Uncle Jerry said, rubbing his chin. "You probably recognize our friend in the robe from TV."

"Not from television, but I saw the movie you did with the trains. And the guy and the girl."

The Actor's face lightened. "Oh. Oh, yes. I was proud of that one."

"You should be," Enrique said, putting his hand on his heart. "It was very beautiful. And you were brilliant."

"Thank you, Enrique."

"But can you do roles like that as a little woman now?"

"*What?*"

"You're right," our host said. "Not my place."

I glanced over to Anza, who was still eyeballing Enrique. I couldn't help but smile. Uncle Jerry was a bit slow. Clumsy. Strange, sure. But give him a little time, and he could continuously surprise you.

The old butler came back for follow-up drink orders but everyone waved him off. He shrugged and began to sweep up the nearby leaves and small branches that littered the circular patio space. Once he finished, he kicked at them and began sweeping it up again.

"I am sorry, though, my friend." Enrique said. "My answer is not one you will like."

Uh oh.

"But… I cannot help you."

Uncle Jerry looked at all of us quickly, then back to his dealer. "Hey, hey… Enrique. The actor's worth millions. We're good for it."

Another shrug. "Not my call."

"It's your plane, though, right?"

"*Si*, but I don't take it out on whims," he said and shook his head. He laughed, but there was no joy in it. In fact, I sensed something else entirely.

Fear.

"We just need to do a quick run—under the radar—to Brussels and back." Uncle Jerry pointed at the Actor. "He can't go by commercial airliner, you know… this is supposed to be secret."

"But…" Enrique stared at him uncomfortably. "It won't be a very good secret when he's coming back with tits and a vagina."

"I will not have tits and a vagina!"

Anza waved her hand in the air. "They are not so bad. You get used to them. And sometimes men buy you things."

"Still! Still, my friends," Enrique said and laughed his empty laugh again. "It is my plane, but, *mi amigo*, I have no say in the matter." He lowered his voice. To me, I sensed this man was a fan of theatric, but this seemed sincere. There was real concern in his voice. "This… uh, territory… we are beholden to the boss."

"Boss?"

The drug dealer's eyes flitted to each corner of the darkness around us. "Yes, yes. The don, okay? One Mr. Arduino Vencentio Cheetle."

"Oh, right. Of course," I mumbled, nodding as my mind drifted out of my own body slightly. "Makes total sense. Just hours into my quest to save my dying wife, and I'm sitting in an inner-city forest belonging to a Honduran mob drug dealer with the stoned non-uncle of my best friend and an illegal alien Ph.D. candidate."

The Actor looked at me. "What, I don't get a billing in your little horror story?"

I shrugged. "You don't even wanna be here!"

Enrique popped up and again scanned the darkness. A moment later, his too-large smile was back.

"My friends, it is out of my hands, for I am in the service of Don Cheetle."

"What?" This time Uncle Jerry stood up, incredulous. "*Don Cheadle*? I can hang with drug lords and mobsters… but I didn't know you were in cahoots with some Hollyweird *actor*, for crissakes!"

"Um…" the Actor said.

"Don' speak thataway around me, Uncle Jerry," Anza said. "Please, that is all I asking of you."

Our host popped back down on his chaise, knocking his glass to the stone paving. It shattered, and he simply glared at his ancient manservant, who slowly waddled over and began to pick up the tiny pieces with his fingertips.

"So," he said, his smile returning, "I am very sorry."

"I bet," Uncle Jerry said, looking like he was chewing something.

"Don Cheetle is a man not to trifle with. Don Cheetle is very powerful and not kind to those who would do trifling."

"Listen," I said, "if you could just not say his name, it's just very… distracting."

"The word of Don Cheetle surpasses that of even the Word of God," Enrique said and laughed. "The only reason, I believe, I am lucky enough to be in his employ is, well, my pedigree. There is a certain *authentico machismo* that a gentleman from my country has in this particular business."

"Your parents must be very proud," I said and looked away from Enrique. A dead end. Day One, and failure was right there, fully within my grasp. My task would have me circumnavigating the globe, and I couldn't get out of the Atlanta 'burbs.

Anza steeled a look at our host and said, scowling, "*Sus padres nunca se casaron.*"

Enrique threw his hands up, "Whoa, whoa… we are in America now, my love. No Spanish in my house. It makes the gringos very nervous. And as I listen to you… you could certainly work on your English!"

The prick laughed again, this time much harder. My desire to put a foot in the guy's face was nearly greater than my need to breathe.

I may have already failed, but it was *my* failure. These three people joined me (okay, one not *entirely* of his own free will) on my quest. For me. The least I could do is not let mustachioed asshats belittle them.

But there were, of course, men like Don Cheetle to consider. And we all saw how he got Terrence Howard booted from *Iron Man 2* and *Iron Man 3*… not a guy to mess with.

Anza stood and declared, "My English is just fine, prison toilet!"

This was the first time I'd ever heard real anger in Anza's voice. Anger steeped in malapropisms, but anger nonetheless.

She kept at him. "But I have been having to notice—"

"Yes, my dear, such a command of the English language you have, obviously," Enrique laughed again and looked at the rest of us.

"—that your Spanish sucks dog *huevos*."

Had to admit—that was one pretty appropriate.

Anza stood up, and the tiny woman strode up to the chair of Enrique, the Honduran drug dealer.

"What if Don Cheetle found out he'd hired a fraud? What would he do, then, huh?"

"Hopefully whatever he did," Uncle Jerry said, "he didn't do it in an English accent like in *Ocean's Eleven*. I couldn't take it."

The Actor nodded to Uncle Jerry. "Hear, hear."

"Not Don Cheadle, it's Don *Cheetle*!" Enrique growled, his face quickly turning a deep shade of pink.

"Well, what if Don-Cheetle-not-Don-Cheadle found out you came from—" Anza stopped midsentence and turned to the ancient manservant, still sweeping up the glass. "*Onde é que esse idiota vem? Qual cidade da América?*"

The old guy looked up slowly, his mouth hanging open slightly. Then his expression turned sour. He looked to his boss, then back to Anza.

"Bakersfield."

"Ha!" Anza said and kicked Enrique's chaise with a flourish. "So what if the great Don Cheetle finds out his Honduran drug pusher is from California? Not even a very good part and *not* from Honduras, after all! Huh? What then, *pendejo*?"

"That is a lie! Now, you all need to lea—"

Enrique was trying to take back control of the conversation, but at this point there was no stopping the little woman. She advanced on him again. He stood and took a step back.

"I have seen all three *Godfather* movies," she said, "and have gave them very high ratings on the Netflix! I can tell you what such men do to underlings who make them look the fool, embarrass them!"

"I won't listen to—"

"You ever hear of a Mexican necktie?"

Enrique stumbled over a small stack of branches and looked to the rest of us. "Can you call off your…"

She leered at him.

"… *friend*! Call off your friend! Please! I will not be treated this way in my home."

I looked over at Uncle Jerry, who then looked at the Actor.

The Actor sighed. "I think you better give us your plane."

Chapter Thirteen

We'd driven to McDaniel Airport, Fulton County's *other* airfield.

For those of us who have not experienced private air travel, lemme school you on the finer ways to hit the *more* friendly skies.

First off, there was sort of an unspoken rule at the smaller airports. That is, if you didn't spoke it, it didn't happen. So, the "haves" of the world were often rather inclined to not declare *what* they had. So, boarding the modified Gulfstream G-550, the four of us got on with no baggage claim, no security check, no pat down, and me twirling a one-liter bottle of water the whole time.

"I only beg of you to not get a scratch on her," Enrique the fake Honduran drug lord from Bakersfield said, standing in the brightly lit hanger.

Uncle Jerry gave him a wave. "Wouldn't think of it. I'll take care of it as if it was my own totally unnecessary personal possession."

"Twenty-four hours, yes? No more! You said—"

"Right, right," Uncle Jerry lied. "You take that to the bank."

As Anza, the Actor, and I climbed into the spacious passenger area of the Gulfstream jet, we heard the *thwack!* of a seventies muscle car kiss the interior of the cabin below our feet.

"And do not fire up that piece-of-shit car on my airplane," the man on the tarmac said.

Uncle Jerry's voice went flat. "You best not talk about Cujo like that. You don't want to make it... angry."

Listening to the other man talk, I couldn't help it. "Why the hell are you still doing the accent?" I yelled.

"That is my level of commitment," he said, smiling underneath his big mustache. "You lose it if you don't keep it up."

From inside, deeper in the cabin, I heard the Actor bark: "Hack!"

A moment later, the old Portuguese manservant appeared from the rear of the jet, having parked Uncle Jerry's car as best he could in its belly. He walked past us, across the steaming black top.

He bowed his head when he caught sight of Anza, and from the third window from the front, she kindly blew him a kiss.

We watched as he walked the rest of the way to the hangar, striding as if his feet did not touch the ground.

"I bet he does selfie to that tonight," Dan's wife said as Uncle Jerry, the Actor, and I buckled in. None of us had anything to contribute to that particular statement.

A commercial flight from the ATL to Brussels, Belgium would have taken more than twelve hours, accounting for flight time, boarding time, disembarking time, et cetera, et cetera.

The modified G550 was going to do it in about seven and a half.

Still, of my four days to pull of this insurmountable task, when we landed in Brussels, it would just about mark the end of Day 1.

And I was still so far away from achieving my goal.

What if we can't find all the pieces?

What if we get all the pieces but can't assemble the lamp?

Breaking my concentration, I heard the practiced tones of a seasoned dwarf performer: "Rasputin, I was hoping to have a quick word with you before I get too drunk on this excellent Beaujolais and pass out."

What if one drunk-to-the-balls member of my crew bails out on me before I can even get the first piece?

The interior of the plane was dark, save the light above my seat and another on the other side of the cabin.

On my side of the cockpit, there were three seating areas. Each pod had three plush seats, which could quickly convert into a sleeper. In the middle of each cluster of seats was a table, and I initially wondered if their shape had been crafted in the profile of Enrique of Bakersfield (or, possibly, his boss, Don Cheetle).

A quick Google on one of the aircraft's web-connected tablets told me that shape was, in fact, that of the country of Honduras.

I wondered if this had been Enrique just playing the part or if he held some sort of false pride to be from some, as it were, exotic homeland, because no one is proud of being from Bakersfield.

With our pilot up in the cockpit, the three of us had wordlessly each picked our cluster of seats. Mine was closest to the cockpit; Anza's was farthest back.

Once we were in the air, the Actor stood from his area, which was between mine and hers, and jumped up onto one of my two opens seats and gave me a *tsk-tsk-tsk*.

I frowned, bracing for him to dig into me.

"Oh, my little sad clown, don't be so glum," he said and sipped loudly from a large wine glass he held gingerly between both stubby hands. "We don't even know each other, and here you are quickly assuming I've got something negative to say."

"Fine," I said, tossing down the pen I'd picked up, planning to craft a master plan for getting all of the pieces in time. I hadn't yet found any paper. "I can hear that... tone in your voice. Yeah, early days for you and me, man, but I think you relish in hurting people."

He'd begun to say something but stopped. Instead, his mouth hung open, like a computer stuck on a bad sector. He just stared at me.

I kept at it. "I'm not a shrink, and I hate when people try to get all Dr. Phil on somebody they don't know well, but in over fifteen years on the radio, I've had hundreds of conversations with those in the psycho-babble industry. And I don't know if it's because you got teased as a kid or as an adult or whatever..."

"Raz."

"… but I'll tell you one thing about me: I may be a screw-up and get a lot wrong, but I am loyal to my friends. I don't have a lot of love left in my heart, granted, but the little I do have is intense. And I don't have a lot of friends—but those I *do* have get all the love I've got to give."

The Actor smiled unevenly, sighed, then spread his arms. "Now who's being negative?" he said. "You ever heard of the Schrodinger cat? Tell me you haven't so I can impress you with my story."

"I'm not a cat person."

"Neither was Herr Schrodinger, it seems," the Actor said and took another purple slurp. "So his thought experiment was this: You put a cat in a box with a canister of poison gas and a trigger to release it. The odds of the gas being set off and killing the cat are random, fifty-fifty."

As he paused, the plane shifted as if it had hit a low speed bump.

Uncle Jerry called out from the cockpit, "Sorry. Little turbulence. Nothing to worry about."

"Okay, we're fine," I called up to him.

"Good," he shot back. "I'm going back to sleep, then."

The Actor continued. "Schrodinger suggested there were in fact two cats, essentially. A live cat and a dead cat."

"Nice. Now you've got two cats. Shitty experiment."

"So you've got live cat *and* dead cat." He put his wine glass down on the table shaped like Honduras and leaned forward. "Depending on your mindset, that determines which one 'pops' into oblivion and which one remains."

"Ha, so you're a big shiny, happy fella? Didn't have you pegged like that, I guess."

"The power of positive thinking expressed in quantum physics. Or string theory, I'm not entirely sure. I kind of get them mixed up," he said. He leaned over and dipped two fingers into his wine, then put them into his mouth for a moment. "It's not fantasy. It's science."

He grabbed his glass and went back to his pod of seats.

I took a deep breath and stared out the window. It was night now, and the moonlight shimmied off the dark, watery dance floor below us. Under better circumstances, it would have been the most beautiful of sights.

Looking back at the Actor, I briefly wondered what made me dislike him. Yeah, he'd busted Anza's phone in a real dickish way, and that was what had probably soured me on the guy. But if I'm being honest, I hoped I wasn't harboring any sort of prejudices based solely upon what nature had done to him.

Whether or not he was a jerk, I shouldn't really dislike the guy until I really knew him. It shouldn't matter *what* he was. I mean, I suppose, it's not his fault he's an actor. I guess you're born that way.

I called over to him. "You're staying positive because, as a team, we'll all pull through this and save my wife. Very kind of you."

"No," he said, then slurped. "I wanted to tell you that once we're in Brussels, you're on your own. I'm catching the first flight I can back to Sydney."

"But I need you, man! You have to tell us where we gotta go!"

"No can do," he said and grinned an empty grin. "This is your little adventure, not mine. Just… think positively."

The plane shifted again. I looked to the cockpit just as Uncle Jerry slid out of the pilot's chair and slumped to the floor, fast asleep.

"So I was right. I knew you had nothing to drop but bad news."

"Ah," the Actor said and flipped off the light above him. "But think of it this way: According to Herr Schrodinger, it could have gone either way. Ultimately, *you* decided which it would go."

I considered that for a moment. My thoughts, my mindset, my attitude controlling the world around me. A man of my own destiny. I looked toward the dwarf actor as he eased back one of the seats into its bedding position.

"Fuck you, that Dingleberry dude, *and* his ghost cats," I said.

In the dim light, I saw the Actor shrug, then dip his head toward me in a low, theatrical nod. "It is as you say."

He pulled a thin blanket up to his shoulders and turned away from me.

"What the hell does that mean?"

"I don't know," he said and punched at a button, extinguishing all light from his part of the cabin. "They have me say it on the show all the time. I think it's a fancy way of saying 'whatever.'"

While all three of my companions were drifting off into sleep, I found it impossible to cross into the world of dreams. After a half hour of fidgeting in my seat, I stood up and walked toward the rear of the jet.

As a courtesy—and because it was right—the rear third of the main cabin had been converted into a makeshift room and given to our female companion. Initially, Uncle Jerry had suggested she take a private room at the very rear of the plane, but after a quick inspection, she returned, shaking her head.

Trust me, I love Dan. And as much as a dog as I can be, as I told the Actor—and I meant it—I am imbued with strong loyalties. Probably something my mother had instilled on me by whispering over my crib when I was a baby or something.

So I had no thoughts toward Anza but gratitude and a responsibility that she remain safe.

She was fine. Resting. And after how handily she'd reduced Enrique of Bakersfield to a whimpering apologist, she deserved all the rack time she could get.

Walking toward the aft of the aircraft, I passed a full-size bathroom complete with bathtub.

In the very back was the private room which, given the manner of the plane's owner, was likely for midflight "entertaining." It looked like the Champagne Room at a Las Vegas strip club.

First there was a low-slung, U-shaped wraparound couch made from a dark brown leather. Didn't seem very comfortable, but it was, I suppose, splatter-proof.

"Ick."

On the back wall were two large screens where you might expect windows to be. Each flickered slightly but only showed darkened images. There was another screen on each of the two remaining walls.

The screen to my left was also mostly black. However, as my eyes adjusted, I could pick out some sort of flooring. Odd, fluffy carpeting. On the monitor to my right, the same flooring, but I could clearly see the rising moon.

Scanning them from right to left, I realized that with these four screens, I had at least a three-quarter view of the outside of the aircraft.

"Cool."

In front of the couch, a little more than an arm's length away, was a stripper pole.

Of course there was.

I could see now why Anza had given it a big check in the no box and decided she wasn't setting herself up back here. Plopping down on the couch, it was clear she wasn't missing very much. It wasn't terribly comfortable, and parts of the leather looked a bit… crusty.

"Ick."

The brass pole, however, I found fascinating.

Like most men, I'd seen probably several dozen in my lifetime (could be more) but had never actually touched one. Touching the brass pole in a men's clubs is verboten and makes the big man in the tight T-shirt hopped up on a steroids-and-speed cocktail come over and do hurty things to you.

So this was what I learned in the back of a jet over the Atlantic: The brass pole is really fuckin' cold. Like Ralphie's little brother from *A Christmas Story* tongue-tip cold. So for all the gyrating, partially clothed, and then non-clothed ladies who made a living off the pole? Much respect.

Another fun fact about stripper poles: They're very squeaky. Maybe that's why they crank the music up so loud. All that squeaking is not so much sexy. Sounds like a ten-year-old going down the park slide in a dry bathing suit. Not really the image they're going for, I don't think.

And naturally, if you've got a pole in front of you, and no one else is around, I mean… right? You're gonna give it a quick try.

That doesn't make me weird, does it?

Listen, I had several more hours of flight time and nothing to do. Maybe it helped with jetlag, what did I know?

So anyway, since I couldn't crank up squeak-covering music—and because you need to drop the phat beats when you're workin' the pole—I came up with what my stripper music might be, if it ever came to that. (Note: Humankind would be on the last several paragraphs of *Revelations* if there were a world where I'd be a rockin' the pole as a stripper)

So… Rasputin's stripper music.

I felt "Girls, Girls, Girls" by Motley Crue was a bit passé. So done, right? In my head, I cranked up "Butt Town" by Iggy Pop, which I realized after a few shakes-o-my-tail-feathers might be a bit too fast paced for a butt as large as mine.

For my body, it seemed far more appropriate to drop the needle on something like "The Wreck of the Edmund Fitzgerald."

Honestly, after about twenty seconds, I'd had all the fun I could squeeze outta the brass pole. And I was winded.

And horrified that someone might walk in on me, and I'd have to, at that point, open a door and jump out of the plane to my death.

For the hell of it, the last thing I did was climb to the top of it—wasn't far; it was short—and tapped the metal ring like I'd seen done time and time again.

Two things I realized as I did.

One: I don't climb well. Especially cold, squeaky stripper poles.

Two: Once I touched the top ring, it triggered the pole's metal skirting to retract into the floor, leaving a pitch-black circle below me. Having no grip left in my hands, I proceeded to slide down with a long, extended squeak.

Standing in the dark beneath the floor, I was a bit spooked. "That was unexpected."

My feet had touched a flat pad at the bottom, and a second or two later, the lights flickered on. Looking up through the circular hole, I could see the dim lights of the room I'd just left.

Now I was in the cargo area, which was mostly taken up by Uncle Jerry's Trans Am. I laughed. I still couldn't believe he'd named it after the rabid dog from that Stephen King novel, but with its tapered headlights and a snout that dipped toward the ground, it was hard not to see the canine resemblance.

"Hey, Cujo," I said, stepping off the pad of the stripper-pole-cum-fireman's-pole and petting the black car on its shiny quarter panel.

I walked toward the opposite wall of the cramped cargo area. There was a long, low recessed panel that had the words "emergency use only" in surprisingly calm, green lettering. I didn't see any way to open it—and thought it probably would be a bad idea if I did—and moved deeper into the bay.

At Uncle Jerry's insistence, Enrique had reluctantly disengaged the biometric security on the G-550. He'd said several times that this meant the jet was an "open book" but that we shouldn't snoop around. All we cared about was that the damn thing didn't seize up on us halfway across the Atlantic.

Near the rear wall, there were three large blisterlike protrusions, one on top of the other. Like some large embedded chest of drawers.

I pulled open the top drawer, and it came away easily, lit by a tiny light inside. I opened the two below it as well, and each was empty. A simple assumption might be that this was just more storage. But given this was a drug runner's aircraft, that might mean this was a place where they could store, well, drugs.

Opening the top drawer again, it slid free with a hiss. I stooped down and examined where the drawer's bottom hit and where, from the outside, the drawer should hit.

"Ah, sure," I said to no one. Except maybe the rabid dog car behind me.

I reached into the drawer, and since the biometrics had been disengaged, the panel slid back easily enough. The hidden compartment was lined with a thick black oily material, which I could only assume was designed to hide the scent of its contents from drug dogs. The inside was mostly empty.

But not entirely empty.

"Oh, damn."

I wasn't sure why Bakersfield's Enrique would have left three plastic bulbs of cocaine in the aircraft. Maybe in case he wanted to entertain a few young ladies on an impromptu trip to Miami.

"Oh, damn," I said again.

Each pretty little bulb must have been at least an eight-ball of coke. Shaking my head clear, I realized that I was likely underestimating the quantity. Each was about the size of the Actor's fist. More blow than I'd ever seen in my life at one time. And for a while, only a few years earlier, I'd seen quite a bit of cocaine.

"Oh, damn," I said one last time and slid the drawer closed.

Pausing for a moment, I held my hand against the darkened drawer.

No.

No.

Too much was riding on this.

Still, something tugged at an area between my heart and stomach. Just…

"No, no, no, no, no," I muttered aloud.

Enrique had said that the Gulfstream aircraft had been "customized" to his needs. And yes, I should have assumed that meant designed for serious drug-cartel-level smuggling.

But I hadn't given it any thought. My plan had been to essentially keep moving at such a pace that didn't allow for me to second-guess my plan. That likely gave me a false confidence, but you can get pretty far on that as long as you don't stop and start thinking about it.

So, not thinking.

Just *moving*.

One of the wisest questions I'd been ever asked was "Are you running to something or running away from something?" Now, that was years earlier, and sure, at the time I may have been running naked through Midtown Atlanta. And the individual posing the question may have been an officer of the law.

But setting that particular *alleged* indiscretion aside, the question was a great one, very revealing, so I did my best to avoid asking it of myself a majority of the time.

I slowly turned away from the panel of drawers and petted Cujo the black Trans Am again as I slipped past.

Behind the lower length of the pole was what looked like a dark closet without a door. Inside was a short metal, two-stage ramp that led back up into the Champagne Room through a flip-open hatch under one of the leather cushions.

In the small space, the ramp was very short, but the incline to the floor above was so great I was sucking in big, gulping breaths by the time my body finally tumbled out and splayed out onto the carpeted floor.

After catching my breath, I went up to the cockpit. Fortunately, Uncle Jerry was awake again (however, it took several swift kicks to the back of his seat to become that fortunate), and he kindly helped me with the satellite phone. When I called my wife's hospital ward back in Atlanta, I got news that didn't come as any great shock. Soul-crushing sadness, yes, but not shock.

My wife had fallen into a coma and was not likely to wake back up again. Calming the screaming in my head as best I could—because I had to think clearly—I thanked my pilot and went back into the darkened cabin, laid myself down on a reclining seat, and tried to dream of my Carissa.

What joy can be the world of sleep and dreams. Whatever it is, sleep is not an escape from life but simply living it on a different plane. More emotional. Less rational. Less *tactile*.

So my dream was of the day I'd met her.

At that point, I'd just lost my disk jockey gig in Atlanta. And how does a guy with nothing but a high school diploma convince people they should let him shoot off his mouth, play music, and—here's the tough bit—*pay him to do that*?

Birthdays. Bat mitzvahs. And the worst: weddings.

One in particular included, despite it being Carissa's. But that night, she wasn't yet *my* Carissa. As of that night, she'd never met me. And I only knew her name because it was written down next to some other asshole's name. It was on a card in front of me, you know, so I didn't forget it when I had to call them out for the first dance.

But that night felt different. Even before I saw her, it felt different.

For a DJ, nearly every wedding reception centers loosely around two pivot points. And it's not the best man's speech. Nor is it the eyeroll-inducing father-daughter dance. Or the toss of the garter (ugh).

No, it's two other specific moments, both of which indicate it's time to take the level of class down a notch. First is when you play that fucking "Hokey Pokey" song. By that time the old folks have soaked up enough box wine to forget they'll be dying soon, while the younger adults have each swallowed an entire rainbow of celebratory shots. Because top-shelf whiskey and cheap wine do the same things to people: It encourages them to cast aside the deep-rooted hesitations that both inhibit and define their character.

You'll probably still see little kids in attendance, wandering around having a blast, glee spread across their faces like they've secretly been eating sugar frosting by the grubby fistfuls, simply amazed by how much they suddenly fit in.

The second pivot point is later in the evening—sometimes much later—when you've fired up "Blister in the Sun" by the

Violent Femmes. The old people are gone, passed out in their hotel rooms. The little kids have fled, making chatty excuses about prescribed bedtimes while being quietly and deeply concerned for their own physical and mental well-being if they were to stay.

What's left are the twenty-, thirty-, and even fortysomethings that feel they've been given carte blanche to get blind drunk and dance like nobody's watching (or nobody should be). If you look closely, you can usually see some manner of digital penetration on the dance floor. And sometimes this happens even when the person is dancing by themselves.

Ahem.

At this point, I'd been out of full-time work for about ten weeks when a one-time listener had discovered that "Raz Danger" (my horrible air name, not of my design) was now spinning at—*can you believe it?*—wedding receptions. Prior to this night, I'd worked about a half dozen events. But this night was different. This was the *first* time she saved my life.

When I show up at the reception, I'd already put down a six pack of some high-octane beer disguising itself as "premium lager." The only thing "premium" was the heroic level of alcohol in each can.

A guy I'd known back at the start of my illustrious radio career made a habit of working weddings each and every weekend for the extra coin. After getting canned, I'd reached out to Midday Dimond, a jock from a small Missouri town. After we reminisced about old times and remote broadcasts at rundown car dealerships for twenty-five bucks a pop, he said he'd be more than happy to email me several wedding reception playlists he'd constructed over the years.

He had three, primarily. The first: The New Lovers. That one was heavy on the slow dance music for the white guys who didn't know jack about what to do on the dance floor.

The second—these were his titles, just so we're clear—was called The Circle of Life. This was a bit more upbeat, still easy to dance to, but it was more celebration than ceremony. Good for folks who were remarrying, giving the whole thing another shot.

The one I gravitated to was the one he'd dubbed They Ain't Gonna Make It: an amalgam of Top 40, hip-hop, and eighties rock tunes, heavy on the saccharin power ballad.

As I said, *something* was in the air that night. I could feel it. About an hour after "Hokey Pokey" and a short time before "Blister in the Sun," I'd gone into the bathroom. The *thing* that had been, at least momentarily, in the air that night was the shaft of one of the groomsmen.

At least they were in a stall. But with the bridesmaid on her knees, her gawd awful purple-yellow dress spilt around her like a clown car roadway accident, the latch had unfortunately been broken and the door left half open.

Above each urinal, there were advertisements for renting out the wedding hall, along with the business cards of local religious leaders who "specialized" in matrimonial ceremonies, cab companies, and one or two escorts. These notices were all held in place by thumbtacks and some cheap, transparent craft-store plastic.

Peeing at the urinal, shifting from foot to foot to keep my drunken balance in check, its reflective surface was just about at eye level. On first glance, it looked like she was rocking out— head-banging, even—to some metal rock tune only she could hear.

The expression on her recipient's face, though… that told a different story. He was more R&B. Think Luther Vandross performing at the Apollo: squinted eyes, beads of sweat across the brow, and a contorted smile that looked more like pain than pleasure.

Through his expression alone, you could almost hear the guy sing. "Baby, oh, baby, why?… OH, damn, baby, where? Oh, baby, there? Oh, you shoulda trimmed those fingernails, baby, baaaaabeeee…"

Thankfully, I left the bathroom before the crescendo.

It's strange, because the next half hour or so was just a blur of light and sound and acid twisting in my gut. I wish it hadn't been, because ultimately it was a very important half hour. At least for me.

I remembered clearly the *clink-clink-clink* of forks to wine glasses, imploring the new loving couple to make smooch face. It was as if the bride and groom had not come to their reception but instead to a rhesus monkey lab, and every time the light came on (*clink-clink-clink*), they were encouraged to punch a certain colored button (smooch face) and get rewarded with a tasty morsel (smattering of polite applause).

The waitress hadn't come back with my next beer yet, and I'd been sort of cursing under my breath because of it. I found out later that the father of the bride had instructed her to not let me drink anymore.

In retrospect, good call on his part.

When my gaze came back from searching for my drink bearer—and waiting for the newlyweds to finish their G-rated kiss—I noticed their table for the first time. The two of them.

She. Was. Gorgeous. Not just in the classical "perfect" way. Her face held such light! Such intelligence! She was a beautiful woman, no question, but that beauty was enriched by what was *behind* her eyes, what was behind her intoxicating smile.

What kind of guy scores a girl like that? I though.

After they broke apart from their kiss, I caught his face.

Of course.

It was the guy from the bathroom. Luther Vandross. The guy who'd been treated by the trumpeter-bridesmaid only minutes earlier.

Now, forgive me, because the next few sequences are a bit hazy.

According to the police report, I'd grabbed the mic to fire up the next record and played "Two Timer" from the *Dressed to Kill* album (the former KISS Army, now God's Undamned Army [Wardoff Chapter] would have been so pleased). And, baby, it's got a bassline that would rattle the balls of even the most devout eunuch.

And, it seems, as that bass slapped from my cheap speakers, I'd said something like this:

"Ladies and Gentlemen, we wish the bride and groom a full, satisfying life replete with love and luck. We are witness to their discovery of joy in each other and are reminded of the joy we discovered in our own partners. Of course, it is a journey that does not come without challenges. There will be hardships, as many of us with a few extra miles on the odometer can attest."

At that point there was some polite laughter, and I coughed into the mic, spit something out, then continued:

"However, take heart, I have already seen our celebrated groom embrace *hard*ship! Well, not so much him as the third bridesmaid from the left—if memory serves me. She, in fact, embraced *his* hardship in the men's stall about an hour ago… and had two fingers straight up his joy to the second knuckle, as far as I could tell."

The room sat stunned, so I'd added, if nothing but to fill the void, "To the bride and groom!"

Ultimately, not my best moment. Not in the top one thousand. At that point, darkened by what I'd already seen in my life, I felt what needed to be said should be said. Consequences be damned.

A short time later, I learned that the "drunk tank" smelled, not surprisingly, a bit like puke.

Nice.

I called a couple of my friends but only got voicemail. Without bail, I was spending the night at the gray bar hotel.

But a few hours later, a cop is banging on the cell's Plexiglas, trying to get my attention. Just before midnight, I was released.

I came out to sign the paperwork, and that was when I'd realized my friends had *not* come to bail me out. Instead, I saw the most beautiful woman of all time. Her face turned toward me, and she smiled.

Standing there in the public area of the police station, she was still wearing her wedding gown.

She shook her head slowly as I approached, extended her hand, and said, "My name is Carissa. And… despite your dreadfully foul vocabulary"—she smiled at me—"or maybe *because* of it, I think you're probably someone I should get to know."

Chapter Fourteen

Lying stretched out on my seat in the jet's darkened cabin, I was so mentally exhausted that deep sleep kept its distance. Over the next few hours, I twisted and turned, frustrated mostly by the impressively loud snoring from the Actor.

Actually, his snoring hadn't bothered me as much has his ability to fall asleep the instant his head hit the tiny travel pillow. For a while, I drifted in and out of a strange state of mind, watching the moon's reflection outside my window.

What an odd thing, for a creature denied wings to be hurled through the air at hundreds of miles an hour over a mind-boggling expanse of water... only surrounded by the pleasant whirring hum of the jet engines, a warm envelope of air and silver plates of cocktail peanuts placed strategically around the cabin.

Outside, only the moonlight and water. The former cut its unsure gaze toward me, the beam quivering at its edges in the currents of dark sea.

If I looked long enough, maybe I'd see a whale? (Probably not)

Or a flock of birds which might have been chasing my moon friend, lured toward its unspoken promise. (Not likely)

The night was so calm, so peaceful, outside my window. Breathing deep, I tried to take some of it in and let it soothe the ache in my chest.

I missed Carissa.

My eyes watered and I swallowed hard. Was I doing the right thing? How could it be right if it had taken me so far away from her?

"I wish you were here now, babydoll," I whispered. To share my serene, beautiful sight. The shimmer of moon. The starlight pinpricks sprinkled across on the water's surface. The tiki-bar restaurant with its flickering torches.

The...

Wait.

Instantly wide awake, I spun in the seat, dropping my feet onto the floor, to stare out the window.

Sure, there was still water below us. But we weren't out on the ocean anymore.

"Uncle Jerry!"

Mostly it was dark outside my window. Nighttime. But now it was apparent some of that "starlight" was actually streetlights. I ran up to the cockpit and half stumbled through its open door.

In the very low light, Uncle Jerry was humming away, tapping his foot, eating an apple.

"Jer—"

Out the front window, I saw… Christmas lights coming toward us.

No, not Christmas lights.

"Wha… what is, what is all… that? There?"

Our pilot looked forward-right, I guessed so he could see my reflection in the cockpit window.

"Lights," he said and cracked off another chunk of apple.

"Yes, yes, yes… but… is that…?"

"Yes."

A hand gripped my shoulder, and I nearly jumped out of my skin. Anza had come up behind me, blinking the sleep from her eyes.

Leaning into the cockpit a little, she looked to the right and left. "I seen a tiki bar."

"Me too!" I said, a little too shrilly.

"Maybe we can get a bite on the way outta town, then, huh?" Uncle Jerry said.

"Hey," Anza said, thumping our pilot on the shoulder. "Is that some bridge coming up there?"

He looked. "Yep."

I turned to her expectantly, hoping she was right there with me, sharing my fear/outrage/anger.

"Okay," she said and went back into the cabin.

Jerry tugged slightly on the controls, and the jet arched lightly upward, the bridge with its dotting of lights passing below us. A push forward and we settled back down.

"We're flying over a river," he said.

"Right, I see that."

"The nav software says it's the best way to get into Brussels without being noticed."

"But—"

"The exterior lights are out. Ex-tinguished." He finally turned toward me, and I saw his eyes lit sea-green by a pair of heavy goggles. "We're like the Batplane, man. This baby comes with *night vision!*"

I nodded, left the cockpit, went back to my seat, and pulled the blanket over my head until we landed.

Twenty minutes later, we were walking away from a shuttered railyard just north of the city. It had been listed on the special onboard navigation software as a potentially suitable landing area because of its long strips of concrete. Just had to keep an eye out for the rusted track.

We'd left Cujo the car behind because everyone agreed the Georgia license plate with the giant peach in the center of it might attract attention from the local gendarme. As we walked, Uncle Jerry came clean that he'd only known about Enrique's jet because he'd actually been tapped to fly it on "trips" a couple of times in the past.

And by trips, of course, he meant drug runs.

The Gulfstream listed at sixty million bucks. Jerry said that from what he'd heard, they'd rounded it up to 100 mil with "enhancements" to keep the thing off radar and out of sight.

One of its most valuable perks was a GPS navigation system built on some open-source mapping architecture out of the Middle East. Using a safe-from-government-eyes Tor network, these maps were updated not only so that they included real-time tracking of international authorities (as in *literally* tracking the mobile phones of some of the more prolific drug-busting agents, which could be pinpointed on the map and was accurate up to three meters!) but also so they could show you the best places/routes to slip in and out of hundreds of countries around the world.

Additionally, it had a fairly accurate local weather feature and could recommend some very nice restaurants. Many of the map updates came from crowd sourcing. The "crowd" in this case was the international drug, weapons, and whatever-else-they-could-sell community.

Whereas their moral compass was nonfunctional, their *actual* compass worked pretty damn well (because getting it wrong for the wrong person in the wrong place was often terminal).

As we walked toward the city of Brussels, remnants of a low, light fog dissipated under thin rays of sun that began to peek over the eastern horizon.

"Today, they expect partly sunny skies," Uncle Jerry said, scratching his three-day-old beard. "A ten-percent chance of rain and a high near 22. And there's a really nice deli, I understand, about six blocks east of here."

The Actor pulled at the cloth tie of his red robe. "Jesus, it's going to be 22 degrees?"

Anza held her hand up to him. "I don' like the talk like that, not even from you."

Just ahead, we saw the edges of a marketplace. Old folks were sweeping stoops, rolling up awnings, firing up street kettles. The smell of morning in this very old city was, even this early in its start of the day, intoxicating. Plenty has been written about how the olfactory sense brings up the most powerful memories. The smell of the market as we approached, the hustle and bustle of opening for the day, brought a warmth to every fiber of me. Despite being unfamiliar with this particular mix of aroma, it was comforting. Like some genetic memory arching across some never-before-used synapse, a very personal experience handed down from an ancestor I would never know.

"I think he's talking Celsius," I said.

"Ugh!" the Actor scoffed. "Barbarians."

"Um, actually—"

Anza shushed us all. "So, where do we go to get this piece to your Lamp of Life?"

We all looked toward the Actor, who walked a little more strained than the rest of us, shuffling along in a pair of oversized slippers. He huffed, rolled his eyes, and said: "I'm wearing a fucking *bathrobe*. The first thing we're going to do is get to a clothier and get me clothes!"

Uncle Jerry rubbed his face, frowning.

Anza threw her hands in the air. "No, no. We've got no time for the Walmarts."

The Actor stopped. "Oh, witness me, the sad clown. No Walmarts, you say? Oh, how you've cut me deep, Little Miss Undocumented."

"Listen," I said, snapping away from my day dreaming. "You have an idea where we go from here, man? Brussels is a big city. I think."

The Actor put a finger and thumb to his forehead. "It's fuzzy without… Pierre Cardin. I wonder if there's a store nearby."

Uncle Jerry huffed.

"Come on," I pleaded with him. "You may not take any of this seriously, but this is my wife we're talking about. She's dying."

"You've said," he said, looking away.

"And, it doesn't look like you have any plastic on you."

Not looking over, I heard his pace stutter for just a brief moment. When I turned, he was absentmindedly tugging at the fabric of his robe's lapel. "Your point?" he said finally.

"I need the first piece of the lamp," I said. "You need your Garanimals."

"Raz," he said breathily, "you are a douche."

"Whatever," I said. "Tell me where I need to go, and I'll hand my credit card to Uncle Jerry. Me and Esperanza will get what we came for while you… go shopping."

We all walked in silence for a moment. Then, a full minute later:

"Fine! It's… Shit, it's not, you know, entirely clear."

"I said, don't do—"

"Hey, I'm not trying to be coy here, Raz," he said and looked at me. He was an actor, sure, but still, it looked like… it looked like this really did pain him. "But it's not like I'm being passed a Post-It note or something. It's just… images. No, not that. It's a feeling. A feeling that raises up like, hell, I don't know… it just eases toward me."

"Okay."

"It's unsettling, frankly."

"I'm sorry."

"Don't do that, " he said. "You don't mean it, and you—"

I spun toward him and took a knee, meeting him eye to eye. "No, I really mean it. You didn't want any part of this, and I pulled you in. I wish that this unsettling feeling, our next step, was my burden, not yours."

The Actor squinted, turning his head slightly but not taking his eyes off me.

I continued. "But for now, I have to rely on what's coming into your head. I wish it were another way, but th—"

"Park!"

My mouth hung open, stopping midsentence. I didn't move.

"I think it's… in a park," he said, calmer now.

Uncle Jerry had kept walking with Anza but now turned toward us, taking his steps backward. "National park?" he said. "Parking lot? Park-n-Ride?"

The Actor grunted and pressed his fingertips to his closed eyes. "Does your boss Enrique have a hitman in his employ? I'd like his number."

"He's not my boss, ya Meisner moron!"

"It… hmm," the Actor said, sighing. "Just wait for… If you just give me a moment—"

I put my hand on his red-robed shoulder. "We're running out of moments, man. I mean, we're already a full da—"

"Dog!" the Actor said as if remembering he'd left his iron on at home. "It's... shit."

"That is finally some honesty talking from your pretty face," Anza said, slowing her pace but still leading us toward the awakening marketplace. The smell of fresh baking bread was pulling all of us in.

"Dog... park," the Team Raz-compelled dwarf said. "That's... dammit, that's it, but not... it."

It was all I had to go on. So be it. I clamped my hand on his shoulder and smiled. "Dog park. Got it."

"Sorry," the Actor said, apparently surprising himself with that utterance, instantly turning a little wide eyed, not meeting my gaze.

In deference to his ego, I slid past it and moved on. "No, that's more than the rest of us have. So it's what we've got. We gotta find a dog park. Cool."

I stood up, dug into my pocket, and fished out my Mastercard. Flipping it to Uncle Jerry, I mouthed *Don't let him out of your sight.*

Not surprisingly, I only got back: "Huh?"

Anza and I were going to search for Brussels's premiere dog park, while the Odd Couple were about to hit whatever little-person clothing store might be open at the crack of dawn.

My gut reaction: Their task might be harder than ours.

Before we split up, Uncle Jerry handed us all what looked like a Bluetooth earpiece. You know the ones—curved, long, and rectangular that a few short years ago urban asshats would stuff into their head and walk around wearing, even when they weren't talking on it.

"Really?" I said. "I don't wanna wear this."

Uncle Jerry's smile fell like a flan cake. "Wha? Why not? They're so cool! It's actually a two-way radio, not cellular. Drug-lord-level encrypted. No one can listen in!"

The Actor held his earpiece gingerly between his forefinger and thumb, staring at it as if were a disliked pet, recently deceased. "You don't have a red one?"

Anza quickly slipped hers into her ear. "This is neat. I'm like that Geordi guy from *Star Trek*."

The Actor and I quickly corrected her. "No, no. He didn't have…"

I looked at him and motioned with an open palm across my face and said: "It was an eye thingy."

Anza shrugged. "Is still pretty cool."

"No, it's not." The Actor tossed his back to our pilot, striding toward the road. "I'm not wearing it."

As much as I hated to admit it, I was on his side and handed the one in my hand back to Uncle Jerry.

"Seriously?"

He stripped his own off and dropped them into a pocket. He glanced at Anza, but she shrugged him off and left it in her ear.

"I look very cool with this here."

Our pilot gave her a thumbs-up, spun toward the marketplace, raised a fist in the air, and barked, "Actor. Let's get you outta that robe."

Anza sidled up next to me, tugging at my arm. The Actor looked over his shoulder toward us, nodded, then followed my childhood friend's not-uncle.

Twenty minutes later, the Actor and Uncle Jerry found themselves weaving through the streets of Brussels, which had become impressively busy and crowded for such an early hour.

The Actor walked past a vendor's cart, reaching up and snatching a strand of breaded sausage that had been swinging in the light morning breeze.

"Beautiful," he said, taking a bite. His eyes rolled back, and he groaned in a way that made Jerry feel a little sick. "God, I love this city."

They walked down the middle of the street, scanning the darkened shops, looking for anything that looked like it might sell clothes. There were no cars at this time of day, just vendors, merchants, and their customers.

Uncle Jerry made an unpleasant sound that resonated deep in his chest. Eyeballing a street performer in a black beret and striped black-and-white shirt, he put a hand on the Actor's shoulder and moved to the far side of the street.

The Actor frowned. "Uh, you can't be serious. *Mimes*?"

Jerry shrugged. "Let's get in and out of here."

"Right. Quicker the better."

"Agreed."

Looking straight ahead to avoid any eye contact with the street mime, the Actor sighed.

"*Awful* little city."

After the third frown and shrug from our queries, Anza and I were both wishing we had a lot more to go on than "the dog park."

It actually became a little more frustrating when the fourth person, a thin, bespectacled guy somewhere in his late twenties, was able to talk with us in breathy, staccato English.

He said, frowning (no shrug, so it was a minor improvement), "We don't have places for only dogs *here* and only people *there*."

"Okay," I said.

"We share it with animals and respect all space and all creatures in it," he said, his tone turning more aggressive. "Not having some fenced-in, partitioned, elaborate *cage* for animals to run in."

"Yes," I said, "but the dogs like them, too."

The young man started to talk, then stopped. He recomposed himself. "I was talking about the dogs."

"Right."

The young man spat some words between his teeth—something in either French or the regional Flemish. Interestingly, it was our miscommunication with that fourth Belgian that garnered the attention of an older woman in a wool coat that would have kept you warm in deep space, who set us off in a promising direction.

"*Excusez-moi, je'n compreds pas.*"

After several attempts, she smiled sweetly and started to turn away. Anza closed her eyes and knit her eyebrows together. A moment later, she stuttered a few words in French.

"*C'est*... uh, dog park. *Parc*... uhhh, *parc chien. Oui, parc chien*... uh... *à proximité? S'il vous plait.*"

The old woman in the coat looked to me, but I had nuthin', so she looked back to Anza. The woman shook her head slowly, then, as if on a ten-second broadcast delay, she smiled and clasped her hands together.

"*Oui, oui!*" she said. "*Marc Chene! Monsieur Marc Chene! Vieux salaud, oui, il—*"

"Uh, *non*..." Anza frowned.

"*Il est encore quelques pâtés de maisons. Une maison mauve. Étrange,*" she said and shrugged while smiling. "*Mais il est là.*"

In a burst of joy, the woman raised her arms and embraced Anza and then me, placing a small kiss on my cheek. Despite her apparently getting it utterly and completely wrong, the sweetness of the gesture put a lump in my throat. I smiled at the woman and nodded. Blinking away some dampness in my eyes, I thanked her in one of the few words in knew in the language: "*Merci.*"

Anza put her hand to her chest as she caught sight my brief emotional moment. She hugged me and whispered soft, reassuring words in my ear. A moment later, I cleared my throat and recomposed myself.

"Let's ask that girl over there," she said, scanning the street.

"I have a better idea."

"I doubt that," Anza said and smiled. "I am very smart!"

"True," I said, then corrected myself. "I have a *different* idea."

"Okay, what is different idea, then?"

Walking in the direction the old woman had pointed, I said: "Let's go ask Marc Chene."

As we headed that way, Anza filled me in on what the old woman had said so elatedly to us.

"He's an old man in a—*pinche chingadera*, my hair—I..." She stopped and tugged at one side of her head. "This *Star Trek* ear phone is getting caught in my hairs!"

"You have lovely hair," I said and smiled kindly. "Now what the fuck were you saying, dear heart?"

She laughed, threw her hands up, and let her hair fall where it would. Which, as it turned out, was half in her face. She tucked the earpiece in her pocket. A few minutes later, we were standing in front of a hideous purple house.

What the hell, I thought. *Why not?*

Anza trailed behind me, something up the street catching her eye. She muttered something low in Spanish.

"What?"

"I do not like this trend where everything is... *Walking the Dead.*"

After climbing a half dozen wooden steps, our footfalls echoed below us as we crossed the porch toward the front entryway.

There was no bell. In the middle of the door, a simple brass knocker.

Realizing she'd said something expecting a reply, I only muttered a "Huh?" back, then knocked on the paint-peeled door. Inside the darkened home, a light came on.

Anza continued her undead rant. "Everything now, zombie this and zombie that," she said and looked off. "So common, even this family walking past the zombie mime doesn't even notice. I'll be glad when all this creepy ugly is over with."

Above us, despite it being daytime, a yellow-orange porch light clicked on.

The heavy door was pulled back, just a crack, and a tall gray man with thick glasses regarded me and Dan's wife.

"Do you speak English?" I asked.

He sighed and leaned against the wooden door's jamb. "Yes. Do you speak French?"

"A little," I offered. "Enough to order a beer and get myself slapped."

Anza smiled and punched my shoulder.

The man called Marc Chene laughed. He nodded and said, "What is it you want?"

Ah. In truth—and this is strange for a guy who spent more than a dozen years as a broadcaster—I hadn't even prepared for what I might say if the door to the purple house opened. So when I spoke, it came out like this:

"Well, my wife is terminal, on her death bed, and it seems the only thing that can save her is this lamp, very old, that has been broken into a couple pieces and scattered across the planet, so I am attempting to collect these pieces, despite having no idea, really, where they might be and having to rely on a dwarf actor, so I can reassemble the old lamp in hopes it might save *her* from death and *me* from, you know, losing her."

The next few moments were unbearably quiet. Then the heavy wooden door slowly closed, leaving the two of us shut out on the sagging wooden porch.

Shit.

Then... a delicate scraping sound. It was the sliding of metal against wood.

With the small chain-lock disengaged, Monsieur Marc Chene opened the door wide. He was a few inches taller than me. He crossed his bony arms, tilted his head back, and regarded me down the bridge of his nose as if it were a rifle sight.

Finally, he said, "Well, it certainly took you long enough."

The Actor pressed his nose against the darkened window of St. Boniface's Nina Meert store. The silhouettes inside—sure, these particular outfits were too large for his body—taunted his mind and broke his heart. He lifted his head and let it fall back to the tempered glass with a soft bang.

"Why must Belgian couture hide itself from me until…" he said, then craned his neck to a placard near the locked door. "11 a.m.? This is a tragedy."

Uncle Jerry would have normally snapped back with some dismissive line but was instead taken by the odd Belgian appetite for street mimes. And not just normal street mimes (a thought he allowed, despite the obvious contradiction). These were hideous. Ugly. More than ugly. Terrifying, really.

"What's wrong with this place?" he said, watching as three of them walked the street in one direction. Another two (then three, then four), slowly ambled from the other direction.

The Actor shook his head, his eyes squeezed shut. "Right, right! It's *cruel*, in fact. I should *not* be denied! We finally agree on something."

Uncle Jerry saw a little girl approach one of the mimes from the first group, unafraid, but she was rebuffed. The street performer simply walking past her without even a wave.

The Actor traced the gaze of his middle-aged partner and said, "Who the hell wants to see, uh, zombie mimes?"

Chapter Fifteen

There are stories about the final minutes and hours aboard the *Titanic* that sound apocryphal, which leads me to believe they're absolutely true.

Most of us have heard the heart-swelling tales of how the band played on as the ship broke apart and slowly sunk into the black waters below. Still, if you've known a musician, no matter the skill level—from the fourth grade, first-chair recorder aficionado to the Carnegie Hall Asian prodigy concert pianist—there's frankly something a bit... *off* with these folks.

Not trying to be ugly, but it's probably best if maybe some of them were blowin' bubbles during the *Titanic*'s trip to the bottom o' the sea. But you can imagine the first-class people, can't you? Ship's busted, people screaming, water rushing into the lower decks...

Listen, my dear, why don't we get some tapas before the long row to the East Coast. (No, I have no idea if they had tapas back a hundred years ago, but it seems like a posh, asshole-type food, so I'm going with that).

So here's the waiter—in tails, naturally—approaching our impatient couple. He's going on seventy; she's a pretty thing, simply waiting for him to die. And as the windows explode around them, the light fixtures burn brightly, then fizzle away. The server, he's looking corner to corner but is obliged to take their order.

This is how I felt, albeit in reverse, as the elderly Marc Chene poured me and Anza a hot cup of tea each. My world was imploding, crashing down around me (and something else close by, but I couldn't put a finger on it), and here was an old Belgian man asking if I'd like a wee bit of sugar in my warm cup of watered-down leaves.

"Oh, yes, please!" I said and smiled.

Anza waved him off, blowing steam from her mug. Outside, the sun was warming the morning air, its rays sneaking through heavy drapes into Monsieur Chene's quiet home. Once he'd sat down across from us, in a chair that wrapped around him like he'd spent decades cradled by it, he began his story.

"In his later years, Andreas Chene, my great-grandfather, he was sort of, *comment dites-vous?* Uh, he was the town kook."

Anza smiled. "Oh, a local celebrity! You have a famous family, then!"

Marc popped an eyebrow and looked toward me. I nodded, imploring him to continue.

"I'm told that after great-grandmama died, Andreas… his, uh, facilities, his brain, didn't work as well as before."

Anza looked toward me. She reached for my hand and held it. With the other hand, I rubbed a spot between my eyes.

"Yes," I said. "Yes, I can understand that."

He stood and walked to the living room fireplace, which was glowing with dim red embers. It looked like it had been burning all night. "Well, she had died in the overnight hours, at *l'hôpital*, but he, alas, was not allowed to visit her in her room. He had begged the administrators, even tried to sneak in but was threatened with incarceration."

"This is barbaric to do," Anza said. Her hand began to tremble, so she put down her tea. "How could they keep a man from his wife as she…" She stopped for a moment, and I think she edited the next words from her mouth. "He had no choice but to being by her bedside as she died. And they denied a husband of such a thing?"

Marc grabbed a metal poker from an old upright canister. "No, the fact is that they were… that is, by law he did not have the right."

I closed my eyes and nodded. "They weren't actually married." Marc looked to me, scanning my face. He saw only compassion and then thanked me with a small smile. "So he could not say goodbye."

"Oh, that is the *most awful* to hear."

He continued. "At night, that's when his delusions were at their worst. A family member or a neighbor, and sometimes, even a police footman, would find him wandering the streets."

"In the street?" Anza said, her voice barely above a whisper.

Marc half turned toward us, the deep red embers reflecting in his moist eyes. "He was looking for her. Because he never got to say goodbye."

My chest tightened, and I fought the urge to press a clenched fist between my ribs, grinding it there in hopes of releasing whatever fat metal spring had suddenly begun to twist there.

"So my grandfather, he would wander the streets at night. The crazy old man looking for his dead lover."

Anza and I both fell silent, stole a glance at each other, then turned back to our host.

"In August of 1883, he was out. It was a hot, suffocating night," Marc said, his words thick with emotion. "He'd become even more disorientated with the heat and wandered to the far reaches of town. Too far." The old Belgian looked at us with bloodshot eyes. "That's when it hit him."

"He realized… he would never find her," I said, my voice cracking as I looked at the back of my own eyelids. "He realized that she was truly gone to him."

Marc shook his head. "No. No, I said that's when *it hit him*."

We both stared at him, and he, in turn, looked between the two of us. Motioning to his head with both hands, he tried again. "*Hit* him. Out of the sky, it came. Too fast to see. And it hit him right in the head."

I shrugged, confused. "What did?"

Marc moved away from the fireplace, and shuffling across the floor, waved for us to follow him. "Your *lamp*, Monsieur Rasputin. In August of 1883, my great grandpapa was knocked out cold after being hit in the head by a piece of your lamp."

"I don't suppose you'd let me—"

"NO!"

Uncle Jerry and the Actor sprinted down a road called Portealsstraat, which at this hour was lined on both sides with drowsy, happy citizens of Brussels. Markedly less happy and definitely more awake were the frumpy man in the rumpled sweats and the dwarf in a fashionable red robe running down the road, barking at the locals to "get the fuck out of the way."

As a young couple just in front of the odd-looking pair did, in fact, get the fuck out of the way, Uncle Jerry surprised himself by lifting his front foot, leaping over the propane tank that was lying on its side and feeding a small confectionery stand.

The Actor did not fare as well.

"Un... Un-cle Jerry!"

The paunchy American spun his head back to see the Actor facedown in the street, rocking from side to side, moaning. Just beyond him, a small army of street mimes, looking ghoulish and ghastly, were running full steam toward them. Lifting his head, the dwarf tried to regain his vision.

What he saw was the only person he knew who could help run from sight, taking refuge in a shop buried in lattices covered in very tiny clothes.

"No," the Actor said into the street below him.

Then a burst of noise drew his attention to where the two of them had just come.

He felt like a fool. Too proud to, (*oh god*), let Uncle Jerry carry him (*for chrissakes!*), but regardless of how very well he'd done in life despite those who'd pegged him for nothing but a future circus act (*pricks, every one of them!*) on rare occasions, he was reminded of his physical limitations.

Running was one of them. Not that he wasn't out of shape. He was.

Not that he wasn't in a pair of slippers three sizes too big after being snatched from a delightful time with two Australian cocktail waitresses and dropped into this nightmare. Check.

But if pressed (or, say, if he were lying facedown on a Belgian street with murderous, demonic street mimes growling and snarling as they clamored toward him), he might quietly admit that his legs were slightly too short to win any forty-yard dashes.

Or effectively get away from a horde of murderous, demonic street mimes.

The horde was causing a terrifying racket—the crash of toppling metal stands, the cries of shock, the shrieks of anger (none from the street mines, naturally, true to their craft).

He knew that they'd finally seen him, and they were picking up their pace, eyes boring into him, shoving their way through the clutch of people, just seconds away from—

"Get in!"

The Actor's heart nearly stopped. He twisted his head forward once more.

"Uncle Jerry!" he said, a smile splitting his face from ear to ear. Then he saw what the frumpy fiftysomething had apparently stolen from the store. He looked back to the pack of mimes, then to Jerry. Then to… it.

"No fuckin' way," he said.

Uncle Jerry reached down, yanked the Actor from the road, and tossed him into the red-and-white all-weather jogging stroller with stubby off-road tires. Immediately, the dwarf tried to crawl out but was hit by a bolt of pain in his side from where he'd fallen and slumped back inside.

Jerry grabbed the crossbar of the stroller, and like a suburban mom on a lose-21-pounds-in-21-days diet and exercise routine, spun in the opposite direction and ran down the bumpy cobblestone Belgian road, carting a grown dwarf actor in a waterproof, nylon, all-terrain baby buggy and a dozen mimes from Hell snapping at his heels.

After the chaos and pace of the last twenty-four hours, I actually found it a little unnerving to be enveloped by so much quiet.

Marc Chene led us through his home. He was a man obviously offended by negative space. While not exactly cluttered or cramped, every open space had been summarily dealt with by the old Belgian man.

It was possible that the place would have been more suffocating if it had been less inviting. Family pictures were everywhere, along with decorations and wall hangings that looked as though they'd sprung straight from the hands of well-loved children.

He caught me looking at them, and I was surprised to find my cheeks reddening in embarrassment. What he couldn't could see, however, was the knot just behind my ribs that tightened as I stared at the drawings. Would my Carissa and I ever have this?

I forced myself to look away and found Anza's smile.

"My nieces and nephews," Marc said. "And their two kids now. In at least five households of my family, when they can no longer see the front of their refrigerator, I get a box stuffed with all this…"

"… art?" Anza offered.

"… finger-paint psychosis?" I asked.

Marc Chene looked at the both of us and said simply: "Love." He then leaned toward Anza, pointing at me. "Is he always like this?"

"No, but his wife, she is on her deathbed five thousand miles from here, and that makes him a little jumpy."

Our host looked me over, his deep chestnut eyes watering slightly, and he gave me a single nod, which I returned. If he and I had spoken for an entire year, our words would have never conveyed the sentiment we shared with that brief, silent moment.

We walked a little more, winding through the dark house until Marc reached a set of wooden stairs, each step covered by a thin rug that likely ran from the bottom all the way to the top. Looking up, I couldn't see the end of the stairwell.

He lifted a foot to the first step but then stopped and turned toward me. "What… what do you know of this lamp?"

White lightning skipped across my nerve endings, drowning out some voice in my head that seemed to be screaming at me.

"We know very little about it. In fact," I said and put on a smile I didn't feel, "I was hoping you might have a few answers for us."

He nodded slowly, turned up the stairs, and began to climb. Each step complained under his foot, kicking up dust as if coughing out particulate with each plaintive cry.

"I have very few answers," he said. "In fact, my grandfather, the son of the family town kook, owned this piece of the lamp for only a very short time."

"Oh?"

"He didn't even know what it was! But he knew it was very special."

Unsure what lay on the floor above, I followed directly behind the old man, with Anza behind me. That may seem brave, but having Anza just a step behind me made me feel safer. I wasn't sure why it suddenly felt as though we were in danger, but it did.

Marc stopped after a few steps and drew in a couple deep breaths. Finally, he began to climb again. "I found out… what the piece was… This I found out. It's called a wick manifold. It is the, uh, compartment that houses the… uh—"

"The wick?"

"Yes, yes," he said as he breathed heavily. "See? You do have some answers of your own."

Anza filled the brief silence. "So did he give it to you?"

"No, to my father, who stuffed it into a cupboard. After Papa died, I simply inherited it along with this house. As I mentioned, it had struck my great-grandfather after traveling some great distance, who knows how far. Maybe thousands of miles. Maybe farther."

"That must have left very big head lump."

He laughed. "Yes, it did. It also killed him within the hour, Esperanza."

"Oh. I am sorry, Marc."

He stopped again, briefly, to catch his breath. "Don't worry. It was a long time ago."

"I'm sorry," I said. "I can't help... It's strange, but I just can't help but feel in some way responsible."

"No, no," he said. "It was long before you were born, Rasputin." Again, he stopped. But this time, not to draw in deep breaths. "But still, they all knew someone would come for it."

He turned to both of us and smiled.

"He knew you would come. My family has waited one hundred and thirty years... and now you've come."

An old emotion washed over the Actor. Being short, as singer and misanthrope Randy Newman once waxed melodically, makes you, as a person, a bit of a nonstarter.

Your feet dangle whilst in tall chairs, you sit precariously and dangerously close to the car's steering wheel, and the cookie jar is, alas, always out of reach. In the end, if life were a carnival, you would not be tall enough for the best ride.

Being a dwarf, the Actor had fought not only the stigma of being "bite sized" but even worse, most other short people *literally* looked down on him. Still, through his childhood, toddler, and teen years he had steeled himself against bullies big and small. By the time he hit his twenties, he'd developed an edge (a "crust," he'd called it privately), a cynicism that disarmed and often dismantled all attackers.

But there were still moments. Those times that his smallness would overwhelm him to where he could feel his insides turning to liquid, spilling out through fissures in his self-composed crust.

Banging down a Belgian cobblestone street in an all-terrain baby stroller, his pink willy flopping around in and out of his red robe as if it were a freshly born panda cub, would indeed qualify as one of those doubtful times.

He'd covered his face with both arms so that he would not damage "the goods," or more correctly, so that no one might recognize him, and the buggy sped up, faster and faster, as he and Uncle Jerry raced down the hill.

He stole a quick glance backward through a clear plastic baby porthole and saw that they'd pulled away from the horde of ghoulish street mimes pursuing them. Each one of them clawed the air as they ran, pulling themselves forward (or fighting some imaginary mime wind?). None made a sound from their mouths, all agape and gory.

The sight sent a shiver through his body, and now even more on edge, he nearly screamed when he felt the thud next to him. He then barked over the metallic rattle of the racing carriage, which was moving faster and faster: "What are you doing?"

Uncle Jerry smiled, hunching over, his face crushing into the other corner as he gripped both sides of the carriage. The fanny pack around his waist was straining at its buckle while the strap appeared to be cutting off the blood supply to the man's legs.

The dwarf, now pressed against the opposite vinyl wall of the buggy by the oversized man, repeated his question as loud as he could.

Uncle Jerry smiled again, yelling over the din, "Downhill, man! We'll go much faster this way!"

The Actor looked back, unable to even blink, then looked forward again.

About a hundred yards ahead of them, he saw a problem: The road ended in a "T," and they were heading for a line of shops. Proud and oblivious, Jerry gave him a thumbs-up.

The Actor tried to put their challenge into words. "Who the hell is going to steer, you dipshit?"

A shrug. "Not me, man! You ever driven one of them little Shriner cars in a parade or anything?"

"No!" he said, then almost corrected himself but thought better of it. *Not the point.* "No, but... Uncle Jerry, how do we steer? From in here?"

Another shrug, the smile fading only slightly. "Beats me."

At the top of the stairs, the air heavy with both the smell of dust and mold, Marc Chene swiveled to his left around the banister and briefly out of sight.

"I used to watch my father as he stared from the window," he said from the darkness. "He seemed... *quell que dit don?*.. uh, paranoid, yes?"

Anza and I got to the top of the landing and stopped, waiting for our eyes to adjust.

He continued. "Yes, before grandfather died, he said someone would come for our part of the lamp."

Something in his voice troubled me. What seemed a bit old and feeble moments ago now sounded different. More jittery.

"It's... I don't know how to really explain it," I said. The old man was somewhere ahead of me down the hallway. The upstairs lights had not yet been flicked on. When I searched for a switch, I found none.

"No, no," he said. "No need to explain."

My gut told me something was wrong. "We're not here to harm you. I hope you know that."

A laugh cut through the thick, heavy dark air. "No, no. I don't expect you are."

"Good."

"But, you've been sent on a mission, no?"

I froze. Behind me, Anza's hand clenched on my shoulder.

"I... I'm just looking for—"

"Yes, yes!" He moved forward now, out of the darkness, toward us. "As you said. You are here for the lamp!"

"Right, we—"

"And," he said, moving into the light, an ancient pistol now in his trembling hand, pointed at my chest. "You were sent by the Devil himself! Tell me that is not true! Tell me!"

"I, uh, that's..."

"Tell me the Dark Lord did not send you to me! Or maybe *you* are him?"

I turned and flung Anza to the floor and spun back to see, then hear, the shot burst from the gun in his hand.

The Actor and his moronic companion were, if they'd checked the inner affixed warning label, exceeding the maximum speed designated by the manufacturers of the Urban Jungle, All-Terrain Polar Stroller (all weather) with Anti-Bottoming Needle Shocks and Semi-Active Biaxial Carriage Suspension (Limited Edition).

However, neither were in a position—or mind—to check warning labels, as they were fast approaching (see above paragraph) a long row of individual shops, built one next to the other, each shimmering in the sun with their large, inviting bay windows.

"Christ, you idiot," the Actor yelled over the whining and banging of the fast-moving baby buggy. "We're about to be knocked unconscious or dead because of you!"

Uncle Jerry lifted his head, and with his fingers bent over the rolling bassinet's lip and reminiscent of a wartime Kilroy, peeked out of the rocketing carriage. He thought for a moment. Then: "You ever ridden a surfboard?"

The Actor frowned and shook his head. "You... you want to ride this thing like a surfboard? That's stu—"

"No, no," the other man said. "Just would be a shame if we died and you hadn't never ridden a surfboard." He turned back to see their reflection in the approaching bay window, their all-terrain baby buggy growing larger by the second. "Pretty fucking awesome, man. Freedom."

Stumbling ahead of me, Anza was, to her credit, halfway down the old wooden steps by the time a second shot rang out and blasted a plate that had been hanging on the wall opposite the stairs.

"Wait!" I shouted, a half step behind my best friend's wife. "It's not what you think, Marc!"

Another shot pinged off a candelabra, sending it spinning to the floor, its thick, yellowed candles breaking free like so many broken bones. Anza called for me to follow her to a small room, and once inside, I spun back and slammed the door. This was some sort of receiving room, and unfortunately, there was one way in and one way out.

But at least there was now a thick plank of door between us and the homicidal octogenarian. Outside the door, I heard the floor creaking.

"Please, Marc, we aren't... we aren't the bad guys," I said and waved Anza away from the door in case he tried to shoot through it. Unable to find any lock, I gripped its handle tightly, my body pressed against the adjacent wall. "Really, man, it's not what you think."

A cough outside the door. "I think it's just as grandfather warned my father and how my father warned me. I think the Devil did send you!"

"Okay, it is what you think."

Blam! The shot rang out and stripped away a panel of wood just above my clamped fist.

"Please!" I shouted. "Please listen to—"

Anza's eyes grew wide, and she gasped. I looked down to see a small bloom of red growing on my shirt.

"*Monsieur, ce n'est pas qu'il y paraît!*" Anza shouted to the air, her eyes watering. "*Nous sommes dans une quête pour sauver l'amour vrai de cet home!*"

I glanced at her, and she nodded, spreading her hands.

For a moment, it was silent. Then from the other side of the door: "Lies!"

Blam! Blam!

Wood splintered, and the air filled with dust and the smell of cordite. Holding tightly onto the handle, I could feel the old man trying to force it open from the other side.

Blam!

"Shit," I said to Anza. "Your French must suck as bad as your English."

Both men looked out of the buggy.

Behind them, a herd of hellspawn devil mimes, arms flailing in the air, running at full speed. In front of them, no better: The cobblestone road was coming to an end, and they were seconds away from crashing through the picture window of a family bakery, which had just opened for the day.

Inside, through the glass, an old, barrel-chested man with a salt-and-pepper mustache stood frozen, mouth hanging open, staring toward the oncoming and out-of-control all-terrain baby carriage.

Bouncing violently in it, the Actor and Uncle Jerry caught sight of him and gave a small wave, trying to look like everything was just fine. Thirty yards between them and closing, Uncle Jerry yelled: "Hiya!"

Seconds from impact, the old baker ran toward the door, looking as if he'd assessed what was about to happen, liked absolutely none of it, and was about to sprint away as fast as possible. But when he got to the door, he didn't exit the store.

Instead, the Actor thought he'd grabbed... a sword?

It was at that moment that the world in front of them, which had been so bright and brilliant and gleaming in the sun, turned dark.

The gunfire on the other side of the door had stopped, and I wondered if the old guy had run out of ammo. I concentrated, trying to recall exactly how many shots he'd gotten off, assuming he was packing a six-shooter.

"Dammit," I whispered to Anza. "If TV taught me nothing, it was to count how many shots they fire!"

"So?" she said, her eyes never losing sight of the door, as if another round would split through it at any second. "How many?"

"Like four or five."

"*Like?*"

"Maybe six. Could be nine."

From the other side of the door, we heard a clattering of limbs, then a groan. I threw the door open and saw the old man had collapsed on the ground.

"Mister Chene!" I yelled and ran toward him.

When I was only a few steps away, he sat bolt upright and leveled the pistol at me. His eyes were drooping, tired, and he was breathing heavily through his teeth.

Anza was frozen at the door behind me, her hand over her mouth. "*Non*, monsieur!" she said, sobbing. "Please."

The old man looked to her, then to me. Finally, he waved the gun, motioning me toward him. As I helped him to his feet, he said, "I never gave the Devil very much credit, but if you two are his agents of evil helping an old man, you are not very good at your jobs."

"Sir, please... we're really not."

"Yes, yes, okay. Fine," he said and looked at Anza, who hadn't yet moved, turned, and dropped his pistol, letting it clatter beneath a side table. "Let me take you to what you've come for."

It was such a strange sensation. As a kid, he learned early on that he really wasn't like all the other kids. He would never be.

Counselors told him he wasn't exactly different—he was "special." Not special enough, mind you, to merit padded headgear and weekly class outings to the zoo. And he was fine with that, despite how cool the zoo could be. But just special enough to stand out. That part... that wasn't so good.

Once he got used to the taunting, the other school kids then began tossing things at him as he passed by. Once he acclimated to that, that's when they stepped it up to physical attacks. They were often quick, cowardly bursts, sometimes done in groups. But always painful.

He knew defending himself would be a joke. Instead, he learned to brace for it, endure it. And once he learned of that magical power, to *endure*, he could render all those bullies powerless. They couldn't get in. They couldn't bruise his spirit nor his heart, even if blue-purple marks eventually did rise upon his skin.

He'd gotten very good at bracing for it. Enduring.

So when the full, undoubtedly painful impact was imminent, when every cell of his body—and that of the Actor's, crouched into a ball next to him—was supposed to collide with the metal and glass of a Belgian confectionery, he braced for it.

Jerry had readied himself. But this time, it had not come. Or maybe it had.

Maybe his imagination, his wandering, dreamy mind, that thing that had made him "special" enough to warrant physical beatings from other schoolchildren all those years ago… maybe it had finally played a trick on him. Maybe he simply imagined he and his short companion had bounced—*bounced!*—off a wall of thick glass, concrete, and metal.

But there he was… floating, floating, floating… drifting through the crisp, cool Belgian morning air. The sun warming his grizzled face. A cool breeze playfully tousling his thinning hair.

An angry dwarf repeatedly punching his ribcage.

"Get up, you crazy bastard!"

The Actor's head then blotted out the sun, his hands pulling hard on the strings of Uncle Jerry's hoodie, slowly lifting the middle-aged man's upper body from the cobblestones.

His mind returned, drifting back into his head, as it always eventually did, and it snapped alert when he caught the frightened expression on the Actor's face.

"We're okay," the dwarf said. Then he released him and started running for a stairwell between two shops. "Let's go, man!"

The spongy man wobbled to his feet and looked down the road from where they'd come. Halfway between where he stood and the shop they should have hit was the Urban, All-Terrain Polar Stroller, on its side, wheels still spinning.

The baker with the salt-and-pepper mustache was now standing on his stoop, staring at him. Behind him, snapping lightly in the wind, was the awning to his store, which he'd released with a long, metal handle, dropping down in front of the glass. They'd ricocheted off the awning and bounced down the adjoining street as if they'd hit a trampoline.

"I'll be damned," Uncle Jerry said and gave the man a wave.

The bakery man did not smile back, instead raising his arms and fanning them. A silent warning: *Go go go!*

At that moment, a dozen, then a dozen more, ghoulish street mimes ran around the corner, heading toward them. The baker ducked back into his store and locked the door.

Uncle Jerry raced after the Actor, crossing the street quickly, then chugged up the stairs after his friend. At the top of the steps, a long stone corridor was lit by a succession of dim yellow bulbs.

There were recesses along each wall, possibly more doors, then another landing of stairs. Jerry stopped and held his breath. Behind him, the only sound he heard was the stomping of feet, growing closer and closer. Above him, the dirty bottoms of two slippers appeared on the top step.

"Jesus, man. Let's go!"

Once he'd caught up, one level higher, both he and the Actor began looking around for a way out of the twisting concrete passageway. Each time they were confronted with what appeared to be a way out, another corridor would simply lead to another. And another.

"What is this stone labyrinth before us?" said the Actor.

Uncle Jerry turned to his partner, huffing as they trotted along. "Wow, you sound like someone in a Shakespeare play!"

The Actor, brow knit, couldn't help but allow himself a little smile. "I think I overdid it a bit."

"Nah, nailed it."

"Hardly," the dwarf said and waved him off. "What the hell is this? Who builds things—"

"It's just corridors that lead up to the back of these shops. Then another row of shops, another row of corridors," Uncle Jerry said as they took another corner, this one slightly darker than the one before. "This is like what they got in the States in all the malls. I used to work at a Pizza Pete's at the mall years ago."

"Uh, you did?"

They leaned back on opposite stone walls, catching their breath.

"Yeah," the older man said, then shrugged when he caught the expression on the Actor's face. "It wasn't so bad."

"The ones with the, things that... move... and..."

"Right, robot animals dressed in Old West get-ups in the pizza joint that come alive every quarter hour to play robot instruments."

"And," the Actor said, pushing off the wall and starting to run again, "what was the appeal in that?"

"Well, it certainly wasn't the pizza."

"I'll bet."

"Yeah," Uncle Jerry said, trying doorknobs along the concrete corridor until he found one open. "How bad do your pies have to be that someone says, 'We better get robot animals in here playing fake guitars?'"

"Whatever works."

"Hey." The older man smiled, flashing yellow teeth and motioning to the open door in front of him. "That's my motto!"

The Actor took a step into the dark room, searching the wall for a light. He didn't find one.

"That's not a good motto, Jer," he said, then looked down the corridor. The shadows of their silent predators danced on the far wall. "We better go this way, huh?"

He looked up to the other man, got a nod, then went inside a bit deeper. A moment later, he said from the dark, "It's not a room. Another damn corridor."

Uncle Jerry started to answer, then stopped. The *pat-patta-pat-patta-patta-pat* of patent leather shoes was echoing off the walls in the corridor behind them. Spinning his body inside, he closed the door behind them and insisted they simply move forward.

In the dark, feeling with only their hands, they found another door and went through it.

"What's wrong with it?" Uncle Jerry whispered.

"There's no switch, I can't se—"

"Nah," he said as they shuffled forward. "My motto is a damn good one. Works for me."

They found another bend in the corridor, with flecks of light occasionally flicking out of ancient bulbs to occasionally orient them.

Stepping quickly, the Actor whispered, "You're unemployed, living in your nephew's spare room, smoking pot all day, and far as I can tell, the only money you make is from the occasional bone thrown at you by some moronic drug dealer with a fake Spanish accent."

At yet another bend, they took the corner, moving as fast as the low light would allow. This pattern went on for several minutes, and all the while the clatter of shoes and slams of doors crept ever closer.

Finally Uncle Jerry said, "You're kind of a mean bastard, you know?"

"Sure. Don't you remember? I'm the one in the group who's the most not good."

Behind them, there was a loud slam, and they both jumped, then froze for a moment.

"Up there," Uncle Jerry whispered loudly, pointing. "There's light coming from under that door."

They ran ahead and threw the door open, their eyes instantly assaulted by an aggressive sun, and both men shuffled forward into the light. Ahead of them, another winding corridor, damp piping down the walls. But there was light! And in the distance a soft, playful churn of music.

The two men ran as quickly as they could, slipping occasionally in the damp corridor, until another break in the passage offered up a strange succession of doors above them, lined at their edges with sun. They were nearly out!

Uncle Jerry pointed to one door, small and irregularly shaped. The Actor went first, and Jerry followed, closing it behind them.

"Shit."

"This isn't a corridor," the Actor hissed. "There's a gap between the corridor and here. Dammit, this is a frigging broom closet! Get ou—"

The door handle began to turn, and Uncle Jerry leapt for it. It rattled hard as he fought to keep it secure, but he could feel it already slipping in his sweaty grip. On the other side, no words, but the snarls and heavy breathing of several of the ghoulish mimes—maybe all of them—told them enough.

They were trapped.

For the first time, the Actor could see that his partner was scared, and that in turn terrified him deep into his bones.

"Find something, man!" Uncle Jerry said in a strained whisper.

The dwarf searched for another knob, a weapon, anything, but only found a succession of ancient levers and switches and recessed buttons. Nothing he could make out too clearly in the dark.

"Hey, man," the Actor said. "There's another door here!"

"What?"

He struggled with the door, both hands clasped over the knob. "Look at my feet, and along the wall here. There's a door or something recessed into the wall."

Just above Uncle Jerry's lower back, the Actor saw it: a thick pipe with angle welds. It was a lever for the second door.

He squeezed behind the larger man and gripped it with both hands.

"When I tell you, let go and jump back."

"*Let go?*"

"Yes, otherwise I can't close the second—"

"Ah, right, gotcha!" Uncle Jerry said and then let go.

"Jesus, not until I say go!"

The first door swung open a second later, and the entire ghoulish mime horde of Hell, Inc. stood there, momentarily surprised it was now standing wide open. Then, catching sight of the two terrified men inside, they all lurched forward, too many at once, and jammed in the doorway.

"Get back!"

The Actor reached up and grabbed Uncle Jerry by his fanny pack's strap, pulling him inside the metal closet, then yanked as hard as he could on the pipe, praying hard that the secondary door would close.

It did.

The thin slab of metal slammed into place, and the next moment, the devil mimes advanced, clawing and banging at the rows of tiny, pinky-sized holes drilled across the top third of the door. They pushed so hard it seemed like the entire room swayed.

"What... what's all this— *Hey!*"

Their tiny room lurched sideways, and slowly the snarling horde slipped from view. Through the metal window, dark patches passed by on a concrete wall, speeding up from one moment to the next.

Then, a queer sensation: It was if they were now swaying freely in the air.

Moments later, they could feel the tiny room lifting them up, up, up. And then the entire space burst with light as the sun's rays drilled through the holes. Uncle Jerry stumbled over, shielding his eyes with his hand, and looked out of the rudimentary window.

"Neat," he said.

The Actor frowned, arching up, trying to see, the bright light punishing his eyes. "What?"

"Huh," Uncle Jerry said. "We're on an old-timey Ferris wheel."

Here was the moment that I'd risked my eternal soul for. Or at least, it was the beginning of that.

I'd commandeered two friends—or rather, the relatives of two—and uh, absolutely shanghaied a third. Arguably, my crew fell well beneath even the definitions of motley and ragtag. But here we stood, me and my best friend's wife, staring at the first big win in my quest to save my Carissa's life.

"Is that really it? That leetle chunk of metal?"

I looked at Anza with an unsteady gaze. She'd voiced the fear in my own heart. "Mr. Chene…" I said.

"Rasputin," he replied, and kindly put his hand on my forearm, "I shot you. We are closer for it. Please call me Marc."

"Yes, Marc. Right, okay." I nodded quickly. "It's just… that doesn't look like, well…"

Anza tried again. "It is not that either me or him is lamp experts…"

"Certainly, right!" I said. "But it doesn't look like much of, I dunno… a lamp."

The old Belgian ambled toward the smudged window of the upper floor's back room. He held the clump of metal up to the muddied sunlight. "It's not, of course," he said.

"But—"

"As I said, this is the wick manifold of the lamp!" he said, eyeballing the two of us. He then lifted the lamp part a little higher, as if it were a sacrifice to some dusty attic god. It was made from some sort of pockmarked metal. Maybe brass? It looked heavy.

But maybe that was just because the old fella's arms were trembling slightly as he held it up. Or he could have just been a bit weak after shooting me. Marc looked at us both and then burst into laughter, nearly dropping the cluster of metal.

Anza moved forward to make sure he didn't fall, but he waved her away.

"No, no," he said, wiping tears away. He raised his hand, assuring her he was not going to keel over. Leaning against the wall, he repeated himself, softer this time, "This is the wick manifold of the lamp." For a few seconds he was gone, somewhere far from us. Then his eyes cleared again. "I certainly would not have known what such a phrase meant had not this been in our home for so many years. So many, many years."

My chest twinged slightly, and I said: "You have... your family has my deepest gratitude."

He looked at me now, his eyes still damp. After a moment, he nodded and accepted my thanks. "This has been in my family for three generations now."

"I'm sure... I know it has great value," I said, my voice quivering.

The Belgian took a few steps and dropped into an old wooden chair, shooting silt up through the attic space. "This? This is a piece of junk." Marc tossed it to me. "It has no value whatsoever."

Anza eyeballed me, her face saying, *We got it. Let's get out of here!*

"Still, I appreci—"

"Its value is only to your family, Rasputin. And mine," he said, his eyes staring off at middle distance again. "My grandfather knew of its importance but *not* of what that importance was."

Nodding, I took a few steps toward the door. Outside the window, the sun was beginning to arch higher in the sky. I caught the edges of people moving in the street as dawn transformed into a lovely Belgian morning.

Marc continued. "It seems your family and mine have been unknowingly linked over the past century and a half, Rasputin. I... I'm sorry."

I walked over and kneeled before him in the chair, the sun from the attic window draped across my shoulders. "No, please, Marc. I'm so appreciative of everything your family has done to take care of it. You could have tossed it out, and it may have been lost forever."

Lifting his chin from his chest, he looked at me, and I grasped his shoulder. He blinked away more tears and smiled. "I know, my friend. I just wish my father were here." He then looked at me with a longing, an emptiness that seemed even beyond the years of his own lifetime. "What is it for, Rasputin? Why have you now, finally, come to claim it?"

Anza opened the door to the attic space, and I stood to leave. As we walked away from the old man, he seemed so small. He and his father, and his father before him, had carried this burden, waiting for someone to one day claim it. I was that someone, and that burden now needed to be lifted.

"My wife is... she is very special. But also very sick. And this is part of a lamp that will bring her back to me."

Marc's mouth hung open, and the old man's eyes did not blink as he listened to me. He was motionless, as if I were some apparition, a trick of the light, and if he were to move, some dust particles might stir and whisk me away.

"I've got a short time to get all the pieces together to save my wife. Or there's a chance I could end up like your great-grandfather. Wandering, searching for my lost love."

He held steady for a moment, half of his gray face illuminated by the sun shining through the window. Slowly, he nodded. "Then that is the greatest of all quests." The old Belgian folded his hands together. "When I leave this place, when I die and join my father and grandfather, I'll tell them that we, our family, were a part of saving the life of an angel."

The word hit me like a hammer. *Angel.* I nodded and tucked the lamp's wick manifold under my arm but felt my legs go slightly weak.

Anza's hand found mine. She offered a goodbye and helped lead me out the door, leaving the old man to his moment of peace—something that had not been granted to his father or grandfather. As we left the room, he wished us luck.

I called up to him: "Thank you! Thank you so much!"

"You're welcome, my brave friend," he said, then I heard him laugh. "Brave and *fortunate*. Fortunate that some kind soul has shown you the path that returns her to your side."

As we headed for the front door, I couldn't help but think that what he'd just said wasn't true at all. I'd *not* been put on this trek by anyone *kind*. Of course, it had been just the opposite. A thought began to swirl around in my head, looking for something tangible to latch on to.

I'd made a wager that might get me a most unique device. One so powerful it could snatch my wife from the cold embrace of the Grim Reaper.

What was I putting up in this wager? This big prize: my everlasting soul. Really? Trust me, I have no illusions about my own self-worth, so even I was thinking the Devil was getting the short end of the stick here.

As we exited the purple house and stepped into the sunlight and fresh air, I voiced my conclusion, my dreadful rationalization, aloud.

"What did you say?" Anza asked.

Shaking her off at first, I then thought better of it and repeated myself. "I said, 'They must be desperate.'"

She shrugged and looked at me, seeking more.

"Nothing," I said and smiled. Then I held up the wick manifold. "We got one, Anza."

She squeezed my hand and beamed at me. "Let's go get the rest!"

"Right!"

"And we should go quickly beforing the old man shoots you again."

"Okay."

The words I wanted to say got caught in my throat. I could only nod and smile, blinking away my tears. Then a lot of those mushy feelings simply got pushed aside as the ugliest street performer I had ever seen rounded the side of the house and made a beeline for the two of us.

Anza looked over casually. "What is with freaky mime?"

The moment Uncle Jerry left the Ferris wheel's small cabin, the Actor regretted, *deeply* regretted, agreeing with the plan. However, something told him that it wouldn't have mattered if he'd agreed or not. The wild look in the man's eyes told him that the choice had already been made.

The only contribution to that brief, frenzied moment of decision-making the Actor had offered was not even a complete thought: "But *where did you get...* I mean..."

That was when Uncle Jerry pointed to his fanny pack with a toothy grin that would have prompted even the Cheshire Cat to say, "Please, for decency's sake, can you dial that down a notch?"

Only a minute earlier, when the Ferris wheel had reached its apex, the Actor had pointed four or five blocks in the distance and said, "Jesus, is that Raz and Anza coming out of that house?"

Jerry had squinted through the metal caging. "It, uh..."

"Not good." The Actor leaned closer to the steel screen, wrapping his fingers through its holes. "They've got one of our creepy mime fucks on 'em."

After that, Uncle Jerry had hatched his plan. And by any objective measure, it was a terrible, terrible idea.

It seemed that there was, tucked away into the nylon bag affixed to the middle-aged man's waist, a lump of plastic explosives he'd once gotten as a thank-you gift from a mid-level Colombian cartel worker.

Yes, the Actor had also rolled his "yeah, right" eyes at hearing that wee nugget. And yes, the first question any rational person would ask was, "Unless you are a suicide bomber, why the fuck would you have plastic explosives strapped to your waist?"

But before that obligatory question could be uttered by the Actor, Jerry had opened the door and *stepped outside* the moving Ferris wheel cabin. For the Actor, the next full minute was a long, long minute. And it was as if, from an unseen grandfather clock, each second (*tick...*) rang off the thin metal walls of the ancient ride's cabin (*tick...*).

It wasn't that he terribly *liked* Uncle Jerry. However, all alone in the metal car now, he quietly admitted to himself the guy was growing on him.

A little.

Or that the act of climbing down the scaffolding of a moving Ferris wheel by a guy who looked like he got winded opening a bag of potato chips was, by all accounts, a prelude to death. In that moment, he couldn't remember feeling more alone and stared up at the sun-white dots of the door's metal screen, hoping the stupid, fat man would soon return.

(*Tick...*)

The Ferris wheel jolted slightly, and the Actor stepped up onto the uncomfortable metal seat, then looked out the metal mesh window behind him. Below, group after group of the ghoulish street performers were loading into the cars. One after another.

"What are they thinking?" the Actor muttered. "It's a Ferris Wheel! They can't catch up, for crissake." Then he thought, *Can they?*

(*Tick...*)

The ancient carnival ride then picked up a bit of speed as it swung the car through the air. Briefly, the sun was blocked by the line of shops they'd just come from as the metal chamber dipped toward the ground, then back up once more.

From outside came: "Oooohffff..."

The sun rose again inside the small car, and pushing his fear deep into his stomach, he tentatively cracked the door open. Below, Uncle Jerry was hanging on a steel lip by his fingertips.

"Oh my god! Uncle Jerry, what the he—"

"Just help me up, man!"

For a very long moment, he stood there hunched, frozen. Then, as if waking from a spell, the Actor quickly gripped an interior strap, reached down, and pawed at the spongy man's fingers. A moment later, a hand was locked onto his. His other hand burned, straining against the weight of the man as he held the strap. It hurt like nothing he could recall.

(*Tick...*)

Still, the dwarf held on tightly, trapped in Uncle Jerryworld, where up seemed down and down seemed apricot-ferret lip balm.

"Pull, ya little bastard!"

"Fuck you!"

"Pull!"

With cacophony of grunts, groans, and whines, Uncle Jerry inched upward until he got one elbow secured onto the cold, metal floor. Then the other.

It took all of his remaining strength—and that of the man desperately pulling him back inside—but he finally tumbled into the car. He flopped onto the floor, breathing heavy as the Actor pushed the tiny door closed. The man in the red robe stared at the heaving, sweating fat guy on the floor. He looked like he might die from the physical exertion. Or worse, shit himself.

"Hey... you okay?"

Still heaving huge breaths of air into his lungs, Uncle Jerry smiled. "Thanks for saving my life, man."

For the first time in as long as he could remember, words failed the Actor. He offered only an awkward smile. Then, still struggling for his breath, the man on the floor added: "You best hold on to something."

"Wha—"

Boom.

In a world where we base our measurements upon our ten fingers and toes, while at the same time relying on little devices that sadly can only count to one (starting at zero, mind you), it's strange how very often the number three pops into everyday life. Obvious examples that ran through my mind as Anza and I slowly descended the old Belgian's rickety wooden porch were things like the Christian trinity.

Or Taoists, who have the Great Triad: Heaven-Human-Earth. Time is separated into past, present and future. Matter is made up of solid, liquid, and gas (screw plasma, that's just a wishy-washy solid).

There are three primary colors. Rock, paper, scissors? Three. Or how *Star Wars* was broken into three *tri*logies. Even our survival limit is expressed in a rule of threes: three minutes of air, three days of water, three weeks of food.

So as I walked from a man's home carrying a 150-year-old piece of a lamp that was supposed to save the life of my dying wife because the fucking Devil said so, I counted that collectively as *one* big damn weirdness (BDW).

But is three the mind's limit to simultaneous BDW? A person, I would hope, would not have to answer such a question. Because just *one* BDW at any given time is truly and honestly one too many. But given that life does throw us the occasional curveball, it would seem that at any moment we might be faced with a singular yet tricky little odd moment.

For example, right then, I noticed that my companion and I were being converged upon by, of all things, street performers.

Mimes.

And as I caught sight of their faces, ghastly and ghoulish, it was clear that they were also operatives of the hostile-takeover-minded faction of the down below, Hell, Inc. Now, it can't be determined that *all* street-performing mimes are in fact not, by design, hellspawn. But I will venture to say, having no proof to support it, from Marcel Marceau on up to little baby mimes, that they are, each and every one, servants of evil. I feel I can say this, if for no other reason than I was fairly sure not a single one of them would contradict this determination. At least not outloud.

So, looking around and taking it in. At that moment, converging demon mimes would have to be counted as number *two* when considering concurrent moments of Big Damn

Weirdness. And *two* seems like far more than anyone should have to embrace.

Honestly, it was.

However, I think it can be stated correctly that the human mind may bend or even break if a third BDW were to be introduced. And obviously just slightly less deep-core rattled than myself, Anza was the one who vocalized and identified the human psyche limit. The third concurrent BDW event.

"Huh," she said, standing next to me on the bottom step of the old man's front porch. "Is that a tree-hundred-foot Ferris wheel rolling toward us?"

"Yes. Yes, I believe it is."

"Oh, good, I was thinking it was just my imagining."

"No," I said. "Your imagination? No, who would do that to themselves?"

"Right. That is good point," she said and nodded. "We should probably run like hell. That is probably best?"

"Yes. Yes, I believe it is."

Chapter Sixteen

The Devil had become—and rightfully so—a little paranoid in recent years. Because the secret to the power of evil (note it was not a very *good* secret, as it's written out explicitly in Section III of Hell, Inc.'s "So Now You're a Minion" welcome packet) wasn't the *power* that evil wielded but the *perceived* power it actually had.

Now, in the Early Days, Satan was all kinds of fire and brimstone. Good ol' fashioned reign o' pain stuff. He'd welcomed tormented souls into the lava pits of the Underworld, at times even personally assigning the torturous to-do list to new arrivals. And while their bloodcurdling screams did still stir him a little in his pink bits, it all just had become so... routine.

For a time, he'd even turned it up a notch—harsher beatings, more James Joyce readings, bigger teeth on the man-eating maggots. Still, sometime in the midtwentieth century, as he stood above his main Colosseum of Suffering, Anguish, and Intermittent Belittling, staring down at his domain, he announced his feelings in a booming, echoing voice:

"Bored. *Borrrrred*," Satan said. He added: "Bored, bored, bored."

Then, hearing his own lovely voice bounce back at him, he had an idea. The Devil called his lieutenants together at a condemned stand-up comedy theater in St. Paul, Minnesota.

They were less than receptive.

"So, wait... you want to get rid of the fire pits?" one said.

"Yes, fill 'em with sand."

"And the torture chambers, those are gone, too?" asked another.

Satan nodded excitedly. "We'll convert them, it'll be—"

"Wait," another of his seconds asked, his voice quivering slightly. "So the giant anthills with the, you know, fire ants with the snapping, poisonous pincers...?"

"Throw them in the fire pits before the sand."

They all gasped.

"No, no," Satan said, putting out his hands, trying to calm his troops. "I've got something better now. Woo *hoo*, this is hot!"

They waited. They looked at each other, then back at their boss. And still they waited. Until someone finally asked, "So what is it?"

Satan jabbed a finger in the direction of his inquisitive demon and said, "I'm glad you asked." He took a deep breath, filling his barrel chest, and explained: "We're going to bore people."

His huge smile was met with complete and utter silence. Then a voice, somewhere in the third row: "Bore people?"

"Yes!"

"How?"

The Devil took a breath and exhaled; he could feel himself getting agitated. He didn't want that. Last time he got a bit miffed, he had to hire an entire new staff (as well as a crew to clean up what was left of the old one).

"I don't know the particulars; it can't be hard," he said. "Listen, we torture souls and bodies, but are we really getting the goods here? I mean, after a while, what's yet *another* electrified fondue fork to the testicles going to do?"

"Jesus, no!" a demon's voice cried out, almost in pain. "We're getting rid of the electrified fondue forks?"

"Listen, listen!" Inhale, exhale. "Take away all stimulus, all joy, all pain, so there's nothing. They'll go mad. The wonderful, lovely anguish of madness! That's fertile soil for all-new *mental* tortures!"

Again, the room was quiet for a moment.

"Just... sir, a bit of guidance. All we're asking."

Deep breath. "Just... you know, put 'em in a room," the Prince of Darkness said. "A gray room with a table and chair, maybe," he said, then lit up. "Ooh! And what about a writing tablet? You know, some paper, but no pen or pencil."

Again, they all stared.

"Sir," a demon in the front row with his feet up on the stage said, "that's... sorta what they're doing now. On Earth. Like, for a lotta these folks, you just described their jobs."

The meeting then ended in a flash of light and several wisps of smoke.

Sadly, for the man in charge, the only thing to come out of that particular confab was the necessity to again hire a new group of lieutenants (and another crew to clean up the remains of the second group). However, in the end Satan did not act on his bold new plan, something he regretted soon enough.

Because one of the pillars of Hell, Inc.'s Tripartite Strategy was in fact to bring a type of Hell on Earth, just as Satan had envisioned years earlier. That wasn't a coincidence.

One of the demons who'd been in attendance at that meeting was not, in fact, smote into a pile of ash and tar. Well, partially. Mostly. But he was still able to slink away. And that demon had taken Satan's idea to a burgeoning underground group with plans to overtake Hell and snatch it from the Old Man.

His intellectual property! Stolen via corporate espionage!

And so the Devil had become a little paranoid in recent years. Not only wary that his good ideas might be snatched up and employed elsewhere, but as he slowly lost control of the Underworld, he was incrementally becoming less powerful. Less scary.

Sure, he could still deliver a good fingertip smiting, but it didn't rattle the world below and above like it used to. So he now held most of his board meetings in a place where he was relatively powerless.

He was still the Big Dog—he could retain a modicum of power. However, his lieutenants, if they as a group got any ideas about a revolt in their heads, they had no power at all. Not on *semi*-hallowed ground.

They couldn't go in a church—that was a hellspawn no-go zone—but they could instead attend, say, a church function. A favorite of the Devil's was the Our Lady of Fiduciary

Exemption bingo hall, because it gave him something to do when he got bored with the meeting.

Yes, the group of demons got the occasional stares from the old ladies coveting their paper cards and ink-filled sponge blotters. His small crew sat at the back, out of earshot of most of the old folks who had bad hearing anyhow.

And if there arose any octogenarian suspicion, well, the Devil wasn't entirely without power, he could stamp that out like Justin Bieber wandering into a Deep South Rolling Thunder motorcycle bar.

"Report," Satan said, fiddling with the array of paper bingo cards before him.

Seven demons sat at the lunch table around him, each representing a continent on Earth. They all looked to Europe.

"Well, he has now the first of the pieces," Europe said. Regrettably, Europe had decided to adopt a French accent. He was not terribly good at accents, however, and it was more a dreadful blend of French, German, maybe Portuguese, and a touch of harelip. "T'ree more t' go."

From the front, a priest called out, "B-18. If you get caught late at night in a car downtown with a member of the opposite sex, they better B-18!"

The Devil searched the sixteen cards in front of him and placed a blot on one on the top row, two on the third row, and another one on the bottom. He looked up to Europe.

"Any more trouble with... them?"

Europe shifted in his seat, partially because he was nervous and partially because they were cheap metal folding chairs and dreadfully uncomfortable.

"Hell, Inc.? Some, but I zink Rasputin und his team can 'andle it."

"*Team*?" Satan said, and as he did, he'd inadvertently spat onto the table, and one of his cards burst into flames and turned to ash. "Dammit! I was close to a diagonal there!"

"Yes, team. The old stoner guy, the illegal—"

"I know who's with him!"

An old woman spun toward the Devil and his seconds and let out a "shhhh."

Satan nodded with a mocking smile, spread his hands, and when she'd spun away, he flicked a finger. A moment later, the miffed lady turned to the woman seated beside her, pointing to her cards. "What? Where did my ink blots go? I was close to... Valerie, did you do something?"

The woman named Valerie either ignored or couldn't hear her.

Satan turned back to his group. "Is he on track, though? Will he get the lamp?"

North America nodded confidently. "I think maybe so."

"Why do you say that?" asked Africa, frowning.

"American know-how and stick-to-itiveness."

The Devil looked toward North America with plans to give him a good eye-rolling, but then got briefly distracted.

"I-21," the priest sang out. "I-21. I-21, so I would like to buy a beer, bartender!"

The group of seven gathered around their boss waited until he'd marked his cards.

"What makes you so sure they can even get out of Brussels?" Satan said, simply eyeballing North America since the moment had passed where an eye-rolling would make any sense.

"Well," his lieutenant said, thumbing the brim of his cowboy hat, "it's gonna get weird. But I did have my people place a couple things along the way that might help. If all Hell breaks loose, the very last resort is this inflatabl—"

"I don't want 'ifs' from you!" Satan hissed.

Another woman in front of them, this time Valerie, turned and gave them another "shhhh."

The Devil, frustrated, couldn't help himself and jabbed a crooked finger toward her. Valerie tensed, then slumped and fell face first onto the lunch table in front of her. The woman next to her looked at her friend, collapsed and life extinguished, and put a hand to her mouth. She then slid the dead woman's cards over in front of her, quickly lifting Valerie's head to get the card underneath it. It fell back on the table with a soft *thunk!*

Satan scanned his group. "This lamp is the key to finally ridding ourselves of Hell, Inc. Not only that, it's—"

"G-61! G-61! Gee, you're 61? I wouldn't have pegged ya for anything north of fifty!"

The Devil blotted his cards, mimicking the sound of Dead Valerie's head. *Thunk, thunk, thunk...* "Listen, the lamp is our chance! This is it! I've seen its power." He looked toward the second across from him. "Europe will be all ours in a day!" Then, he looked at Asia. "Your four and a half billion people in maybe two!" With a quick glance at Oceania, he shrugged. "Shit, what would we want with New Zealand and—*what?*— Papua New Guinea? Meh. And of course, we've had all of Australia for years, so no big whoop there."

All seven looked to each other then back at their boss.

"How is this possible?" Antarctica said.

"I waited," the Devil said. He looked around the table, nodding slowly. "I waited billions of years to get this planet. And I found just the thing, the lamp, that will get it for me."

"But," South America said, "why did it take until now to get this thing? This lamp."

At the front of the room, the priest began to speak but then stammered as the Devil twisted his fingers round and round.

"It...the..." the priest said. He looked at the ping-pong ball in his hand, put it in his mouth, and then swallowed it. "O-69. O-69." He then swayed a little unnaturally and crooned off-key: "You play me like a flute, I'll toot ya like a trumpet... and that's oh-69!"

The Devil turned to his crew. "I waited a long, long time to find someone who loved so hard they'd be blind enough to risk everything to find the lamp for us. You see, the seeker couldn't be anyone like us or anyone working for us. *Un*affiliated. So I waited." He blinked slowly. Then he added: "And I got bloody tired of waiting, so I... well, I went and got the ball rolling. We got our guy. And soon we'll have all of Earth."

Satan then stood up, parted his arms and said, "Bingo."

What the group of silver-haired ladies in the bingo hall all said after that brought the warmest smile to the Old Man's lips.

Chapter Seventeen

So there I was, running down a street in Brussels, Belgium with my best friend's wife, eyes locked on a giant Ferris wheel that was chewing up concrete walkways and garden paths like some sort of steampunk Pac-Man as it headed toward what initially appeared to be a field of tall, unwieldy white trees.

Of course, they weren't trees. None had branches, leaves, or a flock of crooning sparrows with charming French accents. They were, in fact, the masts of several hundred high-dollar boats from the Brussels Royal Yacht Club.

What distressed me, of course, was that yachts meant water. And that concerned me because I knew that my two friends were undoubtedly on that rolling Ferris wheel.

"We've got to get to them before they get to the water."

Anza, pumping her arms as she ran, looked at me and said, "Who?"

"Uncle Jerry and the Actor."

"You think they are on dat crazy wheel?"

I looked back at her and said calmly, "Can you seriously imagine any scenario where they're not?"

"I don't feel so good."

"It... OW... why, then... SHIT... Christ, I'm going to break something... DAMN."

The one item in the "assets" column for Uncle Jerry and the Actor might have been that the Ferris wheel had been constructed at a time after World War II (although likely not long after) when steel once again became abundant.

The wheel's beams, its individual carriages, the struts between the beams... all of that was flexing the muscles of the post-war steel industry.

Which also meant it wasn't likely to slow its roll anytime soon. As The Actor bounced from top to side to bottom to side and back to top again, he got the occasional fleeting glimpse of their hell-pledged, street-performing pursuers.

He could take solace in the fact that those guys were in as bad a position as he and Uncle Jerry were... albeit silently. If he'd had his choice, which he didn't, the Actor would have elected to pass out and endure the banging around as conscious as a rag doll in an industrial-sized clothes dryer.

But no, he'd stayed alert and felt the battering from every angle in succession around his body. Then, when he'd seen the boats through a small slit in the body of the carriage, and subsequently, the river beyond it, he'd not been entirely surprised.

To the rather nihilist dwarf, it made perfect sense.

Of course it would end like this. Dying in a multi-tonned steel behemoth, with an idiot partner, pursued by Belgian street performers who'd pledged allegiance to Satan, unable to escape.

"Typical," the Actor mutter to himself.

The rolling metal tumbleweed was moving too fast for my pumping legs to catch up to it, which in truth simply meant it was moving. Me, I'm not really a big runner.

Anza was ahead of me, naturally, and was quickly widening the gap between the two of us. But it was clear as she fell back to a trot, shouting something *en Español*, that there was no way she could catch it. Not on foot, at least.

Now, there's a contemporary proverb, a maxim, if you will, that is altogether shameful, disrespectful, and wholly true.

Fat girls 'n' mopeds. Fun to ride, but you just don't want anyone seeing you do it.

See? An awful, awful thing to say. But then again...

Anza, it seems, had caught sight of the same thing I had. I lumbered up to her as she desperately tried to talk a chubby Belgian lass into letting us borrow her Vespa.

Sure enough, as I approached, the girl stepped off the moped and handed it over with a wave of her hand. I looked at Anza and said, sucking in deep breaths, "What... why... did she just give that to you?"

"Is okay, I am bi," my best friend's wife said.

"Wuh, wha... it... What?"

"Actually, tri, I think."

Dan, you ol' rascal!

"Spanish, English, and French," she added as she got onto the moped.

"Ah."

"The girl, she speaks French."

"Trilingual."

"Even though she is Flemish, I think."

"Yeah," I said, climbing on the moped behind Anza. "But she carries it well for a girl her size."

Because our friends were about a minute away from being submerged in the river, we did not take the offered helmet. At least Anza hadn't, and I was already sitting in the bitch seat. No need to add insult to injury and be the only one aboard wearing pink headgear.

As I sat, a streak of pain rippled through my side where the old man's bullet had passed through me. Wincing a little, it occurred to me that it should hurt a lot more than it did.

"Nice move getting the moped," I yelled over the wind rushing past us.

"*Si*, thank you!"

"What do we do if and when we catch up to the big spinning wheel of death?"

She shrugged and gunned the little engine harder. "I came up with first part of plan, the rest is for you to work it out, Rasputin."

As I've said, while I do believe there is a Devil, I may not entirely believe in God. And no, that's not some thought force-wriggled into my brain by Ozzy Osbourne backwards-masked lyrics while I air-guitared to "Over the Mountain" years ago.

Like I've said, evidence-based. Just look around you. If there were a God (capital g), I believe he'd be the kind of god (small g) who probably got really tired of our shit.

God said: "I give you a river."

Man says: "Cool, now I've got a place to pipe the runoff from my factory."

God said: "I give you a beautiful, rolling meadow."

Man says: "And I'll put the bleachers over there, dugouts over there…"

God said: "I give you songbirds."

Man says: "Just need some mustard and two slices of bread…"

And then God said: "Aw, fuck this."

So we haven't heard from him a long while, but I think he may pop back just to mess with us from time to time. Which may have had something to do with why I was prompted to tap on Anza's shoulder and say: "Veer right."

"What? Why?"

"Head toward the hill over there!"

"Wh—" she began to say but stopped mid-thought. Because she saw why.

Uncle Jerry splayed out his arms and legs, trying to hold on to the inner walls of the Ferris wheel's carriage. For a brief, strange moment, the Actor thought the man looked like an album cover he'd seen many years earlier.

The older man's plan to repeatedly secure himself inside the small metal carriage ala da Vinci's Vitruvian man worked reasonably well until they reached the apex of their fun-wheel orbit.

Upside down in the tiny cabin, he would inevitably fall down hard onto the brushed-steel seat and its restraining bar. Occasionally, he'd land on the Actor. This was softer, albeit not by much, and often came with a sort of asthmatic verbal tirade, as the little man was bounced from wall to ceiling to wall to floor and back again with each rotation of the Ferris wheel, mostly because he was unable to brace himself in the same manner.

Uncle Jerry kept his eye on the door, as if at any moment it would be flung open and a cool superhero like the Green Lantern would beckon at them. "This way, my friends!"

Then they would ride out on a ribbon of green light and maybe get ice cream!

But if he was being honest with himself (something Jerry was stridently against), he knew that it was from there, from where the blade of light danced and sliced, this would not in fact be where his salvation came from, but his end. Whatever force had been assigned to end him and the dwarf, it would be coming from that direction.

Which was why it took him a moment to register that the insistent voice in his head was not, in fact, in his head. Granted, there were a good number of voices rolling around in there, and he'd gotten to know all of them too well since they'd first shown up in his early adolescence.

This one, however, was not one of them. This voice, he was sure, belonged to Rasputin. And he listened intently without responding because there was no way Raz was saying what he was saying. It just made no logical sense.

Staring dumbfounded, the racket from a dwarf actor bouncing around the interior of the metal cabin making it difficult to concentrate, he listened again.

It sounded like Raz was saying (but of course wasn't saying): "Get in the Zorb!"

This was what I'd been talking about when I said I was convinced the only reason God might have hung around was to mess with us now and again.

What could Anza and I do when we caught up to the Ferris wheel? Nothing. There was nothing, short of ramming it with a Vespa (which would be on par with a Georgia stinkbug "ramming" a Ford F-150's radiator grill), that we could do to help our friends.

Then on offer was the smallest of possibilities: stoned Belgian students messing around with the most idiotic invention since the lawn jart: a Zorb. A Zorb which I commandeered from the aforementioned stoner students.

As we approached the Ferris Wheel, I held on to the man-sized inflatable ball above my head with all the strength I had. The Vespa had nearly pulled off a wheelie because of the drag, which I think may be technically impossible.

From an upper atmospheric vantage point, we must have looked like a couple of teacup mice on one of those mini-skateboards that were so popular some years back, with a fat glazed doughnut held high aloft, chasing after our mouse cousin's runaway exercise wheel.

As we sidled up to the spinning metallic wheel, I could feel them. That was the queerest thing. I could feel my friends, where they were. My eyes locked on to their enclosed car, and I told Anza to hold on—whatever that meant, since she was simply steering the minibike.

It's odd because as reckless as I can be (or more correctly, as I try to portray), the idea of blindly leaping at a spinning metallic wheel of doom with a Zorb on one arm is not, as they say, my thing.

As we kept pace with the massive rolling Ferris wheel, now less than 300 meters from the river, Anza was trying to figure out which compartment contained our friends. This was somewhat easier than it sounds, because the rest of the metal cabs had outstretched arms clawing at the air.

The only way I could get the giant human hamster ball close to Uncle Jerry and the Actor was to anticipate their car on the downswing, hop off the moped, and run with the wheel, latching on to it with my fingers before it rose back up again.

Right. No damn way I was pulling that off. Still, it was the only shot we had.

"I'm not feeling very confident about this move, Anza," I yelled over the whine of the Vespa's engine.

"Is nothing."

"No, it is not nothing! Is very dangerous thing to do this!"

She smiled at me, white teeth glimmering in the sun. "And selling your eternal soul to the Devil is not so dangerous a thing?"

Looking up, I got a bead on where their car was. All in. This was all in or nothing. Feigning a bravery that I did not wield, I yelled over the wind: "The Devil don't got it yet!"

She yelled back: "You know dats right, Rasputin!"

A moment later, she nodded quickly, giving me the *go-go-go-go* move with her dangling fingers.

I hopped off and instantly fell forward, mistakenly slipped and tumbled inside the Zorb (which I can only compare to what one might endure if one were to visit the time of one's birth, in reverse), and bounced like an idiot.

"Son of a…" Still rolling, the only move left was to embrace my inner hamster. "Okay, freaky ball of weirdness. Let's go, let's go."

With the inflatable walls lifting me as I ran, I could take big Elasticman-type strides, and given that I was already moving at a fair clip when I left the Vespa, I was—as they say in the cooler parts of America—hauling ass.

Too fast. The hamster ball was going to get in front of the big metal wheel and get crushed if I didn't get a grip on it.

Anza had gunned ahead, getting smaller as she approached the river. I wasn't sure what she was up to, but it didn't matter. I rolled up to the spinning wheel, my heart pounding like a trapped animal trying to break free from my chest, and I saw their car arcing back toward the ground, so I bounced the Zorb and outstretched my arm, fingers extended, latching on to the side of the ancient spinning Ferris wheel.

"Oh, shit!"

I didn't have a good grip—just two fingers and a thumb threaded through the metal slots of their door, but I knew it wasn't not enough. With my body at an angle, I could see I was about lose my grip and be dragged underneath the hulking metal frame.

When your life depends on it, you can find strength you didn't think you had. Not me, mind you, but I've heard that happens to others. The lower half of my body was within the Zorb arc, near where the giant wheel was chewing up grass, leaving behind it a scar of sod, soil, and crushed rock.

I waited for the bite of it, but it didn't come right away. I knew there was no way my grip was strong enough to be able to hold on for those few seconds. And then I realized that my wedding ring had caught along the lines of the metal frame, effectively keeping my hand from losing its grip.

That was how I was, in that moment, not being dragged underneath.

But I knew it couldn't hold—within the next second, I was going to arch upward and that meant…

"Gotcha!"

I looked toward the darkened car and saw that I now had one hand gripping the car and a hand from within the car gripping me.

"Raz!"

Uncle Jerry!

He had a death grip on my wrist. It hurt a lot, but I would take that hurt any day over the alternative. I saw the Actor not doing well, banging around in there like a dwarf in a runaway Ferris wheel.

I shouted to them again: "Get in the Zorb!"

This seemed, on the surface, like a simple command, a simple task. But, see, I was holding on to the door's mesh window, and Uncle Jerry had a hold of my wrist. They needed to open the door to get out and then into my big blow-up hamster ball. Which meant once he swung it open, I was back to staring down death's wheel.

I glanced ahead. Anza was waiting at the river's edge, holding something I couldn't see with all the spinning.

Bam!

When we hit bottom, I bounced with my hamster ball, and it felt like my fingers were being stretched beyond the limitations of muscle and ligament and skin. Then my hand began to scream at me as we arched back up again.

I could hear Uncle Jerry helping the Actor toward the door, and I got a quick glance down. "Whoa, that's a long way…"

"Okay, when you bounce on the bottom in about three seconds," Uncle Jerry shouted, and it felt like everything was going in slow motion. "I'm gonna let you go, and we'll leap out toward ya!"

That, of course, was ridiculous, and I was about to tell him that when I hit the ground with a *BAM!*

A second later, he and the dwarf are bundled into some sort of combo Jerry-Actor that may have come out of the second pod in the end of the movie *The Fly*, and they launched out into my hamster ball.

Near my feet, the Actor, who was clamped onto the older man's chest, yelled: "Let go of the wheel!"

The strange part was that I thought I *had* let go. When I looked up, two of Satan's mimes had crawled from their capsule and were now holding on to us.

"Let go of my Zorb!"

One of them pulled a long knife from his belt, and he didn't fill me in on what he was planning to do, but, well, he wouldn't… right?

I looked down toward the Actor, who was watching me and the ghoul mimes and realized the little guy was beat the fuck up from all that bouncing around inside the wheel carriage.

They're going to need a little more pancake makeup on this guy before the next season can get off to a good start.

Blinking, he slowly shook his head. "Raz."

"Yeah, man. Sorry about all this."

Just behind my head, I could hear the grunts and heavy breathing of the two Hell, Inc. ghouls starting to climb inside.

"You should bounce."

"Right, man," I said as the knife-wielding mime started hacking away at my hamster ball. "We'll be gone soon."

"No," he said, opening his bloodshot eyes wider. "'Bounce."

"Boun…"

Me, I'm slow. But when I get it, I get it.

Gripping both sides with my arms, I lifted my body upward. The mime with the knife drew it down onto my forearm and hit pay dirt—there was a burst of blood, but I still held on.

"Fuuucckk!"

Then, when my fat legs and ass were as I high as they were going to go, I let go.

Bonnggg!

Floating, floating, floating… just the sound of the wind. A soft, pleasant intoxicating feeling. Like a bird adrift on columns of air.

And in the middle distance, I saw the giant spinny Ferris wheel hit the river and topple sideways into the water. We bounced, bounced, bounced, and slowly rolled to a stop.

In the Belgian sunlight, I saw a woman approaching us, holding something in her hand. Anza had her phone out.

"Dat was amazing!"

She'd been taking a video of us.

"I is gonna YouTube you guys, and then we should get out of here before evil hell-mimes that did not drowned come to kill us."

Exhausted, I closed my eyes, if only for a moment. "Good call."

Chapter Eighteen

"What is it?"

"A wick manifold."

"Cool."

"Yeah."

"What the hell is that?"

We'd gotten back to the drug dealer's jet with our first piece of the lamp. After extracting me and Uncle Jerry and the Actor from the bouncy Zorb, we were all tired of our dip into Belgian extreme sports.

Inside the aircraft, we'd gathered around one of the small tables, examining our prize. Uncle Jerry had been in the cockpit for a few moments, ran through an impressive array of cursing, then exited the aircraft, hands up in the air. "I got it, I got it…" he said. "Y'all just play with your toy."

Which we were, in fact, happy to do.

Since the walk/run back to our getaway vehicle had been bordering on panic, I hadn't noticed the Actor still dressed in his fluffy (albeit less fluffy) red robe.

I pointed at him. "No Neiman Marcus?"

"Yes, but we ran into a bit of trouble with the locals," he said, sipping a whiskey that I would have assumed could kill a man his size.

As I turned the wick manifold over in my hands, Anza's chin was propped up onto my shoulder, as if her head were a parrot searching for a pirate. Looking at the Actor, I couldn't help but smile at him. "I'm actually starting to get used to the robe on ya."

He regarded me with a nod. "You know, it's freeing. Liberating. I'm enjoying… the dangle."

"Okay," I said, clearing my throat. "Got it."

He took a big slug of his drink and poked a toothpick into some chocolate-covered cherries he'd found in the galley. We all sat and enjoyed the silence together for a moment.

It didn't last.

"You know, the trick with whiskey... or any other alcohol, really," the Actor proclaimed in a slow, measured tone, "is finding the best accoutrement, depending on the flavor of what's in your glass. Some, you go with oily meats or maybe a smoky cheese. But every drink has just the right... companion."

"Too much think about your drink," Anza said, waving him off. "I like a nice red wine sometimes."

He sat up and said, "Rolos."

She sat up too. "Wha' did you jus' call me?"

"A good, full-bodied red wine? You can make it infinitely better with Rolos. The little chocolate candies with caram—"

"I know what is a Rolos!"

"Pop and sip, sista," he said and raised his eyebrows with a lascivious grin.

I put the wick manifold on the table and got a small twinge of pain from the hole in my side. "What about... a martini?"

"Depends on your palate. For the Kmart-shopping type, you can't go wrong with lemon drop candies. For those who are a little more... refined—"

Back in the plane again, Uncle Jerry offered, "Like Target?"

"—capers can be very nice."

Running my hand gingerly over the spot where I had been, you know, *shot* in my side, I scrunched up my nose. "Capers and gin?"

"Oh, god, no. *Vodka* martini. I don't drink gin martinis because I have no desire to have a taste in my mouth like I've snowballed someone who just blew a Christmas tree."

"What is 'snowballed?'"

"SO," I said and cleared my throat again, really kind of disappointed that with all my wincing and grunting that no one was asking about, you know, me being *shot*. "You know, by the way, I got shot."

The Actor poked at another brown blob on his plate, popping it into his mouth. Looking at me intently, measuring up my expression, he made his professional determination: "You don't look like you've been shot."

"You see this patch of blood here, don't you?"

They stared at a small red bloom on my T-shirt. Then I lifted the shirt, and they finally offered a slightly more appropriate reaction.

"Gross," Uncle Jerry said, looking at me over his shoulder from the pilot's seat as he fired up the jet engine. "You sure you didn't just didn't get grazed? You ain't bleeding anymore. Maybe it cauterized as it went through."

I thought about that for a moment. "No. I don't think it works like that."

Anza bent down to get a better look. "Do it hurt?"

"No, for the most part, it doon't, actually. That's the weird bit."

"Then you probably fine," she said.

"I mean, *at first* it did."

"But not now?"

"No, not really."

"Then you probably fine."

As far as I knew, I should be panting, feverishly sweating with someone standing over me, wide eyed and in a panic, as they dug into my open wound looking for a piece of life-threatening thin cloth in the shape of the hole in my T-shirt... but no, nothing like that. It was a wee bit tender where, you know, I'd been *shot*. Other than that, nothing.

So for the moment, that was the end of it. About, you know, me being *shot*.

Whatever.

The Actor hadn't been the center of attention for a solid half minute, and so he righted the world once again.

"Don't get used to me being around, Rasputin," he said. "Already too much adventure for this guy. I mean, I've heard of people doing their own stunts..."

Anza's head snapped up from the magazine she was thumbing through. She looked at him, waiting. Then she broke: "Are juu gonna say, '… but this is ridiculous.'"

"No, hell no! I wasn't going to say that."

"Because, that's what normally people say after a first part that sounds like that one you said."

"No, no, and no," the Actor said between punctuating crunches of ice.

"Why not?"

"Because we're not in a wacky, eighties TV adventure-comedy, illegal alien."

Anza waved him off, tucked the magazine away, then watched me twirling our first piece of lamp in my hands. "We're in Belgium, leetal man. Snuck in past a tiki bar. So today, we are all illegal aliens."

Laughing, I punched a fist into the air. "Je suis illegal alien!"

And as it happens, I was the only one laughing. Outside the open cabin door, I heard a motor fire up. As I leaned back in my chair, searching for the source of the sound through the cockpit windshield, Anza took the opportunity to snatch the wick manifold for a closer look at our prize.

Outside, a hundred meters beyond the nose of our craft, there was a large fence cutting off our part of the yard from the rest of a long concrete road. As I pondered if we would need that extra bit of runway, it seemed I'd gotten my answer.

Uncle Jerry had commandeered a forklift and was racing it like an iron fist toward the fence at a speed that, if he'd had a permit to drive a forklift, it would have been revoked before he could even extract himself from the cab of the vehicle.

Watching as he closed in on where the two large gates were bound by thick, rusted chains, I was transfixed and worried that this was one of those moments where you realize only later that your intervention was desperately needed because physics was obviously not on your side.

But as I mentioned, I was transfixed. My brain's wiring was preventing any intervening, and frankly, even if I'd wanted to help, what could I do?

A few moments later, my concerns were at least partially addressed. Uncle Jerry, moving like a medieval jouster racing toward his opponent, raised the fork of his way-too-fast machine just as he closed in on his opponent.

I'm not sure if he let out a primal yell or if I simply heard that in my own head. What I am sure of is this: He hit that fence with mind-boggling speed, and with its fork up, got wedged between each side of the gate, and while he impressively hit it dead center, bulging the gates to some stress limit that would have given any competent structural engineer the vapors in a moment I can only describe as retro Coyote-of-Roadrunner fame, he and the forklift stretched the fence like a tennis net, reached the upper limit of how far it could be extended, and then was launched back in the other direction like a racquetball spat out by an angry camel.

"Oh, no." I put my hand to my mouth.

Anza, who I hadn't noticed, was now standing in the cabin with her phone out again. "That's soooo going on the YouTubers!"

A few seconds later, I flinched as an incredible crash rattled the thin interior walls of the jet, sending a sharp wave of reverberations down its hull.

"Jerry!"

Running to the door, I was halfway down the steps when I saw my oldest companion jogging up toward me. The forklift was on its side, wheels spinning as if it had lain down to rest and was now merely breathing heavily from the exertion.

He waved and smiled. "Let's go, brother!"

Looking back to the mess of fencing, I saw where the horrendous noise had come from: While the chain actually held in the middle of the fence, the tall structures that had been secured to either side of the gate had buckled under the strain and had then fallen to the ground.

Dust rose around the fence as it lay there in a heap, as if taken out by a nuclear blast. Which, as Uncle Jerry's nature was becoming more familiar to me, I felt wasn't too far from the truth. Huffing as he climbed the stairs, I could actually smell freshly smoked pot on the guy.

Did he get stoned before or after he tried that?

Helping the spongy man back into the plane, I hugged him briefly. A silent thanks. A bit wiped out, he simply patted me on the head but still gave me a beaming smile.

As he climbed back into the pilot's seat, everyone else began strapping in. The dust that had arisen from his fence assault was beginning to settle. As it did, in the distance, I could see the red-blue-red of local authorities.

I pointed to them.

Jerry nodded. "Why d'you think I was runnin'?" He gave me another smile. "We're good, man. We'll be back up in the clear blue before they get here."

Lifting my hands up, I smiled back. But before joining the others, I asked: "How'd you know the fence would go down?"

Uncle Jerry flipped a few rocker switches above his head, and the jet engines began to roar. After a moment of checking a series of readouts, he finally answered.

"I didn't, man. There just didn't seem like a lot of options."

"There's a 'forklift' option? Didn't know about that one."

"It's like that ol' thing they used to say on TV. 'It's so crazy, it just might work.'"

From her seat behind me, I heard Anza yell over the engines: "But thees is rediculous!"

Then I believe the Actor swore at her in French.

I turned back to Jerry. "Yeah, but that's... sorry, man... that's a dangerous way to find solutions. No offense, and it worked out, but... that idea, doing something crazy, that may sound like a really good idea, but it's actually, you know, kinda stupid."

He shrugged. "Yeah, but sometimes with all the big thinking, you never end up getting around to actually making a choice.

And when things go all haywire, sometimes you just gotta…
do."

Reaching under the seat, his face suddenly lit up, and he
strapped on a wholly unnecessary pair of leather goggles. The
big, big smile was back.

"Sure," I said, "but you get it wrong, and that's it. Game over,
man."

"Nah," he said, and with one hand on the control wheel and
the other on the throttle levers, he got the jet rolling forward.
"It's only over when you stop playin'. Maybe being a bit dumb
sometimes ain't so bad. I'm too stupid to yield."

"Yield?"

"Yep. Me, I just keep at it until I get it. You don't never yield,
and whatever you're up against will fall, man."

Something about that sounded profound but still really stupid.
Or at least impractical. Tired, I let it go.

Sort of.

"Sure," I said and lightened my tone. "But I noticed your 'do
not yield' policy doesn't seem to apply to getting gainful
employment."

"Well, it's a work-in-progress type of policy."

"I see."

Before leaving the cockpit, I returned the pat on the head he'd
given me on the airplane's steps and headed back to the cabin.

When the faintest rising tone from one of the Belgian
emergency vehicles entered the cabin, our pilot punched the gas,
and we rocketed forward, which launched me off my feet toward
the rear of the craft. Thankfully, I landed in the dwarf's seat.
Unfortunately, he was still in it.

From beneath me, his muffled voice rose over the engines:
"Okay, I yield, man. I yield. Can you get off?"

Leaving Brussels behind, we'd flown far too low for anyone's
comfort but our pilot's, until he'd found another river—all this
directed by the customized onboard navigation system—which

we followed until the land below us was relatively unpopulated and the hints of mountains rose on the horizon.

Now in the clear, I smiled at Anza and raised my hands in the air. She smiled back. We'd actually done it. One down… three to go.

But that had cost us about thirty-six hours of my four days. We had to pick up the pace, or we'd never make the deadline.

Then I remembered. "Hey, where to next? Do we know where we're going?"

"Hidden Buddha," the Actor said, slurring slightly, a sleep mask already in place.

I waited for a moment. "I'm cringing against some terrible sexual imagery, but I'll ask anyway: What is that?"

The Actor waved his small hand toward a ten-inch tablet that was propped up against the wall. Anza grabbed it and sat next to me. Luckily a phrase like "Hidden Buddha" doesn't get a lot of hits on Google, and it seemed, thankfully, very few of them were East Asian "chubbies porn."

You take the wins where you can.

According to the wiki, the Hidden Buddha was not in India as you might think but instead at an ancient temple in Japan. And no one, absolutely no one, had been allowed to even see the statue in over fifteen hundred years.

"Is walled up or something," Anza said. "No way inside."

I nodded. "Sure, of course. Of course, it is."

Steve Janus looked up to the video monitors on the wall directly in front of the large circular conference table—a table that looked like a big flat doughnut with a tiny hole.

A staggered array of screens flanked a very large hi-def screen, which ran from ceiling to floor. On that main screen was a fish.

The chairman and CEO of Hell, Inc. sat in the center of the circular table; it was from this perch he always ran the daily morning meeting for his television, mobile, and web "infotainment" platforms. The setup ensured all of the others around the table—those at the outside edges—knew they were just as equal (read: expendable) as the person sitting next to them.

There was no second in charge. No, no. Janus made sure of that. Guys with titles like vice-this or deputy-that too often got their own ideas about running things. He should know. That was how he'd first created a shadow leadership within the bowels of Hell decades earlier. And he'd worked very, very hard to create a takeover entity that could crush the tragically underperforming Satan *and* his old guard. And no fresher-faced little upstart was going to be in a position to take Hell, Inc. away from its chairman!

Janus was seen both as a savior and pariah to those who made up the infrastructure of Hell. Sometimes both to the same people. For countless millennia, the Devil had been spinning his evil wheels as he'd desperately tried to turn the good to bad, the light to dark, with the ultimate goal of taking Earth and all its inhabitants, with the overlords of Hell finally running the show.

However, it was always just out of grasp. The closer they got, the harder it became. When Janus had passed from Earth and arrived in Hell, whereas most saw pain/torture/eternal suffering, he saw more. Steve Janus saw opportunity.

Over the years, he'd taken those skills learned on Earth—before choking on an errant lump of foie gras ended all that in a blinding moment of irony—and created a corporate culture so massive and so pervasive, the Devil himself had to get into the game or risk becoming entirely obsolete.

Janus had not done it alone, however. As with any corporate entity, he'd needed backing if he were ever to get off the ground, and he had found it in some of the Old Man's lieutenants. Sure, there was fun to be had for the seasoned and energetic sadist, but most had long ago resigned themselves to Hell's place as the eternal also-ran.

But Steve Janus had a vision. He was not going to just take over Hell and Earth. It wasn't enough to simply darken humans, as Satan had done. A long, long campaign of soft, breathless whispers into the hearts of men had not only caused some misery on Earth, but each new recruit had fueled Hell's fires in the afterlife.

In the *big* good-versus-evil picture, this had basically done fuck all. Like some game of chess (or *Stratego*) using human pieces, for every time a Hitler was born, there was a Churchill or FDR. For each Vlad Dracula, there was a Professor Van Helsing and likely some lesser-known guy with a name like Geoff the Pointy Wood Pole Maker.

Janus's plan was more pervasive. After securing himself at the top of Hell, Inc., he'd systematically purchased small, then bigger and bigger, companies on Earth that would collectively ooze greater and greater amounts of misery into larger and larger portions of the population.

Not the big Blue Chips, at least not at first. No, at the beginning it was just little players. First off, it was like the tool company that manufactured millions of low-priced and brightly colored screwdrivers, which after a few turns become useless as the soft metal tip frustratingly stripped into shavings that flaked to either side of the unscrewed screw.

Or the Nashville-based plastics firm, whose ice-cube-tray molds never released full cubes, just freezer-burned chips that never quite cooled your drink.

Now he was on to much larger entities like their global communications empire.

Still, though, he had to deliver to those original backers, his shareholders. That meant showing gains each reporting period, drawing larger and larger percentages of human souls.

Of course, Janus had realized one of the most efficient manners of doing this was through television, and he had, over time, acquired a handful of the world's big networks. But to make his nut, the ratings had to grow.

And at the moment, he was in a slump, and it seemed marathons of *Golden Girls* and *Boy Meets World* wasn't going to help this time.

He needed a winner.

"New York," Janus said, an edge creeping into his voice. The seventeen men and women in the room with him, seated around the table, watched their leader's mood grow darker by the second. Most were happy it wasn't directed at them this time. "We can see you guys there at the conf— Hello? Hello, New York." He turned and looked to the tech sitting at a cubby on the far side of the room. "Gina, can they see us?"

"Uplink says we're all good."

"Why can't they—"

"Because they're a box of tools, twats, and taints," she said, then added: "Sir."

Janus scolded her with a look she did not see but wouldn't have cared if she did.

Unquestionably, he worked harder than anyone else in the establishment. And as you would assume in one who headed up a corporation trying to supplant the leadership of Hell after billions of years, he was ultimately cold, calculating, and harnessed a temper that not only powered his very prolific megalomania but could crush those who displeased him so entirely that anyone besmoted by Hell, Inc.'s Steve Janus would not only be reduced to a small stain of black ooze, but often a generation or two of those relatives who'd *preceded* his victim would be as well.

Many believed he'd honed his unequaled, ruthless style from his years as the CEO and chairman of Baby Gap. However, Gina the tech pretty much had carte blanche with the guy.

Really, really good tech people were just way too hard to find.

"New York," Janus said, his volume increasing. "Can you hea—"

"Yes, yes, hel-*lo*!" An electric-fried, over-modulated voice suddenly crackled into the room. On the monitor marked New York, a balding man who had been sitting at his own (albeit rectangular) conference table, along with about a dozen others, had gotten up and moved closer to the camera. He was actually talking into the conference room camera itself, instead of the microphone that was on the table, so the entire room around Janus—and likely the other dozen bureaus also patched in— were getting the same view of the fried-egg sandwich he'd had twenty-five minutes earlier. "Gotcha loud and clear, Chief."

"Okay," Janus said and rubbed his temples with the heels of his hands. "We got everyone else? Paris? Tokyo? LA? Ottawa?"

A man just off Janus's left shoulder rapped the table— possibly to stop his hands from trembling—and said, "Ottawa is going to be a little late. They're battling a snowstorm, apparently."

Janus threw a withering glance in his direction. "It's August."

"Yeah, yep, yeah… could have been a, you know, Canadian metaphor. Maybe. It's unclear."

"Fine, fine," Janus said and spun back to the monitors on the wall. "Shanghai, do you have the fish where you are?"

The video image on the screen representing the Chinese contingent rolled once, and four men and three women looked at each other. A graying woman spoke up: "No, no. We've got bagels this morning, Chairman."

"Bag—?"

A man with jet-black hair sitting next to the woman chimed in eagerly: "However, one of the spreads is indeed… smoked *fish*, sir. Best bet, it's salmon. Possibly strawberry." Across the electronic divide, the man's huge grin fell after catching the expression on Janus's face.

"Gina," the chairman said to the tech, his eyes beginning to crease around their edges. "Is there something wrong with our feeds or the audio?"

"Just the cunts watching the feeds and listening to the audio, sir."

Janus took a moment to compose himself, then began: "If you would look at the monitor just below where you see me talking," he said, momentarily pausing for effect, "you will see a fish in a bowl."

"London here, sir. We've got a goldfish, I believe."

Janus sighed. "Right, that—"

"It could be carp, but I daresay they may be the same thing."

Paris chimed in, "I believe it is a koi. Koi fish."

The lid holding in Janus's steam momentarily buckled. "It's not about what kind of goddamn fish it is!"

The room fell silent as their leader took a deep, cleansing breath. He steepled his fingers and continued. "Our little finned friend—"

"New York here. You know, that fish looks just like the one we had on Channel 137 for the past couple weeks."

Janus nodded. "Yes, yes, Darius. Don't get ahead of me now."

The well-dressed black man did anyhow. "Some sort of alt-channel, like a business newser or UGC video or something. They had just a camera pointed at the fish bowl to set up the cable net's carrier signal. All day long, just a fish swimmin' around in a bowl."

"Right, yes!" Janus said, holding his hand up. "Exactly, so—"

Darius was on a roll. "My kids loved the fish," he gushed. "They damn near cried a river when they took it—"

Janus had had enough. "*SMOTE YOU!*" he bellowed, pointing a crooked finger at the man in New York.

Darius stopped midsentence, drew a queer expression on his face, which disappeared nearly the moment it formed, along with its owner, in a wisp of dirty smoke and a twist of ash.

It seemed, Hell, Inc.'s boss finally had their undivided attention. He took another deep, cleansing breath, not because he felt he needed it, but it was an impressive mannerism after a good smiting. A sort of warning to others: *I'm just barely keeping my angry id in check... Don't test me further!*

He waved lazily toward New York's monitor. "Andreas, please move into Darius's seat. No, no, don't dust it off, just sit. Embrace the ash, my friend. It'll let others know you got yourself a promotion today."

Big smile from the big man. "Okay, Darius had it right—but in a wrong way. Once we cut the video feed to the fish and put up the 24/7 car chase channel we were quietly test marketing in New York, viewership went down by"—he sifted through papers for effect—"ninety-nine percent."

An appropriately concerned-sounding murmur bubbled through the room.

"Marketing tells me, the fish had a *fucking twelve* share in four of the five boroughs!"

Silence. None of the shows the network programmers and producers had put on the air in the last year had broken double digits. A stupid little fish in a dollar-store glass bowl had crushed them all.

Janus stood, raised his arms, and took a slow spin. "People, I want answers. Our TV nets have always been one of the best performers, ratcheting up the Misery Index quarter after quarter. But the past eighteen months, you guys have been in a serious, serious slump."

Again, a murmur of agreement. Then, all was quiet as Janus only stared, waiting.

On the monitor from Sydney, a hand went up. "What if we get our own fish?"

Another voice: "Wait, maybe the original fish is available. Anyone know if he's repped?"

"Is it a *he*?"

The newly appointed leader in New York, Andreas, rubbed a small patch of ash into his slacks and offered: "What if we get our own fish, but it's... you know... evil."

Silence.

"A, you know... *bad* fish," he added.

Janus eyeballed him from several thousand miles away. "You know, I still got more smite left in this here finger."

From the seats lining the back wall, a gray-haired, ponytailed man named Tommy spoke, the timber of his voice demanding immediate attention. "Bring the original fish back, same channel. Doesn't have to be the same fish, just one that looks like it."

Janus stammered for a moment, then said, "Sure, that's good for the ratings but the fish actually made people happ—"

"Right," Tommy said, nodding slowly. "Give it about two weeks, so people get all excited... tweeting and Facebooking 'the fish is back' and whatever. Then one afternoon, you put a cup of bleach in the bowl and let the thing thrash for about four seconds."

The room was quiet. All eyes—even the ones on the monitors—stared right at Tommy.

"It floats to the top and starts to rot. Leave it up for about a week until all its little fishy flesh has sloughed off to the bottom."

Janus interrupted the next silence. "Oh, that's... shit, that's really good. A short-term gain, but I like it."

"Nah," Tommy said casually, leaning back with his hands behind his head. "After that, put another fish in there. Give it a few weeks, then pull back a hair and show that the bowl is on a stove. Hit the burner and bubble, bubble—another dead fish."

"Gross!" a young woman said. A room of scowls turned toward her. Several emotions passed over her face until she added, "Um... Yaaay!"

"Right, and by this time people are waiting to see how the next fish dies. There'll be Facebook pools, online betting, viewing parties. All morbidly waiting to see how the next finned friend meets its end."

Janus was getting into it. "Oooh, there may even be copycats trying to cash in on YouTube!"

Voices chimed in across the room and from across the globe.

"And I bet they won't stop with just fish!"

"Hamsters!"

"Gerbils!"

"Grandmothers!"

"Gross!" A pause, then: "Yaaay!"

"Exactly," Tommy said. "We can ride that train for at least a year."

The room burst with applause, and Janus decided to dismiss everyone on the high note. There'd been so few of them recently.

"Uh, Tommy… your team, you guys stay," he said, raising his eyebrows. "Another matter."

Once the conference room was empty, the grumpy audio-visual woman in the denim overalls closed both doors as she left. Janus sat back onto the curved edge of the table while Tommy and his two content development team members stood at the table's outer edge, facing the darkened monitors.

"How goes this Rasputin business?" Janus asked.

"He has the first piece," Tommy said evenly. "And he's headed to get the second."

Janus squinted. "You don't sound… troubled by that."

Tommy shrugged. "Five years of vocal training, sir."

"Ah, okay." The Hell, Inc. chairman nodded. "So what's the plan to take him out?"

"That is what Troy here wanted to talk with you about," Tommy said.

Troy, a tall white man with hair like a Marine (the only thing about him like a Marine), went a shade whiter. Janus waited.

Troy found his voice and spoke. "Well, we were thinking… this year, you know, we've seen the Mix start to flow in our favor with some of our other non-traditional revenue-style projects."

"*Mix*? You mean MX? Since when is it Mix?"

"That's… you know, what the younger staffers have been calling it. Gotta say: It's got a fresh-groove feel to it."

"Don't ever say 'fresh-groove feel' to me again. Ever."

Troy nodded and swallowed hard. "Well, our team has done a real deep search on this whole lamp business…"

The young woman next to Troy added, "A dead dog search."

"What… what the fuck does that mean?" asked Janus.

"It means a real deep search," Troy said. "And it seems that the lamp the Old Man is after could theoretically, you know, wipe us out entirely."

"WHAT?"

Janus unconsciously cocked his finger.

"Well, it's a rare thing, an Artifact of Light. Leftover from the Dark Times a few centuries back. Heard about them, but this—"

Janus waved him off. "Get back to the part about how it can wipe us out entirely. That seemed important."

"Sure," Troy said, shifting his tall frame for a moment as he thought. "It's a construct of some minor deity, long since gone. Basically a mega-amplifier. A person of Light holds it, and it concentrates that Light, jacks it way up, and casts it out. That Rasputin dude wants it to cure his sick wife."

"Why does the Old Man want it?"

"Because if a person of Dark holds it instead, it does the opposite. And in the hands of someone very powerful, the Light or Dark energy it amplifies could affect entire cities. Continents, even."

Janus ran his hand over his mouth slowly. "And the Devil wants it to darken souls in his favor. Thousands… maybe *millions* of people at a time? That *would* wipe us out entirely."

"Yeah, and get this: That kinda rapid super flow? Man, for the first time, the Earth could conceivably go Dark."

"With the Old Man running the show!" Janus stood, spun in a circle, and ran his fingers through his white hair. "All the more reason to eliminate this moron, Rasputin. Hell, all the work we—"

"Wait," Tommy said calmly in a voice robust with a velvety timber, "what if we instead waited until he collected the pieces and then we just stole the lamp from him."

Janus stood, pacing his small cut-out circle. "Risky. Risky, risky."

Troy was gaining steam. "Yeah, but you know, the rewards— in a day we could not only take over the Downtown, all of Earth would belong to us! Beat the Old Man at his game with our better game, man!"

"Wha… 'The Downtown?'"

"Oh, that means—"

"*I'm not a moron, Troy*! I get what it means. From now on, no more coming up with catchy words and phrases without my approval!"

Tommy looked toward his team, nodding slowly.

"Got it," Troy said.

Janus sat back down on the edge of the table. After a full half minute, he said, "Why can't one of you just go get the pieces before this Rasputin does?"

"First, the locations are secret and only revealed to those who seek it for selfless reasons."

"Fuck a duck."

"Yeah," Troy agreed. "And second, we can't go into the places where any of the parts are. Verboten, man."

Janus eyeballed Troy, his smiting finger beginning to itch, but then let the moment pass. Instead, he asked, "Do you really think we can get the lamp before the Old Man does? Won't he be ready for that?"

"No," the young woman said, "he'll think we're just on Rasputin's tail to take him out. We already tried once with that idiot reporter and his cameraman."

"Like you said, it's really risky. But they won't see it comin'. The moment the dude puts all the pieces together, *whammo*, we take him outta the picture and snatch up the lamp."

Janus nodded. "It reminds me of my years running Baby Gap."

The three people sitting across from him inadvertently slumped a little lower in their seats.

"What?" Janus said, then waved them off. "I came up with a new onesie design. Much cheaper, with a lining made entirely out of wool. They said I was crazy, risky. But what a payoff in our secondary aloe vera market."

They stared, waiting.

Triggering a sensor as he passed his hand over a panel on the armrest of his chair, he slowly and dramatically began to lower into the floor to his office below. When he was about waist high, he spoke.

"Do it."

This likely goes without saying, but if you have to travel from country to country—or continent to continent—if you can arrange it, you should do it by private jet.

Sure, you do miss the indeterminately long wait in the airport queue, and once aboard, there is the nice lady who comes by and disapprovingly whips a small bag of salted nuts at your forehead forty-two days past its BEST BY date…

But instead, you have a refrigerator. And a pantry. And a wet bar.

That can be nice, if you have the means. Or if you don't, you then blackmail a drug dealer into letting you use *his* means for a while.

Another nice bit about flying privately—and believe me, I could go on and on—is that you can sleep in the prone position. As in, you know, lying down. In the world of commercial airliners, that isn't possible unless you go with the first-class option, which likely means you have, as it were, the means.

But still, one's own private jet. Surely this tops even the swankiest of accommodations aboard an *icky* public airline.

First off, there's the comfort of a built-in fireplace if one were to get cold. Yes, admittedly, not all private jets have afforded their owner such a luxury, and in truth, I can't imagine the necessity of said fireplace… but it's jolly nice to have if one is available to you.

Ah, to stare into the gas-fed flames, lulling one's mind into a calm and restful place with only a few inches of metal separating you from the outside atmosphere and near-instant death.

But the best part of one's own private air transportation—and let me again be clear that there are so many, many good parts— is that when you need to use a lavatory, its actual purpose is of your choosing.

You want to smoke? Go right ahead—the only quandary is choosing *what* you might want to smoke whilst inside. Hell, you want to join the mile-high club? Actually, you could just use one of the lounge chairs. Why rock your lust within arm's reach of where people poop, for chrissakes?

But the airplane bathroom—whether you're on a commercial flight or a private one (again, *preferred*, if I might just hammer that point home one final time)—is like your own temporary private inflight suite. It's a chance to just get away from it all for a brief moment, whether one is enduring a weeks-long business engagement or traveling the planet searching for an ancient lamp to save your dying wife.

A little mile-high me time.

And it was there that I sat, but despite my pants being bunched around my ankles and me sitting on a toilet, I really didn't need to use the bathroom. There was just something safe and familiar about the deed in that particular moment. Which is exactly what I needed right there and then. A quiet moment of temporary solace. A respite fifty thousand feet in the air.

Until, of course, Uncle Jerry came on the overhead speaker and said: "Hey, we're about two hours out from a little airstrip in Kusatsu, Japan, with fuel that'll last us about ninety minutes. I never really pushed the fuel reserves in this bird to its limit before, but there's a fifty-fifty chance we might die, falling from the sky like a rock."

Jesus.

Jerry added: "Just, you know, FYI."

I hopped up and did the obligatory tissue rake, cinched up my jeans, and bolted out of the bathroom into the main cabin.

The Actor, still mostly sleeping, had found a way to wrap the seatbelt around his little body while still in the prone position. Anza was halfheartedly battling with her buckled restraint— which was less to do with the complexity of the device and more to do with her temperament as she tried to secure it. The "adventure" in Brussels was likely more than any of us had ever been through. And this was just the beginning.

That realization was manifesting in different ways for all of us, it would seem.

Seeing me, she broke, and tears fell onto her cheeks: "I can' do it. Seat belts is broken."

If nothing else, for whatever reason, I'm damn good at comforting troubled women. I think, if I'm honest with myself, it's because most of those aforementioned 'troubled women' had found themselves in such a state because of something I had done. But that aside, I know mostly when to talk, when to smile, or when to just extend a kindness like a hug or stroke of the hair.

I walked over to Anza and dropped to one knee. The buckle looked like it had taken a bit of a beating in a previous 'fun-filled' outing. In fact, there appeared to be *lubricant* inside the clasp.

Could be jam. Probably not.

Once I got the metal bits to behave and got them back to where they were supposed to be, the latch clicked, and she was good. My best friend's wife put her hand to the side of my face, more thankful for my understanding than for the mechanical fix.

"*Gracias.*"

"*De nada*," I said and smiled.

Anza held my face for a moment, and I saw her eyes were damp. "Your Carissa must be an amazing woman."

"She is." I nodded. "Me, I'm a screw-up."

"No, no. Rasputin, you a good man."

I shrugged. "Still, no matter how many times I get things wrong, she's always there with me. On my side, you know?"

"*Si*, yes. I know."

There was a pang in my chest as I realized she was missing Dan. Because of me, she was thousands of miles from home and away from her husband. Then a chuckle grew in my chest, and Anza lifted her eyebrows.

"You know, my girl, she doesn't really frame photographs," I said, thinking of home. "Instead, she's taken to framing my apology letters."

Anza laughed softly. "The wha?"

"Well, not just apology letters. But you know, cards I'd get her for birthdays and stuff, too. All around our house are letters I've written to her over the years, beautifully framed, of me saying sorry for something I did—"

"And you also telling that you love her, yes?"

I nodded.

"Rasputin, dats why she has all of them there. When you're not around, she can look to a picture frame to remember, to feel how much you love her. Is a girl thing."

A smile bent my lips. "It's also probably a reminder to *me*, in every room, of all the wonky shit I've done."

"Yes, probably a little bit of that, too." She kissed my forehead and turned over to get some sleep.

Slipping from the darkened hum of the main cabin (and now a quiet snore from our thespian companion), I joined Jerry in the cockpit. As a courtesy to those sleeping, he'd dimmed the lights, and his features, more wrinkled and ropey than I remembered, were lit by the dull, warm amber glow coming from the instrument panels.

When I flopped down into the copilot seat, Uncle Jerry briefly tapped away on a keypad just out of my line of vision. Less because it seemed we needed a course adjustment and more likely that he wanted to be sure his "pilot hat" was firmly affixed as I entered his domain. That humbled me, actually, because it was a kindness.

In a more bitter mood, I would have seen it as showing off. Showboating. But knowing the man a bit better, I realized he was silently assuring me that he was taking care of all this flying business. No need for me to use any of my limited brainpan RAM to worry about the trip.

"You wanna try your lady again on the sat phone?" he said.

I stared ahead, looking at the man in the curved reflection of the cockpit windshield, his features elongated and distorted.

"Nah, the doctor said he doesn't expect her to wake up again," I said. "Probably for the best. If she knew what I was doing, I think she'd die."

Jerry looked at me sideways to see if I was smiling at my own gallows humor. I was, and this allowed him a short laugh, something it seemed he needed.

"How can you keep going, man?" I asked him. "Everyone else back there is spent. You're still plugging along."

My companion lifted a doughy arm and flexed it, the strongman of the skies. "You should grab an hour of shuteye yourself, if you can, Raz. That's an abandoned airfield I'm heading toward, old wartime relic. Not on any of the charts anymore, but it's on the drug-network nav software. When we get there, I'm going to hafta scare up some jet fuel."

My wife's life was in part dependent upon a patchwork of secret, low-flying highways used by drug runners, smugglers, and arms dealers. "Yeah, I heard you mention the low fuel bit. How screwed are we in that department?"

"Dunno. But I'll be honest," he said and scratched the scruff on his chin, "sometimes it's better when you don't think on things too much. Then you don't realize how truly screwed you are. That way you're so truly clueless about the situation… you might actually pull it off 'cause you don't know no better."

Too tired to nod, I blinked and said, "Man, you ever thought about writing some of those corporate motivational posters?"

He laughed. "Nah, those are all part of the incessant indoctrination to keep us enslaved, man!"

"Whatever."

"You wanna see the real work of the Devil? You'll find it hanging on the walls of Fortune 500 companies around the world! With big, bold captions like COURAGE and LEADERSHIP and PUNCTUALITY."

"I don't think they make motivational posters about punctuality, man."

I stood and stretched my arms as far as they would go in the cramped cockpit and felt a couple satisfying pops along my shoulders. "Uncle Jerry, you are a fountain of positive vibes. I love you for it, man."

Smiling big, he sat up a little straighter. "I do yoga. It's a good way to focus your energies."

"You do yoga?"

"Well." He hesitated, tapped something into a keypad again. "I watch it on TV. It's on kinda early, out of Hawaii or something. But there's this chick on there with these amazing curves and a real nice beach behind her."

"Classic."

"Very Zen, man."

"Well, if that's what helps power your ability to keep on keepin' on, then I'm grateful," I said, stepping out of the cockpit.

"Yeah, that and the half eight-ball of coke I did while you were in the bathroom."

"Naturally."

Anza and the Actor were both knocked out. Given that he'd fallen asleep within a few minutes of takeoff, I briefly wondered what sort of hidden substance the Actor might have found in the aircraft to help him rocket to dreamland so quickly.

Easing into a leather lounger, I lifted a fluffy, zebra-striped blanket from the floor and pulled it up to my chest. Sleep wasn't going to visit me, that was obvious, so for a brief moment I just sat and stared out at the sky above and the clouds below us. The stars winked almost imperceptibly.

They were, I'd heard it once said, time machines to the past. That the light we saw had traveled thousands, millions, or maybe even billions of years to get here. I was catching beams of light that had begun their journey such a long, long time ago.

Above the clouds, I was the only one staring up at the sky, and it was as if this starlight was only for me. I felt obliged to keep watching. That pinprick of light had traveled so far, and in the end it had only gotten to one person.

Me.

Strangely, it seemed wrong to turn away from it. Because then it would have traveled billions of miles, millennia after millennia in the cold quiet of space, only to be lost in the clouds of a dozing world that simply hadn't bothered to look up.

Nevertheless, eventually my eyes did close, and they only came open when I heard the tones blaring from the cockpit warning that we were crashing.

The Font

17 May

Dearest Carissa,

I'm sorry for making your ex-fiancé go permanently bald.

There's really no excuse for me being so childish.

You know how upset I was that he was still calling and harassing you after you annulled the marriage? And I kept my promise not to beat him bloody again with my commercial-grade garden rake, so I hope you can see that I'm really trying to make this work between you and me.

Yes, breaking and entering his apartment was wrong, I get that now.

And yes, putting the Nair hair-removal cream into all of his hair products, soap dispensers, and hand lotion (let's face it, single guys only use hand lotion for one thing) was beneath me and a very mean and silly thing to do.

Thank you for keeping it our secret.

However, it's not entirely clear why his hair won't grow back. I'm sure there's some clinical explanation for it, but you've told me to steer clear of him, so I'm washing my hands of this (but I won't do it with his hand soap! (okay, no, that's mean and no longer a laughing matter. I'm sorry)).

As a bit of a meaty mea culpa... you've been working hard, so I bought a bunch of those weird Australian frozen pot pies you like—the beef and pepper gravy ones!—and put them in your freezer.

Each one has a note taped to it, but please don't look ahead—the idea is to have a nice note with lunch each day. Or you could pretend that a different Aussie beef pie is professing its love to you every afternoon... whichever floats your boat, babydoll.

Listen, I know you've got some wrapping up to do of your former life with your ex, and I respect that. You do what you need to, and I'll keep my distance on the matter.

Just do me a favor and don't open any of his closet doors or take a ride in his car that exceeds thirty-two miles an hour.

Just as, you know, a precaution.

Forever Yours, Rasputin

Chapter Nineteen

"Whazzat mean, we are crashing?"

"We're not crashing," Uncle Jerry assured Anza. "Yet."

It should have troubled me more than it did, but instead I blinked against the harsh fluorescent track lighting that had automatically come on and thumbed the electric panel in the lounger's arm to raise myself from the sleeping position. I waited as the chair whirred and hummed upright, listening to the negotiations between two of my companions.

"But dat voice, it was saying—"

"I know what it was saying!"

"That people sounded like they know what they was talking about!"

Uncle Jerry said to Anza through clenched teeth, "*That people is a goddamn computer-generated voice!*"

"I don' like..."

She is right, I thought. There was a voice, repetitive but not overly insistent, saying: "Fuel reserves nearly depleted. Land the aircraft or it may crash."

Those two sentences again and again. And every now and again "Attention! Attention! Attention!" preceded the recording.

For a moment suspended in time, I wondered what the person who'd been hired to recite the words of that voice clip had been thinking at the time of recording.

"I got a voice gig, honey!"

"Oh, really? Doing what? A movie? Cartoon, television show?"

"No, it's for an aircraft manufacturer."

"Ah, well... a gig is a gig, right?"

"Yeah, they've got about a dozen scenarios where when some pricey jet is about to hit dirt, my voice comes on to warn them."

"Oh, so anyone who hears your work will likely end up dead shortly after?"

"Pretty much."

"Does it pay well?"

For a brief moment, not measured by minutes or seconds but by the traverse of emotion across time, I feel that as the voice actor had read lines like "Pull up, pull up…" they couldn't help but think, for an instant, while blinking away a slight dampness in their eyes, *I hope they make it.*

In the cockpit, Anza and Uncle Jerry continued to argue over the veracity of the words spilling from recessed speakers. I looked over at the Actor, who was at the compact minibar, plinking some ice cubes into a couple fingers of whiskey. He had a strange look of contentment, which for the life of me, I couldn't account for.

Then when I saw an item resembling a knapsack clinging to his back, like a canvas-skinned super leech, I realized he'd simply been immensely proud of himself for finding a parachute aboard the crashing/not-crashing aircraft and then hit the bar in a casual celebratory drink of top-shelf liquor.

He turned toward me, grinning serenely.

Beneath his right elbow was a small length of rope with a bright orange triangle affixed to the end of it. The Actor spotted me staring at it, clinked his glass against the plastic bauble, and it swung happily as he sipped his drink.

What he apparently hadn't seen, which I had before he'd turned around, were the tiny words imprinted across the top of the "parachute," which read "In case of a water landing, this may be used as a floatation device."

The Actor twisted a wry smile at me as he leaned back against the lip of the bar with the CO_2-powered, inflatable life jacket strapped to his back, and a dark part of me wished he'd have a chance to use it. Because seeing the pain in the ass hurtling toward the ground at terminal velocity, wondering why the parachute wasn't coming out of his life preserver… the look on his face?

Classic.

My plummeting dwarf fantasy, which was simply a way of not actually coming fully awake, was interrupted by a sudden immersion into total darkness. Hurtling through the atmosphere in the dark, I briefly thought back to my lonely starlight.

"Turn back on th' plane, Un-call Jerry!"

Snapping fully awake, I leapt to my feet, and in the dark, unfamiliar space, crab-walked toward the cockpit. Halfway there, I tripped over the Actor.

"Raz, delightful," he said after I'd toppled onto him, happy that the life preserver he'd strapped on had cushioned my fall. "Somehow you didn't say a word but delivered me one of the most demeaning insults I've endured in quite some time."

"Sorry," I said, and meant it.

In the dark, I saw only the glimmer from his widened eyes, and he muttered, "Don't worry about it."

In the cockpit, Anza had taken over the copilot seat, her arms waving in the air like she was fending off some elusive, unseen flying pest. All the lights had been doused, even the instrument panel—the only glow was a green that spilled down the cheeks and chest of our pilot.

He turned toward me, briefly freezing me in my steps at the sight of the eerie, probing light of the night vision goggles. Realizing how he probably looked, he began to grin at me in a mad but not menacing manner. I smiled and kneeled onto the single stair that led down into the cockpit.

"Is there a reason for stealth mode, Batman?"

"No, Wonder Boy, don't worry about it," he said, his focus back on what was approaching from the other side of the glass. "It's just there ain't any runway lights or nothing."

"See, that's troubling, because those two sentences are in perfect conflict."

"Thank you."

"So, back to what you were saying about no runway."

"Right," he said, then tapped something out of sight. Actually, it was near pitch black, so damn near everything was out of sight. "Since we don't have the runners, I need to be able to see in the dark. Like a creature of the night."

"*Si... la cucaracha*!" Anza said, seething.

"No, no," our pilot muttered. "No time for campfire songs. I gotta focus."

Anza said something else in Spanish under her breath. Ahead, I saw nothing. A moonless night. Only stars had lit up the vast landscape of clouds. Below the cloud cover, not even fireflies breached the darkness, as if they were afraid of being seen, easily singled out. I forced myself to exhale the breath burning in my lungs. Then I remembered something.

"Oh, hey, you said we were low on fuel. We got past that, then, huh?"

"No," Uncle Jerry said slowly, drawing out the word. "We are on fumes, son."

"But we're close enough to glide in, right?"

"Yeah, basically anything that can fly can glide. But you gotta have enough air between you and the ground to make it to the runway."

"We got that?"

"No," he said and looked at me again with those wild, luminescent eyes. "But I like to live dangerously."

At that point, I felt my entire body calm, and my muscles went smooth. In another situation, I may have taken that for accepting that matters were out of my hands, Uncle Jerry was a good pilot, and that it would be best to trust the hand we'd been dealt.

But the newfound calm was actually because my body was suddenly no longer humming with the hi-rep, jet-engine vibrations of the past few hours. The fuselage below my knee was still, the sound of the engines only a memory.

"Okay, shit, so much for living dangerously," Uncle Jerry said. "We just ran outta fuel."

I stood and braced myself against the cockpit door, looking from our pilot to Anza, then back.

"Wha-what do we do?"

He waved the two of us back to the main cabin, and my best friend's wife was up and out of the copilot's seat before he could even get the words out.

"Strap yourself in and maintain a seated, crash-landing position," he said with impressive professionalism. Had it not been pitch black all around us, I would have thought he'd read that off of a quick, break-seal emergency-instructions pamphlet.

Anza and I both quickly got to our seats; the Actor was already strapped in.

"What is crash-landing position?" she asked.

The Actor cleared his throat. "Depends if you want open or closed casket."

Over the next few dreamy minutes, I felt something between my chest and stomach begin to ache. As emotion began to steal my calm, I realized that more than anything I just wanted a drink.

No. Forcing the thought from my mind and looking around the cabin, I saw the silhouettes of the three people who were risking their lives to help me save my wife.

Then it hit me. That wasn't right: *I* was putting them at risk. Sure, they'd each agreed, but it was clear to me for the first time—maybe because one's awareness of mortality sharpens the mind—that my quest for the Lamp of Life should be my risk, not theirs.

But I'm no Rambo or John McClane or even Paul Blart, Mall Cop. Part of me knew that I needed each of them if there was any hope of fulfilling my contract with the Devil, but I also knew it was grossly unfair for me to very likely be setting up a meeting for each of them with the Angel of Death.

Every moment they spent with me put them in deeper and deeper in danger. And not just from the fact that Uncle Jerry was about to crash the plane in rural Japan. When I looked out the window, I was struck at how much *nothing* was on the other side of the double-paned glass. Then something flitted across my vision and went away.

A bird, a *bat*?

Whatever it was, it knew better than hang around Team Rasputin and was gone the next instant.

"Hey, Raz?"

"Yeah, Uncle Jerry?" I said, disturbed at how loud my own voice sounded now that the engines had died.

"Can you come up here into the cockpit?"

"Sure."

He added: "I don't wanna die alone."

Oh, Jesus.

My skin tingled slightly as I crossed the threshold back into the cockpit. I drew a breath in and exhaled it slowly as I sat down in the only other chair.

"I'm just kidding," our pilot said. "I need you to look out for a road or a highway or something we can land on."

Exhale.

Inhale.

Exhale.

"How dire is it, man?"

"Depends on how soon we can find a road or a highway, Raz," he said, his head tracking from left to right, searching the ground below, which was getting closer by the second.

From the cabin behind us, the Actor said, "How remote is the airfield?"

The green light flickered around as the response followed a shrug: "Very. Like lookin' for a Rib Shack in New Delhi."

"Helpful."

I looked back to the cabin. "What difference does that make?"

My answer from him was at first only the tinkling of ice cubes in a low-ball glass. "Because there'll be at least one road leading to the bloody place. And if this is west of Tokyo, my best guess is that your road would be then coming from the east."

Damn. That made all kinds of sense.

Turning toward Uncle Jerry, I asked: "Which way's east, then?"

He chuffed. "On the right side! Duh."

"Only if you're going north, man!"

"Well... yeah. Of course."

Anza chimed in. "And we are going from the west, from Brussels, so the east is father away from where the airstrip will be!"

Damn. That made all kinds of sense.

I shook my head. "None of this is helping!"

Our pilot did a quarter turn of his head to me, grinning. "See what I mean? Better not to know, right?"

The nose of our craft dipped, and I had to quickly reach toward the cockpit paneling in front of me to not faceplant into it. My stomach dropped as we fell from the sky.

"What are we doing, Uncle Jer'?"

He cleared his throat and stripped away the infrared goggles. Turning toward me, I saw starlight reflect off the watering of his eyes.

"We're on a quest to save your lady. There'll be a road below us that leads to the airstrip. I know it."

The lump in my throat stopped any words from passing my lips for a moment. Nodding, I finally said: "But then why do you have to take the night vision goggles off? Don't you need those?"

The glimmer off his eyes winked for just a moment. "Shit, you're probably right." He laced the goggles back onto his head.

For the next five minutes or ten minutes, or infinity, we glided lower and lower, a vast, yawning darkness below us. Ahead, even without the night vision goggles, I could see the clearing of the airstrip. We were so close!

As we flew, inch by inch, the blur of darkness below us sharpened, and I could begin to pick out treetops of the Japanese countryside.

Just when it seemed the tips of them were about to lap at the belly of our plane, I heard Anza call out: "To the port side! Look, is road! Uncle Jerry, is road there on the left!"

"Got it!"

In that instant, I nearly somersaulted out of my seat. Somehow I held on, but I still ended up with my head on the step between the cabin and cockpit. Then we straightened out.

Something told me I could sit up, but another something (far more persuasive) said it was best if I didn't look out any windows for a while.

"Hold on to something, we're about to touch down!"

Crack!

It was more of a bounce than a touch down, and we hit hard. Then, as if clawed back down by some hungry, earthbound creature, we went down again, bounced a little shallower, and the next connection put us on a path that felt strewn with tiny stones. The aircraft didn't seem to slow as we rocketed down some apparent road.

Outside, I heard the banging of tree limbs smacking the wings, a sound that terrified me. I closed my eyes. Then, only left with the *banga-bang-banging* outside, I tried to estimate how close we were to stopping.

Nope. I was lost to the man stomping on pedals, which controlled the tiny nose wheel out front.

"Hold on!" he yelled, and time slowed to a crawl, whisper, whisper, and then *boom!* as we jolted hard upward, then slammed back down again. The world began to spin, as if we were toppling end over end, and I heard Anza scream, though it may have been the Actor.

The next moment, it was all over. I lifted my body, which felt unnaturally frayed and tender, and looked out the cockpit window.

An airfield.

We'd made it to the airfield. Sure, we'd taken a service road to get there, but we'd made it to the airfield.

Jerry yelled out again, but this time it was pure joy: "How about that, man?"

Anza prayed with her eyes squeezed shut. The Actor leaned over the side of his chair, held suspended above the floor by his safety restraints, and threw up onto the floor.

"Not bad," I said.

"How does it look?"

We'd all climbed outside to take a look at our ride.

To me, the drug dealer's airplane looked a bit like the old American space shuttle. And I don't mean all hi-tech and glittering and could possibly traverse the boundary between Earth and outer space. No, more what the space shuttles began to look like a few years on.

Yes, in the beginning, the shuttles were very gleamy and space shippy and exactly the sort of thing that someone like Arthur C. Clarke would have approved of. But near the end of the program, they were just getting old… the space shuttles began to look a little like the truck that belongs to that one weird uncle the family doesn't really like to talk about. Sort of beat up, inexplicably dirty, and something that would look right at home up on cement blocks in front of some rundown, one-story rambler on Alabama's gulf coast.

Uncle Jerry was running his calloused hands up and down the wing on the left side of the plane. "It looks like hell, but it seems intact."

We all watched as he rubbed his frayed goatee, inspecting this bit and pressing on that bit.

A minute or so later, the Actor spoke up. "You have no idea what you're looking at, do you?"

"Yes, I do! Mostly."

"I can drive a car, but if the car broke down on the side of the road," the Actor said, sitting on a suitcase he'd dragged outside, "I wouldn't know the first thing to do. Other than buy a new one instantly because I have quite a lot of money."

"Uh, your talking, it makeses my stomach turn, sometimes."

I agreed with Anza. "Yeah, it makeses my stomach turn, too, Mr. Crabbyapple." The plane looked ragged out but not busted up in any noticeable way.

Except in one case.

There was a small pool of what appeared to be hydraulic fluid next to the left landing gear. Of course, I don't know for sure what hydraulic fluid looks like, and I may have initially simply guessed that the onboard toilet had dumped, the plane simply doing what we'd all been doing the previous ten minutes.

Except there was a black hose bit that hung down onto both the rear landing gear and the front, but the difference was that the left rear one was flayed like some exotic vegetable you might see on an Asian cooking show.

It was beneath this that the pool of fluid rested, growing slightly larger from the *drip-drip-drip* that had been coming from the flayed bit.

"Yeah, hmm," Uncle Jerry said, rubbing the side of his head. He then stiffened as if he'd been hit by a bolt of electricity, spun around, and ran up the stairs and into the aircraft.

The three of us looked at one another, not saying a word.

A moment later, he came back down the steps, now in a brightly colored Hawaiian shirt, and obviously having realized the partial solution to a problem that he'd been struggling with.

Walking past us, he smiled and blew smoke at the Actor. He then put the joint back between his lips, smiled again and got on his hands and knees to get a better look at the landing gear.

In truth, I had no faith whatsoever that he'd be able to fix the problem, identify the problem, or even describe the problem to a qualified airline mechanic, but that wasn't the most pressing thing on my mind at the moment.

Anza said it before I could.

"You better go find the second piece, Rasputin," she said, taking a step toward the man pretending to know what he was doing beneath the plane. "I'll stay here with him."

"Yeah, I just… I mean, how are we going to take off if the landing gear is screwed up?"

"And we're out of fuel," the Actor added. "Don't forget that wee nugget, darlings."

He was right, of course. The plane was damaged *and* outta gas. And still time was marching ever forward into the future. More specifically, my precious few days and hours were ticking away, and I could feel the lamp drifting farther and farther out of reach.

Anza saw the look on my face and gave me a hug and one of her warm smiles. "Go find the next piece," she said. "I deal with Bob Marley pilot here, and we make to work something out."

A minute later, I was firing up Cujo the black Trans Am and driving it down the ramp, out of the belly of the plane. When I got to the bottom, I heard a banging on the passenger-side door, reached over, pulled the handle, and pushed it open. The Actor climbed in. Swallowed by the black leather bucket seat, he cinched the small terrycloth robe tighter and then reached for the seatbelt, which collapsed in a heap. He tossed it to the floor.

"If we pass a Macy's or something, we are stopping for some real damn clothes, for crissake."

"If you wanted to come with me," I said, "you could have just said you wanted to come."

"I do not! I just can't wear this *thing* anymore," the Actor said, tugging at the lapels of his little red robe. I looked up to see Uncle Jerry walking toward us, his eyes darting between his car and me at the wheel.

"Understandable," I said.

"Can you imagine traveling endlessly in a bathrobe?" he said. "I've had enough of it."

Uncle Jerry came to the window and leaned over. His face darkened as the floodlights of the plane bathed the tarmac behind him.

Clearing his throat, he said, "Uh, you be good now. Don't do anything crazy."

"I will, don—"

"He's talking to the car, Raz," said the Actor.

"Oh."

The man softly rubbed the shiny, black door and nodded, forced a smile, and then patted his beloved Cujo on its quarter panel. Calling back to me as he walked away, he said, "Take good care of my baby, Raz. She's all I got."

In that moment, I once again became acutely aware of how much I was putting these strangers through. All I could offer in return was to allow the shame to course through me and fight the urge to dull it or push it away. But there was something more. A fleeting glance at something important. And wonderful.

I looked over at Anza. Here she was in the middle of a cold, dark airfield in the middle of Japan, thousands of miles from her home and her husband.

The Actor, a pain to be sure, but he was there by my side in a ridiculous and increasingly soiled bathrobe. A man that was likely already overly conscious of his appearance, made to feel more self-conscious all because of the dangerous quest of a man he'd met only a day earlier.

And then there was Uncle Jerry.

For as much as I'd dismissed him so easily and completely in previous years, he'd already been incredible… from being our pilot to even very nearly killing a guy—along with his German cameraman—to protect me.

My vision rolled slightly, and I wiped my eyes with my sleeve. I'd known them just one day, and these were the best friends I'd ever had.

And they were risking everything for me. From what I knew of the world? This just didn't fit. But despite that, there we were.

A hand on my elbow stirred me out of my thoughts, and I heard the Actor say softly, "Come on, man. Let's head out."

Looking at him, I saw something I hadn't before. And in truth, it looked like it was a little uncomfortable itself, stuck on his face. A moment later, it flitted away. I nodded, coughed, put Cujo in gear, and pointed down the same road that we'd come down in the plane. The two headlights acted like sharp-edged spotlights on either side of the car as we drove. Every couple of yards above us, there were bent or broken tree limbs.

The Actor broke the silence. "Ah, this is far less terrifying in a car. On the ground."

"Agreed," I said. "Do we know where we're going?"

My copilot put the name of a temple into the cheap GPS plugged into the car's cigarette lighter.

"Zenkoji Temple," he said. "We're about an hour out. Hopefully there's a mall along the way."

"Not likely."

"Or at least a Starbucks."

"Not likely."

The Actor put his feet up on the dashboard. "At least let a little man, dream, won't you?"

Anza raked a fingernail between two teeth as she watched Uncle Jerry. The running lights of the aircraft cast a spotlight on their small corner of the landing strip, as if it were in a display case in a darkened hobby shop. At the edges of that curvature of light was only darkness.

Shifting her weight from foot to foot, she eventually decided she would have to venture out into the dark to see if she could find the fuel storage that the nav software said would be there. They would be stuck on a Japanese runway if she couldn't.

Rummaging around in the cargo hold, she eventually found a flashlight, sighed heavily, then told Uncle Jerry, who seemed to be trying to scoop up some of the spilled hydraulic fluid with his hands, that she was going to see if the airstrip had jet-fuel tanks. She walked away.

Uncle Jerry looked toward where she was heading but saw nothing but an inky black void. "Well, if you get into any… I mean, if you need any help, just, you know, whistle or something."

Calling back, she said, "No, if I get into any troubles, I will be screaming, Uncle Jerry."

"Right. Probably much better."

He looked back down to the flayed tubing near the base of the airplane's wheel and sighed.

Had he still been looking at Anza as she walked away, he would have been very curious—or more likely, instantly petrified—that someone or something was now following her in the darkness.

Zenkō-ji is a seventh century Buddhist temple serving as the veritable county seat of Nagano, Japan. In fact, the original city of Nagano was built around the temple. These days, it's said to be weighed down by stifling bureaucracy, co-managed by thirty-nine priests from two different sects of Buddhism.

That bit I got from a monochromatic paper pamphlet tossed aside on the outskirts of the temple grounds. Sounded a bit like it had been clipped from some local alternative paper.

Although it won't say it in the standard tourist literature, fourteenth-century Japanese temples have totally shit parking. I mean, I'm not going to pretend to know what they rode around in, but there's no way they walked everywhere. Like Jesus. Or the guy from *Kung Fu* (which is Chinese, not Japanese, *I know*, so you can stop your internal monologue).

But you would expect they'd have some sort of park-and-ride setup, at least on the outskirts of the temple for their variation of a cart. Horse-drawn cart, slave-drawn cart, panda-drawn cart, slave-panda-drawn cart (Yes, *I know*, Chinese again!).

Still, nope. We had nowhere to tuck Uncle Jerry's Trans Am so it would be less conspicuous. Then again, how conspicuous could we— in an 800-year-old ancient place of worship, driving a 1976 black Pontiac with blood-red lights spilling down its quarter panels and giant orange eagle on its hood—be?

"You realize that this car idles as if it were a snoring giant? With a sinus infection?"

The Actor was right, so at the temple's massive gates, I pulled as deep as I could under the awning of a stall that sold Buddha-themed chachkies—key chains, necklaces, mantel pieces, back scratchers—each additionally stenciled with the image of what I could only assume was a silhouette of the Zenkoji Temple.

Before we could get close to the temple, we had to pass through a huge, three-story-tall exterior gate that was "defended" on each side by a type of soldier called (according another, more glossy brochure) a Nio.

Sure, they were big stone statues that may have at one time scared away cowardly robbers, but despite their size, it was sort of hard to really get frightened of tall (very tall, actually), muscular, and able-looking warriors whose job, assumed or implied, was to burst to life if someone were approaching to do harm or steal—like say, try to make off with a part of a priceless ancient lamp entombed within its walls—from them.

"Jesus," the Actor said, his eyes locked on the left statue as we approached. "That's a terrifying thing, isn't it?"

"Is it?" My eyes had not broken from a hard stare-down with the guy on the right, so I couldn't really tell what his big, scary stone guy looked like.

Just beyond the gate was a long courtyard, flanked on either side by more shops, which according to yet another pamphlet I pulled from a wooden box next to the Niomon Gate, would eventually lead us to Zenkoji Temple.

I looked up at the length of the rod iron gate between the two stone guardians. Huge. No way either of us was climbing that. I briefly had a vision of tossing my companion over the gate so he could unlatch it from the inside but, *ahem*, quickly shooed that thought away.

The Actor squinted at me. "Why are you giggling?"

"Nothin'."

Crossing his arms, he leaned back against the gate and looked around. A few inches from his head, a large padlock secured the gate. Tugging on it a few times, I felt it was pretty solid. We'd have to find another way—

"Hold on," he said. He walked over to Cujo, asked for the keys, and then caught them in one hand with barely a look in my direction. He opened the trunk, reached under its carpet, closed it again, tossed them back. As he got closer, I could see he had a tire iron in his left hand.

"What are yo—"

In one quick move, he leaped up, threading the tire iron into the lock's loop, and his full weight came down onto its mechanism. The Actor let out an *ooof* as he rolled and tumbled onto the ground, the tire iron still in his hand.

The lock now hung open.

"Dude, wow," I said. "I'm impressed."

He stood, dusted off his increasingly grubby bathrobe (yep, no Macy's along the way), stripped away the lock, and pushed open the massive gate with a flourish.

As I walked passed him, he pointed a thumb to his chest and said, "I'm the evil one, remember?"

I laughed as he walked into the courtyard, pressing the tire iron into my hand. Tossing it into the dirt, I said, "Evil *ninja*, man! That was awesome."

It *was* awesome!

Until an alarm went off and a series of floodlights turned night to day above us with a *pop-pop-pop*.

"Quickly," he said, pointing upward. "Take out those lights with the tire iron."

"I, uh… it's back there. On the ground somewhere."

"*What?*"

The Actor was bathed in the white light, his red robe looking cartoonish and surreal as he took a half step left, half step right, unsure where to run to.

"I… man… Hell, even if I had it, I couldn't take them out. No way," I said, shielding my eyes from the brilliant light. "They're very high up there."

Behind us, we heard voices, so we ran in the only direction we could: up the courtyard toward the temple. All along the way there were small shops to the left and right of us but no hiding options; each was boarded up for the night, padlocked closed.

I really could have used that tire iron.

We rounded a dark corner and skidded to a halt as the temple came into view. Even in the very low light, it was impressive and awe inspiring. Its giant double doors were closed for the night, but hints of light floated around their edges.

The voices behind us were getting louder, calling out. I noticed a very large pot at the mouth of temple, as big as a Dumpster, likely just ornamental. It looked like it may have at one time been for offerings. I pulled at the Actor, who slapped my hand away, and we ran toward it. Leaping up onto the huge stone tablet it rested upon, I grabbed its rim and looked inside.

"Can't see a thing," I said, and the echo of my voice agreed.

"Yeah, so?"

From the direction we'd come, I could see the left-right-left swiping of flashlight beams heading toward us—security guards or samurais with light sabers, or who knows, the giant stone guardians from the front of the gate, reawakened and pissed off.

Jumping back down next to the Actor, I said: "Get in."

"What? No."

"Come on!"

"*You* get in, motherfucker!"

I'm not proud of it, but I picked up my friend and tossed him—yes, it was a toss—up and into the giant pot so that we could hide. A moment later, I scrambled up after him, landing flat on my back on the surprisingly soft interior.

We were both in complete darkness and near silence, except for the rhythmic sound of him punching me in the kidneys repeatedly, as the men pursuing us ran up. It became immediately clear that we had not jumped into some sort of offering chamber or donation pot.

It was obvious at that point that it was, in fact, the largest incense burner I'd ever seen. Huge. Like as big as a septic tank, though it was infinitely more pleasant smelling than a tank of human waste (I can only assume). Upon landing, the air around us had immediately filled with the remnants of centuries of incense ash. Maybe more.

I also knew it was an incense burner because a man's voice outside said, in English: "Please come out of the Zenkoji Temple incense burner."

Instead of arguing with the man—which we couldn't have done anyway because in truth, surrounded by ash, we couldn't breathe—we gasping-panic-climbed out in the same order we'd gone in.

The Actor was covered in white ash from head to toe and looked a little like that friendly cartoon ghost from TV. That little observational nugget, by the way, I decided to keep to myself in deference to my kidneys. Stumbling out of the giant pot after him, I fell to the ground hard. The Actor helped me up and then planted his fist in my stomach.

Looking up from the ground once again, and through the haze of dust and light, I was happy to see that the half dozen uniformed guards surrounding us weren't ghoulish and eerie, which would have revealed them to be homicidal hellspawn from Hell, Inc. and would have meant me and my punchy friend were in even worse trouble.

"Well," the lead man said in heavily accented English, "at least you did not miss the blessing."

The other men behind him laughed. The Actor looked at me, slowly nodding and feigning a chuckle. Me, less of a thespian, I shrugged and said something unintelligible, ending that panicked utterance with a small amount of ash-laden spittle dripping from my face. I was covered head to toe in a thin layer of ash.

Except for, of course, a small line from my lip to my chin.

The leader leaned forward and extended his hand. "You are American?"

I hesitated, then nodded.

He turned to the men behind them and said something in Japanese (I can only assume, but I think I'm on solid ground with that one). They approached, cheerfully smacking and slapping us both on the backs, as if one of us had accepted the other's proposal of marriage or something.

The ash dust rose quickly from our clothes, and we all took turns coughing.

Once or twice, I burst out with a giggle because it tickled, and it was hands-down the strangest moment I could recall in recent memory at that time.

It only got marginally stranger when the lead guy said, "You are on the wrong side."

My turn to be sly. "…Oh?" I cleverly said.

He nodded as several of the men tugged us by the elbow, leading us into the temple.

"The other side," the leader said, motioning his arm in a long up-and-down arc. "The race starts on the other side."

"Right," I offered, again playing the cool customer. "The other side. Gotcha."

But of course, my mind only went: *The race?*

Anza wasn't a big fan of walking great distances in the dark. Not that this particular apprehension set her apart from the entire human population. If you are a fan of walking in the dark, you're possibly up to no good. In fact, it's very likely you are. Bad things often happen in the dark, and more often than not, they are perpetrated by the aforementioned people who like being in the dark.

As for Anza, she could trace back to the very instant she became soured on strolls through the night air. When she was a kid and part of a very large family in Juarez, Mexico, there wasn't a whole lot to keep a young, active, and curious mind entertained for a terribly long time. These days, when she drove past Atlanta's parks, basketball courts, and playgrounds, she couldn't help but wonder why kids preferred to stay indoors all day.

Other than, of course, to avoid stray bullets.

As a little girl, she and her friends and siblings would run around outside all day. And very often they would play hide and seek endlessly. One New Year's Eve, they'd played all day, then *all night* long.

Anza had been doing well, evading discovery until her cousin Ronaldo started closing in. She'd been up a tree, which was technically cheating since Ronaldo was twice as wide as he was tall. The only way he could even possibly pursue her was in the unlikely scenario he could scare up a ladder from somewhere.

He found one.

Climbing hand over hand and rung by rung, sweat had begun to burst from his face from his very first advancement up the tree. However, once he came close enough to her perch to tag her out, Anza had simply hopped down and sprinted away, passing between a wooden fence and a long, dilapidated shed which had recently been relieved of its only functioning ladder.

Always a fierce competitor, she ran away from Ronaldo at full speed, and he was making an awful racket as he stumbled back to the ground. The space between the shed and fence just accommodated her skinny frame. Even if Ronaldo had been right on her tail, he wouldn't have been able to squeeze through without a thorough lathering of animal fat and possibly a sizable cache of pyrotechnics.

In the pitch black, arms and legs pumping away, her destination was a spray of light 150 feet ahead, and she ignored the threat of jagged rock, errant rake, or busted two-by-four to get there as quickly as possible.

Then something odd happened. Her hand had hit something on an upswing.

It hadn't been hard like a jagged board or discarded piñata entrails or anything like that. It was solid, sure but soft. It had felt more like hitting an overripe tomato with her wrist.

Then, and this bit was odd, as she kept running, she felt the tomato begin to crawl up her arm. She could feel each of its eight legs individually as it slunk up toward her shoulder. Naturally, she screamed very loudly, spun back the way she'd come, and ran even faster. This alerted Ronaldo to her whereabouts, and he appeared in the light ahead, ready to pounce. His huge, sweaty grin flattened the moment she exited and flung her arm forward, hurtling a furry palm-sized tarantula, *adult* palm-sized tarantula, away from her. It landed squarely atop his upper thigh.

The young Anza, shivering with fear, rolled to the ground and looked up in time to see her cousin take off running in an attempt to get away from the spider, which was, of course, on his body. It had been the fastest she'd ever seen her cousin run.

And she'd even felt partially responsible that it had taken him nearly a day and a half to find his way back. For her part, Anza never forgot that such creatures lurk in the dark.

Walking down the uneven Japanese tarmac, she shone the flashlight ahead of her, her pace slowing as if the darkness were in fact some viscous fluid wrapping around her puddle of light. Just ahead, she saw a couple glints reflect back. She raised the flashlight slowly, and the light revealed a series of long utility sheds.

She whispered to herself, "I don' like sheds."

The third had its double doors hanging slightly open, one side hanging a little lower than the other. Both doors were rotted, rusted, and close to collapse. She inched toward the gap and felt a tingle ripple across her skin. Taking a deep breath, she pushed forward and closed in on the shed's opening, steeling herself for what might lurk inside. She peered in, but her view was blocked by a fallen piece of corrugated steel just on the other side.

She made a little fist, then opened it again and gripped the handle, dragged the door farther open, and cast the beam of light inside. Within, she saw a collection of what an overactive imagination might describe as fat, lazy ghosts.

Dusty gray tarps covered several dozen mounds of what was likely metal and plastic, optimistically discarded with designs that whatever might be beneath their coverings might be used again. She sighed.

"Yeah, nuthin' in there worth a damn, huh?" a voice said.

She tensed like a cat in a bathtub, then spun around and screamed, "Get go away from me, tomato spider!" She went down on one knee and threw her arms up, crossed at her wrists.

The old man took a half step back and raised his hands in a surrender motion. He did this mostly to show that he meant her no harm, yet it was also because he was pretty sure he'd just heard her say something about a big spider.

His deep voice, thick with a syrupy American southern drawl, eased toward her from the dark. "Whoa, I'm... I was sent here to give y'all a hand."

She squinted to see his face, but it was too dark; the only illumination was a tiny pool of light in the middle of the runway with a stoner pilot lying under a jet. Twisting her flashlight toward him slowly, she was first surprised to see that the man appeared to be wearing overalls. Not something you'd necessarily expect to see from some stranger coming out of the dark at a Japanese airfield.

When the light hit his face, he smiled. Or it seemed like he'd smiled, but all Anza really saw was a face that looked like he'd first bludgeoned himself with a claw hammer and then washed up with handfuls of broken glass.

"Ruined," Raz had described it earlier.

This was an agent of Hell.

She leapt up and sprinted away, cutting through the darkness as fast as she could, tomato spiders be damned.

I wasn't exactly sure how the Actor and I had ended up standing near the starting line of a Japanese temple's footrace with more than one hundred other guys, but it seemed to be a favorable result over being arrested for trespassing, so the two of us were both happy to pretend it had been a part of our master plan all along.

The rest of our master plan, well, we hadn't gotten all of that worked out yet.

The second piece of the lamp was not only inside the Zenkoji Temple, but it was likely in what we came to learn was called the Forbidden Room. That is, not just forbidden like you had to pay extra on a temple tour to get to the special room. Nor was it, despite its arguably provocative name, any sort of temple stripper Champagne Room with red-velvet-rope cordon and bikini-clad temple nuns (which I was pretty sure they didn't have, with or without bathing attire).

Forbidden as in, no visitors were allowed in. Ever. In fact, none of the priests were even allowed to go in. Ever.

Turns out, it had been this way a very, very long time…
which concerned me a great deal.

"Yes, hello. Billable hours begin now depending on your
individual contract. Who's this?"

"You know who this is."

"Why does *everyone* assume I know who's calling? I can't
stand that. If people—"

"It's me. Rasputin."

"Oh dear, that explains the sudden throbbing of my anger
boil. Absolutely dreadful to hear from you again, my little fried
afterbirth. What can I do to quickly make you get off the line?"

I had tucked myself in the most secluded area in the crowded
gathering hall—between a couple of wooden carts selling fruit
and a small group of spectators waiting for the race to begin.

"You said that the lamp was blown apart, all four pieces jetted
off in different directions."

"Yes."

"A couple *hundred* years ago."

"Uh, I'm so looking forward to you being dead," he said.
"Yes!"

"So how come I've been led to a hiding place that was sealed
way *before* then? More than a thousand years before you say the
lamp blew apart!"

"Oh," the Advocate's voice oozed from Raz's fingertip, "such
a curious burrowing weevil, aren't you?"

"I'm running out of time, and we were guided to the wrong
place! That's not fair, you fat f—"

"No, no. Ugh, listen… you're familiar with physics?
Einstein?"

"The dog in *Back to the Future*?"

"And to think somehow you've lasted this long in the world. I
mean, how have you not simply swallowed your own tongue
and expired by now?"

"Whatever."

"Briefly, then, because talking to you gives my hives hives:
The lamp was blown apart by forces, let's say, beyond your

world. Some of the pieces may have traveled so fast that they not only crossed a great distance but back across time."

"Impossible!"

"Says the man with a finger in his ear talking to a demon in the lower bowels of Hell."

Okay, sure. He had me there.

"Just get your piece and move along to the next," the Advocate said. "Chop, chop! You're right: Time is running out.
"

Click.

The Actor had learned that the Hidden Buddha was in the Forbidden Room, which had been sealed for over thirteen hundred years and was likely somewhere behind the main altar.

"We just have to get down the hall leading to that altar; there's a couple of rooms to get through, and then the secret sealed room is behind that."

"Holy, shit, Sherlock Holmes! How'd to find that out?"

He held up a glossy, full-color brochure he'd pulled from a stack on the table just behind him.

"Ah, good thought," I said. "I tell you, these various brochures lying around have been terribly helpful."

"Indeed."

The trouble would be, of course, somehow getting to the main altar without being stopped by ninjas or shogun swordsmen or just really irritable night custodians.

The Actor tapped my hip to get my attention again. He was looking up at a giant woven map of the temple, twenty feet high, hanging from a stone wall. On it, the race route was laid out. We both saw it at the same time: The very last turn of the race went past the hallway leading to the main altar.

From the glossy brochure, the Actor read the race's history. It was called the Lucky Man. It had been run every year for hundreds of years, and the winner, the first one to reach the temple's priest waiting at the end, would win the coveted title of "Lucky Man."

And along with the title, they'd win an entire *keg* of sake. Not joking.

I snapped the brochure from my friend's hand. "We're running the race!"

The Actor looked at me, shaking his head slowly. He then grabbed my wrist and led me between the folds of two huge hanging curtains. "What... what are you talking about? Running? We are *not* running, for crissake. I thought you wanted to get your piece of the lamp? You want to run a race?"

"This is the perfect opportunity," I said and began walking toward where we'd been standing, pointing up at the huge cloth map hanging from the ceiling. "Look, we run right past where we need to be."

Stronger than he looked, he quickly pulled me back to the curtains. "No, no, no... listen. We can sneak over there while everyone is *watching* the race, Rasputin. It's a perfect distraction."

"Not without being seen. There's people lined all up and down that area to watch the race."

"Raz..."

"Getting to that hallway with a pack of runners is the best way to do it—we could peel off from the chaos, and no one would see anything," I said. "We walk that way whistlin' and we get nabbed, for sure."

"Raz..."

I looked toward the big map, tracing in the air with my finger. "We just need to get to the outside lane in a group and peel off."

"RAZ!"

My enthusiasm on pause, I looked at the Actor and wondered why his eyes were jumping around like two eggs in rolling boil.

"I..." he said, then stopped. After a breath, he started again. "Unless you haven't been paying close attention... you may have ascertained that I am not exactly the running type."

My heart sank. Obviously I'd missed a small issue.

In a quest to save my wife's life, I was asking my new friend to embrace what appeared to be a lifelong humiliation, its scars apparent from the expression on his pleading face, one that had likely haunted him from childhood.

"Fuck it, you're running," I said.

"Come on…"

Leaving the curtains, I said, "We're running! Stretch a little or something, so you don't get a charley horse or whatever your little legs might get."

I was being tougher than I wanted to be, and frankly, much tougher than I felt. The look on his face as he followed me, staring up at that big map, was crushing my heart.

Arms wrapped around his knees as he crouched on the oil- and dirt-stained tarmac, Uncle Jerry stared at the hydraulic tube, split in the middle and frayed at its ends.

Unsure how to fix it, he'd resorted to busying himself with picking out leaves, twigs, and bits of vine that had gotten snarled into the landing gear after they'd touched down on the auxiliary road.

He noticed a residue of fluid on his hands and licked his index finger. It was an oily taste, mixed in with a smoky sort of rubber taste. Then he wondered—obviously a little later than such consideration would have been properly useful—if the hydraulic liquid was poisonous. What if it caused brain damage, organ failure, or some sort of sensory injury?

He shrugged. "Damage done." And he licked his fingers clean.

He'd been locked in a crouch too long, and getting up, his knees popped and cracked like a silver-haired Orson Welles rolling around in a swimming pool filled with Bubble Wrap. Then something in the distance, in the darkness, stirred and called for his attention. In the deep black night before him, he saw a mystical, magical, beautiful dancing beam of light.

The beam of light knew him and was calling his name. "Uncle Jerry!"

He looked down at his damp fingers, whispered "Dammit… I hate brain damage" and wiped them off on his Hawaiian shirt. When he looked back up, Anza burst from the dark into the light, letting out a breath she'd been holding, and nearly stumbled to the ground.

With visions of monstrous tomato spiders dancing in her head, she ran up to the middle-aged pilot and threw her arms around his neck.

"Whoa, girl… You okay?"

She looked up, but before she could speak, another voice lifted out of the dark.

"Tha's my fault, sir," the old man said, ambling into the light. "'Fraid I scared your friend, but I swear to ya, I was just saying hello."

He stepped further into the light, and Jerry stiffened at the sight of him. An agent of Hell, his face—at least to their eyes—was twisted and wrecked.

Jerry, unsure if he was seeing what he was seeing, whispered: "I think I mighta given myself a little bit of brain damage, Anza. Some of that airplane juice, uh, spilled in my mouth."

Anza frowned at him. "Airplane juice?"

"Yeah," he whispered again, his eyes locked on the man in the overalls who'd now taken another step closer. "I'm seein' weird things. And not, you know, the usual weird things."

"Trust me," the stranger said and chuckled with a deep, warm laugh. "You don't look much betta to me."

Releasing her grip on Uncle Jerry, Anza spun around and crossed her arms, scowling at the man (now that he had turned out to not be a tomato spider, just a demon).

"Now you get out of here," she said, "because I know, and Uncle Jerry know, that you are creepy devilspawn."

The man looked at her, then to Jerry. He said to him, "Wha's a matter with yo' friend?"

"She's an illegal."

"*I am not a illegal!*"

Jerry shrugged, and the old man standing before them nodded. "Listen, I ain't here to cause you folks no trouble. Just came to help."

"From where did you coming from? We don't need any of your demon help!"

Jerry stepped forward. "Yeah, we do, actually. Hydraulics are all busted on that landing gear, and that's kinda outside of my, um, skill set."

Still a few yards away, the tired old guy hunched a bit to get a better look at the damage. "I hear ya. And what exactly is your skill set?"

Uncle Jerry smiled. "Avoiding real work."

Anza shot him a dirty look.

His smile fell. Jerry hooded his eyes and said, "I mean… assassin."

The old guy pointed to some of the luggage Raz had dragged out when he'd moved the Trans Am. "You mind?" he asked.

Uncle Jerry opened his mouth to answer, then looked to Anza. She shrugged and patted her friend's spongy arm and nodded.

He sat down with a grunt. "Thank you kindly."

She took a step forward. "You work for the Devil, then?"

"No. Other side they call Hell, Inc."

"So why would you want to help us, then?"

The man pulled a rag from his overalls and wiped his brow and neck. Tucking it back away again, he said, "Well, I could lie to ya, but I'm too old and too tired for nonsense like that. Truth is, my side wants your man to get that lamp pieced together as much as the Devil does. Maybe more."

"Why?"

"'Cause once you do, we plan to steal it."

Anza laughed. "Do you think we're stupid?"

"No," he said and frowned. "But I did see your friend licking hydraulic fluid off his fingers a few moments ago."

"You are not good guy," she yelled, pointing a finger at him. "You are not trying to save Earth from the Devil or help Rasputin and instead want only bad Hell things with the lamp!"

"Now, I didn't say we wanted it for anything terribly good, no."

"Wait," Uncle Jerry said. "I thought the lamp was supposed to save Raz's wife."

"From what little I heard, yeah, it can do that," the man said. "From what I heard."

"So I don't get it," the pilot said. "Why would anyone else want it?"

"That's above my pay grade," the old man said, slowly standing again. "I just was told to help y'all keep movin'."

Anza put her hand up. "Hold the horses! Why you tell us all of that about the plan to stealing the lamp, then?"

He shrugged. "Guess there's no point in stayin' quiet. They never said not to tell ya. And, frankly there probably ain't gonna be a whole lot y'all be able to do to stop them." The old guy pointed toward the darkness. "If you need to top up your tank, out there yonder, about one hundred fifty yards, looks like a big ol' cylinder of jet fuel. I was surprised, since this airstrip is outta commission, but it's actually well stocked."

"Well, let's say this is one of hundreds of little airstrips than aren't exactly as out of commission as they look, man." Uncle Jerry took a step forward, nibbling on a fingernail. Then his eyes got a bit big, and he yanked his finger from his mouth and spit a few times. "Any thoughts on the landing gear there? That hydraulic line is pretty wrecked."

The old man waddled over to it, bent down with a creaking grunt, and took a good, long look at it. After studying it for a moment, he finally spoke. "Y'all got maybe a sheet or some old linens you don't care so much about?"

Anza's eyes went to slits. "Why?"

"That an' some heavy oil or something like it."

"For what?"

The old black man straightened and then pressed a fist into the small of his back and rubbed. "Cause'n, your fix here? What you need is tar tape."

Chapter Twenty

Years ago, I'd taken some singing lessons because I began to think that since I played rock music on the radio I could naturally be a font-o-rock, too. My vocal coach was a skinny old hippie in his seventies. Very Zen. Think Buddha meets Jerry Garcia with a secret methamphetamine habit.

About ten minutes into our first session, he'd said to me: "Your biggest problem—other than lacking any talent for singing—is your breathing. I'm afraid if you really want to do this, you're going to have to quit smoking."

"I, uh, don't smoke."

"Well, damn," my vocal coach said. "Damn, damn. If you'd smoked that would have been a lot easier to fix."

Finally, he'd come up with a solution. He decided I should sing while running. This would help teach me to breathe properly when I did sing. However, the only song I seemed capable of singing while running was "Ohmyfuggin'God, please, someone call an ambulance, I'm going to die!", which may be an old Ike & Tina track, now I think about it.

So I eventually ditched the singing, but for a while, I kept up with the running. Given my profession, it seemed like music should still be a part of my jogging routine. Well, not music per se.

For someone who plays music on the radio, it can be less than inspiring to essentially bring your work with you on a run. Music was no longer a calming, meditative endeavor for many jocks, so instead I settled upon what seemed like a pretty good alternative. I created the "My Predators" mix tape.

Not just music, but the sounds of various bloodthirsty creatures as if they were chasing after me. As I ran, my ears were filled with snarling, angry creatures like wolves, lions, hungry hippos, zombies (not the *Walking Dead* stumbly ones but the sprinting, speed-freak ones from *World War Z*), and English soccer hooligans.

You'd be surprised how quickly you get your second wind when you've got a snow leopard or T-Rex snapping at your heels in Dolby surround sound.

Stretching as I walked the dusty floor of the Japanese temple, I was loosening up so a dwarf actor and I could run a centuries-old race in a twenty-one-hundred-year-old temple to steal a piece of the Devil's lamp from Buddhist priests.

Arguably, it was a bit surreal.

"I wish I had my mix tape," I said.

"What?" The Actor's eyes were still jumping around from other runners to the big map on the wall and back to the runners again. "Raz, I don't see how this helps us."

"It does, and you know it."

"I-I have awful memories of foot races."

"Hey, perfect! Time to create happy new ones, then!"

He looked around. "That seems... unlikely."

He was right, of course. And not just because of his stubby little legs. It seemed we weren't the only ones there who'd earned their Hell merit badges. It was a mixed group of students, factory workers, farmers, and Japanese corporate climbers.

In this last group, at least a dozen of "the ruined" had entered the race. Standing there, young business types, with their near-identical dress shirts and rolled-up sleeves and power ties, all of them had collars slightly loosened at the neck as if they'd come straight from whatever Hell-affiliated shell company they'd been working for that day.

Whatever side they were on, they weren't interested in me and my friend. It seemed they were all about winning the race. Or, like the nasty bellman at the hotel, they had no idea who their true boss was.

As he walked away from the registration table, the Actor stared at the yellow racer's ribbon in his hand like it was a death spoor waiting to burrow into his body the moment he looked away.

"I can't believe this is happening."

"You'll be fine," I said and walked up to the woman at the table. Before I could speak, she slammed the long wooden box closed. "Whoa, hey. I'm here to—"

"No. Closed."

"What? No? No! It can't be no closed!"

"Closed," she added, not even looking at me. "All entries in."

"But he just got one," I said, pointing to my friend.

"He last."

"No last!"

"Yes, last!" She dismissed me with a tired wave of her hand, as if she'd had this very conversation many, many times before.

"No way! That is not… good. For me."

She stood up and disappeared through the folds of a curtain on the back wall before I could come up with a more compelling argument.

The Actor looked toward me and his eyes briefly lit up. "Raz, totally fine, you can take my place."

I snatched the ribbon he was holding out for me and looked at it. Printed lengthwise on the ribbon was the date, some Japanese characters, and then, most distressing, a monochromatic printing of the Actor's face. This, it seemed, was the Buddhist temple's twenty-first century anti-cheating measure.

"Ah, hell."

"We're cooked, Raz! If you can't run it with me, we'll never get to that damn Hidden Buddha. We'll have to come up with Plan B. Not even worth running it. No, not a bit. I'm taking off these running shoes."

"No, leave them…" I said and stopped. "Hold on. Where'd you get running shoes? You're still wearing your robe."

"I pushed down a nine-year-old, stole theirs."

"Wow."

"Little bitch punched me, too." He touched his cheek. "If this thing rises into a bruise on my face, I will kill you as you sleep."

I thought for a moment and decided we had to work with what we were given.

"Listen, this is perfect when you think about it," I lied.

"It's not perfect, far from it, and I don't want to think about it."

Crouching down, I dropped my voice. "You come waist high to most of these other runners. You could peel off at any time, slipping down a corridor to the hidden room and no one would know."

"Waist high?"

I shrugged. "Yeah."

"*Waist* high? These are all *guys*. You mean *cock* high!"

"Naw, not…"

"Yeah, man! There'll be more cock wigglin' in front of me than from a gay pride float in West Hollywood on Wiggle Dick Day!"

I gave him a moment to calm down… and then I slowly escorted him to the starting line as if I were his trainer.

Nodding toward the other runners (and avoiding the scowls from the demon-spawn corporate types), I tried to be encouraging.

"Don't get trampled, man."

"That is not helping!"

Associated Press: "Lucky Man" Chaos

The "Lucky Man" race in Nagano Prefecture at the Zenkō-ji Temple became unexpectedly unlucky for a majority of the runners who'd dared to run in the 21-hundred-meter annual event.

Thirty-seven men entered this year's footrace, competing for the celebrated title of "Lucky Man" and the award: a keg of fine sake prepared by the priests from the previous year's rice harvest.

In what started out as a predictable competition of fastest man wins, it fell apart on the very final turn.

"He was a little guy," said Senjo Iridaki, a banker from Matsumoto city. "My guess is his tiny legs tired and he was trying to make it to the sidelines."

Another witness, who asked not to be identified for fear the man, reportedly a dwarf, might put a curse on him, said: "It was like suddenly they are running and this mass of men, some tripped up by this amanojaku (a small wicked demon), others stumbling as dominoes might fall, this group of men comes crashing down, every last one of them."

But reportedly, the little person in question had been the first to fall and then first to get back up again. But instead of looking for a path to safety, he did a most surprising thing.

"The little guy runs across the backs, heads, and shoulders of all the guys who'd fallen on the floor," said Iridaki. "Heading straight for the finish line!"

Tiny legs pumping along, he was just meters away from the finish when three others leapt up quickly and were set to easily overtake the crafty fellow.

Then the second most incredible moment of the race transpired. Another man, unshaven and dressed in a decidedly unkempt American way, hurled his pasty, pudgy body at the dwarf's three pursuers, taking the small man's last competition out of the race.

At full speed, the dwarf leapt to the finish, which was where the awaiting head priest had been standing to greet the winner, knocking himself and the holy man to the ground, to the cheers of the spectators looking on.

During the award ceremony, the man who'd toppled the three runners just before the finish line was reportedly jumped and sustained some slight facial bruising.

The dwarf may have also been slightly injured in the melee, for witnesses say this year's Lucky Man was wiping tears away from the tops of his cheeks.

The Actor sat atop the wooden keg of sake, languidly kicking his feet in the air with an expression so obscenely self-satisfied, if there had been small children around, I'd have ushered them a safe distance away, covering their eyes whilst uttering calm reassurances to each of them.

Sipping from a tiny glass, pinky extended, he slurped on his sake and kicked his legs again.

"Don't for a minute think you're bringing that in Uncle Jerry's car," I said.

"Oh yes. It absolutely is coming with us."

So used to him being a bit of a miserable prick, I found it hard to hang with Mr. Happy Face.

I caught him repeatedly looking down at the paper "medal" encircling his neck.

"Japan's 'Lucky Man!'" he said.

"Yes."

"Lucky man!"

"That's just an expression."

"I'm feeling very lucky," he said and jumped down off the keg. "I've never in my life won a race before."

"Well…"

"Ever," he added, but he wasn't saying that to me.

I had to break his spell to get us moving. "I'm pretty sure that as some of those guys punching me were talking about wanting to kill you."

"Pfft," he said and slurped from his drink again. "My line of work, I get death threats all the time."

"Really?"

He shrugged. Sip.

"Well, okay… so, Lucky Man, now we're kinda screwed, huh? We lost our shot back there. Now there's no way we'll get back into the hall without being seen."

The Actor thought about that for a moment. "We'll go around from the other side."

"Right. How?"

He lifted the other string around his neck, holding a carved wooden key as large has his palm.

"We can get into any room in the temple, I'd wager."

I laughed. "That is a ceremonial key!" I snatched the drink from his hand, spilling some of the clear liquid on the floor. "No more sake for you."

"No, no. Not with that key," he said, eyeing the cup. He lifted his other fist from his red robe's pocket. "This key."

"Where… where'd you get that from?"

"I stole it from the priest when he was awarding me this other stupid wooden key."

"How?" I said as he plopped the key into my hand. "How did you do that?"

The dwarf took the opportunity to snatch his glass back and refill. "Like I said. I wasn't always an actor."

A few moments later, we'd stashed the keg and were making our way through the darkened halls of the temple with the stolen key.

The layout of the inner rooms of the temple was a little like those cute little Japanese nesting dolls. That is, if cute little Japanese nesting dolls were not dolls but instead a goddamn labyrinth of rooms with no windows and no reasonable pattern to how they'd been laid out. Each door we unlocked and went through only led to another. Then another.

"This can't be right, man," I said. "We've been at this for a half hour."

"And this place isn't very big."

"Right."

The only answer had to be that, despite apparently traveling in one direction, somehow we were going in big circles. But that didn't make sense.

Anytime we'd enter a room, we'd seek out a door on the wall opposite to the one we'd entered. If there wasn't one— let's say just a door leading to the "west" and we'd been heading "north"—we'd take the next "north" door, being sure we'd headed back "east" by one.

"Hell, we should be damn near Tokyo by now."

"No," I said. "We're just going round and round."

"How's that possible?"

Opening the next door, I went through, then returned. "Hold on." I stepped into the next room again as the Actor took a moment, sat down, and watch me hop from room to room.

After a half minute, he said to me: "Seriously, Raz. If you're waiting for me to ask what you're doing, you're wasting your time."

What a dick.

"Because, thirty minutes ago," he added, "I was seriously happy to be sitting on a keg of Japan's finest sake, sipping myself into extreme happiness."

"You were more likely going to slip into an alcohol coma."

He looked at me. "What's the difference?"

Leaving him behind for a moment, I did a very Third Reichy kind of goose step into the next room, to its far wall, then spun back. Then back in the room with the grumpy dwarf, I repeated it.

"In that room, compared to this room, they are different sizes."

Without missing a beat, he said, "It's probably just colder in there than in here."

"So that—what?" I said, then scowled. "Um, whatever. Too easy."

"Hey, my buzz is fading. You're not going to get the A material."

I explained to him that with the rooms being different sizes—likely due to some cunning, early Japanese hi-tech design—every time we thought we were righting ourselves on the north-east-south-west pattern, we were actually drawing ourselves into a circle.

"Probably," I added.

The Actor stood up slowly. "You're running out of time. You don't have the luxury of probably."

I rubbed my face, so tired. I purposely wasn't looking at the countdown on my watch. "You don't have to remind me."

"So if these rooms were designed to keep you from finding the Hidden Buddha on this floor—"

"Of course," I shouted. "We should just retrace our steps in the opposite direction!"

The Actor frowned. "No, that's... I don't even understand that."

"Don't listen to me, my blood sugar's crashing."

"No, if we're being led around by the nose here... it means, I think, it's not here."

That was a truth I couldn't handle and expressed that thought with a flagrant dismissal of all the facts available to us. "No, way. It's here."

"It's not on this floor, I mean," he said. "It's here but not... here."

"So..."

"It would seem no one has breached the hidden room for, what, more than a thousand years, right?"

"Right."

He crossed his arms. "Then we give up."

"What?"

"Raz, I'm an actor—a great one, sure—and... you're an out-of-work deejay. People that passed through these halls were generations of philosophers, engineers, master sake-makers..." He looked at me and sighed. "You and me? We are not that."

For some reason, I had to fight back tears. Not for me (although I am more than capable), but just that thought...

"I... I owe her everything."

"I know."

"You don't," I said, my vision blurring. "She gave me everything. *Her*, you know? A woman like that!"

"Raz..."

"No, this girl, she's an angel on Earth. And she hitched her wagon to a slob like me. I am nothing."

"Come on."

"No, it's true. I don't deserve her. I have nothing… Who am I? You're right. An out-of-work deejay. I regret she ever had to sacrifice and slum for someone like me."

"Not true."

"Pity," I said, wiping my damp face with my sleeve. "That had to be it. Must've been fucking pity."

"No," the Actor said and took a step toward me. "You are worthy. Here sits a man who, upon discovering his wife cannot be cured, wagers his very soul with the purveyors of Hell, then enlists the help of total strangers to travel the planet in a plane he stole from a drug kingpin."

I sniffed. "Yeah, shit. That ol' chestnut."

"Most men… hell, *every* other man I've ever known would have given up. You didn't. That's a man any girl would want beside them."

I gave him a smile. I could only nod then stupidly smiled again. We'd started into the next room when I finally found my voice: "Did… did you do the acting thing a bit there to ramp me up."

"Yes, and I was damn good."

Another door, and we found nothing, of course, but with no other choices being offered up, we simply moved to another. From a small end table, the Actor picked up a faded brochure for the temple. It appeared to be an earlier printing of the one he'd shown me earlier. There wasn't any turn-by-turn map inside (one can dream), but he read it for a moment.

"'No priest has laid eyes upon the statue for more than a millennium'," he said, scanning the folded paper. "So maybe it's in a sealed-off room. Encased in concrete or something. Guarded by stone ninjas."

Again, the suggestion of failure drained me, and I plopped down on a short stool, thinking about what he'd just said.

"Stone ninjas would be pretty crap ninjas. Walking all slow and always looking for snacks… giggling when one of them made a noise."

The Actor looked at me, confused, then gave me one of his frowns (I was going to start categorizing them). He ignored my comment and suggested that the room could be made unavailable but not necessarily sealed off.

Then I froze. Outside the door, I thought I'd heard scuffling sounds and signaled to him to be quiet. We sat for a full two minutes.

Nothing.

"If you had a one-of-a-kind religious artifact," he whispered, "where would you put it?"

"eBay."

"Be serious," he said, and I raised my hands up in surrender. "Where?"

"If I were religious… I would… put it somewhere special."

"Why?"

"Somewhere… where it could help me, I dunno, commune with God, right?" I said. "No?"

"Buddhists don't believe in a god." I stared at him, and he added: "I dated a girl who was a Buddhist."

"Wow, that's… oddly convenient."

"Wasn't for me," he said and stretched his little legs. "Too hard to tell when she had an orgasm. She was so conflicted at what she should yell out."

"Fine. Then you tell me where you think it might be, ya jerk."

His eyes got wide, which surprised me.

"Okay," I said. "Sorry about the jerk thing."

A voice behind me said: "He is a jerk."

A white-hot bolt of electricity seized my muscles, preventing me from turning around to see who had found us.

Several feet shuffled behind me until the head priest's skinny body whizzed past my shoulder, and he impressively lifted the Actor from his feet.

"Key! *Key, key, key!*"

"Um, I don't exactly speak Japanese," the dwarf said, then added with a cocked eyebrow: "*Kone-ee-chiwa.*"

He dropped my friend to the ground, and in his hand was the key that had been stolen from him. Less than half a minute later, several large priests wound us through a series of rooms, and before we knew it, a large set of double doors was slamming closed behind us, and we were left outside in the cold, standing in a light dusting of snow.

I took a few steps forward, then stumbled back and looked at the big wall in front of us. "*Fine*. I'm going to give this place a really shitty Travelocity review."

"Raz," the Actor looked at me. "What do we do?"

"I'm… I'm lost, I think." My emotions crashed down upon me like damp snow that had broken away from the eaves. I felt like crying, screaming, roaring… and for a moment, it felt as though my head simply lifted from my body. I whispered, "I think I'm lost."

You're not lost.

Baby, I am. Jesus, I am.

You're not. You're always right here with me.

But I'm not. You're in a hospital bed thousands of miles from here, while… I'm, shit, I'm on a stupid, impossible trek to nowhere.

No, every time you take a step you are a step closer to somewhere. You might not know where that is, but you are getting closer.

Sweetheart, I am… I am lost.

Then head back toward where you started until you find yourself again. You are there along the way, somewhere.

Like, turn around? I can't, there's no—

No, you go back toward your start.

Okay, babydoll.

All the way if you have to.

I smiled for no reason.

Then I fell away from the temple, dropped flat to the ground, and my back thumped onto the snow-covered pavers. I stared up at the cold, pin-lit night sky. For a moment, I just lay there.

Then, slowly, my arms and legs began to move. Up and down. Up and down.

The dwarf stared at me, his expression momentarily frozen in panic. Then his face softened, and he dropped to the ground and lay next to me. He began making his own (somewhat smaller) design. Neither of us spoke for a full minute.

Just lying in the snow with a gentle misting of tiny ice crystals cooling our upturned faces, it was dead quiet except for the sound of two lunatics making snow angels.

"I haven't done this for a very long time," he said in a soothing voice. "Surprisingly, it's a bit of a stress reliever."

We both stared up at the brilliantly clear night. Both of our arms and legs: up and down. Up and down.

"Beautiful, isn't it?"

"Amazing," he said, and his voice hitched momentarily. "I don't think I've seen a sky like it in my entire life, Rasputin. It's breathtaking."

"Good word for it, brother. Yep. Breathtaking. It really is."

"I think you could nearly see the whole universe if it wasn't for that steeple bit on top of the temple."

"It's not a steeple, I don't think..." I said, then struggled to properly find the right word. "It's... it looks like..."

"A room."

Yep. That was a good word for it.

Uncle Jerry inspected the newly wrapped hydraulic hose as it hung down from an opening just above the landing gear. Scratching his beard, eyes darting to the other two landing apparatuses, he grunted in a manner he hoped sounded affirming.

Standing, Uncle Jerry wiped his fingers off on his shirt and shook the hand of the man who'd helped them. The old black man then introduced himself as Alvin Stoddard from Wardoff, Mississippi.

"Well, not Wardoff, exactly," he said quietly. "Right near there. A road right near there."

Anza was less convinced of Alvin's good/not good intentions—and maybe still a little bit cross over the scare he'd inadvertently given her when he'd first approached—so she kept a safe distance. In her hand, she had one of her shoes, which she fiddled with a little, ostensibly because there was something on it that needed her attention, but really, it was so she was armed in case the stranger was trying to pull a fast one.

All the same, Alvin gave her a nod and a smile.

"There's a rusted ol' tank over yonder," he said. "I gave it a knock earlier and heard a sloshin' inside. Like I said, I think it might be the fuel you need. Lucky break for y'all."

"Oh, not really," Uncle Jerry said. "This airstrip is on kinda this international drug-trafficking network. Looks all run down, but it's got millionaires, maybe billionaires, who got people making sure it's stocked up."

"They from your side?"

"Our side?" the pilot said, then got it. "Oh, no. Um, freelance misery dealers far as I can tell."

"And you fly for them?"

"No, I don't think so," Uncle Jerry said. "Not anymore."

Alvin nodded, and his small smile wavered. "Well, I don't know about all of that, but if you'll help me hitch that tank up to the bobcat over there, we can haul it over to ya plane, and I'll be off."

"Alvin, you're a godsend."

"No, I don't think so," he said. Then added after a beat: "Not anymore."

The two men laughed as they walked into the darkness. Uncle Jerry looked over to Anza, and after a moment she gave him a smile and waved him on. Her shoe, however, was at the ready, if necessary.

"So, if I can ask, why you out here running around on this here, uh, quest," Alvin said. "Man in his sixties gotta take care himself."

"I'm fifty-four, man."

"Ah, well. My eyes ain't what they used to be. Don't mean to offend."

Uncle Jerry slapped the old man on the shoulder. "I don't offend easily—built up thick ol' alligator skin against that sorta thing over the years. Don't worry about it."

"Glad to hear it."

The pilot thought back to Alvin's question, which he'd dodged with a quick joke, then said, "Well, I don't think answering your question would make any difference to what we're trying to do."

"Wouldn't change nothin', no."

"We are out here for a friend who's trying to save his wife," Uncle Jerry said and cleared his throat. Then cleared it again. "In fact, our guy is wagering his eternal soul to save his girl." Jerry stopped, and in the darkness, he turned to Alvin. "What kinda man would I be if I didn't help a guy like that?"

This time, Alvin gave Uncle Jerry's shoulder a warm pat. "That might make all the difference, now I think about it," he said. "Me, hell, I did… well, I did something just like that, oh, a long, long time ago. Lifetime ago. But I went all lone wolf, gambled, and lost. That's a tab ya work to pay off for a long, long time. But, hell, ya never do. Ya just keep payin'."

They started walking again. After a full minute, Jerry said: "I'm sorry to hear that for ya, Alvin. I really am."

"Your boy's got a chance, though. He really do. 'Cause'n he got friends that love him on his side."

"You're right about that."

"And that's a powerful thing, that is," Alvin Stoddard said. "Love, that is a powerful, powerful thing."

"Rasputin, I fucking hate you!"

"Don't worry! You're nearly there," I said and pulled again. The little guy was much, much heavier than I'd thought he'd be.

It had taken the better part of an hour. After we'd looped some rope from the Trans Am's trunk over the top of the first-floor roof of the temple, I'd pulled him up. He'd tied it off, and I climbed up clumsily and slowly, huffing and puffing the whole way.

From above, he helped me up onto that first roof. By the time my body flopped up there, my hands were both bloodied, and I was exhausted. One more to go.

"Jesus, I didn't realize how far up this was," the Actor said.

"What? Oh, right. Sure."

"'Oh, right,' what?"

I shrugged. "Naturally you're afraid of heights."

"Fuck you."

"Yep. I totally deserved that."

"Man, I do not like the sensation of swinging," he said, little puffs of moist air bursting from his lips in the cold night air. "Hate, hate, hate it!"

Ten minutes of trying later, the rope was again looped under his shoulders, and I finally draped the other end of it over the landing above. Once we got up top, we could carefully climb the sloped roof and get to the room at the building's peak. That would be where the Hidden Buddha was.

The temple looked a bit like a two-tiered cake, with each roof ending in a flair. Getting to the first landing had damn near taken every last bit of my strength. I was now dipping from shallow reserves trying to get him up to the last one.

I yanked hard, ignoring the searing in my hands. A bit higher up, the wind was stronger, and my friend began to sway back and forth. Every foot higher, the arc along which he swung got larger and larger.

"I'm getting a bit queasy, Raz. Can you stop with the swaying?"

"I got one move here. Just pulling," I said and grunted. "I can't control anything else."

Another half minute and he was closer to the top. But my pulling was slowing, and he felt like he was getting heavier by the second.

"What if the next piece," he said, "you know, isn't up… way up there?" He then said, just above a whisper, "Jesus, this is really high."

"It is," I said, puffing my words. "It's where the Hidden Buddha is, so you'll be the first man to see that thing in, like, thousands of years. What… what a lucky, lucky man!"

"Go slow!"

I nodded, exhausted, and sent snot and spittle flying from my face, gave him a sarcastic salute, and lost my grip. Then I fell over the edge.

Hitting the ground from four stories up? I'd be dead. Or wish I were dead.

The distance between each second and the next grew exponentially, while my eyes fixed downward as the ground raced toward me like a predatory animal, about to pounce and smash the bones within me. But just a few feet from the ground, I stopped, hanging from my end of the rope tied around my waist.

Then, briefly, *impossibly*, I got yanked upward for a few feet, held there, *tick-tick-tick*, then once again dropped like a rock, this time hitting the ground.

It stung, but the second fall was so much shorter, I made it. I was okay.

"Holy cats, that was close," I wheezed.

Oh shit.

So with me all worried about, you know, *me*—you are likely way ahead of yours truly on this—it was only at that next moment I wondered: *Hmm, what happened to the little guy?*

Here's what happened:

The Actor saw his friend falling, and his heart leapt into his throat as he thought, *That fat fucker is going to take me crashing to the ground with him!*

Raz fell into the darkness below, and then, not surprisingly, the rope which had been looped up and over the corner of the roof grew taut, and the Actor was launched like a rocket into the night air.

Given the weight difference—and it was significant—plus the speed at which the man below was hurtling to the ground, once the rope grew tight, the equivalent force was like a fluffy bunny rabbit sitting on the lowered seat of a teeter-totter while, upon the other raised seat, jumped the Sydney Opera House.

On a sold-out opening night.

Sponsored by "Weight Watchers".

Rocketing up past the rooftop, the Actor briefly hung way up in the sky, until the weight below pulled once again, causing his trajectory to then bank hard, arching him toward the very hard exterior of the temple.

"Shit-shit-shit-shit-shit!"

Heading forward and down, he looked beyond his little feet and saw he was heading for clapboard wood.

Since there was no use in swaying, running, or flapping his arms at this point, the dwarf did what anyone else would have and squeezed his eyes shut, hoping he would at least die quickly.

Instead, he crashed through the boarded-up skylight, hung at the end of the rope for a moment in a musty dark room, and subsequently passed out.

Unconscious, his arms raised like a doll's, and he fell to the floor below. The rope whip-snapped out of the room, and in the distance, in the quiet night, if he had been fully awake, he would have heard the distant, soft cry of "motherfu-ohhwwwnpt!"

A few seconds after landing, his eyes opened again. The Actor looked up. The moon shone bright through the hole in the roof of the tiny room. Rubbing the spots under both arms, he knew he'd bruise pretty badly, but other than that, he seemed fine.

Except he felt that he wasn't alone. There was someone else in the room. From above, wood splinters were sprinkling down upon him. Damp, they smelled slightly rotted. Not wanting to be there any longer—quest or no quest—he looked around, through the dark, to see if he could pick out a door.

Someone stood there, watching him. Menacing and still. The Actor backed up to the wall and bumped into more rotted wood. He spun around and pulled at it. It easily came away, but behind it, more wood.

"Shutters," he whispered. "They boarded up the shutters."

He threw the pair in front of him open, letting a little more moonlight into the room. Along the next wall, he did the same, stripping away a couple wooden boards, and pushed another set open. He did this again and again until each of the five walls could draw a fresh breath of air into the room, the first in more than a thousand years.

Still, quietly standing in the middle of the floor, the man stared at him. No, not a man. A statue made from stone. One arm was raised, the other outstretched. In the upturned stone palm in front of him lay the brass, disklike font of an old paraffin lamp.

"Oh my God." He then looked at the Hidden Buddha, twisting his mouth into a frown. "No offense."

It was good to be back on the jet and in the air again. I looked at my watch and saw we'd nearly burnt through half of the time I needed to collect all the pieces of the lamp. Turning to my friends, who were understandably still elated at finding the font, I couldn't help but be down.

"I still have three pieces to get. Three damn pieces," I said and looked out the jet's window into the starry night that had looked so peaceful as I had lain in the snow. Now it just looked cold. "Man, I just... I'm not going to make it."

"How you are having three left?" Anza said from her swivel chair, sipping a small glass of sake. "Two. Two left."

The Actor, who once again sat perched atop his wooden keg, getting a bit drunk, chimed in: "Dear sweet Anza. The contract, which you read to us, listed five. We have two. Surely"—he slurped loudly—"in your country, they have people that teach arithmetic? Maybe missionaries or the occasional benevolent pirate?"

"We've got the wick manifold and the fuel tank," I said to her.

"It's a font," the Actor corrected me and slurped again.

"Right. And I still need the glassy globe thing, the spindle that moves the wick up, and then the damn fuel."

Anza shook her head. "The fuel is not a part."

"It's in the list of things Raz needs to get."

"But fuel is not metal or glass, it is fuel! It doesn't preserve. You can't fill up your car tank with gas, put it in your garage for one hundred fifty years, and think it with start up again with that tank of gas!"

We sat quietly for a moment. It was Uncle Jerry, from the cockpit, who broke the silence. "You know, she's probably right."

The Actor, to his credit (or the fact that he was getting bombed), leaned back onto the bulkhead and said, "Well, I'll be damned. There sure won't be any sort of ancient jug of fuel you can use."

Anza smiled, slurped from her glass loudly, and looked directly at the Actor. "See, where I came from, they not only taught us maths but logic with an emphasis on inductive reasoning. *In elementary school.*"

I laughed. The man across from me hopped off his keg, turned and refilled it with a flourish.

"You'll have to excuse me," the Actor said. "I'm in the middle of getting properly pickled."

Anza sipped and shrugged. "Is no pickle. Is gherkin."

All I could do was look straight ahead and focus on a point in middle space. *Just keep staring, just staring, no laughing, not funny, just staring.*

"You see?" she pushed. "Because *half* of a pickle…"

"I get it," the Actor said, and despite being the butt of the joke, couldn't help but smile.

"… one *half* of a pickle, tha's a gherkin!"

"*I get it.*"

A big, lovely smile slowly bent her lips. "How is dat for arithmetic?"

To his credit (or the sake's), the Actor began to laugh until he couldn't breathe properly. And sure, he's a performer, so he probably did the next bit on purpose, but he fell right off his damn keg, which finally sent me and Uncle Jerry into hysterics.

The Globe

23 Aug

My Baby doll,

I should have known our vacation "cabana by the sea" was such a good deal, mainly because of the ongoing armed conflict between the paramilitary and guerrilla factions battling for control of the country's illicit drug pipeline.

However, scout's honor, that was *NOT* anywhere on their travel website.

Still, of course, you were awesome.

We had some lovely dinners, and I don't think I've ever been happier in my life than simply walking down the beach holding your hand, with the sun dipping into the sea, turning the water to amber.

By the way, I looked up "minas terrestres" (remember that crazy old lady yelling at us, ha!) and no biggie, but it was good that we turned back around.

Carissa, when we'd lie there at night after making love, with only the wind whispering through our cabana, I will always remember how you looked, lit only by the starlight reflecting off the lazy, rolling ocean waves. I've never seen a woman more beautiful.

That said, you were also pretty hot with the assault rifle strapped across your back when the "Omega Amanecer" guerrillas were rushing all the tourists who'd paid the "taxi fare" to the airport ahead of their three-point offensive against the "fascist paramilitary pigs."

274

And, hey, good thing I brought my Lars Ulrich-autographed copy of "... And Justice for All" by Metallica after all! Otherwise, we might have ended up like that mouthy Australian couple three cabanas down.

Even with all the civil unrest, concussive blasts of military-grade ordnance, and remote possibility of, you know, being shot in the back of the head, you were there with me hand in hand the whole time.

I know that couldn't have been what you would have described as your dream honeymoon, but looking back, to me, it was close to perfect.

You are my perfect.

And I've got fifty or so years to love you and make up for booking that godawful trip.

Viva la Revolution,
Your Rasputin

Chapter Twenty-One

"How we lookin', Uncle Jer?"

I'd dimmed the cabin lights, mainly so Anza could sleep. Impressively, once again, the Actor was already passed out. But he'd been great, and I wouldn't have had the second piece without him. So yeah, he deserved the rest.

"We're doing good," our pilot said. "I suppose. Our dwarf divining rod wasn't entirely exact on his where-to-next tip."

"Mexico."

"Yeah," he said. "Big place."

"He'll narrow it down when we get close."

Our pilot nodded slowly. "Roger."

I dropped into the copilot seat and stared out at the blackness in front of us. It was tranquil. Soothing. Every now and then, a puff of a white cloud would slip past the cockpit windshield.

"You know," I said. "I never said thank you."

He grinned. "And I never said you're welcome, so that makes us even."

"Listen, I'm sorry if I underestimated you."

"You did? Nah, don't worry about it. I don't really give off a good first impression. Part of my charm."

He made me laugh, again. "I couldn't have done this without any of you guys."

Jerry punched a couple of buttons, flipped a few switches. I'm not sure if it was necessary or if it helped fill the unsettling quiet of the moment. Then he thumbed the light on the console, dimming it by half.

"It's on auto. We got about seven hours until Hawaii."

"Hawaii?"

"Yeah, can't do Mexico in a straight shot. Gotta touch and go on Oahu."

I grinned stupidly. "You're the pilot."

He looked out the window for a moment, then back into the darkness of the cabin behind us. "You know, Raz, as you said, we got just two pieces so far. So we may be a little behind the clock, so to speak."

"I'm hoping for a miracle."

He laughed. "Tall order for a group working for the Devil."

"Subcontracted!"

"Oh, right."

"Subcontracted, man, not working directly *for*."

"Splitting hairs."

"Yeah," I said, "while I got 'em!"

He smiled at me kindly, grabbed a gray blanket from under his seat, then pulled it over his ample tummy.

"And, Raz... no need to thank me," he said. "You'd do it for me."

Slowly, I nodded, and it struck me. "Yeah, you know. I would. Really, I would."

I started to head to my seat but turned back. "Hey, so that guy at the airstrip back there. He just came outta nowhere?"

"Like our lady said, he's working for Hell, Inc., but he helped. I'm damn sure we'd have not gotten off the ground without him. Or at least, it would have been hours later."

"But the guy said—"

"Alvin."

"Okay, Alvin said they wanted to *steal* the lamp?"

"Yep. Right honest of him for a demon seed."

I leaned on the bulkhead. "What the hell would they want it for? To mess with the Old Man? What use of it would it be to them?"

Before he could answer, Anza's voice drifted up to us from the dark. "Maybe, I think, that lamp is more powerful than they are saying to you."

That made a lot of sense. "Right."

Jerry added: "In your hands, it heals your wife. In the lands of... the lords of the underworld? Who knows?"

"Maybe this is a bad idea," I said.

"Of course it is, man. But even a bad idea can do a little good. We're gonna help your lady, Raz. That can't be a bad thing."

I nodded, tried to say something but couldn't.

Taking a half dozen steps away from the cockpit, I settled into my lounger in the middle of the cabin, my head stuck on what my friends had just said. As I closed my eyes, alarm bells were going off in my skull, and I wondered if I would be able to sleep with all the racket.

"We got about seventy-five minutes before we're back in the air," Uncle Jerry called after us, reminding us for the third time. "If you're late, I'll go without you."

"No you won' not, Uncle Jerry," Anza said, her tiny feet tapping quickly down the jet's stairs. She'd said she was going to try and find a Skype terminal in the airport and call Dan. I'd asked her to say hello for me and to let my friend know I was taking care of her. "How are you taking care of me?" she'd asked.

"It's a guy thing," I answered, eyes hooded a little as I followed her down the steps. "So he doesn't worry."

"No, you forgetting he knows you, Raz. I don't think the idea of you looking out for me is much comforting."

"That hurts."

She shrugged. "Truth hurts," she said. Then added: "Love hurts." Then: "Hitting your funny bone, also this hurts."

The Actor rubbed a small patch between his eyebrows as he followed me onto the tarmac, squinting at the sun's glare. "I don't think the English language is your trouble, Anza, just the use of language in general."

Taking the quickest, longest strides her tiny frame could pull off, she called back, "This is coming from a guy who is making a living from strangers who are writing every word he's ever said."

"Damn," I said and laughed. Spinning on a heel, I couldn't help wanting to catch a glance of his face. He looked like he'd been stung by a bee. When he caught me looking at him, his expression softened. I stood there, grinning stupidly, with the only the *click-click-click* of Anza's shoes echoing in the hollow of the airplane hangar.

He walked past me, brushing some invisible fluff off of his red robe. "I'm going to find something a little more modest."

"In the *airport*? They don't have clothing stores in the airport."

"Raz, have you been to an airport in the last decade? They're like the Beverly Center, but with less armed security."

"You got an hour."

"Seventy-five minutes according to our stoned pilot," he said and turned away. "That's plenty of time for a visit to... oh, I wonder if they've a Jimmy Au's here?"

"An hour!"

He waved and stopped, then turned halfway toward me and said, "Remind me not to get involved in any more verbal tête-à-têtes with our illegal friend. She doesn't fight fair."

Still standing at the foot of the jet's steps, I tilted my head, considering his request. "Nah. When she's crushing you, man, the rest of us are safe."

As he slipped from the sun into the darkened hangar, heading for door, he lifted his arm and raised his middle finger, shook it languidly in the air until he got to the door and walked into the terminal.

"We gotta fuel up, man," Uncle Jerry said, his body in a swayed arch, hands clasped to the inside of the door of the plane. "Little crew will come out here and get us set up. I been to this one before a little while back. Won't take long. Shouldn't be, you know, any foreseeable problems."

I nodded. "I know you got it under control. Gonna head inside and see if they'll let me do some takeout."

"Good," he said. "I'm starvin'." Uncle Jerry smiled back at me, but his eyes were locked on the door where the Actor had just gone through. Watching him for a moment, I asked him if he wanted to go inside, stretch his legs, but at first he didn't answer.

After I'd asked a second time, he brushed me off with a grin and assured me his legs were adequately stretched.

Years earlier, the Actor hadn't been the upstanding model citizen that his earlier resumes had implied.

Once things began to take off in his career, he left behind the occasional petty larceny; his brief stint of short cons partnered with a low-rent, B-movie location scout; and the entrepreneurial forays into transactional perspective enhancement (he sold a little acid).

Yes, as the cash began to flow in the proper direction for the first time in his life, he'd decided to put his dark past in the past. At least, that's what he'd told the judge at age twenty-four, in what was not technically his "third strike" hearing, but it could have been considered a full-count with bases loaded in the bottom of the ninth.

However, once tempted by the dark side, it can be too hard to completely leave all of that back in the shadows. Instead of minor crimes, the Actor turned to the moral ones. Specifically, sleeping with the wives, girlfriends, sisters, and friends of other cast members and production staff.

In some ways, it hadn't been his fault—nearly every young man growing up in the school systems across the world finds himself cumbersome with those of the fairer sex. A happy few work it out before graduation. Most don't, and many never do.

So now that he was seeing his name climbing higher and higher up the playbill and earlier in the on-screen credits, he found getting girls to be almost effortless. But not wanting to get "duped" into a relationship (as he'd once drunkenly described it), he'd made the conscious if flawed decision to sleep with women who were already in a relationship with other men. Or with other women; he wasn't terribly choosy.

One evening, after enjoying a second bottle of wine with a young blonde production intern—when all was going quite to plan that night—her boyfriend, who was also the second-unit director on the Lifetime movie they'd been shooting that week, stormed through the front door and caught the two of them naked on the living room floor.

The director was supposed to be in New Jersey. Instead he was standing, fists clenched at his sides, towering over the two of them. The girl jumped up and began yelling and waggling her finger in the man's face, while the Actor looked for a way to get the fuck out of there and not die.

Unfortunately, his clothes, which held his wallet, were back in the bedroom. A little buzzed by the wine, the Actor wasn't sure if they'd ended up under the shower curtain he and the young lady had laid upon the bed or if they were balled up next to one of the large empty Wesson vegetable oil bottles on the floor.

Then, it seemed like he would be okay. The boyfriend was storming once more, but this time in the other direction—out the door.

She turned to the Actor, who had covered up with an oil-soaked sheet, and said, "Ugh, I hate when he's coked out of his mind. Totally out of control!"

Before he slammed the door, her coke-fiend boyfriend shouted back: "I'm gonna get my rifle out of the car."

The dwarf froze, wide eyed, and waited for her to contradict that parting statement.

"He doesn't have a rifle in his car…"

Oh, good.

"… it's actually a shotgun."

Oh, shit.

"Don't worry," she added. "He's too blasted to even get the trunk open."

Just as he'd taken a breath to consider his next move, the door handle exploded, sending splinters into the apartment's foyer.

"Damn," the pretty blonde said, hands on her lovely naked hips. "He musta had it in the front seat."

Over the next twenty minutes, the Actor ran eleven blocks wrapped only in an oily sheet, tripping on it at least a half dozen times. Both his feet and pride hurt, but what he'd realized was that he would not have had to run eleven blocks if he'd had some way to pay for a taxi. So an amendment to his personal standard operating procedure was to always, always have a small stash of cash or credit card tucked away on his person at all times.

When he'd started to really do well, that meant sewing a credit card into the lining of each of the robes, house coats, and pajamas in his collection. Standing in Honolulu International Airport at a kiosk buying a pair of sunglasses and a counterfeit LA Dodgers hat, he'd been pleased to find that the red robe had one of his Amex Black Cards sewn into its cuff.

"No limit," he mumbled to himself. "Choice."

Next, it was straight to the Departures board. If there was time, maybe a quick change of clothes, but most importantly he was going to get off of this crazy, messed-up merry-go-round he'd been drafted into.

"I got goddamn shanghaied," he mumbled to himself.

"Whassat, man?" the man examining his charge card said. "You going to China?"

"No, it—" he said, then waved the man off. Putting on his cap and glasses—he was not yet an A-lister but still commonly got recognized on the street—he signed the receipt, leaving the man in the tiny airport kiosk behind.

When he'd been selected for Raz's quest—"*fucking shanghaied*!"—the Actor had been in Sydney shooting an independent film, which his agent had said could be just the type of role the Academy might consider for an Oscar nod.

The Actor had discovered, in this case, that meant plenty of screen time but not a lot of dialogue. A lot of staring. Wistful staring, pensive staring, saddened staring… but less dialogue meant less time spent memorizing the shit, so he was just hunky dory with the entire situation. That and the Aussie producer's wife was smoking hot. And as he'd discovered in his Sydney hotel room, mostly made up of original parts.

After winking away and ending up in, of all places, Georgia, he'd left behind her and another woman (who he couldn't remember the name of) all sharing a delightful champagne bubble bath. Of course, the girls would have left and the bathwater would now be cold, but it was time to get back to his life.

"Sydney… Sydney…" He stared up at the monitors, scanning the flights out.

Then he quickly ducked back behind a married Asian couple with their four young children, all of them dressed exactly the same—*Hey, you guys up before or after the Von Trapp family?*—who'd also been looking up at the electronic board.

Slowly glancing back, he saw Anza at one of the airport's Skype terminals, the dopey husband he'd seen back in Atlanta on the screen with a big, stupid smile, and naturally she was talking fast, and hands were going up all around and everywhere like she was telling him about how much fun she and her girlfriends were having at Disney World.

"Jesus Christ, how does he put up with all that?" the Actor said, and the young boy in front of him turned back, popped his gum, and walked off with his family.

The boy kept staring back as he walked up next to his mother. *Kid looks like a moron.* When the child reached up and grabbed his mother's hand, which had been waiting at her side, the Actor was surprised to have to swallow down a lump that had formed in his throat.

He looked back up to the Departures board and only glanced over at Anza a few more times before finding the flight that would thankfully take him away from all this craziness.

Uncle Jerry didn't trust him. Nope. Not one bit.

Sure, the little guy had helped Raz pick up their second piece at the Japanese temple, but something about the Actor just never quite sat right with him. The guy was sneaky. And according to Hell types, also the worst person on their crew. He couldn't argue with that because those folks seemed pretty reputable judges on the matter.

The refuel crew was set up and doing their thing. No words were ever exchanged in these types of drug underworld transactions—the plane's owner would quietly be billed. Plausible deniability was just one of the many non-monetary currencies traded in the shadow world. Uncle Jerry was just fine with that arrangement.

He scrambled down the stairs leading to the jet without much concern about locking the craft. Who'd be stupid enough to steal from a drug lord? Of course, technically *they* had stolen the drug lord's plane.

Jerry put that thought aside. It then joined legions of other thoughts, considerations, and concerns that had been regulated by the man to the sidelines of his mind. In fact, if one's mind were a playing field, the combined weight of the sheer number of thoughts that had been benched by Jerry would have created entirely new tectonic faults and very likely subsequent splits on both sides of the mind field.

"Ha, mind field," Jerry mumbled to himself. "Like mine field. Damn near same thing."

Back to the mission at hand—recon on the Actor. How hard would the guy be to find? A dwarf dressed in a red robe can't exactly slip into the crowd.

Jerry stopped and said to himself, "Unless he's changed clothes already—then I might never find 'em."

Whoosh! Off went that thought, quickly crossing the transom of his mind. Tucked away. Somewhere in the ether was the slightest of tremors. The airport was pretty crowded, but being a little taller than most, he had no trouble scanning the throng of travelers.

Passing an Asian family all dressed alike, Jerry smiled and couldn't help himself: "You guys look awesome, man!"

The six of them turned toward him, all grinning, and the father pointed at Jerry's shirt and gave him the thumbs-up.

"Hey, man," he said. "When in Rome. Or Hawaii, right?"

Jerry didn't mention the fact that he'd been wearing the shirt since they'd left Japan.

Jerry heard her before he saw her—Anza, talking to a computer screen that was displaying the loving face of her husband. Dave? Delbert? From this distance, he could see the man was smiling, but her eyes were a bit red.

Good woman, that one there, he thought as Anza leaned forward and kissed the screen and waved goodbye.

It only took another couple of minutes of searching. And the cap and sunglasses didn't fool Jerry. Not one bit.

The Actor could have booked the ticket at a kiosk, sure, but it was always so much better to talk directly to the little people working for you. However, when he got to the counter to book his one-way ticket to Sydney (getting an odd look when he'd said "no luggage"), it left him... unsatisfied.

He'd had a brief moment of hesitation after the ticket clerk asked him to remove his hat and sunglasses. After complying, he was met with a big, lipsticky smile of recognition. She looked left and right, then said just so he could hear: "I love your show!"

The problem would be, of course, that he didn't actually have a passport to get back to Sydney. It was in his hotel room. In Sydney. She apologized, blathering on about rules or laws or something.

And sure, it was highly irregular, but as long as he picked a flight within the fifty US states, she was sure they could arrange something so he could get back to one of his various homes scattered around the country.

After a weak attempt to argue, his feather-trigger anger disappointingly was failing him, and he agreed to keep it domestic and booked a flight into LaGuardia.

"*Not* Kennedy," he said sternly. In that, at least, he'd been able to throw his weight into.

She'd handed him a ticket and said something about using the picture on the back of Amex card for identity verification at the gate, which she assured him would go smoothly. She would call ahead to get the ball rolling.

Donning the cap and sunglasses again, he stuffed the ticket into his red robe and began walking toward the gate. He felt odd. Something was missing. Maybe it was because he was traveling alone—he'd begun to hate that in recent years and avoided it—or maybe it was because he was just a guy in a robe walking through the airport. Catching his reflection in a departures monitor, he saw no one was reaching for his hand. No one was fighting back tears as he left.

For a moment, he just stopped and stood there in the middle of the airport as travelers whisked past him in all directions, hurrying to see somebody waiting for them or say goodbye to someone else, going to and from one place to another.

"Get a grip," he growled to himself.

Then, ahead, the big, lanky, graying pilot with the boiler-pot belly in the incredibly stupid Hawaiian shirt was taking huge strides, splitting the crowd of travelers like a stoned, WASPy Moses parting the Red Sea. Within seconds, Uncle Jerry was right there in front of him.

"Thought you were gettin' a suit, Actor."

The dwarf casually looked away and shrugged. "They didn't have any in my size. A hazard of someone—"

"Don't care," he interrupted. "We gotta go. On the clock, as—"

Uncle Jerry stopped, frozen, and his eyes flipped downward. Then, unbelievably fast for a man with pot resin partially blocking major arteries, his hand darted into the left pocket of the red robe, then came back out again. Scanning the airline ticket, he scowled at the Actor.

"Get movin'," he said and swung sideways as if his body was a door back to where they'd come.

Anger returned to him once again, and the Actor was warmed by it. At least, he was pretty sure it was the anger that had done that. He planted his feet and said, "This is not my responsibility, Uncle Jerry."

"It is."

"No it sure-as-fucking-well is not!"

The older man shrugged. "Making up curse words don't mean you're not getting back on board."

"Why should I?" the Actor barked loudly, and it felt good. "This has nothing to do with me!"

Uncle Jerry's brow creased, and he hooded his eyes for a moment. He then squared himself back to the Actor.

"The man needs your help, and he can't do it without you."

"Not my problem, dude."

"Nah, but it is your ride," Uncle Jerry said, his voice lowering. "No matter if you didn't choose this and if instead it chose you, whatever. This here's your ride."

"*I* choose!"

"Life don't always work that way," Uncle Jerry said, frowning. He knelt down and put a hand on the dwarf's shoulder. "Our guy back there needs you. *You*, man. Not that dude over there with the homeless-guy beard, not the chick over there squeezed into her pajama jeans. Raz needs *you*."

His voice shook unevenly. "So what?"

Uncle Jerry's voice hitched for a moment, and he said, "You don't get what a gift it is to be needed by somebody? I don't mean somebody just wants something from ya. I mean when somebody needs, you know… you."

The gray man stood up and cleared his throat, rubbed his bulbous nose for a moment. "That don't come 'round too often," he added.

The Actor closed his eyes slowly, then waved his hand forward, and once again Uncle Jerry turned, opening their path back to the jet.

Chapter Twenty-Two

"I think this flying is more exhausting than all the running around when we eventually do get somewhere," the Actor said, slowly spinning in his seat.

Anza agreed. "I am quite crampy as well."

"Few more hours," their pilot said. "It would help a whole heckuva lot if we knew exactly where the hell we were going."

The Actor frowned. "It's still a little muddled."

"Unmuddle it."

Looking to deflate a bit of the building anger in the room, I said, "We got a few hours."

Uncle Jerry muttered to himself something I couldn't hear. But like all of us, I suppose he was on edge. Actually, it sounded like he was specifically really pissed off at the Actor, but we were all just tired.

"We'll find it," I said.

"Just... just let me clear my head. It'll come to me."

The look on the man's face didn't convince me even he entirely believed that.

We were about an hour off the coast of Mexico when I yelled out, "Holy shit, Jer! What are you doing?

"Me? Nothing! It's not responding!"

"Man, what? We got only ocean down there!"

Slowly, the Actor cracked an eye open. "What's going on?"

Anza had both hands over her face, trembling so badly I thought she was going to hit her skull on the bulkhead and knock herself out. She said, muffled: "Out of petrol."

"WHAT?" the Actor was fully awake now. "Wha-what? What-what?"

Uncle Jerry yelled over his shoulder from the cockpit. "We've run dry, son... all goin' in circles out here."

"Now, we are going to crash," I shouted. "In the ocean!"

The Actor stood and stumbled as the plane shifted and began to point downward. The windshield went from clear blue sky to deep blue ocean.

Wide eyed, he looked at me in the copilot's seat as I fumbled with the seat belt.

"Jesus, tell me you're kidding!"

I shook my head and said, "Yeah."

"No, it can't..." he started, then stopped. "Wait, what?"

"Yes," I said and stopped juggling my restraint. "We're kidding."

The Actor stared at me, eyes still like those of a Chihuahua in the middle of a sixteen-hour coke binge during a *Hellraiser* movie marathon.

A moment later, Uncle Jerry leveled the plane out. He turned to the Actor: "Your head clear yet?"

The dwarf swore in some foreign language, then stumbled a few paces and fell back into the lounger he'd been sleeping in.

Anza pulled her hands away from her face, still violently trembling.

The Actor looked at her flatly. "*Et tu*, Broomhilda?"

She pointed a pointy finger at Uncle Jerry and said, "He told me to do it because you was jerking off!"

"Jerking around," Uncle Jerry barked from next to me. "Good god, I said jerking *around*!"

I stepped back into the cabin of the plane, slapped the Actor on the shoulder, and grabbed the seat directly across from him.

"Sorry, but we're getting low on time, man. Had to rattle you a bit."

"No, you did not *have to*, Raz."

"I did."

"No."

"Did it work?"

"That... that is not the point!"

I smiled. He looked away from me and then tugged at the lapels of his dingy red robe.

"Come on," I said. "Tell me the next location, and I'll buy you some pants."

The man crossed his arms, still not looking at me.

"For the record, Anza didn't want to trick you."

"T-tr-tr-tricking fine, okay," she said. "I am n-n-no good at lying. Always get caught."

The Actor looked at her, eyes at half-mast. "Gee, it's not like you have a tell or anything. A moment ago, I thought we were going to have to stuff a wallet in your mouth to prevent you from biting your tongue off."

"Leave her be," I said, glancing at the countdown on my watch. "I'm running outta time, man."

"Fine."

"Great. A pair of pants coming your way. They got 'little people' stores, right?"

"Yes, they do," he said and walked to the window and looked out. "I've a favorite in Vienna."

"Great."

"But you'll be buying me an entire suit," he said coolly. "Maybe even a *chapeau.*"

"Oh?"

"Yeah," he said, looking at me. "Because I've got two locations for you."

"The *last two*?"

He nodded and bounced a fist off his lips, but despite that, I could see the hint of smile. "Yeah."

Uncle Jerry cheered, Anza clapped loudly, and I actually gave the little bastard a bear hug. He pushed me away, but it didn't seem like he was trying too hard.

The Mexico stop, where we hoped to find the third piece of the lamp, was about ninety minutes east of where we were at that moment.

"This is good," our pilot said, "'cause we only got another two or three hours of fuel."

"Good news, then," I said.

He shook his head. "Not all good."

Bringing up the World Drug Lord navigation system, he showed me the trouble. Our first stop was near Mexico's eastern seaboard.

A very tiny community called—

"El Tajin," Uncle Jerry said, giving the 'j' a Spanish 'h' pronunciation, which drew a warm look from Anza.

He pointed at the display. "Look here. That's it there. That's El Tajin."

The digital map animated our path, and after a few moments the digital representation of the area gave way to a satellite photo of our destination.

Squinting, I said, "Looks like... like a mall."

"Ha, no mall," Anza said and sidled up next to me. I slid over to give her half of the copilot seat.

"You know it?"

"Sure," she said, tapping the screen. "The town is Poza Rica... well, closest town. El Tajin is actually a—"

"Skating rink?" I offered.

"Cheese factory?" Jerry said.

"Alpaca clothier?" the Actor said from the back.

My head rocked toward our friend in the cabin. "Wow, nice one."

Anza wasn't having as much fun with her story as we were. "Stop talking weird things! El Tajin is a pyramid."

I stared at the flattened cubish shape on the display. "You're shitting me."

Anza explained to us that El Tajin had been around for thousands of years. "I don' think nobody knows who builded it."

"Aztecs?"

"No, this is before them. Maybe Olmecs."

She said that various histories of the region claimed it had likely been a temple built in honor of the thunder and lightning gods. Looking at the ground surrounding the ruins, it all seemed pretty arid for a bunch of natives making their mascot a lightening god.

Anza thought about what I'd said for a moment. "Well... where there is lightning, there is rain sometimes. Maybe they prayed to lightning god for rain?"

It made sense, sure. Still, something nagged at me.

Our pilot took his eyes off what he was doing and looked at the satellite map more intently, which I found unnerving, despite little fear of hitting anything tens of thousands of feet in the air.

"What's there now?" he asked.

"Ruins and shops, mostly. Tourist attraction," she said. "Fat, drunken white people get off cruise ships, pack into buses, and visit sometimes."

Uncle Jerry perked up. "Sounds like my kinda place."

Anza talked to herself for a moment, manipulating the digital map in front of her. "I don' think..." She paused, lost in thought. "It's so small, there isn't even teentsy airstrip there."

Uncle Jerry flipped through several layers and maps on his drug-kingpin nav-sat layout but only found options to the north and far south.

"Sorry," he said. "No runway, no landing."

"Wait," the Actor said and walked up from the back, nibbling on a bag of potato chips. "Can't we land on an interstate or something?"

We all looked at him.

"Like back in Japan," he added, "but you know, this time on purpose."

Ninety minutes later, when we got to El Tajin, Uncle Jerry did a couple of large circles, looking for a field or road that might serve as a place to land. Staring down on the pyramid, this time in the real world and not a satellite image, it looked like something from an alien world.

Anza came up next to me at the small window, halfway down the fuselage.

"Is still considered a sacred place. I have heard there is a cult that still worships there... when all the fat white tourists have gone for the day."

"Would they be dangerous?"

She frowned. "Zealots is always dangerous."

"Sure, but would they be, uh, hungry zealots?" She gave me a blank stare. "Cannibals?"

"Yech, no."

"Good."

"But human sacrifice was big thing back in the day."

"Great," I said. "But, um, not so much *today*, right?"

"Who knows with zealots? Today, tomorrow. I don' know if those guys got really good calendars. From what I remember, all their old ones seem to end very bad."

We had the option of dropping in or around Mexico City, not necessarily at the international airport but just outside where, as Uncle Jerry put it, "We got some under-the-radar-type choices."

"So, that's good," I said, then saw his expression. "Or… no?"

"No, not really. Two things."

"Shit," I said. "Give 'em to me in reverse terrifying order."

"Okay," he said and thought for a moment. "First, if we land then take the car to El Tajin, we're not talking about a bang-on interstate system."

"Many of the roads are shit," Anza said, surprising the rest of us into silence. She added: "Silt, I mean. Silt. All dirt, in places."

"Uh, huh," the Actor said, eyeballing her. "You musta misspoked."

"So we're talking like three or four hours just to get there by car after we've landed," said Jerry. "Then, same trip back to the airport."

I closed my eyes. The countdown on my wrist read just over seventeen hours. Option number one was just too big of a chunk of my time left.

"Okay," I said. "Seems like not a great option."

"To make it worse," he said, "number two is our plane here."

"What about it?"

"She's been to these parts before… not some stopover, but on, you know, business."

"Oh…"

"Right. Which means when we drop in there may be some questions as to why the not-Honduran drug dealer isn't aboard."

"That doesn't sound promising," the Actor said.

"And I guarantee our not-Honduran drug dealer hasn't posted an Instagram picture of his empty hangar, hashtag-takegoodcareofmybaby, letting everyone know that we've borrowed it."

"Well, no," Anza said. "Instagram is for food, anyhow."

We all looked at her.

"What?" she said. "Totally true."

As we stared, the Actor said what the rest of us were thinking, "I can never quite tell when you are joking."

She shrugged, and I saw the tiniest smile come to her lips.

Back to the problem at hand. "So we either have eats up too much time or possible death at the hands of definitely not happy drug dealers."

"Sorta rules it out."

"Right."

We decided that if we were going to get the next piece in time, we'd have to find a way to get the plane down near the El Tajin pyramid.

Circling the site, I looked down and saw the various stone structures surrounded by fields, brush, and grassy steppes. Cutting between parts of the site like some ancient one-to-one scale blueprint were pathways carved out in the grass, either by design or by the wear of thousands of feet over time.

An incongruously new building sat on one edge of the site: a long rectangle which, according to Google, was the tourist pavilion.

The El Tajin website showed pictures of a miniature display model of the ancient ruins and said it could be found just inside the gift shop. There were also headphones for rent for walking tours, or every ninety minutes, a guided tour (for a few bucks more).

Gazing out the window again, the entire site was really breathtaking. However, as a structure, the pyramid wasn't all that impressive. Most of the surrounding site was a suggestion of something more grand, so much more powerful.

I frankly couldn't tell if it was something of a false promise.

Like *Oh, you shoulda seen this place back in the day. Yeah, most of what's left is just dusty footprints, but back then?,* punctuated with a rising whistle.

Maybe that's the cynic in me. Or too many years of being let down by advertising. But how many times do we discover too late the carrot is made out of stick?

Still, the crumbling pyramid was hard to take your eyes off of. It was a pyramid, but not in the junior-high-school history-class sense. No apparent golden triangle or perfect proportions coming to a pointy tip at the top.

Square at its base, it rose up with a series of blocks, each hollowed out. Then, far before coming to a peak, it stopped and flattened out. Like the folks working on it had shown up one day, hung over, and said "Aw, fuck it. That's high enough" and crawled home to climb back in bed.

"It's really beautiful," I said to Anza, who'd joined me again at the window.

"Our next piece is there?" she asked.

I nodded.

"That's interesting, Raz. The last place was a temple. This here, we call this a pyramid. But it's also a house of worship."

"Huh."

"So this is why the devilspawn cannot go inside to get the pieces, you think?"

"Jesus."

She smiled. "Exactly!"

"Wait, what about the first piece?" the Actor chimed in. "We found it at an old Belgian guy's house. Not exactly hallowed ground."

Damn, he had a point.

After a moment, I said: "You know, the old guy said his great-grandad got hit in the head by it. Maybe it was on the way to some cathedral and an old Belgian dude's skull got in the way."

"Could be," Anza said and smiled at me.

"So I guess holy places are kind of outta bounds for them. Only way they can get inside if some a schmuck like me goes in, not as minion, but someone not directly affiliated… by free will."

She smiled and tapped her temple.

We broke away from our circling, and Uncle Jerry arched the plane a bit north.

Slipping up into the cockpit, I wearily sat down in the copilot's seat again, despite having no responsibilities at the helm.

"You know, for as often as I've sat here in the past few days, I should know something about how to fly this thing."

"You wanna learn?"

I thought about that for a moment. "When I was younger, I wanted to learn how to fly."

"Yeah?"

"Well, yeah. And I wanted to be a physicist… and a lawyer. And a hockey player."

Uncle Jerry laughed. "There always seems like so much damn time, huh?"

I smiled and felt a selfish lump raise in my throat. "Until you realize you're running low. You're racing toward forty, and you're not going to be a lawyer or physicist or hockey player."

"Did you really want to be any of those?"

"No," I said and had to laugh. "Not really. But it was nice to believe I still had options."

Uncle Jerry looked at me, then back out the windshield.

"Raz, listen, I don't know much. And the stuff I did find out, hell, I've burned away half of that with weed and booze."

"Just half?"

"Maybe more, I dunno. Burned away a lotta my math skills, too," He laughed and threw a crumpled napkin at my head. "But nobody makes it through life without regrets. Nobody."

I looked at my hands. *Right.*

"You gotta remember, the only thing a regret is… is wondering what would have happened had you done something else. But that says you *did* something. You made a choice. Right or wrong, you picked a path and went that way."

For a minute, I was quiet. "But what if you… maybe you picked the wrong path after all?"

"Who can tell? Just because there was another path, that don't mean it was the right one because yours didn't turn out so good. You make the best of the path you're on."

"You think that's the secret?"

"Brother," he said, banking slightly toward the midday sun, "that's why you're out here. I'm proud of you for it."

"Then why are you out here?"

He shrugged. "I wasn't doing nothing special. Between employment opportunities. And this sounded really nuts." He gave me one of those Jerry smiles that makes everything okay.

Which, of course, it wasn't.

A few minutes later, he pointed to a long streak of highway. Not *very* long, however. "We may be able to drop her there."

The Actor stepped up into the cockpit's doorway and said, "Really?"

"Maybe. Then y'all can pull Cujo out and get the next piece while I find somewhere to fuel up."

"Okay," I said, mostly because I felt that if I affirmed what he'd just said it would make the plan more concrete, more possible.

Luckily, as we began to drop, the road ahead seemed completely clear.

Eduardo Loza, standing at front the tour bus, tipped the last of the El Presidente forty-ounce bottle he was holding into a small paper cup and handed it to a nearby passenger who looked at it with a blank expression.

Tucking the empty bottle into a paper sack so he could refill it later, he then reached down into his beat-up Styrofoam cooler, grabbed another large bottle of beer, uncapped it, and poured out another tiny portion for his next guest.

Despite the promise of a wonderful day at "a fifteen-hundred-year-old Mexican pyramid," what brought many of these pasty tourists from their cruise ships onto his native Mexican excursion had really been the phrase "free Mexican beer will be provided."

And free it was. But less glamorous, it would seem, was that a sweaty, sixty-something tour guide would be doling it out in little wrinkled paper cups from large, warm bottles.

When Eduardo looked out the window and caught sight of the charred shack that had at one time been a roadside vegetable stand, he said, "In about ten minutes, we will arrive at the amazing El Tajin pyramid."

There was a smattering of applause, and the tour guide smiled politely, briefly gripping the back of the driver's seat as the bus shifted on the crumbling road.

He spat a few words to the man at the wheel, smoothed his dark mustache with a thumb and forefinger, and once again offered his practiced smile.

"We will break into two groups, and I will lead the first group. The sec—"

The driver tried to interrupt him in a low, harsh whisper but was once again dismissed quickly. Eduardo's smile wavered but did not break.

"Okay," he said, "it seems our second guide, Miss Carmenia, has been hit with a touch of amoebic dysentery."

The entire bus gasped.

"Don't worry, she stayed home. If she has not been hospitalized, she may join us for the second half of the tour."

The bus driver twisted the wheel again, and Eduardo, off balance, gripped the tourist sitting in front of him, nearly tossing the man into the aisle.

He growled at the driver, "Ramon!"

"*Señor, la—*"

"Shh," the group leader said and again addressed the crowd. "So this will mean for those in the back, some people will have to repeat what I am saying to them."

He nodded, and as if on cue, they all waggled their heads in return.

"And please, try to get it verbatim. I have worked very hard on my presentation for accuracy and maximum cultural impact."

The harried bus driver tried again, this time more aggressively. "*Señor!*"

Eduardo once again shushed him and turned toward his cruise patrons. Just past the road's shoulder, he caught site of a rusted out '67 Ford overturned in a gully and silently cursed, because he should by now be somewhere between the fourth and fifth paragraphs of his Approaching Monologue.

"*Eduardo!*"

Ignoring the driver, he couldn't remember where in his memorized script he'd left off. He covered by asking: "Are there any questions?"

One hand slowly went up.

"Yes?"

"I was only wondering…" a woman in a pink polyester pantsuit said shakily, pointing to somewhere behind him. "Is that plane supposed to be there?"

Eduardo spun around to see a beautiful, gleaming white jet growing larger in the windshield and forgot about his speech entirely.

He could just make out the expression on the pilot's face.

Inexplicably, the man seemed to be laughing.

Not getting an answer, I asked again, "Jesus, man, what's so goddamn funny?"

Uncle Jerry's hands trembled as he gripped the jet's wheel. "It's like… the worst possible scenario."

"That's funny?"

"Nah, it's kinda terrifying," he said. "I don't do so well with emotional extremes."

The Actor took three long strides from his seat into the cockpit, got a look out the front windows, and yelled, "Pull up, man, pull up!"

"Roger, doing that."

Our jet wheezed and then revved as it arched upward again, missing what looked like a tour bus packed with people by about fifty feet.

We banked hard, and I caught sight of a heavyset man near the front of the bus, inexplicably holding a large bottle of beer in one hand and a tiny paper cup in the other.

Our eyes briefly locked as we passed over, and we were close enough that I witnessed him making the sign of the cross, his lips moving in what either seemed to be an uttered prayer or a curse, and then he was gone from my sight.

After a few moments, our pilot got a handle on the plane again, and we fell into a low holding pattern—a large circle above El Tajin.

Locking in the auto pilot, Uncle Jerry joined us in the back cabin.

"Well, I gave it a shot," he said, plopping into a comfy lounger. "But man, we ain't landing here."

We all nodded.

Discouraged, I tried calculating our time back to Mexico City, then the return drive.

The Actor vocalized a version of what I'd come up with— "We're screwed."— and stepped up to his sake keg once again.

"Pour me one, *por favor*," Anza said.

We sat quietly for a full minute until Uncle Jerry finally spoke.

"You know… shit. Uh, there is something else we could try."

"What?" I said, unsure if I'd heard him correctly. "What do you mean?"

"There's another option," he said, wiping his face with an open hand. "But to be honest, it's not a very good one."

"What is it?"

The belly of the plane was cold, dark, and smelled like damp steel and motor oil.

We'd followed our pilot down in hopes of a miracle, but in truth, the weight of our reality was already gripping my heart.

Standing behind his beloved 1976 Trans Am, Jerry traced a finger across its glossy black spoiler. "This is a smugglers' plane," he said. "They plan for contingencies."

"Okay."

"Like, say, if a pair of US Air Force F-111s rocket up and flank this plane, forcing it to land."

"Uh," I said, "and...?"

"And the emergency contingency then—only in an emergency—is to drop from a trapdoor in the jet's belly, and in theory, parachute down to safety.

"In theory."

"Yeah," our pilot said, crossing his arms and leaning against the rollaway door behind him. "Far as I know, he's never been desperate enough to do it."

"Oh," I said.

"Because it is pretty batshit crazy."

"Right."

"Wait," the Actor piped up. "You expect one of us to strap on a parachute and drop like rock from some hole under the plane at ten thousand feet? No one here knows how to do that, man! You could fucking land in the fucking desert fucking miles from fucking anywhere and *fucking die*. That's ludicrous!"

Anza's eyes widened, but I don't think it was because he'd sworn a little.

"Nah," Uncle Jerry said, walked to the opposite wall, tripped a set of latches, and yanked back on the low paneling labeled, in green lettering, "EMERGENCY USE ONLY".

"No one's gonna be wearing a parachute."

I considered messing with the volume button on the radio but knew, of course, that wouldn't make a difference. Just one of those male habits, I think… You get a bit confused, turn the volume down.

Except, of course, the radio wasn't on.

I checked both tiny windows—yep, both were rolled up. But in truth, I wasn't sure these ones went down in the first place.

"Raz!"

My dull focus was on the noise, so crazy loud, thinking that if maybe I could somehow fix that, then all the rest would work out. But it was just all some sort of avoidance, of course.

"*Raz!*"

To be fair, I wasn't sure if I was actually trying to ignore the extreme terror of the situation or the dizzying nausea that was washing over me.

Damn. I really didn't feel good. And not just because of the endless spinning and spinning and spinning—my stomach was already a twist of nerves before I dropped from the plane.

"*Raz-PYU-tin!*"

"What?" I said over the scream of the wind. "Uncle Jerry?"

"Yeah… whattya doin', man?"

Trying not to puke, that's what I was doing. That was pretty much it. All that whoosh noise and the spinning. Jesus, the spinning. I was definitely going to barf.

No question.

My friend's voice, I realized a bit absentmindedly, was coming out of the radio. He was still back in the plane he'd just dropped me from.

"I'm… man, I'm falling. Really fast."

Obviously.

"Did you *crank the fever*?" he asked.

The wind was roaring and banging against the windows, like I'd somehow made it angry and it wanted to get in to settle some score. Uncle Jerry was yelling again, but I could still barely hear him over the angry wind.

"What?" I said. "Um... what? Crank the fever? You stoned or something, man?"

I could hear the urgent voices of Anza and the Actor, hollow and echoey, in the cockpit behind him. But they were talking so quickly that I couldn't make out any of what they were saying either.

To their credit, back on the jet, both had offered to join me in the weird little vehicle, however, I'm pretty sure the Actor felt safe to volunteer because I'd already so adamantly turned Anza down. Just too dangerous.

Uncle Jerry yelled over the radio, "Did you *spank the beaver?*"

"No," I said, oddly sleepy. "Not really the time or the place, man. What—"

"RAZ," he yelled, and the fear straining his voice sobered me up a little. I finally found the volume control on the tablet-sized screen in front of me and thumbed it as loud as it would go. "You've got to *yank the red lever* next to your head! C'mon, man, you're... Christ, man, you're falling like a rock!"

No, I was falling like I'd been pushed from an airplane at ten thousand feet in what could only be described as half motorcycle, half Tylenol capsule. Two wheels, moto-style body, with a sort of enclosure-slash-fairing that was a thick, clear clamshell above me, locked down by a wraparound fiberglass body.

If *Mad Max* had been dropped onto the grid in *TRON*, this was the type of light cycle he would have ridden.

"Yeah, yeah," I said and looked up. The looped metal handle hung down, clanking and twinkling inches from my skull. "Yanked it, man! Didn't do anything cool."

There was silence over the phone-radio for a moment. Then I heard: "*Oh. Oh, shit.*"

My chest was beginning to ache as the weird motorcycle actually slowed its spinning and settled into a sort of tilt forward, nose down. The bike's curved windshield looked as though it had turned into a terrifying wraparound HD screen. A television with just one channel and only one program called *Falling to My Death.*

I couldn't help but laugh a little.

"*Raz!*"

Ugh, this guy with the yelling all the time.

"Cable's out, man." I laughed again. Whatever.

"*The chute... it didn't open yet!*"

"Ya think?"

"*Well, shit man,*" he said, shushing the voices behind him. "*Can... can ya wiggle it?*"

"I don't think wiggling it is going to make a difference."

"*Do* something, *man!*"

"I... it just..." I said and closed my eyes and thought of Carissa. My wife. I was glad, so glad, she couldn't see me. I was happy she never really saw me for the fool and screw-up I was.

"*Raz!*"

Maybe it was better like this.

"*Raz, please, do something.*" Anza's voice. It hurt my heart a little to hear her so distressed.

"It don't work, Anza," I said and tapped the hanging red metal handle with my fingertips. "Just... doesn't work." It chimed like an old-timey doorbell each time it was tapped. *Ring ring, ring ring ding.*

"Do something, don' just... please, Raz." She was crying.

"Might be better... just... like this."

She said something else, but the wind was growing so much louder. Couldn't hear.

"*No, let me. Let me!*" It was the Actor. "*Raz.*"

"Geez, let it go."

"*Listen—*"

"Nothing... really left to do here," I said.

"*Listen to me. If you hit the ground, I'm having Jerry fly me directly to Atlanta to see your dying wife.*"

"That's cool of you, man. Tell her—"

"*I will tell her, Raz, that you gave up on her.*"

Wait.

No.

My vision darkened.

He kept it up. "*I'm going to tell her that like usual, you got halfway there and gave up. You gave up on her.*"

I wanted a moment before answering so I could properly compose myself. "Fuck you."

"*Raz, I will tell her you were within sight of the finish line, but you simply gave up. You gave up on her.*"

Light refracted off the water in my eyes, making it nearly impossible to see.

"*You gave up on her, right when she needed you most.*"

I screamed at him. I screamed and thrashed and screamed more. My fists were aching, and I could taste blood in my mouth.

I lashed out around me, slamming the console, punishing the vehicle's ceiling and felt the heavy iron handle smash against my hand and saw a small splatter of blood hit the windshield.

Although I wanted to tear at the seat beneath me, my breath shot out of me as an incredible punch socked me in the lower abdomen, and my body rocked forward and then flung backward again. I saw stars and light, then, for a brief moment, only darkness.

I was floating, floating… and my vision spun slowly, then cleared. The wind… still there… was so much quieter now.

Lifting my head from beneath the enclosed motorcycle's handlebars, I had to wait a moment for my mind to follow. My thighs stung where a double set of belts kept me strapped in place. Through the windshield ahead of me, I saw the horizon. Just below, a long expanse of dead grass.

I sighed. "'Chute's open."

Over the radio, my friends cheered between loud snotty sobs. I then became aware of tears spilling down my own cheeks. Yep. I was so lucky to have people like them on my side.

"*Okay,*" Uncle Jerry said, again shushing the others, only this time they were happy shushes. "*There's a sat phone embedded in radio. Bring up the keypad, and you should be able to just mash down on the 'one' key to ring me right here in the cockpit."*

"Got it."

The very next moment, my wheels hit the Mexican ground with a thud.

Waiting for the bike to topple over, I looked down and saw instead that some sort of flexi landing contraption had broken my fall and was now holding me and the weird bike upright.

From a distance, it probably looked like the bike was up on a stand on some kid giant's dusty shelf somewhere.

"Got it," I said again and took a few deep breaths to try to get my brain back in gear.

"Okay, we're heading out to find the next piece. You got... about fifteen hours to get there."

"Right," I said and sucked my stomach in, clicked away the restraints, then found the latch to release a gull-wing door on the bike's right side. "I'll see you guys in New Orleans."

My landing had been in a large, flat field, but being the dry season in this part of the world, "field" simply meant "long expanse of dead grass and possibly creepy snakes."

Between the two handlebars was a rectangular touchscreen display that appeared to control everything related to the bike. With a couple taps, I was able to coax a Google map out of it to show me where I was.

Only about a mile and a half from El Tajin. I just needed to get to a road a little south of me and truck along. Fortunately, because the drug kingpin who owned the weird superbike knew that an emergency escape might mean he'd land in a remote area, the vehicle was completely over the top, even for a drug kingpin.

In my limited experience, bigshot drug dealers were kinda like everyday people who've just got a lot more money than they've got sense/taste/class/laudable driving records.

It seems the run-of-the-mill uber wealthy (a snap judgment here, sure) blow their dough in ways to say, *"Hey, look at me. I have so much more money than all of you!"*

The difference is drug dealers aren't necessarily after that sort of attention. Attention can lead to FBI sting operations, federal incarceration, and subsequent amateur jailhouse proctology.

But they *were* drug dealers. And a good businessman will keep up with the quality of his product, often daily or even hourly, to where one might witness conversations like, *"Someone is stealing my dryer time! Clothes,* listen, listen, *clothes go in wet and come up frickin' wet, man! You know, they got guys, engineers, right?... that calibrate those machines to the frickin' second, man. The muthaluvin' second! So, if my clothes are coming out wet, someone or some*thing *is stealing my goddamn drying time! Mine! Time, man. They're stealing my TIME!"*

So...

One could assume a drug dealer at the top of his game would be prone to making some rather excessive (read: paranoid delusional) choices.

The knobby tires on the motorcycle were almost as large as the bike itself. The tires were so huge, in fact, I was convinced that in the event of a water landing, the bike would bob down once, then inevitably float and allow me to simply drive to the nearest coastline.

I mention this because you might question my choice to forgo the Mexican road system and instead take a more direct route, as the crow flies... if the crow didn't fly but instead piloted a drug dealer's $300,000 tricked-out super cycle through semi-desert scrub brush.

"Super cycle." My voice bounced back to me off the curved Plexiglas of the bike's interior, and it sounded oddly hollow. "Nah, that name sucks."

I pressed my thumb onto the touchscreen display over a small square emblazoned with the word START, complete with an animation showing tiny clouds of exhaust puffing from the bottom of the letter S, as if it were a tailpipe.

The rocketbike—Ugh, no. Rocketbike sounds like something from a bad eighties movie—roared as it fired up, which told me it had a bit of kick under the hood. Or maybe more accurately, since it didn't have a hood, under the flabby guy riding it.

The navigation software directed me to head southeast, so I turned the front wheel until the golden line on the plasma screen was right ahead of me like Dorothy's yellow brick road.

However, without a real road, naturally the going was a bit uneven. But it seemed I could ride at a safe, twenty-mile-an-hour clip without too much concern about cliffs or giant holes or small spiny animals with razor-sharp teeth.

The sun was already making its move toward the horizon. It would be dark within the next few hours, so I didn't have any time to waste. The Actor seemed sure I was chasing after the glass globey bit of the lamp out here, and if I was going to find something like that at the pyramid, I'd have a lot better luck looking around during the daylight hours.

That was the main reason to get there before nightfall. Another reason, though relatively minor, might be that Anza's stories about some killer cult possibly lurking around at night gave me the King Kamehameha willies. Yes, daytime would be better.

Weaving and darting to avoid the occasional bush or tree or rock, I twisted the accelerator and picked up the pace.

The radio came up with a few taps on the LCD display, and I searched for something to listen to. Hitting "seek" tripped the numbers on the FM dial, and it ran through the VHF part of the radio spectrum, its megahertz range, then flipped over to AM and cycled through the kilohertz range.

See what a dozen years of radio gets ya? Very valuable frequency breakdown knowledge right there. Totally useless. My gift to you.

When the radio started filtering through the weather emergency bands, I gave up and looked away. So much for the celebrated "Mexican radio."

With the day arcing toward night, the horizon shimmered with heat pouring in waves toward the heavens. Mesmerized, I stared through the windshield and watched as great and often terrifying figures manifested in the confusion of light and air and heat... beasts of prey that predated even the ruins I was now closing in on with the bi-racer. *No, that doesn't work. Bi-racer sounds like a sexually indecisive marathoner.*

As I approached, the unsettling, wispy figures of the desert would often transform into the skeletal remains of brambles or massive rock outcroppings, then once they were regulated to my rearview mirrors, sleeping giants would shimmy in and out of existence.

Eventually, they were gone from my view entirely, flung back somewhere into their own universe. Lost in thought, I was startled by the radio. A solitary female's voice reading a steady stream of numbers: "*57, 42, 17, 36...*"

The numbers appeared to have no particular pattern. At least none that I could immediately discern.

No music accompanied the solemn reading. Just a distant, lonely woman's voice running through a list of what sounded like random numbers. I tried to concentrate on them to discern their purpose. A list of coordinates? A secret coded message? The world's worst lottery drawing?

No. And like the presumption of the mind that a TV or movie character's mouth is the source of their vocalizations—and not, instead, the television's embedded speakers—I stared at the radio's plasma display, hoping to pick up any visual clues to what the list of numbers was trying to tell me.

Which is why, when the road dropped out from underneath the bike, I looked up just in time to do nothing about it except belt out a shrill, protracted scream.

Uncle Jerry brought the jet down into a smooth landing and was directed to a private hangar on the northwest skirt of the New Orleans airport.

"Hangar 47B-3, Don Cheetle. Nice to see you back. I assume you're not staying very long."

Uncle Jerry keyed his mic back. "Right, yep. He's indisposed at the moment. A bit of an infection after getting his third nipple pierced, uh, so he stayed home."

"Oh," the voice on the radio crackled back. Then, less enthusiastically: "Okay, just drift into the hangar, and the disembarking crew will be there to help out."

"Roger," Jerry said, forcing a smile into his voice. Then he swallowed hard, stared intently out the windows, and mumbled to himself, "Disembarking crew…"

No longer keyed into the radio, he yelled: "Anza!"

Returning from the plane's bathroom, drying her hair with a hand towel, she had finally heard the third time Uncle Jerry barked out her name.

"What?" she said. "What are you yelling for me about, Uncle Jerry?"

He motioned for her to come into the cockpit. Working her arms into an Arizona State University sweatshirt she'd found in a drawer, she asked him what was up.

"Listen, the ground crew will likely know we ain't the not-Honduran drug dealer's crew."

"Is that bad for us?"

"Not necessarily," he said, then continued in a measured tone. "Now, you are… delightfully, you know, Mexican. You could casually suggest you're his, like, sister or something."

"Why?"

"Because, you know, it's kinda similar."

"No, is not!"

"And because, to be honest, New Orleans is a pretty drummed-up town. Sure, they're an easygoin' bunch, but in the stuff they ain't so easy about—like matters involving money—they don't let much slide."

"Cannot you just say to them that we have borrowed the drug king jet?"

"No," Uncle Jerry said and scratched his week-old beard. "No, that would sound like we killed him."

"Really?"

"Uh… yeah."

"But," she said, sitting down in the copilot's seat, then immediately standing up again, "I cannot say I am his sister. I am a terrible liar! This is what was said only just earlier ago! Don't make m—"

"Come on, we need you to pull this off."

"Why?"

"Because if we raise some eyebrows, the local drug lord, a Cajun with bad teeth—I met him one time—he might take us up to some dark warehouse in the marina district to find out why we've got the plane. Peel off our skin, stuff like that. And that's after we tell him."

"This would have been better information to learn before we are landing at the airport," Anza said.

"Yep," he said. "Can't argue with that."

"Uncle Jerry! I can' do tha—"

"No, no." The Actor's voice floated up from the back of the plane. "No, don't ask the *actor* to play a hardened member of some international drug syndicate in your tarmac pop-up theater! No, why would you even consider asking the only *actor* here to play the part?"

Uncle Jerry looked at him. "My thoughts exactly."

Anza, tears beginning to rise, pleaded with the middle-aged pilot as they pulled into the hangar. "Uncle Jerry, please have him do it! I cannot!"

He looked at the Actor. "I don't trust him."

The Actor winced and looked away for a moment. More quietly, he said, "You don't have much of a choice. Gimme a shot here to make things right."

Wiping away tears, Anza cast her eyes down. "This is not something I can do."

"Uncle Jerry," the Actor said, looking into the man's eyes. "I… I'm sorry about Hawaii. I was just… I'm just tired."

Anza took a quick breath and looked between the two of them. "What happen in Hawaii?"

"We're all tired, man!"

"I know, I know. It's not a good excuse. But trust me. Let me make it up to you," the Actor said. "Let me do what I do."

Uncle Jerry eyeballed him as the jet came to a halt in front of a small hangar with its door rolled open. Before they came to a complete stop, a golf cart rumbled toward them containing four large men in matching blue coveralls. Anza and the Actor watched as they disappeared from view. The pilot stared at the Actor, weighing his options.

Outside, there was the sound of metallic rattling as the crew secured the plane's front wheel. Moments later, there was a rapping on the outer hull.

Uncle Jerry exhaled a deep breath. "Okay, what's your idea?"

Chapter Twenty-Three

While doing a header over the lip of some sort of desert-dry gully, there was a brief moment where I unnaturally pitched forward, and my body was actually parallel with the ground. I blamed the Big Wheel-type tires on the motorcycle.

Hanging only by the crisscrossed seatbelt around my waist and legs, I bounced at least twice on the front tire, and my flabby arms flapped like broken bird wings as my fingers dangled somewhere beneath the handlebars. I felt like a baby being aggressively carried from one room to the next by an angry parent.

The front tire finally sank into some soft dirt, which sent the rear of the bike arching back down toward the ground, slowly at first, then much quicker, and my head whipped back against the headrest while my wrist got a fresh battering from the parachute release lever.

Relatively unhurt and upright, I let out a huge breath. And then I watched helplessly as the bike tipped over sideways, taking me with it, and landed very hard against the ground.

For the moment, I was totally good with lying there inside the relative safety of the bike's capsulelike interior. The motor had cut out, and it would have been completely quiet had it not been for the radio.

"72, 58, 12..."

Having earned a big fat D in geography (and *that* was only because we'd all been given passing grades after Mr. Hendrickson beat the shit out of one of the kids in front of us for smashing a half dozen compasses with a muddy Doc Marten), I'm not good with topography or how land masses form, ebb, and flow. However, as I caught my breath watching the dirt settle around me, I would have guessed this trench-type area had been part of a river or big stream at some point.

The flat area ahead just outside my windshield raised back up to a ridge, like an embankment. Still on my side, I twisted my head and looked upward. After sliding the sunshade back, I saw that the dried stream bed ran at least two hundred yards before melting into the horizon.

Here, someone would be sheltered from the desert's cold, harsh winds. Sure, during the day's punishing heat, the wind would be a blessing, but at night the desert is a thief without pockets. When the evening comes and the sand below loses its grip on what it's taken from the sky, it grows very cold. To be sheltered from the wind, then, could mean the difference between living through the night or dying in the dark.

"I bet there's some really creepy ghosts around here when the sun goes down," I said to hear my own voice. Then I kind of regretted those words as they passed my lips.

For the moment, I was happy to lie there and gaze out the windshield as the dust around me settled and tinkled against the plastic and metal of the weird motorcycle.

"It's quiet," I said. "Too quiet."

Actually, it wasn't too quiet. In fact, it was a very pleasant and calming quiet, which I found completely unnerving for some reason, immersed in my little dust cocoon.

I was admittedly simply busying my head, avoiding any chance to properly observe my situation, because my gut told me something was really, really wrong.

Keeping on my path of avoidance, I thumbed the radio's volume.

"*19, 7, 57, 42, 17...*"

"Worst. Song. Ever," I said.

"It's not a song," a disembodied voice said calmly.

I stared straight ahead, waiting for the body of the aforementioned voice to appear.

It didn't. At least, not right away.

By now most of the dust had settled back to the ground, and so I spun this way and that, trying to catch sight of who'd spoken.

"It's a message," the voice said.

Finally pinpointing its origin, I threw my head farther back and saw a shotgun pointing at my head. Instinctively, I put my hands up, but in the motorcycle's little plastic dome, they didn't go very far.

"What is this machine you are riding?"

My answer—and it would have been a good one, only it got stuck somewhere around my Adam's apple—was basically a slightly panicky, squeaky choking sound. The man holding the shotgun took a few steps around the bike, the weapon never wavering from its bead on me. Despite the heat swirling around us, even in the early evening, he was in full motorcycle leathers.

"I think… I think it is quite cool, this machine of yours," he said. "It's a motorbike shaped like a .38 caliber slug. It's some type of… motor… motobullet."

Motobullet? Shit, that's good.

Then my entire world shifted and rocked, and I heard the strained grunts of several other men, some barking in Spanish, as they lifted me and the bike upright. A ragged ball of fear spun in my abdomen, and if I'd had anything in my stomach, it would have likely ended up splattered upon the inner windshield of the bike.

Twisting my neck from side to side and squinting through the light haze still hanging in the air, I saw about three dozen Mexicans on Harleys. Well, that was an assumption on my part. To be fair, I really couldn't tell exactly what they were.

So they could've been, you know, Hondas or Suzukis, sure.

The fact that I'd not heard them roll up must have meant they were already nearby.

Shotgun seemed to be bit agitated with me. He lifted his open hand toward me, and I looked at him and shrugged.

"The numbers?" he asked. "On the radio, right? I said… it's a message."

"Oh, sorry. Right," I said. "So, what is the message?

Looking at me through a squint, he sized me up and lowered the shotgun. Then he took his outstretched hand, wrapped in a fingerless leather glove, and rubbed it across his stubbly face.

"The message? That... that is not yet clear." He said it with such weight that it took me a few moments to realize that he had basically just said he didn't have any idea what the broadcast meant.

"Oh," I said. "Well, good chat. I'll just be headin' out, then, if—"

Seeing my hand move toward the ignition, he cocked the weapon and raised the shotgun to his shoulder again, its stock pressed against his sun-kissed cheek. It was suddenly so quiet you could hear a pin drop.

Or, more correctly, the soft *tink* as the expelled shotgun shell fell to the dirt at his feet.

An older man with a gray beard and ponytail came up beside Shotgun, scowling. "Why do you do that? You waste shells all the time with the *click-click, clickety-click!*"

The old guy bent down, blew the dirt out of the shell, and put it in the pocket of a flannel shirt beneath his open leather jacket. The two glared at each other, teeth bared.

Looking to score a few points with the guy with the gun, I offered: "Uh, I get it... you know. It's a very dramatic sound."

Shotgun broke away from the old guy, gave me an open look, and pointed in my direction. "See? That's what I've been saying all of this time."

"Right," I added. "Really scary sound, man."

He looked over his shoulder at the other man. The gun was still trained at my head, mind you. "All the grief you give me, old man. Listen to the guy, okay?"

"It had the desired effect," I said, my raised hands a little higher now. "A little bit of pee came out of me, I think."

Shotgun finally lowered his weapon and threw a hand in the air. "Too much sharing!"

"Got it," I said.

He took a step back and gave my bike a long look. "What the hell kind of motorcycle is that?"

I shrugged and lied. "Rental."

"Never heard of that kind. It looks…" He stared at me and blinked slowly. He let out a slow breath through his teeth, then said, "… cumbersome."

Hmm. Didn't expect that word. The way he'd built up to it, I thought he was going to say "dangerous" or "beastly" or even "environmentally irresponsible." With this guy, I felt like I was missing something.

Shotgun walked close again and ran a hand down the bike's flank, found something under the fender, and yanked hard on it. My enclosed motorcycle buckled for a moment, then the flexi-stand spread from the base with a *thwack!* The men who'd been holding me up were sent away with a wave. Shotgun knocked on the thick plastic dome, inches away from my face. I unhitched it, and he flipped it open onto a set of hinges just behind the seat, like he was opening a fast-food burger container.

With a hand resting on the back of my neck, his other still holding his weapon (at least it was now pointed to the sky), he asked me, "Why are you here, *puto*?"

"I'm heading toward the… the ruins out there."

He looked in the direction I was pointing, then back to me. His eyes danced as he said something in Spanish and a couple of his friends laughed.

"You," he said and smiled. "You got lost from your tour group?"

"No group." A cold sweat began to trickle between my shoulder blades.

"Right, right."

He wasn't buying it, and that thought was making it hard for me to swallow properly.

Slowly, he began to walk around the newly-christened motobullet. "So… such a strange vehicle."

Calling back to someone in the group I couldn't see—it was growing darker by the minute—a voice answered back in Spanish. He nodded and came around the front spokes, his short legs straddling the tire.

"You maybe are looking for samples?"

"Um... of what? Samples? What... what are you selling?"

"*Que?*"

"What samples?" I said, talking much too quickly. "Samples, like, Little Debbie's snack samples or maybe carpet remnants?"

I was going to die, no question.

Shotgun's face darkened, and he tossed his weapon from hand to hand as he walked toward the side of the bike once again. "You're an oil man, huh?"

I tried to swallow but couldn't. No spit left. "Uh, breast man, really. If that matters at all..."

Unconvinced, Shotgun moved in a bit closer to me. He smelled like sweat and meat and dust.

"Why are you here, breast man?" he whispered loudly.

"I... I'm going to El Tajin."

"*Why?*"

"I'm searching for something," I said, as honest as I could be. "Something that's supposed to be... hidden in the pyramid. I think."

Slowly, he nodded and took a few steps around behind me. I lost sight of him for several long, long moments. I waited until I couldn't anymore, then spun my head around, ready for the worst.

He was calmly strapping his weapon into a holster at the side of his own motorcycle. "Okay, okay," he said, waving at the remaining men behind him. They retreated back into an area sheltered from the wind, just below the bank of the dry river where they now had a roaring bonfire.

That's when I finally realized that I'd happened upon this group of armed desert men in the middle of their afternoon barbeque. However, not seeing many cows nearby, I decided not to ask what was sizzling on the grill.

"Fine," he said. "I believe you are not here for drilling."

"What? No, no drilling."

He walked around to the other side of the bike, stood at my shoulder, and tapped on the touch display between the handlebars. The screen revealed its radio, but after a few more taps the image changed to Google Maps—and it confirmed my destination: the pyramid of El Tajin.

He leaned back and muttered under his breath. "Very weird bike," he said. "So, you are going to the pyramid now?"

"Yes."

"It's getting late. Quite late, yes? Do you know what that means?" He leaned forward, probing the interior of the bike's enclosure with his hands. "Do you know what happens… when it gets late?" he asked gravely.

In a single heartbeat, I went from feeling relieved and safe to being instantly petrified again. I could only squeak out: "No."

"It will be…" he said, reaching into a slender vertical compartment, and I could no longer see his hand. Slowly, he pulled out something long and metallic, and I fought the urge to close my eyes. "… dark soon."

He held a flashlight out for me, and I clutched it, trying not to show him how badly my hand was shaking.

"Helpful," I said. "Thank you, sir."

He began fiddling with the lights and some controls on the touchscreen, then looked through a couple more compartments he'd found down near my shins. Flipping open one square cubby, he found a wad of bills. I gestured for him to take the money, but he just shot me a dirty look and closed it back up again.

He seemed genuinely interested in my vehicle, but with his hands crisscrossing over my legs and crotch for several moments, I honestly felt a little bit violated.

"Maybe, next time you could butter me up with a couple drinks before all that?"

"Huh?"

"Never mind."

He ignored me and then asked, "What are you looking for at El Tajin?"

I thought, *What the hell?* "A lamp."

"A lamp?"

"Well, a part of a lamp. The glassy bit that clamps onto the base of an oil lamp."

He considered this for a moment. "Don't you think a Walmart or Target store or something would have been a better place to go? An old Mexican pyramid… I don't think they got that there."

"Well, it's a particular glass globe. A specific one."

"And it's at El Tajin?"

I shrugged.

He nodded and rapped on the bike with an open palm, as if giving it his seal of approval. "I never saw any glassy things there, but I don't go there much anymore. As a kid, sure. Now, not so much."

"Well, I gotta look," I said.

"Sure, sure." He pointed back to where his friends were. "You want some brisket? For the road?"

"No, gotta go. On a schedule."

He looked off into middle space, lost focus for a moment, then looked back at me. "You know, in Africa, some places they don't even have clocks."

"Huh," I offered, not having any idea his point. Was this a veiled threat? Like he was saying my time was running out? "So, I mean, no clocks? How do you even know if your pizza's late, then, right?"

What am I even saying?

"But that's the thing… with no clocks, so much less pressure." Shotgun stared at me with a knowing glance. He waited, just staring at me.

The most important thing I learned from being married was that when I wasn't exactly sure what I'd done to make the wife mad at me, there was really only one thing I could say to prevent things from escalating.

"You're right," I said.

"I would wager," he continued, "you would be hard pressed to find one single man or woman on antidepressants or antianxiety medicine in Africa."

"Because no clocks?"

"Right. Not a slave to time," he said, nodding. "As a people, they have far less stress."

Still unsure what we were talking about, I thought for a moment, then offered: "Except, you know, lions."

"Wh— Lions?"

"Well, there is the stress of getting eaten by a lion, I suppose."

"Yes, yes," he said, looking back to the horizon. "There are... the lions. And, also, I understand... hippos. Hippos are quite dangerous. They do not come in multiple colors, as we have been led to believe, with appetites only for tiny glass marbles." He looked at me and nodded slowly once again.

Then I realized it. Nearly every sentence the guy spoke was said in a way that seemed as if he were implying something of great weight or hidden dangers, even if—or maybe especially if—it didn't.

So this guy? A total loon.

"Okay, man," I said. "I gotta run."

"Run," he said, taking a few steps backward, lifting his hands up. "Some men walk, some must run."

"Nice chat," I said and fired up the motobullet.

"Remember, amigo, do not be a slave to time," he spoke loudly over the bike's engine. "Even when we arrive at the movies exactly when it is supposed to start, there are still twenty minutes of unbearable previews..."

"Yep. Uh-huh."

"... and often commercials."

"Right."

"... and the 'turn off your cell phones' video, which often contain... sponsor tie-ins."

I thanked him with a nod, and he gave me a lazy, grinning salute in return. I dropped the bike into gear, exhaling a breath I hadn't realized I'd been holding. Giving the bike a bit of gas, the flexi-stand snapped back into a compartment beneath the bike, and I began to roll away from Shotgun.

"Hey," I said, "so why don't you go there anymore, if I can ask? El Tajin?"

"Oh, saw it a lot as a kid. Not much more to see."

"Right."

"And at night there are some certifiably crazy people that I think do sacrifices and wear masks made of human skulls."

As he walked away, I returned his wave with a smile and a nod. Then I realized he'd just said something of actually scary-level importance, which I should have paid much, much closer attention to.

"Hey, *what*?"

But he was now back laughing with his friends. Probably about the joke he'd just played trying to scare the dumb American on the weird bike.

Yep, that was probably it.

About twenty minutes later, after weaving through dry brush, dead bramble, and the occasional skittish varmint (in desert settings, all things that crawl, with or without legs, are varmints, I believe), I was at El Tajin.

What struck me first while rolling up to the ancient site was the size of the place. That is, for the weight and magnitude of the archeological wonder, thousands of years in the making, it was pretty damn small.

Of course, I was standing at just the northern edge of the site. For all I knew, the place could go on for miles and miles. But even from my vantage point, I could see both adjacent borderlines leading to the other end of the complex—one a mere twenty yards away to the west, the other edge about fifty. Sure, ye ole pyramid site wouldn't likely have been rectangular, but still, from here, it didn't look huge. I don't think urban planning was a big deal to the Aztecs or Olmecs as it was to Americans when they first started quickly cobbling together cities.

Parking the Motobullet™ (I'm totally trademarking that) in a dry trench next to the site, I started walking.

Like the early corresponding properties across the international border to the north, various-sized plots of the temple's city seemed to have been long ago knit together in a patchwork style.

Hey, we need a store. Hammer, saw, drill. *Yikes, ol' man Tutamooples's kid just knocked down the lightning god statue, we need a prison.* Brick, rebar, chicken wire.

In the fading light, I tried to make out specific areas of the site that had not yet been worn down by the wonder-twin powers of sand and wind. I didn't see much to help me discern between a small home or storage hut.

Whereas the scrub land I'd ridden across after meeting the riverbed barbequers had been mostly barren and flat, as I approached El Tajin, it appeared to lift itself from the earth as if it were slowly awakening to greet its new visitor. Thick green tufts of grass mingled with wind-washed rock, both looking as though they'd grown in harmony, right there on the spot.

But it all hinted of a time when hundreds, maybe thousands, of people had walked every day along the same path that I did now. Around me, this might all have been a cluster of homes. Families going about their day-to-day business. They were happy, they were sad, they worried about paying the bills, they didn't like the way the neighbor boy looked at their daughter.

And all of those people, their worries and their joys, were gone and forgotten. The only thing left of them was some jagged bit of stone that might have been the bottom of a wall to their home. Now, a guy sets up a kiosk and charges twenty bucks for strangers to trample right through their home and doesn't even know it.

Stopping for just a moment, I crouched down and got very quiet. I tried to listen for the echo of their voices. The ripple through time of their laughter or their whispers. Instead, not too far away, I heard the honking of a diesel bus.

"Aztec Greyhound," I said and stood, and the bus honked again, three short bursts.

Walking toward the sound, I rounded a corner and was met with a familiar buzzing, not instantly able to place it.

Almost a moment too late, I realized it was a lawn mower. Not a riding one but actually hand pushed. Gas engine, sure, but this old, skinny brown guy with what looked like metal earmuffs strapped to his head was landscaping the ancient archeological site with a push mower *by himself.*

Overachiever.

He whizzed past me, bobbing his chin as he slid by, and I realized he was listening to music. Wondering what melody had his attention so thoroughly, I dismissed the easy (and borderline racist) pick of mariachi music and instead decided he was probably rocking out to ABBA.

Why not?

If you're going to spend hours and hours walking and sweating and getting covered with grass clippings, I think you should be doing it to "Waterloo" or "Dancing Queen."

When I looked to where he'd come from, past several crumbling stone structures, I saw an incongruously modern building. The sun was getting sleepy, which was thankfully making the air cooler by the minute. Still, after about five minutes of walking up and down through the site, I was drenched in sweat.

Standing now at the rear of this newer building, I saw two doors on the back with black stick figures designating where boy peers and girl peers were supposed to unpee.

At that moment, on the right side of the building, a dim overhead floodlight came to life just as a room near it clicked dark.

"Señor!"

This looked like the small gift shop/café/museum area where tourists would gather to spend tourist dollars, so they could bring home refrigerator magnets, T-shirts, and pyramid-shaped salt and pepper shakers to let others somewhat less touristy know they had been to such a magical and wonderful place, and that it probably cost a good chunk of change to get there.

"Señor, can you please return to the bus?"

A graying man with a mustache that shaded a pleasant smile was waving at me with a clipboard.

He looked strangely familiar, but I couldn't place it.

The smile dimmed a little, and he waved at me again impatiently, as if somehow I hadn't seen him, heard him or maybe just didn't understand him. Or maybe he thought I was drunk. Had it been in the years before I'd met my wife, the latter would have been a very good guess.

I twisted my wrist and checked the countdown—no time for chatting with the bus wrangler.

Part of me wanted to head into the gift shop for a little El Tajin intel and get a look at the miniature-scale model or even a map that might give me a layout of the site. But how hard would it be to find a pyramid? So I cut a quick left between two steppes of grass and stone, searching for the ancient stone structure that, if the Actor's Hell-imbued radar was any good, would somewhere inside have the third piece of my lamp.

Okay, I wasn't sure why I thought the glass globe might be in the pyramid itself—or how I was supposed to get inside—rather than anywhere else there, but it seemed if there was something important at this site, it would be there.

Stepping away from the gaze of the tourist pavilion's floodlights, it grew darker by several degrees. In the distance, I heard the bus wrangler call again. Surrounded by the life and death remnants of thousands of people that the world had forgotten, it sounded like an echo of some collective, plaintive cry from so long ago.

Despite that wee bit of spookiness, the site was surprisingly beautiful. And the darker it got each minute just made the place feel more and more magical. Quiet.

No, not quiet. I mischaracterized that. It was serene. Calm. An almost assurance to the quiet. An unspoken promise. However, given all those who'd once lived there had died without a trace, it seemed maybe that promise had been broken.

"*Señor!*"

"Jesus!" I shouted and jumped back. For an old guy, he'd snuck up on me like a Mexican ninja. "Whaddya want, man?"

He gave me a practiced smile. "Amigo, we are leaving here. The bus is about to go."

"Uh… I, no, listen you guys go on without me. I'll grab the next one and catch up."

I went to turn, but he clamped his hand down on my shoulder. Again, he smiled. Well, his lips did. His eyes had narrowed.

"Friend, this is the last bus," he said. "Time for everyone to leave El Tajin."

"No, I… uh… didn't come here with you guys. I was with, you know, um—"

"But you rode out here on the tour bus, no?"

"No, I didn't."

He laughed humorlessly, started to speak again, then stopped. He lifted a clipboard (where had he been hiding a clipboard?) and then looked at me.

"Are you not… Moira Silverstein?"

"What? No."

"Abdul Mahem Mohammed?"

"Are you serious?"

"But," he said, squinting in the dim light, "I am sure I saw you on the bus. Remember your face."

Oh, damn. The old guy *was* familiar to me. The dude with the forty on the bus we nearly killed with our jet.

"Different guy," I said, and this time I offered up a vapid smile.

He stared for a moment, and then something briefly flashed across his face, and the grin was back.

"As you wish, señor," he said and turned slowly. "But still, El Tajin is closing. As they say, you don't have to go home, but you can't stay here."

"No worries," I said. "I'm at a campground just up the road."

"There are no campgrounds near El Tajin."

I jammed my hands in my pockets so they didn't reach out to choke him to death. Instead I spun, put my back to him, and just started walking.

From behind me, Mr. I Gotta Get The Last Word In said, "El Tajin is not a place to be when it grows dark. There are… spirits. Unsettled spirits that come out at night. Spirits that would be not pleased with someone such as yourself here."

On that, I spun back around. Facing each other in the twilight, I couldn't see his face but was sure the practiced grin was long gone.

"Oh?" I said, because for whatever reason something in me wanted to fight with someone. "Why is that? Why would they not be pleased with someone such as me?"

"They are still angry, I think. Your people destroyed these people. My people. A long time ago. Their spirits still do not rest. Some of the living still pray to this very day, asking that the lightning god make things right."

"I'm not… *my people* didn't invade here. My mother was Canadian, my father may have been mostly Irish. Unless there was a band of Canuck-Irish conquistadors I've never heard of—"

"*White people*, señor! White people slaughtered these people."

I shrugged. "Racist," I muttered, and I left him standing alone on the dark path.

Chapter Twenty-Four

"Wow. Oh, shit."

Their deceptive plan, as it was, might have worked except for one small, unforeseen problem.

Given some of his previous work in the area, Uncle Jerry was somewhat familiar with the local drug "talent" and knew if any of them were to come aboard, they would be expecting to see the not-Honduran drug lord sitting in the comfiest seat and sipping brandy from a fancy glass.

More importantly, no one locally had been given the heads-up that a lieutenant of Don Cheetle's would be swinging by their territory with the big man's custom Gulfstream 550 jet. That was a bit of a no-no. People got dead that way pretty quick.

However, Uncle Jerry had been the pilot on a few runs to New Orleans over the years and knew that a gift and an offering of apologies (and a promise that you'd leave quickly) could often get you out of a sticky situation such as this.

Of course, they had a problem: the fact that the not-Honduran drug lord was not there to smooth things over.

"So, okay, actor-boy, you'll need to be our drug kingpin," Uncle Jerry had said a few minutes earlier.

The Actor smiled, nodding. "Always wanted to play a baddie."

"Don't overdo it, though, man."

That drew a long look. "Gimme some credit."

Aside from the formidable thespian skills in play here, they were going to take advantage of the local Cajun boys' likely discomfort with this heretofore-unknown dwarf kingpin's rather short stature. And it was begrudgingly agreed upon that the Actor would use a British accent like he used on his current sword-and-schtup cable television show.

Also, Uncle Jerry thought a cool nickname was warranted.

"It'll give you gravitas, man," he'd said.

The Actor frowned. "Or I sound like a clown and they gut me where I stand."

"Yeah," their pilot said, nodding slowly. "Could happen."

"How about British Bulldog," Anza said, already shaking a bit at the thought of what lay ahead of them. "It sounds fierce, and it also is employing some nice alliteration.

The two men looked at her for a moment, quietly contemplating the ridiculous idea. Then both said: "That works."

All appeared settled when the Actor realized something the others hadn't. There was a queer edge to his voice. "Wait! What if they recognize me?"

Uncle Jerry's eyebrows arched. "You been here before?"

"No, no, no," the other man said impatiently. "It… you know, from the show. Or movies, who knows? It could—"

Jerry laughed. "You big with Cajuns, man? You're probably good."

Their female companion rubbed her chin for a moment. Without a word, she quickly disappeared into the rear of the plane, and after less than a minute, returned with black-framed eyeglasses and, of all things, a zippered case with a variety of mustaches inside.

"There was also pizza boy uniform," Anza said matter-of-factly. "In some hidden cupboard under seat next to stripper pole. And rainbow wig, policeman hat and baton, and—"

"Got it," the Actor said, taking the glasses and mustache kit. "How'd you know that?"

"I was exploring," she said. The two men continued to stare, waiting for more. "Before now. Earlier time."

After a moment, they both shrugged. "Okay."

Anza, for her part, was going to tuck herself into Cujo's backseat as a backup plan. The keys would be in the ignition, so if things went very bad—or worse than expected—she could rocket out of the cargo hatch and try to find the last piece of the lamp without them.

"Very bad like wh-wh-what?" she'd asked. Neither man had an answer.

The local drug talent had shown up and were banging on the outside door, demanding to come in. Once they were inside, they would have to move quickly.

Anza was grabbing her things while Uncle Jerry headed to the back of the jet to jam the keys in the ignition and see if there was another eight-ball of coke in the drawers to serve as an offering for the locals (or more correctly, some *part* of any coke he may come across).

Just off the cockpit door, the Actor was walking in small circles, muttering to himself in a British accent, practicing some lines.

And as dangerous as the plan was—as conceived—it might have worked. Uncle Jerry was actually feeling like he and the Actor could pull it off as he dropped into the belly of the Gulfstream and noticed the rear rollaway was still open and the private fuel-up crew was finishing up their work.

When they caught sight of him, that was when everything went south.

"Oh, hell no, look who it is," a heavy man with more hair on his knuckles than on his head said to his two partners. Hairy Knuckles returned the fueling nozzle to an apparatus next to their electric cart. "It's our friend Uncle Jerry! It's our *debtor* friend, Uncle-fucking-Jerry!"

"Hey, guys," Uncle Jerry said, arms raised, palms open, as friendly as he could sound. "This is a real bad time to settle scores, amigos. Can we pick this up—"

"You owe our boss about fifteen still, right?"

Another of the men—tall, in greasy coveralls with a matchstick rolling around his teeth—whistled at hearing the bill.

The third said: "What a good day this will be. We can settle accounts from, what was it? Some drunken card game about eighteen months ago. What fun that was! But finally settling up? That'll make Boss real, real happy."

Uncle Jerry lowered his hands and looked from left to right, right to left. Not waiting for whatever plan was forming in the middle-aged man's soft head, Hairy Knuckles nodded to his two friends, who moved quickly to grab him.

"So you've come to pay what you owe? Very noble of you, UJ."

Uncle Jerry shook his head, his mouth turning too dry to answer.

Hairy Knuckles's face theatrically turned downward. "That," he said, "that was the wrong answer."

I kept myself to the skirts of the Mexican ruins.

And despite the boogeyman-level warnings given to me, I wasn't overly concerned about being strong-armed by the locals. I'd lived about four years in Atlanta, a summer in Kansas City, a year in Dallas, and another in LA—and not the nice area where they make movies, but Hollywood itself, which at the time was a quaint but potentially deadly shithole. Hell, I'd even once strolled through Watts with a busted-up starter of a '77 Toyota Celica to get to the only repair shop within walking distance.

Still, the most dangerous I'd survived was renting a mother-in-law apartment in north Minneapolis. Laugh all you want, but I got shot at twice in north Minneapolis. Sure, the locals all seem *Fargo*-y and nice—*don'tcha know?*—but when people spend more than a third of the year in temperatures that can kill you... it can express itself in all sorts of ways. From my experience, it expressed itself as them a couple times shooting at me. That put the city high on the oh-hell-no-meter for me.

With about nineteen hours to get from the El Tajin pyramid to New Orleans, I was tired and frankly not interested in confrontation, conflagration, or even conversation.

In less than a half hour, the calm, serene site had turned downright eerie once night had taken hold of it. I scoured the ruins, searching for the low-slung pyramid.

There was a howl to the wind, which struck me as odd, since it didn't seem the wind was blowing very hard. Then I could make out voices. Insistent voices, cresting then dropping in the distance.

I moved in several directions, trying to see if I could find where the voices were coming from. It took me a while to properly track them. I'd first moved away from them at every step, the waves of voices fading like big dewy raindrops tumbling from leaves after a summer storm.

With the sun completely tucked under the horizon, it was as dark as I'd ever seen it. An inky blackness seemed to greedily swallow any light, squirreling it away to later use for warmth when the air turned colder.

I briefly set aside my worries about voices and sat on the grass at the edge of what was once possibly an impressive stone structure. All that was left was a jagged trace outline of the place. A home or eatery or store... it was a place people had once called theirs. All that was left now was the base of the exterior stone walls, looking like the rudimentary police-chalk outline of a fallen loved one long, long since passed.

That thought punched my chest, and as I began to feel tears rise up in my eyes—they were coming more quickly in recent days—and I chased it from my mind. I stood slowly, and my aching legs hated me for it, clicking and cracking each inch of the way up.

Walking stiffly at first, I headed toward the voices. For a sleep-drunk moment, I thought maybe a late bus had arrived or had returned with some panicked tourist looking for a misplaced camera or cell phone. Instead, I rounded a corner and finally came upon El Tajin's millennia-old pyramid.

Naturally, now pitch black, the pyramid was lit by the torches of three or four dozen people—men or women, I couldn't tell, because all of them were wearing terrifyingly hideous masks.

Of course they were.

And, just a shot in the dark, but if the merest possibility existed, it could have been the case that each of the masks they wore was crafted from the human skull of former victims.

Which, of course, they were.

Now, despite my earlier declarations of being the deputy mayor of Badassdom, I wasn't a complete idiot. But something told me that to find the next piece of the lamp, I would have to see what the scary mask people were doing.

However, I didn't think walking up with a hand outstretched—"Any y'all seen a piece of a really old lamp? Glassy thing, real shiny, about yea big?"—was the way to go. Not trying to cast aspersions upon a group of anonymous people wearing human skull masks and armed with fiery torches, but I wasn't going to just walk up with a friendly howdy, just as I wouldn't have done had I stumbled upon a Klan meeting in the middle of Mississippi.

Not that they'd toss me from the top of the pyramid (or worse), but there's a reason people get together wearing masks. And in this case, at least, I didn't feel like this was an *Eyes Wide Shut* sort of gathering where old guys were being serviced by willing pretty young women who'd been led to believe they were getting far more out of the evening than they really were.

Turning away from the group, my heart hammered like a silent klaxon because time was short, but I needed to take a moment to let my eyes readjust to the darkness. Then, trotting along, I searched for the floodlights of the pavilion. Spotting them a full minute later, I picked up my speed and ran toward the gift shop.

Through the darkened store windows, I searched the inventory to find anything that might help hide my face and got a bit lucky: On the far wall was a rather comical assortment of hand-painted, if non-skull-based, ceremonial masks.

After a few minutes, I finally found a way into the gift shop through the women's bathroom by standing upon a toilet tank and crawling through the window over the door of a maintenance closet, which was also connected to the store.

Two minutes later, I was back outside with a mask that, while a bit less of a DIY number than the torch people were wearing, would give me my best shot at getting closer to them. However, it was markedly less than authentic, since every single mask on the wall bore the face of a popular kids' entertainment character, albeit slightly distorted, presumably to avoid any licensing costs.

Not running—too dangerous in the dark, especially wearing the mask—I walked/jogged/stumbled my way back to the pyramid, but when I finally returned, puffing and sweating, they were gone.

Disappeared.

"Shit!" I said, my lips sweaty behind the mask. "Dammit!"

Despite how illogical it might sound, I knew they would help lead me to my next piece of the lamp. And it seemed unreal that forty-odd people could just disappear into thin air.

Were they somehow *in* the pyramid?

That seemed unlikely, because from the outside, it didn't exactly look like the pyramid *had* an inside. Just row upon row of what looked like large masonry blocks, each with a dead black center. Stepping twenty yards away and turning back, it looked like some pre-Colombian Hollywood Squares, but with like seventy-five George Goebels and Carol Channings as celebrity guests, except the top tapered toward the middle until it came to a flat top.

In the middle of the wall facing me, it looked like there was a crumbling set of ascending stairs. Maybe it wasn't an inside sort of pyramid and more like some folks had built a nice high spot for community cookouts. But of course, instead of cookouts, they drank the blood of virgins or had, *ugh*, stingray stingers lanced through their outstretched penises to ensure a fertile harvest (that last bit is totally and horrifically true, I found out later. Google it if you don't care much about your internet service provider recording your web search history results).

However, right now, it was clear there wasn't anyone up there doing anything.

"No time for this!" I said, my teeth tapping against the stupid mask.

I ran around to another side, but there was no way in. The next side, again, nothing. But then I caught the faint sound of muffled voices and caught a slight flicker behind the pyramid.

Sneaking up to the corner, I peeked around and saw a handful of the masked revelers disappearing *beneath* the pyramid. That's when I noticed a large slab of flat, rigid earth that had been pushed aside. Beneath it, a short stack of stairs leading below. When the last person had gone down, they dragged the sod above them back into place, snuffing out the light.

I waited a full half minute before following.

While biding my time, I surmised that there would have to be some sort of ventilation to the outside for the folks down there or, with each of them holding a fiery torch, once the oxygen burned away, this group of homicidal Aztec or Olmec followers would soon look like the smurfiest smurfin' cult the world had even seen.

But there was no time to search for some sort of air vent to sneak down, and moments later, I'd slid aside the hidden entrance and was climbing down the subterranean passageway, toward the sounds of a man's voice, joined by the call and return of the faithful.

Step by step, orange and yellow light licking the short tunnel ahead of me, I was walking toward some sort of ancient prayer service. Or possibly one of the first AA meetings ever established in the world.

But really, it was more likely the first one.

And despite my macabre interest, I hoped there wasn't any sort of bloody, sacrificial ritual taking place. My luck, I would be showing up just in time for everyone to draw straws.

As I got closer, the chanting of the faithful grew louder and louder.

Not dallying in the entry hall, I slipped into the meeting chamber without thinking how dangerous it might be, and my breath momentarily got trapped in my chest at the sight of this group, all chanting and swaying. At the front was a person on a short riser, waving his arms emphatically to the encouragement of those around.

Any other setting and this could have been a simple church meeting or a city-level political assembly. Or maybe an Amway rally to get potential recruits jazzed about their goddamn laundry soap.

But this was none of those, of course. These were the descendants of the first lightning god worshippers. Generation after generation praying to the god of the electric sky, seeking a return of the world stolen from them by time and by foreign men.

This I knew because, as the leader spoke, lightning actually flashed across the walls. All around the cramped earthen space, the room was continuously lashed by streaks of lightning.

Then I saw its source: a fat candle on the raised pedestal just behind the preaching man's head.

Around the candle was glass—a perfect crystalline globe bulging at its middle like an ex-boxer—which washed the faithful clean with its dancing ribbons of light, as they stood swaying in the hot, moist air.

"Damn," I muttered, my voice muffled by the gift-store mask. "That's it."

Here was this cherished relic—a treasure of these people. One that had given birth to their lightning god more than a thousand years earlier.

And I was there to steal it.

The moment Anza heard laughing, she knew something was very, very wrong. Not that laughing itself should engender that sort of reaction, but it was several men laughing—and she recognized none of their voices.

Slowly, she inched her way down the rear stairs leading to the jet's cargo ramp, trying to peer around the corner.

Shadows.

Two, no, three shadows of men.

And they looked like they were... dancing?

Why are dancing men back where Uncle Jerry is supposed to be?

Just when she got the nerve to go around the corner, a *flwump!* flattened her back to the wall.

She did not hear Uncle Jerry's voice among the men. Balling her hands into fists—not to fight, but to stop them from shaking—she edged down the ramp past the slick black Trans Am.

Outside on the tarmac, three men in oily coveralls were sitting and laughing on the back of a red fuel truck while a fourth was driving them away. Anza stayed low next to Cujo, keeping an eye on them as they disappeared into the night air.

"Uncle Jerry," she said in a horse whisper.

Then she saw him.

The tall, part-time pilot looked like a folded strawman, crumpled to the floor. Anza's fist went to her mouth, and her eyes began to instantly water.

"Oh, *mia*... Uncle Jerry," she said softly, reaching down for him. He didn't move at her touch.

Inside the jet, the Actor was strutting the floor of the plane's cabin now, really getting his stride. Puffing out his chest, he said in a variation of his current workplace accent: "So, do we have an understanding, gentle—"

He stopped when he heard someone approaching. Turning just his head, he caught a glimpse of Anza's face. At the sight of her, his knees buckled slightly.

Once again, the pounding came on the side of the fuselage, this time even louder. The locals were getting restless, and it should be noted, they were heavily armed.

A moment later, the two of them were standing over Uncle Jerry, who was in an odd twist of limbs just beneath the tailpipe of his beloved car.

"Shit, is he dead?"

"No, but he won't wake up," she said. "We need to get him—
"

"Wait, wait," the Actor said, blood draining from his face. "Who did this? What happened?"

"I dunno," she said through sobs. "I am coming around the corner, the guys were leaving and laughing and our Uncle Jerry is on the floor with bleeding. It's… he's going to be okay, though. We'll make sure—"

The Actor took a few steps back until he felt the wall behind him. He held it with both palms flattened next to his sides. In the distance, he caught the lights of a tiny red fuel truck making a sharp bank around a corner. Then it was gone.

Again, the banging came from up near the cockpit, even louder now, and this time accompanied by more voices. Demanding. Angry.

The dwarf stared, frozen against the cargo bay wall, as Anza wiped Uncle Jerry's bloodied face with her shirt. A part of him marveled at how she hadn't let a teardrop fall, and was just there for her friend.

More pounding above.

The Actor heard himself say, "You… you need to take Uncle Jerry and go."

"Wh-what?"

In a daze, lines were being fed to him from some part of his brain he wasn't terribly familiar with. He pushed away from the wall. "We'll put Uncle Jerry in the back seat of his car, and… and…"—he reached for the handle, but it was locked—"the keys… the keys should be in his pocket."

"Okay, we all go, though," she said. "Help me with—"

He felt his legs grow stronger beneath him. "No. If we all take off, they'll see us, and we're dead."

"No, is a fast car, so—"

"This is an airport," he said, running around the car and searching the pockets of their fallen fiend. "There's no quick getaway. You guys get into the car, and once I bring those…

those visitors up there into the plane, you get the fuck out of here."

"No," she said, her body shaking harder. "Bad plan."

"Unless I get the drug people up there pounding on the door inside, none of us are getting out of here, Anza!"

Uncle Jerry was swimming in and out of consciousness as the two of them helped him toward the car. Straining under the weight of the tall man, they tried to shuffle him across the floor, but he was too heavy. Grunting, they both once again lowered him to the floor, so that he was slumped against the car's passenger door.

Anza stood up, her fists two bloodless balls. Shaking, she said through her teeth, "I do not abandon my friends. We all go or none of us go."

For a moment, the Actor had no words.

It had been a long, long time since anyone had called him their friend.

But what could they do? Uncle Jerry had been a pivotal part of their plan. And Anza, as brave as she was, was shaking so hard she looked like she was about to shatter into pieces.

Then the actor realized that last thought was exactly right.

Despite its appeal, most pros would admit there's very little merit to the role of Radio DJ.

There was no raft of "life lessons" that one could directly pick up from a career of playing recorded music and shooting one's mouth off. You are bestowed a mantle of respect and reverence you didn't likely deserve. The Bossman put you on the air instead of some other schlub. Not necessarily—or even chiefly—because you were better. It's more likely he or she had convinced you to work for less than the other guy.

But a modicum of fame you had. It was usually worth nothing, except possibly getting out of the occasional traffic citation.

However, you did start to believe the bullshit, the hype. Mainly because you had to. Sure, you might find yourself hosting yet another "homemade" bikini contest in a dive bar in an unincorporated part of the city, but there was an owner and maybe a hundred hard-up guys who are looking for you to take the rudder.

And what made you qualified? Someone simply handed you the mic.

However, one minor life lesson you could certainly pull out of being on-air radio talent was this: If you looked like you know what you were doing, nine times outta ten, nobody was going to stop you from doing it.

You want to get into a hard-to-get-into club? Grab a case of bottled beer, put your head down, and walk with purpose— you'll push right past the bouncer almost every time.

Need to get backstage? Slap on a pair of oversized headphones slugging a Radio Shack mic and keep looking at your watch (note: get a cheap watch for this one), and you'll move past security. You *will* be stopped, but most hired muscle monkeys only have one good *Hey, you!* in them. Push 'em off with a bored expression as you keep walking and you usually get in.

That's all there is to it. It's all about the "Hey, man, I am supposed to be doing this!" attitude that sells it. And often a good prop or two.

This was what was running through my mind as I sucked in a deep breath and strode confidently through the mass of sweaty revelers beneath a Mexican pyramid, wearing a horrible mask ripped off from the El Tajin gift shop.

As I approached, a couple of masked faces swiveled toward me, and my eyes focused on the breathtaking prize: the glass chimney of the Lamp of Life. I could see how it had enchanted others for what I gathered may have been thousands of years.

Simple and perfect, the curvature of the glass harnessed the candle's flame and splattered ribbons of pulsing light across the earthen walls, the dirt floor, and every person there.

Beautiful.

And me, I was about to take it from this group of potentially homicidal sacrifice-happy twilight revelers.

The man at the front of the small subterranean room was doing his call-and-response routine with the local folks. Arms punching the air, each breath he exhaled seemed to spike the humidity several points.

Naturally, I couldn't understand a word of what he was saying, and not just because I don't speak Spanish. This sounded very different, very foreign. As a place of worship, I wondered if this was what it was like when Catholics held a Latin mass. Similar, it seemed, except without the up-down-up-down calisthenics.

When he'd reached a crescendo and a cheer rose up around me, I took my shot.

Bursting from the shoulder-to-shoulder crowd, I charged right up to the man at the stone podium, the next piece in my quest to save my wife just a few feet behind his head. Startled, his body stiffened with arms still raised in a draping arch. He turned just his face toward me. Even behind the mask, I saw his eyes widen.

I realized simply grabbing the glass globe at that point would be inviting several dozen masked zealots to drop me where I stood. I had to look supremely confident and find a way to tell a group of people who wouldn't understand me that I was in control and "Hey, man, I am supposed to be doing this!"

I raised my arms, crushed my hands into fists, embraced whatever lunatic thoughts suddenly came to my mind, and yelled them through my comically stupid, gift-store mask:

"HELEN MIRREN'S VAGINA SHOOTS WARM RAYS OF CARIBBEAN SUNSHINE!"

They stared.

And in truth, how couldn't they?

"ADOLF HITLER HAD A SINGLE TESTICLE," I yelled with all the phlegmy, Southern Baptist evangelical passion I could muster, taking the smallest of steps up the riser, "AND ALL THE KIDS CALLED HIM 'WILLY DANGLE!'"

It was complete gibberish, but with each pronouncement, I edged closer to the glass globe.

"PUPPETS! HAND PUPPETS SPOIL YOUNG MINDS WITH THE EARLY SEEDS OF AN UNNATURAL INTEREST IN FISTING!"

I uncurled my left hand and pushed it toward the globe but stopped when everyone's eyes then locked on to my fingers. Holding them suspended in the air, I yelled: "IF GOD IS EVERYWHERE, AND HE FARTED, HOW WOULD YOU GET AWAY FROM THE SMELL?"

Unbelievably, I heard a voice in the back say, "The guy in the Hello Kitty mask makes a good point."

Yes, horrifically, my best option from the gift shop had been a goddamn plastic Japanese kitty cartoon face complete with green bow (to avoid direct copyright violation) and a thin elastic string to tie it to the back of my fat head.

However, when everyone's head swiveled back toward the man who'd spoken, I took my chance and reached forward, extinguishing the beautiful tendrils of lightning that had lit up the room, and as my fingers brushed against its surface (*Jesus, it's hot!*), they turned blood red, and I lifted the Lamp of Life's glass chimney away from the candle. The room instantly darkened.

I ran.

Now, I had never been a terribly proficient runner, but as explained earlier, I once invented an exercise regimen that put lions, tigers, or zombies on your tail. As I charged through the dark, uneven ruins of El Tajin with the lamp piece in my hand, I decided that if I lived beyond that night, that list should definitely include scary, bloodthirsty, masked hordes of Aztecs (or Olmecs).

Running full sprint—at least full sprint for a spongy, outta-shape American dressed in a not-quite-copyright-violating Hello Kitty mask—I knew that if I could get to the weird motorcycle, I'd be home free.

When I looked back, I saw them pouring out of the earth like angry fire ants, coming after me. Who could blame them? I'd stolen their lightning!

But if they caught up to me, I was dead. Not a good dead either. No, it'd be one of them we-need-to-appease-the-angry-lightning-god-type deaths that can get real, real creative and take a long, long time to carry out.

I ran faster.

Chapter Twenty-Five

"What the hell took so long?" said the first man up the stairs and through the door. "You get stuck in the fuckin'—" He stopped speaking as his feet hit the floor, seeing a pretty young woman holding the jet's cabin door open. Her face was red, splotchy. The hand that had opened the door was shaking and covered in dark streaks. Silently, she drew her arms in as he was about to ask her something.

"Welcome, gentlemen," the Actor said from one of the lounge chairs. He was sipping from a martini glass and casually pointed to a wooden keg. "We made a stop in Japan for some sake. These lovely priests make it, just the one keg a year—best there is."

Three men, all in dark suits, flowed into the cabin. As their collective bulk made the air denser, Anza's entire body began to visibly shiver.

The man talking identified himself as Dré Preuss, a representative from the "local chapter".

"And who the fuck are you?" Preuss said to the man lounging casually in, of all things, a tiny red robe.

"Do you not knowing wh-wh-who this is?" Anza choked out. "Iz the British B-bulldog, right there."

The Actor smiled and gave her a wave. "That'll be enough, Carlita, thank you."

The Cajun drug lieutenant looked her up and down and grinned, then chuckled. "You want to sit down, *cher*? You look like you're about to cry."

"Oh, no," the Actor said in a soft English accent, taking another dainty sip of his drink. "That isn't fear. No, no. Don't trouble her. Your business is with me."

Dré looked at his two men, who'd said nothing yet but were tracking from corner to corner of the room with their eyes, and told one of them to head back down the stairs and keep an eye out.

The man, young but balding, winced. "It's hot out there, Dré. Tarmac is about a hundred—"

Dré stopped him with a look. Bald Man jammed his hands into his sport coat's pockets and stomped down the stairs, taking each step louder than the next.

"My niece's husband," Dré said with a half smile.

"Family's important."

"At least harder to kill, right?"

The Actor laughed. "Not, uh, not in the world I live in." With a smile but a subtle edge to his polite accent, he added: "It seems damn near every week some relative of mine is getting their head lopped off."

Dré sucked in a quick breath, then recomposed himself.

"This here… this is not your city," he said. "And you don't have friends here as far as I know."

"It's early. I was hoping you and I could be friends." Another bored smile.

The local drug man took a few steps forward and towered over the Actor. "And this isn't your plane. The man who owns it—"

"Enrique, yes, yes," the Actor said, sighing and sipping. A wipe of the lip. "He owed me a favor. And actually, that is exactly what I now seek from you."

"A favor?" Dré looked at his remaining man, who drew then his weapon. "*Friend*, I've already done you a favor," Dré said, looking over at Anza, whose tremors had graduated to moderate trembling. Wide eyed, she stared at Dré. "See, I haven't plugged both of you nuts and dropped you in Lake Pontchartrain already. That's the only favor you and Shakes over there are gonna get from me." He stepped forward, snatched the Actor's drink, drained it with one gulp, then tossed the glass.

It smashed into the bulkhead just over a window, glass particles raining down like a thin January snow through a bright beam of sunlight.

Anza was now full-on shaking.

"Now, if you got a pistol hidden away in your cute little robe, I don't see it. And I know your friend's not—"

The Actor raised a hand, leaned back, and grabbed a fresh glass. As he filled it, the Cajun shook his head, looked at his man, and they both laughed.

Filling his new drink, he said, "You should have said you wanted one, I would have gotten you a fresh glass." With a self-satisfied smile, he sipped and nodded to the broken glass on the floor. "Don't worry about it, though."

"I'm not," Dré said after a slight hesitation.

"It's just, I have had the nastiest of outbreaks," the Actor said, pulling his mouth back like he'd tasted something bitter. "That's why I'm wearing the dressing gown, mate. It's full on, too. I could roast a game hen down there at the moment. But"—the man with the English accent squinted, looking toward Preuss' chin—"I wouldn't worry much. I haven't noticed any mouth sores."

"Jesus," Andres said and turned to his man with a hand extended, looking for something to wipe his mouth. The henchman, eyes bulging, shook his head quickly and took a half step back. The Cajun settled for wiping his lips with his sleeve.

"Not that the wee bleeders aren't there," the Actor added. "Sneaky buggers, they are. Hard to see sometimes."

A little more wiping, then: "Jesus Christ…"

The trembling Anza knitted her brow and said in a burst, "D-don' swear!"

Dré had had enough. He pulled out his pistol and trained it on the Actor.

"I'm done with this shit. You come into our town thinking you're gonna, what? Poke around? Catch a show? Shit, you ain't even armed!"

"Don't need it," the Actor said, bored, and sipped his new drink. "I've got her."

Andreas began to speak, then stopped. Then he and the other drug man laughed. Anza began shaking violently, eyes never leaving their leader.

"Are you fucking joking? She's so terrified, she—"

"Oh, no," the Actor said, and now it was his turn to laugh. He raised his hands toward his friend. "No, no. That's... as I said that's not fear. I've just spent the last five minutes—with you and your lot out there pounding on the door—trying to calm her down. Rage issues, you see."

"You have *got* to be joking."

"No," the dwarf in the red robe said. "She damn near killed our pilot after a bit of a bumpy landing. Not a big fan of flying, you see. I was back in the hold trying to calm her down before you started banging on the door like... What's the expression that man in Pensacola used the other week? Before you disemboweled him, Carlita? Oh, yes, I would say you were out there 'banging like a screen door in a hurricane.' Ha, *brilliant*! Yes, that was it."

Dré looked from the Actor to Anza and back. Then he looked to his man, who offered what could only be described as an unhelpful expression.

He looked back to the Actor. "Bullshit."

"No. No, unfortunately," the Actor said, crossing his short legs. "If we were going to get out of here in the next few hours, I had to intervene. Couldn't have her killing the pilot. He's, um, 'sleeping it off' in the loading bay."

The Actor nodded to the back.

"Go check it out," Andreas said to the man behind him.

After a brief moment of silence, the Actor launched into the script he'd worked up minutes earlier. "Okay, here it is. My employer back in the United Kingdom has, let's say, made various *overtures* to your employer. About opening up parts of Western Europe for you lads. The owner of this lovely bach-pad in the sky, Don Cheetle, implored his man, Enrique, to temporarily gift it to us. He was kind enough to offer it up for a few days to facilitate what is hoped to be the beginning of... a very lucrative relationship."

The small-time boss took a half step back. "So why didn't I hear about any of this?"

The Actor steeled him with a look. "Really?" Then, for the first time, he raised his voice, punching each word: "Are. You. Joking?"

The man standing before him said nothing. Waited.

From the back, out came Dré's man. He looked toward Anza, then quickly downward. Then he strode over to his boss and whispered loudly. The Actor could easily make out the last few words.

"... fucked up, man! Looks half dead."

At hearing those words, a sound escaped Anza's lips.

Then as if he'd suddenly seen something he wished he hadn't, Dré took a step toward the door and said, "Jesus fucking Christ, look at her shirt!"

They all did. Blood stains streaked the front of her sweatshirt. Her right, trembling fist banged against her side, just below what looked like a bloodied face print.

"D-d-don'...," Anza said. "I say *don' swear around me!*"

"Hey, boss," Preuss' man said, taking a small step away from his employer. "The lady don't like you guys swearing."

For the first time since the meeting began, the Actor stood from his lounger. He then lifted his arms. "Let's give it a push, shall we? Let's see what happens when give it a *god damn* push!"

Anza shot a terrified look to the Actor, saying, "No, I ask you so many—"

"Hey, hey," Dré said, his arms outstretched, his hands petting the air softly in front of him. "She seems... very nice. Doesn't seem proper to, you know, upset the young lady."

"No, no. I suppose you're right," the Actor said, spinning back to his chair and tipping his body back into it with the tiny thud. "Carlita is part of a lesser-known devout religious order. We've got her on loan from Rome."

"Rome?" the goon said. "You mean—"

"Ah, ah." The Actor shook his finger and took another small, dainty sip. "It's best not to talk about it. She's terribly, terribly homesick and upsets easily. Our dear pilot learned that the hard way." He sighed. "I did warn him to tread lightly."

Dré cleared his throat and tried to reestablish control. "Nah, listen, I would know if some other player was dropping in. Something as big as you're talking about? We would know." He looked to his man for some sort of affirmation but did not get it.

The man in the robe said, enunciating each word: "In what world do you live in… that my superior and the vaunted"—he paused—"Don Cheetle would be sharing such plans with men like you… as if it were some sort of fucking Facebook meetup. Click *yes* if you'll attend. Or *no*. Just not *maybe*—" With a quick flick of his arm, the Actor flung his own glass across the room, and it shattered on the far wall, its pieces falling where the others had landed minutes earlier. "Not *maybe* because that's just the version of *no* only the cowards use, don't they?"

The Actor then just stared at the two men without any trace of expression on his face, waiting.

Dré shifted from foot to foot for a moment, then holstered his weapon. The other man did the same. The Cajun looked hard at the Actor, then tried to do the same with the violently trembling Anza but failed.

"You got three hours," he said, pointing to the door. "If this plane is still here after that, it'll be destroyed."

The Actor nodded once.

"Doesn't matter if you're in it or not," Dré said, and he and his man left.

Anza leapt to the cabin door and pulled it closed. She turned to run, then stopped, bent over, and placed a kiss on the check of the Actor. Then she bolted to the rear of the plane.

Sitting alone for a moment in the envelope of quiet inside the plane, the Actor let out a heavy sigh. He said to himself, "Not bad."

He then rose to follow Anza and check on his friend.

I followed another dried creek bed, the spooky-masked people getting smaller and smaller in my rearviews, too fast at first, but then I eased up a bit so I could weave out of the way of any big rocks/embankments/Chupacabra and not end up crashing.

Again and again, I tried to raise Uncle Jerry on the sat phone but got nothing. It just rang and rang. For the moment, I was on my own.

The closest airport was Mexico City, but without a passport (and without a private jet, which, have I mentioned, is the far better way to travel), very little cash, and no interest in burning the valuable hours it would take me to just get to the airport, I would have to find another way to get to the Big Easy.

The Motobullet™'s routing software told me even if I drove straight through to New Orleans, it would still get me there three hours after the deadline.

I needed another plane. And, of course, another pilot.

Which was totally impossible, no question about it. But I'd already done a handful of impossible things over the past few days. Why stop now?

Maps had shown an airstrip near the coast. A town called Gutiérrez Zamora. At my first chance, I left the unbeaten path behind for one a little more beaten. And with my time ticking away too quickly, I rode faster than common sense would recommend, but Mexico's Highway 180 was actually far better than some I'd driven on in Atlanta.

About a half hour later, thirty miles away from the Gulf Coast and without the merest hint of another human being anywhere in sight, I pulled the bike over onto a dark, high shoulder to drain my bladder.

Once the bike's ignition was off and its head lamp dimmed, I simply stood on the road beneath the moonless night and stared for a moment. I marveled at the quiet and the deep, deep dark, having never before been embraced by such a loving envelope of night.

Extending my arm, I could barely see the tips of my fingers. Above me, the sky was a wraparound shag carpet of stars. The beauty of it filled my chest and brought a dampness to my eyes.

There was even a twinkling just a few yards ahead of me in the dark, dark night, somewhere on the desert floor, so pretty. Then I realized, *not* so pretty, because those were *eyes* blinking as they stared at me.

I decided to cut my pee break short.

It took just over twenty minutes to get to the next town's outskirts. And now, closer to people, the road turned from half-century-old blacktop to decade-old blacktop.

At least for the time being, my kidneys—which had been beaten and battered by the road—called off their revolt and settled back into their original cavities.

Along the way, I'd searched for some radio, which, with the sun down, now offered up some American AM stations on the skip. A couple of times, I'd come across the numbers station again—and for about five minutes, with the rest of the AM and FM bands giving me only static, I listened closely to try to find some sort of pattern.

Not that hearing one would help. But to avoid panicking over the Hell-set deadline rushing toward me like a roiling tsunami, I listened to the long list of numbers.

As far as I could tell, the sequence never repeated. Not once.

Thankfully, after some time, I eventually found a news-talker called WWZ out of New Orleans.

Catching the bulletin at the top of the hour—and having not yet heard from my friends despite calling them every ten minutes—I braced myself for some story about a small plane crash or other air disaster.

Instead, my stomach growled upon hearing a deliriously catchy jingle for some place called Sonny's Bar-b-que, and I realized that I couldn't remember the last time there'd been a plate of food in front of me.

As Shotgun had discovered, there was a thick wad of American bills stuffed into one of the bike's many compartments. When I stopped to fill up just outside of Gutiérrez Zamora, a microwave burrito and Coke became my dinner. I asked the kid behind the counter where the airport was. He gave me an odd look and pointed back the way I'd come.

I shook my head. "No, no. Here in town," I said and dropped my voice low and lied. "It's a, uh, sort of 'secret' airstrip from what I understand."

"So then how would I know where it would be?" he said without even blinking.

Right.

"Well," I said, trying to recover from looking too asshole-American stupid, "maybe somebody let you in on the secret."

He frowned. "They won't even tell me the combo for the toilet doors."

"Really?"

"Yes, really."

"How do people get in to use them?"

"The owner, he doesn't want that. People make a mess, and you got to clean it again."

"Right."

"And I don't get paid enough to scrub toilets."

I gave him a knowing look. "Does anybody?"

He thought about that for a moment, but before he answered I dropped a hundred-dollar bill on the counter and was out the door.

There hadn't been any secret airstrip to my knowledge, but—and I was only spitballin' here—there *had* to be some sort of illegal human smuggling operation going on this close to the US border.

Nearing the coastline, I rode around until I found an area that looked like it could be used as some semi-secret airstrip. What I found was promising: a flat expanse of land on which Maps had pinned a tiny, monochromatic bi-plane icon.

So not remotely secret.

On its southern side, there was the familiar barn-shaped hangar with two smaller, squared-off structures flanking either side. If I was getting to New Orleans in the next few hours, my ride was definitely going to be here.

"No planes," the man inside said.

"What? This is an airport. What do you mean no planes?"

"No airport. Is air*strip*," he said. The man had such an impressively bulbous belly that if some joker had drawn three large circles on it in a triangular pattern, a giant would likely reach down from the clouds and toss him down an oiled wooden surface to knock down ten upright pins.

"Airstrip, okay, fine," I said. "So where are the—?"

"No planes."

"You said that."

The man in the coveralls had been eating a sandwich wrapped in wax paper. He hadn't bothered to wash his grease-blackened hands, which I suppose explained why he'd gone to the trouble of wrapping it in the paper.

"Why are you here, then? Concierge?"

Through a mouthful of food, barely giving me a look, he said: "Mechanic."

My inner legs were angry with me, since it had been years since I'd ridden a motorcycle, while my ThighMaster had long ago ended up in the trash after one unfortunate evening known amongst only my very closest friends as "the dog and butter incident."

Behind me was a wheeled stool with ripped vinyl, and I sat slowly.

"So what good is a mechanic if there aren't any planes?"

He was back to his sandwich—which smelled a little like a dead cat left floating in a bog—chewing such a large chunk that I quickly ran through some basic CPR I'd learned on YouTube the year before.

After a full minute, he looked up as if just hearing the question. He then pointed to a door leading to the adjacent hangar. Wheeling my chair toward the opening, I saw dozens of plane parts scattered in a loose circle around a beautiful World War II single-engine fighter.

"That work?"

"Sure."

"Okay, then…"

"Tell me, señor," he said, still chewing through the corner of his mouth. "What do you not see?"

That was an odd question. "At the moment?" I asked. "Um, rainbows? Unicorns? Unrequited love?"

He looked away slowly, gave me a half nod, then looked back toward the hangar. "What do you not see… that you should see when you look at the plane, which is what we are talking about?"

The aircraft was beautiful. Time had taken its toll over the years, but it still glistened under the flickering lights dangling down from the ceiling—wires some fifty feet in length terminating at a bulb capped by a circular shade, like luminescent spiders that hadn't had enough silk thread to get to the bottom and were now forever swinging out of reach of the airplane.

Shit. Now, I couldn't get spiders out of my head. Dammit!

"Sir?" he said.

Staring at the seventy-plus-year-old plane, I realized what Mexican Goober was going on about.

"So, where are the wings?" I asked.

"No wings."

"Doesn't make for a very good plane."

"No planes."

"Well, none with wings, sure."

"No planes."

I crossed my arms over my chest and exhaled. "I don't suppose there's an airplane-wing store close by."

"No stores."

Standing slowly, I said, "Totally knew you were going to say that."

He crumpled up the wax paper and tossed it into a small metal wastebasket, which gave off a soft but satisfying *thunk*.

After a belch that would have made small babies angry, he exhaled and, realizing I wasn't leaving anytime soon, waddled past me up to the door.

"That is a Douglas SBD Dauntless, a single-engine American dive bomber made in 1941," he said. "The exact same kind that blew holes into Japanese carriers at the Battle of Midway."

He stopped and looked at me, as if challenging me to interrupt. Me, I was focused on how dreadful his sandwich breath was.

He continued. "This is the SBD-5, made in Tulsa, Oklahoma. Nearly three thousand were built. Some went to England, some to the Kiwis. And a couple made it into the Mexican Air Force."

"I didn't know you guys had an air force."

He blinked at me. "Why wouldn't we have an air force?"

"Dunno. Just 'Mexican fighter pilot' doesn't sound like a phrase that would come up a lot."

"It does in the Mexican Air Force."

"Right."

He glared at me for a moment. Less for the air force crack, I think, and more because I'd messed with his groove when he'd been giving the old airplane spiel.

Continuing, he said, "Two Browning M2 machine guns in the front. Two more Brownings in the back. Unfortunately, those were removed by a previous owner."

"Against regulations?"

"No, I'm told he mounted them on his truck."

I let out a low whistle. "How'd that turn out?"

A shrug. "It took a while to identify the body, but when they did—dental records—his son inherited the plane."

"Right."

He stared off for a moment, then was back. "Pedal to the medal, she could do over four hundred kilometers an hour."

"Is that fast?"

"Sure, compared to a boat or a car." He leaned against the door jamb. "But other planes? SBD—slow but deadly."

I nodded. It was time to get moving.

Puffing out his chest, he added, "I won her in a poker game two years ago."

"If you got a bit better," I said, "maybe you could win some wings for it?"

Not surprisingly, I laughed alone.

I leveled with the lonely mechanic—whose name turned out to be Hector—that I was desperate to get to New Orleans as quickly as possible but through the least public means as possible.

He told me there was nothing he could do to help. I pleaded with the guy because, at that moment, he was it. The dude was all I had.

"Listen, any ideas you might have, I'm game. I just got a few hours to get to New Orleans, or my wife is lost. And I sort of go to Hell or something."

"*Ay que la chingada,*" he said, punctuating it with a smelly-sandwich whistle.

"Yeah," I said. "Turns out you really gotta read the fine print on those cell-phone contracts, huh?"

He started to say something, looked around, and then seemed to think better of it. "I am sorry," he said, then walked me toward the door without another word.

I was exhausted.

Drained.

With no idea where to go next, I slowly shuffled from the hangar into the darkness.

My mind was fried, I'd been running on adrenaline for days, but now that tank was on empty. My body hummed, and I very likely smelled dreadful.

What do I do?

When I got back to the bike, I reached in to once again try to reach my friends on the satellite phone. Nothing. Just a sad warble of a ring repeating again and again until the line dropped.

"Where the hell are you, Uncle Jerry?"

Nearby, I heard a branch snap.

Since I was in a foreign country, I stiffened, unsure if I should be making a run for it. But then, where would I run?

A phlegmy voice rolled across the night air toward me. "So, you are looking for a coyote, señor?"

The squat man was just at the tree line. A yellow bandana had been hastily tied around his face.

"No, but I think there may have been a few back along the road," I said. "Spooky yellow eyes out there in the desert. Scared the bejeezus outta me."

I heard the man swear softly. Then: "You looking to travel… north of the border," he said between heaving gasps for air.

At first I wondered if the bandana was restricting his breathing, then it was clear: The guy had run around the hangar and through the line of trees.

"Wait, I recognize your voice."

"Not possible," he said, lowering his voice. "We are strangers in this strange place, you and I."

I took a half step closer, then looked back to the hangar. "I was just talking to you, Hector."

"I don't know anybody by that name."

"Yes, you do," I said and caught a whiff of him. "And even from here, I can smell your stinky sandwich."

"Nah, a completely different guy."

"Same guy."

"Listen," he said with a snap in his voice. "Do you want to get to New Orleans or not?"

The mysterious not-Hector "stranger" told me he knew of a pair of young twin brothers who ran a shipping business that "may or may not" pass through the New Orleans area from time to time. If the money was right.

I agreed to go see them—there wasn't much choice—and he handed me a slip of paper with the local address of the guys who might be my only chance left to save my wife. And, you know, prevent me from roasting in Hell for all eternity.

I looked at the paper and thanked him. Then I noticed some printing at the top of the square piece of paper.

"Dude, this even says, 'From the Desk of Hector Perez.'"

"*Que? No lo se!*"

"Whatever," I said. "But seriously, thank you, Hector. I really appreciate it."

"No problem."

I got back on the bike, and the electronic map had me there in about ten minutes.

"Hello?"

Obviously the idea of walking around in the dark in an area that was literally foreign to me while looking for criminals could, on first blush, look like a really, really stupid idea.

"Hel-*lo*?"

But this was it, the last option if I was getting to New Orleans in time to meet up with my friends… wherever they were. The fact that I couldn't get them to answer the phone concerned me. But I decided to deal with that terrifying issue once I'd landed in the Big Easy.

"Hel—"

The pointy bang-bang end of a rifle found its way between a couple of ribs in my back, stealing my breath.

If you've never experienced that sort of nip in the skin, I'll let you in on a secret—your hands go up all by themselves like you're a big meaty jack-in-the-box. No one needs to say 'stick 'em up.' Ya don't even have to think about it.

From behind me: "What do you want?"

"Hector sent me."

Voices chattered behind me, then: "That is not an answer to my question. That is a declarative statement."

I nodded quickly. "Yes, I… I was answering, uh, the subtext of your question."

"What subtext?"

"Your real question is: Should I shoot this nice, harmless man?"

"I don't think it was that."

"See, I was telling you that I'd come here via Hector with the tacit understanding that I, you know, would not be shot."

"Why?"

"Because I don't want to be shot."

"No, no." The young man's voice began to sound irritated. "Why would knowing Hector prevent your shooting?"

"Well, he... Because he's your friend."

"No." This was another man's voice behind me. "That guy always smells like fish sandwich."

I shrugged. "Can't argue with that."

For the next half minute, I felt hands rifling through my pockets, checking my legs and arms and crotch for, I assumed, weapons. Sure, they could have been checking for testicular lumps, which would be really kind of them, however it didn't strike me that armed men, who were likely people smugglers, would be medically inclined in an encounter with a total stranger.

Snap judgment on my part, of course.

"Turn around."

I did. The two twin brothers standing in front of me were just barely men, at best a year out of their teens.

The semi-automatic rifle one of the brothers held looked older than both of them.

"I'm sorry," I said, "but I'm desperate."

"Desperate," the brother on the left said. "Fine. Means you'll pay more. What is it you want?"

"I need to get to New Orleans."

They laughed and glanced at each other, then back to me. "You're serious?"

"Yes. Absolutely."

"Wait. Why don't you head to Mexico City International and take a fucking plane, man?" he said. Then his smile fell. "You're American, aren't you?"

"Well, yeah."

"Just checking," the twin not holding the rifle said. "Had a run-in with some Canadians a while back. We'd like to steer clear of Canadians."

"Fucking ruthless, those guys," his brother said.

"It's all that cold. Goes to their brains," the other brother agreed. Then he was back to me. "Man, we couldn't get you within a hundred miles of New Orleans without the Coast Guard boarding us or blowing us."

"Coast Gu— *Ugh!*" I said. "What did you just say? They, they *what?*"

The unarmed twin smacked his brother in the shoulder and said, "Dude! Blowing us *up*, man! The Coast Guard would *blow us up!*"

"I shortened it because, you know, the sentence structure, it's kind of alliterative—"

"Not worth it," his brother said. "Totally lost the meaning, and now you sound a little bit on the gay side."

"Marginally," I offered, my hands still in the air. "But totally cool if you are, man."

"*I am not*," he barked at me and lifted the rifle higher. Which, of course, meant he was not having any luck reconciling that with his macho, gun-toting, people-smuggling persona.

His brother turned to me. "Okay, so we ain't taking a boat to New Orleans, man, because it's crawling with Coast Guard, who will *blow us the hell up* before we can even see the aquarium."

"No, no," I said. "I don't have time for a boat. I need a plane."

They both shrugged. "No planes."

This.

Fuckin'.

Place.

"That," I said and dropped my hands to the top of my head. "That can't be true!"

"Boats we have. We have boats, but we don't go to New Orleans."

"There are a few possible landing areas just north of the border," the other one added. "Texas."

"No, no. Not Texas," I said, walking in a circle. So tired. Fried, fried, fried, and just so tired. "Okay, Jesus... If we went to Texas, how long would that take?"

"Maybe… twelve hours."

The other twin said, "Fifteen."

"No way," I said. "I just… no way."

"No?" The young man with the rifle raised it again. "You think now that you know where we are, who we are, we're going to let you walk outta here just like that?"

I froze.

"Well, we are," the other brother said and laughed. The other did too, a half second behind him. "We're not killing types. But hey, like our Facebook page, K? We're nearly at one thousand likes."

Barely hearing them, my legs buckled, and I sat down on the ground, all my thoughts crashing into one another.

"Uh, you can't stay here, man."

"No sitting here!"

I lay down.

"No lying down either!"

There was no way this was going to end like this. I couldn't wrap my head around that. Wouldn't. But I was stuck seven hundred fifty miles away from my next piece with just hours to go. My wife was going to die while I was stuck like an idiot and making a fool out of myself, asking impossible things of total strangers.

"I… I can't," I mumbled through sobs. "I have to… I have to…"

"No blubbering, either. Come on, man. You gotta get on your weird motorcycle car and go."

"Motobullet™," I mumbled.

"It's not weird," the other brother said. "It's efficient and futuristic. I like it."

"Yeah, but you're stupid."

The sound of the twins arguing lifted away, and I drifted, so scared for my wife. So disappointed that I'd failed her. Then I heard Uncle Jerry's voice in my head:

You don't never yield, and whatever you're up against will fall, man.

...never yield...

With every bit of strength left in my body, I stood slowly, anger rising up in my chest. "You have got to get me to New Orleans."

"No, we don't," one brother said, his face tensing. "Get outta here!"

"I won't. I won't give up. I can't," I said, but that was all I had left. My anger drained, and my legs folded beneath me.

"He's sitting again."

"Not good."

The one on the left eyeballed me and exhaled a huge breath. "Okay. What's in New Orleans?"

"Mardi Gras," his brother suggested.

"No, no. I…" I thought for a moment then. "What the hell: My wife is dying."

"Bad news, bro."

"Yeah, so… so it's, you know, terminal. She's sick."

"I'm sorry. Tough break, but—"

"So I made a deal with the Devil," I said. "For her life. I get this thing for him, this lamp. And then she doesn't die. I save her."

They stared at me for a long, long moment.

Then, together they said: "Bullshit."

I stood up and went to the Motobullet™ and pulled out the glass globe I'd, um, *borrowed* from the homicidal indigenous Mexican worshippers. I handed it to one brother. Unimpressed, he handed it to the other.

Then my heart jumped to my throat as that guy dropped the fucking thing onto the gravel road! Rage split my mind in two as I saw the globe shatter into a million pieces, but in the next instant, there was a *fwup!* sound.

Before us, the glass chimney reconstituted itself.

Good as new, it was whole again.

Despite being on the Devil's quest for several days, that was really the first instance where I'd witnessed firsthand something totally otherworldly happen right before my eyes. In any other situation, seeing something like that would have been unquestionably life altering. It would have told me that my perceptions of reality were illusions and that far more lay beneath the fabric of our existence than meets the eye.

Breaking the silence, one of the brothers said, "Holy fucking shit, man!"

But for my part, after the past few days, this was a little par for the course. I picked up my lamp piece and held it away from the Mexican brothers, like Gollum coveting his precious ring. Eyes wide and unblinking, they exchanged some quick words, never breaking their gaze from the globe.

I saw my chance. "Seriously. You think I could make up a story like that? I don't expect you to believe it."

"You're right. We can't believe. You'd be so dumb as to make a deal with *el Diablo*."

"Si, stupid move."

"He is not to be trusted."

"You might be right. Actually, I know you are," I said, nodding. "He knew there'd be no way I could pull it off."

"So, why New Orleans?"

Walking in a small circle, I ran my fingers through my greasy hair. "The final piece of the lamp I need to beat the Devil and save my wife. The last part of it is there."

The two boys talked low to each other, back and forth, quickly. It occurred to me this might be a brother thing or maybe a twin thing. I had neither, so I didn't know. I couldn't catch individual words, but they traded desperate tones in what may have been their very own twin language.

Or, another possibility, my hearing had been deadened from twenty years of cranking heavy metal through earbuds, and that's why I couldn't exactly hear what they were saying. Yeah, maybe *that* was more likely than these two guys having their very own secret twin language.

Finally, they looked at me. Their eyes were red.

"El Diablo, he took our father."

I looked at them. "What? The… What do you mean?"

"Our father, a good man until he went looking for something at the bottom of a bottle. El Diablo reached up from the bottom and pulled him in."

The other boy nodded. "You could see it in his eyes."

"Everyone said to us, 'He's a mean drunk.'"

"But it wasn't him. You look into his eyes, and it wasn't him."

"He died three years ago." The young man looked at his brother. "Asshole Devil took our papa."

I just nodded.

And listened.

This was a *good* development—I could feel it. Not good that the kids' dad was a dead guy, but, you know...

"You get to New Orleans and el Diablo loses your bet, yes? How does that work?"

"Well, I get all the lamp pieces, and then my wife, she can be cured. She can be saved. And also, the Dev—el Diablo doesn't get to take me to Hell, you know, for all eternity."

They traded glances again. Then the slightly taller one took a small hop like he'd been stung. "Wait!" he said. "You said you know Hector, right?"

"Well, I don't *know* him know him."

"He still got that plane, right?"

I said, "No plane."

They laughed. "Yeah, you know Hector. He got that crazy old plane."

"Yeah, but no wings."

The taller brother, grinning like an idiot, grabbed the fabric of my shirt at the shoulder and pulled me across the parking lot to a Ford F-150. "Get in the back of the truck." He jumped up front, where his brother was already at the wheel. "Bro, I been dying to try this for ages!"

Thirty-five minutes after the twins took me back to Hector's hangar, we'd returned with his "no plane" plane on a flatbed with the old mechanic in tow.

Ninety minutes after that, we stared at what Hector and the twins had done.

Both young men whispered, "Beautiful."

Pushing the welder's mask up from his face, Hector said, "Loco!"

He wasn't quite as on board as they were.

The Dauntless fighter plane had been mounted inside the thick steel hull of one of the twins' spare boats. They said it was one their father had used decades earlier to help people across the border. He'd purchased it a half century earlier from the government.

Before us was the combination of World War II fighter plane and the shell of a 1950s Mexican Coast Guard boat.

"I didn't even know there was a Mexican Coast Guard," I said before I could stop the words from coming out of my stupid American mouth.

The shorter twin looked at me. "Why wouldn't there be a Mexican Coast Guard?"

Still, despite the impressive, sturdy workmanship, it looked... impossible. But what choice did I have.

"Is that going to work?" I asked.

"Hey, *pendejo*, you said you wanted to get there fast."

"Yeah, *that* will go fast!"

"Loco," Hector said, then pointed a finger at me. "An' you bring my plane back!"

One of the twins laughed. "You're never getting the damn wings if it sits *here*, man. They don't make 'em anymore."

Hector had been all against me taking his no-wings no-plane. But the twins had known him for many years, their entire lives, really. And, it seemed, they knew what would convince the old man to give up his prized plane.

There was an airyard in Houston that could make the plane whole again. The brothers' plan was to have me get the plane there after I got to New Orleans, and then, once rewinged, I could have this pilot I knew fly it back.

"Real low, like," one of them had said, nodding slowly. "So as to avoid detection by the radar."

With the prospect of finally getting wings for the old girl, he'd reluctantly let me borrow his no-plane.

"Will this thing work?" I asked again, pretty sure my question hadn't gotten an answer.

The twins nodded. "You'll be in New Orleans in five hours."

Hector crossed his arms. "*Loco*! She will rattle apart before he gets halfway there."

"Then he needs a mechanic. You go with him!"

"*LOCO!*" he said, walked into the night, then stopped. Standing in the half light, he turned, softened, and gave me a wave. "I wish you luck in saving your lovely wife."

Me, too emotional for my own good, I could only nod a thanks.

"And if I may," Hector added, "I would suggest you consider switching your mobile phone carrier. No contract. Maybe something like a monthly, pay-as-you-go option would be better."

Stifling a snotty, weepy laugh, I gave him a thumbs-up, and he was gone.

"What the hell is that supposed to mean?" one of the brothers asked.

"That old man's crazy, dude," the other said.

"Loco," I said, walking toward the shoreline unsteadily as one foot pulled me forward while the other appeared to have a mind of its own, trying to get back the other way. "Jesus, okay. Okay. Let's go, guys."

The twins raised their hands in unison. "Hell no, man," one said. "We're not going. That's crazy."

"Loco," the other said calmly.

"What?" I said. "Wait, what do you mean?"

"Hey, it's your only shot."

"How do… I mean, I don't even know how to really pilot a boat. Or drive a plane. Certainly not some sort of… boat-plane!

And I sure as hell don't have any idea how to get to New Orleans."

One of the twins pointed to the water. "North."

Right. No more delays. I was out of time. I sloshed through the ocean water toward the boat and said, "Helpful."

"You'll be fine. Your weird bike is in the back for a little ballast. It's not as heavy as the nose of the fighter, but it should help keep you from tipping. You've got GPS on that thing. Just follow the arrow."

"Sure, no problem," I said, climbing into the hulking contraption. *This is total suicide. But the kid's right. I got no other choice.*

"Good luck!"

Walking uneasily toward the back, I had to nearly crawl to get under the fuselage of the plane. As I did, one of the twins went up into the Dauntless and fired up the plane. It came alive with a thunderous roar that both thrilled me and terrified me at the same time.

The young man exited the craft and joined his brother at the rear of the boat. When I reached the boat's wheel, which controlled a pair of rudders mounted on its rear, I turned back to watch the boys push the craft into the water.

Over the noise of the fighter plane, I shouted, "This is really, really, really stupid, isn't it?"

"Nah," one of the young men yelled back, grunting as he pushed me farther into the sea. "You already did stupid when you made your deal with the Devil. This pales by comparison."

"Right," the other twin said. "But you couldn't pay me to spend thirty seconds in that rocket ride."

I yelled back, "None of that is helping!"

Once it was in open water, the plane-boat or boat-plane or whatever quickly picked up speed and was soon traveling so fast that I let my bladder empty where I stood, because it was now clear to me that I'd left little worries like peeing on myself back at the Mexican shoreline.

Chapter Twenty-Six

"I'm fine," Uncle Jerry said.

"I don' know how to driving a stick shift," Anza said, chewing on a nail. The two of them looked at her for a moment as she hunched over Cujo's leather-wrapped steering wheel, fiddling with the controls on the dash.

Uncle Jerry struggled to sit up from his position lying down in the back seat, saying, "Hell, woman, it's not a stick! Get outta the driver's sea—"

"Uncle Jerry, you're not driving," the Actor said calmly from the passenger's seat.

"I'm fine!"

"Your left eye is swollen, and I think a number of your fingers might be broken."

The pilot lifted his hand to his face, gingerly pressing on his eyelid with his palm. "Damn. I thought it just stopped working."

About a minute later, Anza got the car moving slowly toward the airport's exit.

The guard at the gate was compliant, happy to let them leave after stuffing a folded wad of bills into his jacket. ("That's how we do it here in N'awlins," Uncle Jerry had said.)

However, once outside the airport, just a few yards into the street, a squad car was waiting. The headlights flashed twice, and two police officers exited, walking slowly to the Trans Am.

"Y'all fly that Gulfstream over there?"

The Actor leaned from the passenger seat to speak to the cop at the driver's side window. "No, we're part of Harry Connick Jr.'s band—just got back. Gotta run, we—"

"Look at you," the second officer said, peering into the back seat from the side opposite his partner's. "Uncle Jerry. You look a little bit like shit."

The Actor turned toward his friend in the back seat. "Why does *everyone* call you that?"

Uncle Jerry flinched slightly. "It's my name, man."

The other cop looked back and smiled without grinning. "He looks a *lot* like shit."

"And he looks very uncomfortable in that tiny back seat," the second cop said.

"Yeah, you're right. Our car's much more comfortable."

Punching along the radio dial, I couldn't find any good music to listen to.

I'd even searched again for the numbers station. Hell, even that was more entertaining than static.

Getting closer to the Louisiana coast by the minute, it seemed that I should be able to pull in WLS, or any other New Orleans radio station, even better. But with all the electrostatic noise kicked up by the propeller rocketing the fighter-boat across the (thankfully) smooth gulf, I got nothing but a dull whine on the AM band.

FM wasn't any better, so I gave up.

Unbelievably, so far I hadn't exploded, burned to death in a jet-fuel fire, or simply been julienned by the plane's propeller blade. According to the Motobullet™'s GPS, and a little fingers-and-toes sorta math, I was about two hours out of New Orleans, rocketing across the pre-dawn Gulf of Mexico.

The constant rattle made every part of my body numb, but it was marginally better inside the Plexiglas cockpit of the bike because the roar of the engine was just slightly muted.

I'd had to pee twice and, making a proper effort while being sure not to fall over the side, tried best to plug my ears, which were being beaten by about 130db, just above the pain threshold.

A funny note: It seems that very loud, sustained sounds can affect one's capacity to think. It's a little like being slightly drunk.

Not just a bit tipsy but a lose-your-license-and-take-the-bus-loser-type drunk. Which might explain why it took me a few moments—you know, being a wee noise-drunk—to notice that the engine had shut down completely, and I was drifting at sea.

"Oh, Jesus. Shit!"

It had only become apparent to me once the fighter-boat slowed after losing its propulsion very quickly, and I'd begun rocking erratically in the wake it had just created.

"Oh god-oh-god-oh-god-oh-gaaawwdd!"

All I could do was hold on in the darkness as slaps of seawater gurgled over the bike and into the boat. Out of habit, I reached for the lever to get the wipers going but stopped. In truth, at least for a moment, I didn't want to see clearly out of the windshield.

After a few minutes of staring, the boat's crazy rollicking slowed to a town drunk's stumble, and I pulled myself from the capsule. It creaked as I climbed out—all the salt spray and wave chop was doing a number on the bike's suspension.

To the east, just off the bow, I caught the first slivers of light of my final day in my quest for the Lamp of Life.

Glancing up at the hulking aircraft, which was steaming from the heat and sea water, even with my low-grade mechanical skills, I could see the problem.

The makeshift plastic fuel line leading from a set of barrels strapped to its tail section to the belly of the plane had split and fallen away, likely from all the twisting over the past three hours.

I was exhausted, spent.

Scanning the horizon, I searched for a Coast Guard vessel, despite being absolutely sure I'd be arrested instead of helped.

Nothing.

Then I had an idea: if I burned the remaining fuel, that would create thick black smoke. Right?

Maybe another boat would see it?

"Or," I said to myself. "Or maybe I will burn to death trapped on a burning boat instead."

I walked through sloshing water toward the Motobullet™ with the thought of trying Uncle Jerry again, but I kept walking and found myself staring overboard at the boat's stern, drained.

I kneeled down. Not praying, of course (I knew, given my current contractual obligations, *that* road was likely closed to me now). I dangled my head over the water.

Self-pity gripped me, and I began to weep. "I need help."

The man in my dark reflection offered no help; he was just as screwed as I was.

With just hours until the deadline and at least two hours—at the speed of a World War II fighter mounted inside a steel boat's hull—until New Orleans, I couldn't help but fall into total despair.

"No, it can't… it can't end this way. I need…" I said, choking on sobs. "I need…"

Tears fell from my eyes, creating ripples in the ocean water. The man in my dark reflection shimmied and disappeared. Without even my reflection, I was totally alone.

"What you need, if I may say," a voice behind me said, "is tar tape."

Chapter Twenty-Seven

"There!" I shouted and pointed, even though it was, well, pointless. The man named Alvin Stoddard certainly didn't need me to explain the obvious.

The old man from Mississippi who'd appeared on my boat had gotten me back on track with nothing more than strips of cloth and a bucket of black goo. Must be some serious, high-level, Hell-issued shit because it held the fuel line together for the next two hours.

Off the bow was land and my first glimpse of the New Orleans harbor. To the east, we also got the first glimpse of dawn. I had just a few hours until my time was up.

As we closed in at top speed, the biggest concern at that moment was a US Coast Guard cutter, which had been pursuing us for the last twenty minutes at faster and faster speeds.

Alvin was a godsend, or rather, the other kind, and without him I'd still be floating adrift in the Gulf of Mexico. Ahead of us was the shiny port—on either side of the canal, two huge creampuff cruise ships.

I was nearly there!

Over the roar of the now-smoking World War II fighter plane above our heads, I shouted to Alvin.

"They'll have a small flotilla of cops waiting for me, no question."

"Betcha that's the truth."

He nodded at the dried gore on my shirt and said, "Who's that belong to?"

"What? The blood? It's mine."

"Okay, then. I was just seeing how far you took all this. Wonder if maybe somebody got in your way for a spell."

"No, I got shot."

"No shit?"

"Yeah, can you believe it?"

"Sure, I been shot a bunch a times. Shot, stabbed, toss off buildins, set on fire once."

Looking at the guy, sure, to me he had the demon complexion, but he certainly didn't appear to be teetering on the brink of death despite the rundown of hits he'd just given me.

"You look fine. Diet and exercise? Everything in moderation?" I said, which drew a chuckle from the old man.

"Nah, can't kill what's basically already dead. I work for the Downstairs, so no point in lettin' me expire. All that sorta just, you know, bounces off. Raz, you prob'ly got yourself a temporary pass in that regard as well. Our lawyers call it 'death indemnity.' As it was explained to me, it was a bit of a—"

"Loophole," I said. "Yeah, heard about those." Then something occurred to me. "Wait, but why then were some people from your side, Hell, Inc., trying to kill us if they ca—"

"Protection gets a bit hazy in regards to other demon folks."

"Oh. How's that work?"

"Loophole within the loopholes," he said, then smiled at me. "I think the lawyers for your side and mine got too much time on their hands, maybe."

Something in me balked at the idea of me being on any "side" of Hell, but I let it go and scanned the horizon. We were coming up fast.

"Maybe we should head a bit to the east and try to land somewhere less populated?" I yelled over the noise. "And, of course, where maybe there's less population likely aiming guns and stuff at us?"

"Nah, man. This ol' bird's almost done. Besides, that cutter back there's just looking to get close enough to blow this contraption sky high. You go any direction other than straight ahead, and your fighter-boat gets turned to molten steel and sinks."

"Right," I said. "But you said they couldn't kill me."

"Sure, but you'd be the chewy center in all that melted steel as it sank. They'd send you to the bottom of the ocean, and you ain't ever getting outta that.

I looked back.

"I'm no lawyer, but I think that might violate my Miranda rights."

Alvin laughed. "Man, you flying a rocket ship into N'Orleans. Nobody's gonna be mad when they shoot us to bits.

For a long moment, I stared into the man's face, looking for something. Some indication of what laid behind his dead eyes. Finally, I said: "Jesus, man. You just... don't look, you know, *evil*."

He laughed. "I ain't exactly evil, man. Just doin' my job."

"But you work for bosses in Hell for crissake. I mean, by all practical definitions, you're evil," I said. "Right?"

He looked toward the port and then at our pursuers. Then he exhaled a deep breath and laid it all out.

"Whatchu think evil is, man? Who is 'evil' in your mind?"

"I dunno. Bad people, I guess."

"Bad people." He laughed, shook his head. "Man, evil's just, you know... perspective."

"Nah, evil's evil, dude."

"Says who?"

"It... well, that's just how it is. I've known people who were fuckin' evil in my life. And not just the crazy bastards that end up on the news."

"Nah, like I'm sayin', that's just perspective."

The hum of the fighter above our heads had long ago made my teeth numb. For a moment, I bit down, trying to stop the tingling. "Alvin, I get it. You're justifying what you do, who you work for."

He looked over his shoulder at the Coast Guard boat closing in, then looked back at me. "How 'bout this: Momma kills her babies. Evil?"

"Shit yeah."

"What if she's a hamster?"

"That... that's not the same thing."

"It is."

"No, it's not. Hamsters don't know any better."

"You don't know that," he said, and I scrunched up my face. Before I could say anything, he added, "Okay, okay. What if she *don't* know any better. Let's say some human woman does the same thing but is so wacked out on drugs or is so messed up in her brain that she thought her babies were monsters coming to kill her."

"It's still murder."

"Now *you're* talking perspective. War heroes ain't murderers, but they kill people. It's just they killed while aligned to some ideology that says 'we gotta do this.' Their perspective justifies it."

"That is… that's muddled."

"Man, it's all muddled," he said.

"So you're trying to convince me evil doesn't exist?"

"Nah, but evil's the domain of Hell, not Earth. To say someone on Earth is 'evil' is just cuttin' corners. 'Cause, one man's evil is another man's… thing he thinks he's gotta do."

Oh, wait. Okay. I'd been slow to pick up on it. Alvin was trying to tell me something.

"Hold on," I said, "so this is all about *me*, then? You're saying by me trying to save my wife, somehow what I'm doing here is evil?"

"In saving your wife, you got to hand over some magic lamp to the Devil. One that's so powerful, he's not allowed to get it for *hisself*. But you can."

"No, wait. That's not the plan," I said. Then, less sure of myself, I added: "I don't think that's what I'm supposed to do."

"For now, that don't matter," Alvin said. "You're trying to save your girl. Trying to save your soulmate. You're a good man. Keep to that."

I nodded and swallowed hard. "Thank you."

Alvin Stoddard looked at his old, worn hands for a moment, then stared me right in the eyes.

"But you gotta ask yourself: If the Devil's made a deal with you—a wager—he don't expect to lose…"

"He doesn't lose," I yelled over the roar of the fighter. "I get all the pieces of the lamp, and my wife is okay. I don't and he gets, you know, me."

Alvin nodded slowly and stared off toward the approaching port. He said, "Yeah, nothin' personal by it, but he coulda just waited until you died. Don't you think you was heading his way anyhow?"

Whoa. How can a statement like that not be personal?

"Wait. If he wanted the lamp, why didn't he just send one of his people to get it?"

"Hellspawn and their affiliated can't go into holy places. Doesn't apply to you. You just a freelancer. We don't get many of those anymore. Rare thing now." He looked at me. "Devil took a shot to get the lamp when you showed up."

The rule that demon-types were verboten from holy places made sense with what Anza had already begun to piece together. More importantly, it helped narrow down exactly what sort of place I might find the final piece, the spindle.

It was time to act.

Alvin stood and pulled himself toward the front of the boat, and I followed him a bit unsteadily. "You don't think we can ram this to shore, huh?"

"Nah, not happening. I hope you can swim."

"I'm fat. I float, man."

Alvin and I had concocted a very basic plan, but it had a slight problem: It was *our* plan. An agent of Hell, Inc. and a Devil-hired freelancer. If anything went wrong (i.e. death-level wrong), the no-killing protection might be invalid.

Here was our terrible plan: I was going to roll off the rocket-boat into the water, which would likely kill me a little bit, while he steered the boat into the pier, which would definitely kill him.

"Nah, it ain't gonna kill me," he said. "I'll wink outta here as fast as I winked in and be back in Mississippi."

"How can you do *that*?"

"Perks of the job, you can say. Me, I'm afforded some… latitude on which laws bind me."

I smiled. "That's cheating."

"Nah, man. Loophole," he said and smiled a dull gray grin beneath his horrible, ghoulish features. "My side's just got better lawyers than yours, ya see."

He got ready, bracing himself at the front of the boat, just out of reach of the prop, as I considered what the next few moments would look like.

Then I stopped thinking about it because it was about to be *very ouchie,* and too much consideration might mean I'd back out.

"Here," I said, about thirty seconds from where I was supposed to just roll into the bay as the boat roared along at hundreds of miles an hour.

He looked at me as I stood there bare chested with my fingers wrapped around my balled-up shirt. I was handing it to him.

"What am I supposed to do with that?"

"It sells the effect," I said and then just began to wrap it around his head.

"This is stupid."

"Which is why it'll work," I said.

He looked at me, swallowed hard, and gave me a nod—a moment in time, I swear, that made me almost love the guy.

"Hey, Raz-man. Good luck to ya."

"Thanks."

"One more thing."

"Yeah?"

"You right. You are fat. You got little man titties."

"Uh-huh," I said, bracing for what I had to do next. "You need to find a woman, man."

"Had me one. How d'you think I ended up doing goddamn handyman work for Hell?" He then yelled over the roar of the engine: "Go, man!"

Keeping low, I put my body parallel to the starboard lip of the boat. As I clung there with the lamp's globe tucked away in a first-aid kit I'd commandeered from the bike, the water sparkled in the Louisiana sun like diamonds—or like razor-sharp shards of glass.

"*Go now, Raz!*"

I mumbled to myself "Screw it" and rolled off the side of the speeding fighter-boat.

At first, moving as fast as we were, I felt my shoulder blades slapping against the sting of seawater as if I were a happy, happy skipping stone. The next moment, gravity finally noticed the fat pink guy bouncing across the water and gave me a hard yank, and I was submerged head first, then tumbled end over end over end until my stomach churned from spinning and the gallon or two of seawater I'd swallowed shot out through my nose.

For a full minute, I just floated, watching the Hell, Inc. man at the bow of the boat getting farther and farther away from me. I'd strapped the first-aid kit to my chest with some of Alvin's extra pieces of cloth, but the handle had been free and left a red bar-shaped welt just above my naval.

Sucking in a couple huge breaths, trying to not throw up, my head just bobbed above the water.

Alvin had sharply turned the moment I'd rolled off. In fact, I think the turn was what finally put me over the edge of the boat. I saw him heading toward the pier, the Coast Guard cutter just a blur, looking to be no more than a couple hundred yards from his tail. At the front of the boat, one of the sailors had manned a huge fifty-caliber gun.

Ahead, a fishing pier was being cleared of bystanders in a panic of gray and flannel. At least a dozen others stood filming with their mobile phones as cops pushed them in shoveling waves away from the wooden deck.

A moment later, I looked back again at Alvin, as we discussed, standing at the bow with my shirt wrapped around the top of his head.

Moments before he hit the pier, I whispered "Allah Akbar, man" and silently thanked him as the explosion twisted a red-orange-black cauliflower plume into the sky.

Forty-five minutes later, I pulled myself up onto the grassy bank of a New Orleans canal. As I lay heaving, I had the strangest realization: I knew where the next piece was.

Images of an old church popped into my vision, momentarily blinding me. I could see a black choir, a preacher, then a flash of white… dust, darkness. Then… contractors.

Then people drinking and dancing, and then again, darkness and dust. A closed-down church had been turned into a failed bar. It had been shut down and boarded up.

"Angelos," I said aloud.

That's where the next piece was. But where were my friends?

I hadn't heard from them in more than fifteen hours. That probably meant they couldn't talk to me. Which gave me two conclusions: They were either dead or in jail.

Nothing I could do about the former. I checked my watch. Just over an hour to find Angelos and assemble the lamp.

And yet I couldn't leave behind the people who'd helped me get to the finish line.

The Spindle

Dearest Carissa,

I think of you the moment I awake, often because it's your snoring that's woken me up. Not that I mind. They're cute little puppy snores. Of course, sometimes the puppy's obviously got a respiratory infection. But still, I love it.

I think of you when I'm falling asleep, usually because I'm shaking as the warmth drains from my body with your cold feet latched on to my leg. But my heart feels good, really good, when you do that because I know it's me (or the exposed flesh of my hip and thigh) that is pulling you from the night's cold grip so you can drift into peaceful sleep.

It's a little frustrating for you, I know because you've told me that when you ask me to explain why I love you so much I simply respond with "because you're my babydoll." You're an organized person and want a comprehensive and detailed answer.

But love is not like that. At least my love for you isn't.

It's so much more than words could feebly describe.

If I were to ask you why you love Boston cream pies, you might list all the elements of the pie. Chocolate, pudding, cake (so why is this called a pie if there's cake???). But those aren't reasons—those are parts and pieces. You might as well say you like flour, sugar, and water. You ever put a tablespoon of flour in your mouth? Not good. It tastes like you've just come to in a Turkish prison and a guy name Muftar is slumped in the bunk next to you with a sloppy grin, looking blissfully satisfied.

The fact is, I can't explain my love for you by simply pointing out a handful of parts of you—your lovely smile, your wonderfully-too-tight hugs, your eyebrow obsession, or the way you smell nicer before you shower than after.

I've left this letter by your hospital bedside, hoping if you wake up it will give you a smile. Sweetheart, I want you to know that I'm doing something borderline dangerous and potentially stupid, but I'm doing it because I love you. I'm risking everything for you because you are my everything.

And since this may be my last letter ever to you, as best as I can, here's my reason for loving you:

Despite the puppy snores and the cold feet—or maybe because of them—you are the only person I want there when I fall asleep and the only one I wanna see when I wake up.

Still, even if I listed all the wonderful things about you, all the things that make you my girl, any exhaustive list or photographic collage would simply come down to one simple, basic notion.

I love you forever.

And know that right now, I'm out there trying to see if I can make our forever last a little bit longer.

Yours forever,
Rasputin

Chapter Twenty-eight

"Yes, the three of them," a desk sergeant said from behind a scuffed, cracked, and clouded slate of Plexiglass.

"Can I see them? It's pretty important."

"You their lawyer?"

"No."

"Do you know why they were in a stolen plane?"

"Wasn't stolen. A guy gave it to us on loan."

He raised his eyebrows. "Us?"

"Them."

"Right," he said and scanned a sheet in front of him. He then rubbed some spot on the semiclear barrier between us. "Whatever, the judge needs to deal with them. Until then, they're going nowhere."

"When will that be?"

"Monday."

I nodded. "What's, uh, today?"

"Friday. So they got a nice long weekend to come up with a better story."

"You're a dick."

"You wanna join them?"

I crossed my arms so I wouldn't punch something (which would have hurt my fist real bad).

"Unless you've got a damn good lawyer," he added with a yellow-toothed grin, "they're spending the weekend in the graybar hotel, son." He laughed and licked his thumb, then worked a smudge on the glass again.

"Yeah," I said and gave him the finger. He tensed, until I stuck it in my ear. "Yeah, I got a damn good lawyer."

A voice in my ear said, "Hello, who is this? And remember, billable hours begin now depending on your individual contract."

My three friends waited on a bench as I finished up with the Devil's Advocate.

"Rasputin, you've got just a half hour to find the last piece."

"On it," I said absentmindedly.

"But I understand it's here in the city. Get that and…" The lawyer smiled as he said the next words: "… you are home free."

Slowly, I nodded and thought about what Alvin had said to me on the boat.

"So what am I supposed to do with the lamp once it's all put together?"

"Fix your woman," he said, annoyed. "Isn't that why you're doing this?"

"Yeah. After that?"

He shrugged. "Keep it. Put it on eBay. Who cares?"

I squinted at him. "Do people still use eBay?"

"I hope so. It's one of ours," he said. "We don't care what you do with it."

Anza stood up. "That is not true." She walked over, wiping her hands on her trousers. "The contract says he must hand over the lamp once the pieces have been collected and it's been assembled."

"Really," I said and looked back at the man. "Funny how you would have forgotten that. Photogenic memory and all."

"Photographic," the advocate said, nearly growling the word.

"Yeah, whatever."

"Listen, young lady—" he started. However, the next word got caught in his throat because I had my fingers wrapped around his windpipe.

"Don't. Don't. *Ever*. *Talk* to my friends."

"Rasp—"

"NEVER," I said, cinching my fingers tighter. "You understand? You're to never talk to my friends."

"Raz," he said, tongue flicking against his teeth. "Do you really think you're in a position to make threats?" He smiled, pleased with himself.

"I do," I said. "I got something your boss wants really, really bad, I reckon. And here's me thinking—the Old Man is going to be very appreciative of me getting the trinket, not you. Nor any of your kind."

His face reddening, he said, "Self-delusion seems to be a virtue in your world, Ra—."

Squeeze.

"So that makes me a valuable asset. Doin' something others can't. Man, with that kind of cred' in a big ol' organization? Well, that's all kinds of sway, don't you think?"

The fat man simply stared at me, his eyelids flickering slightly.

"So, for now," I said, "let's not make me... displeased with you."

I let go, and he drew a short breath, straightened out his suit.

"As you wish," he said, then turned toward Anza at my side. His mouth opened and his eyes flicked toward me. Then it clamped shut like a hungover bullfrog with cottonmouth. With a nod, he was out the door where his black car, never far away, instantly appeared at the curb.

I looked over at my friends on the bench and pointed to the door, and we all headed to the exit.

"You can't give it to them, I don' think."

"I don't think either, Anza," I said, whispering. "But I think I have to."

She stopped me and turned my head toward her. "You have to breathe. You have to eat. It ends there. Everything else is a choice."

"You also have to poop," I suggested.

She smiled, despite herself.

"You can't keep all that eating stuff in," I said.

"Shut up," she said and laughed.

"Poop... there is no choice. We must."

"Yes, but it messes up my mama's nice saying. Breathe, eat. It's more poetic. Pooping is not poetic."

"Oh, I've had poetic poop," I said, correcting her.

"No more poop talk."

"I've had friggin' *iambic pentameter* poop, lady."

"So gross!"

Chapter Twenty-nine

As previously established, in the beginning, God had secretly stacked the deck in His favor.

The Earth was within His domain, and because of established rules—what we humans call physics—it was going to stay that way.

Them's the rules.

However, ironically, the devil is in the details. Especially a small detail in general relativity—discovered, categorized, and detailed on various worlds by various names.

In its simplest terms, it's a matter of polarity: positive and negative.

Similar to when one begins to reach the speed of light, where one's mass grows toward the infinitely large, the same is true for contested elemental systems that begin in a positive or negative state. If a growing force begins to tip the balance toward its opposing state—say from positive toward negative—an increasingly and exponentially larger force occurs to maintain the original state.

(Note: this is true for that majority of contested zones, where both "sides" have a stake in the game. It doesn't apply to places that, for example, God deemed unworthy and gave up without a fight. (see: Orlando, Florida))

Earth's original state had been in the positive "good" zone and while there were the occasional city-wide fires, prolific serial killers, and James Joyce poetry… theoretically, for the most part, it would always stay there. And in terms of "good" to "evil," in a closed system, the opposing force is eventually acted upon by a force inverse to the distance to equilibrium.

The upshot is this: the closer the losing team moves toward getting the upper hand, the more that hand is pushed back by a powerful and exponentially larger force.

Evil was, in essence, fucked.

However, like Canada, sometimes God hadn't thought it all the way through.

One evening, Niels Bohr was chatting with the Dark Lord over a tawny port (Bohr had been brilliant and mostly good, but there'd been an unfortunate little moment in his early teens brought on by a half bottle of cough syrup, the close proximity of a fireplace bellows, and a morally ambiguous neighbor's cat). Bohr had suggested to Satan this:

Bohr: What if you, instead of trying to tip the scales from Good to Evil, you rocketed from Good to Evil?

Satan: Doesn't matter. As you close the gap, the force pushing you back grows and grows. Can't do it.

Bohr: But what if you approach the equilibrium, approach zero, but then jump past it? Pop on the other side of it.

Satan: Hold on. You can't. You can't pop. No one said anything about popping!

Bohr: But what would happen? You go from 50.1 percent positive one moment, to 50.1 percent negative the next.

Satan: But you can't go from one point to another without passing the middle bit in between. You can't... Right?

Bohr: Uh, tell that to an electron.

Satan: Nah. I stopped talk to electrons years ago. They're so negative.

Bohr: …

Satan: Come on, that's funny shit!

Bohr: …

Satan: Whatever.

Bohr himself had discovered this little quantum loophole back when he'd been, well, alive and not cavorting in the bowels of Hell.

Electrons in an atom essentially move from one "floor" to another—and this is the important bit—*without passing through the space in between.* So Bohr suggested—not because he was evil; he was just spit-balling to pass the time—if evil barreled mankind toward the equilibrium very, very fast, that in a quantum measure, it *could* actually leap *right past zero* into the negative.

From positive to negative. From a reign of Good to one of Evil.

Up until then, Satan's army of demons had been turning souls one at a time. A congressman here. A boy band there. But what if he could turn thousands? *Millions?* And quickly too.

Pyramid schemes? Still too slow. They needed the equivalent of a roaring wildfire of evil. Converting souls, casting misery so fast as to tip the world into the dark so quickly it'd catch the laws of physics with its pants down.

But it couldn't be something that was simply bad and destructive. That was the old-school approach. It would have to be a purely negative and corruptive force, on a massive scale.

Many years earlier, in the 14th century, they actually stumbled upon it. And mankind never saw it coming.

The Black Plague had been considered by many to be the "Devil's doing," and they'd been right, but for all the wrong reasons.

The Plague didn't simply kill indiscriminately. No, it sowed the most dangerous of human desires: greed. If the owner of a parcel of land wanted the neighbor's lovely fields as well? Well, guess who gets fingered as a plague victim?

What about if Grandfather had overstayed his welcome (but the resulting inheritance had not)? Pop-pop's got the plague-plague. That was evil not written about in the textbooks.

The genius of the Black Death, the factor that nearly pushed the Earth into Satan's hands, wasn't the piles of blackened bodies but the black *hearts* it helped create!

Seeing his Earth was on the brink, God, as the Americans say, called an audible:

Norse god (retired): Aye, what cha doing in my pub?
God: Need a solid.
NG (retired): Retired.
G: I'll owe ya.

So how does God (big G) come to ask for help from a Norse god (little g)?

The story goes that for a century or two, God and the Devil had their attentions diverted away from the Earth as they fought over a neighboring galaxy.

Billions fighting billions on either side. While the forces above and below were otherwise occupied, the Dark Ages produced a series of lesser demigods. And during the freezing winters, no one had prayed harder than the Scots.

Sure, when God and the Devil returned, all the minor leaguers had to piss off and find other work. And that's where God had sought out and found Víðarr and asked for a favor. This was the Norse god of revenge!

And almost as important, the Norse god of silence. So he'd keep this shit to himself.

The story says that in his bar, Víðarr went to the wall, and among the many artifacts, ornaments, wooden goblets and pewter chalices… there was a lamp. A last remnant of those demigod days: a small paraffin lamp. When held by a being that projected pure kindness and love, its light could turn even the cold blackness of space all warm and fuzzy.

God entrusted the priests of a secret and uniquely devout sect (and, bonus, with their vow of silence they didn't ask too many questions) with the lamp and with its light, cast the Black Plague from Earth.

Borderline cheating, one might argue, sure, but who's gonna complain? Getting rid of the Black Plague? If nothing else, the entire place would smell a lot better.

And ultimately, with the lamp slamming the brakes and stopping the Earth from tipping into evil? Who could be pissed about that?

Well, Satan, that's who.

So, for years, the Dark Lord tried to get his hands on the Norse god's lamp so he could finally rule and control every human on planet Earth.

And now, an idiot who simply loved his wife more than life itself was about to give it to him.

Chapter Thirty

We took a taxi to Bourbon Street because, if a bit of Hell were lurking about in New Orleans, it'd be there. Anza used her phone to Google "Angelos" and confirmed that suspicion.

We were all following the Actor, who smiled wide when we started down the famous stretch of road.

"I did a made-for-TV film in that bar there a dozen years ago."

"Learning Channel?" Uncle Jerry said and laughed.

"Don't remember. Wasn't a very big network, though. Wasn't a very good movie, far as I can recall."

I spotted an upscale clothing store; suits I couldn't afford hung in the window.

"Hey," I said, "you wanna get some proper clothes, man? You gotta be tired of the dirty robe."

The Actor didn't even break stride. "I'm entirely comfortable strutting in this robe. I started this wearing the red robe, I'm ending this wearing the red robe."

For whatever reason, that sounded like something I should write down and hang on a wall.

I'd already told everyone that we were looking for the boarded-up Angelos. The Actor had been used to leading the way, so despite me grabbing the title of Most Evil in our group, he was blazing our trail, walking down the middle of Bourbon.

He glanced up at me with a half smile. "What did you do in Mexico to become our little group's most bad? Do we even want to know?"

To be honest, I couldn't think of anything that was *really* bad. I mean, except for stealing the holy artifact of a dying race of people (but that was for a good cause).

After thinking it over, I said, "What if it's the opposite?"

"Meaning what?"

"I dunno. Maybe *you* did something really good, man."

For a short time, he was very, very quiet.

Uncle Jerry had been characteristically stubborn about not needing to go to a hospital, insisting he was there to finish what we'd started. However, still very stumbly from his encounter with the goons at the airport, walking wasn't so great for him.

It had been his idea to instead crawl up into an abandoned shopping cart, arms and legs hanging over the edges, while Anza and I took turns pushing.

"There," I said after a couple of blocks.

The Actor looked over his shoulder at me stealin' his thunder a little and said, "Right. That seems—"

"Ras-poo-tin," a pretty black man said, his German cameraman just off his shoulder, filming our approach. The reporter was leaning up against Angelos, sipping a cocktail out of a clear plastic cup.

"Thought you were dead," I said as we walked up.

"Nah, I wouldn't miss this for the world. Whatta day, whatta day!"

"Yeah," I said, the anger slightly draining in me. "But that.. you know, that doesn't explain why you're not dead and all."

"I got two broken ribs, a cracked collarbone, and a misaligned pelvis!" the cameraman yelled.

"That doesn't remotely sound German," I said.

The reporter smiled his pearly-toothed smile. "Me, I was able to pull Gunter on top of me when you ran us down, asshole."

"Gunter?" I turned to our oldest team member as he slowly climbed from the cart. "Gunter! Hey, *that* sounds German, doesn't it?"

Uncle Jerry patted me on the shoulder with a smile. "I'll be damned, you were right."

The black reporter shooed his hands at me. "You go get your piece now, Devil minion." He opened the door with a flourish. I could see he had—or more likely his Nazi cameraman had—snapped away the board that had been securing the entryway before we showed up.

I opened my mouth to say something clever but stopped, momentarily, hearing a song somewhere in the distance. It was… I couldn't place it.

So familiar, though.

Running out of time, we quickly headed inside.

As I said, the place was a bar once called Angelos. And while, as holy places go, that doesn't sound like it would rank terribly high, there had been "Gospel Brunches" at the bar on alternating Sundays—for either the faithful or terribly hung over (or both). Those events were reminiscent of its previous incarnation: a historically black Baptist church.

"Look around," I said. "We got fifteen minutes to find the piece."

"Yeah, but that's only four all together, then," the Actor said.

I nodded. "The lamp is just those four. The fuel is a different story."

"Okay," Anza said. "What is this to look for? A spindle."

"It's, well, it's tiny. Think of a thing that would wind a watch, like a bar, a needle shape, but instead of a sharp point it ends in a squat cylinder. Like a tiny muffin with ridges."

"Okay."

Then, briefly, I heard a smattering of music again. This time, I could just make out the lyrics. Something about a "god of thunder"

Oh damn.

"Rasputin!" a man said from the bar's back door. He was flanked by his two friends and held aloft a large wooden club. I knew without even seeing it that it would be emblazoned with a KISS Army crest.

"Who are those idiots?" Uncle Jerry asked.

"I met 'em a few days ago."

"They look like dicks," the Actor said.

"They mean well," I said.

"Said Neville Chamberlain, returning from Germany in 1938," said Uncle Jerry.

The three men stepped forward into a dust-choked ray of sunlight. For his part, Dr. Love held high, I could now see clearly, of all things, KISS Army-issued nunchucks. Next to him was Love Gun in a wide stance with something glinting in each hand—more throwing stars, of course. Deuce was holding a small piece of paper. He stammered for a moment, and all eyes fell on him.

"This is a receipt for a KISS Army bazooka!" he yelled at me. "However, I am still within the standard seven-day waiting period."

"Rasputin!" Dr. Love said. "You cannot hand the lamp to the Prince of Darkness. It will empower him... as it did once before. He nearly turned the light of our world dark!"

"It will save my wife."

"At the expense of every other person on the planet?"

I looked toward my friends, who nodded back. "Fair trade," I said.

There was a moment's hesitation, and then he said, a degree less cool: "Damn, I wish somebody loved me like that."

"Me too," Love Gun said.

"Still!" Dr. Love had his righteous indignation back. "We can't let you give it to the Devil."

They charged.

I turned to Uncle Jerry and Anza. "Find the spindle."

To the Actor, I handed over the first-aid kit with glass chimney inside. "Assemble the lamp." And then I ran for a set of stairs across the room.

For a brief moment, God's Undamned Army halted their advance and glanced at the three remaining friends.

Anza looked at them, put on her angry face, and said, "He went... thataway, nerds."

Strangely, they all flashed her a smile and chased after Raz, who they'd already seen running.

"I don't think they talk to ladies much," Uncle Jerry said.

"Who still says 'ladies,' man?" The Actor tapped them both, and the three of them swung into a shuttered office. The office looked like it had recently been a sleeping area (and likely a toilet) to a number of homeless people. The tiny room's pungent bouquet confirmed that.

Several empty, crushed, tall-boy beer cans were scattered across the dented steel desk. The Actor cleared them away with a sweep of his arm, revealing scratches in the desk's gray paint, written with various levels of crudity and depravity. The most recent appearing to be: "Your mom swallowed my baby batter on this desk!"

"Nice penmanship," the Actor said.

Anza handed him the globe after she'd pulled it out of the first-aid kit, but when he grabbed for it, it rolled out and fell hard toward the concrete floor.

In a fraction of a second, the Actor was able to reach for it but instead of catching it, he inadvertently sent it rocketing across the room toward the wall.

I was obviously not going to be able to outrun Murderous Larry, Moe, and Curly for very long.

First off, the place wasn't that large. Second, the remains of tables and chairs (not to mention the remnants of food, both rotten and "used") made the actual "outrunning" next to impossible.

Of course, the biggest reason was that I was an overweight lump who'd not seen a proper night's sleep in a full four days. That is, three days, twenty-three hours, and fifty-two minutes. And counting.

I just had to keep them away from my friends so they could find the spindle and get the lamp together.

Kicking through the bramble of broken chairs and tabletops, I heard the *twack-crunch* of splitting wood just inches from my head.

Someone had upgraded their throwing stars.

Uncle Jerry and Anza had both closed their eyes, unable to watch. The Actor walked over to where the globe had smashed against the wall.

"Oh, wow," he said.

"Oh my God, don't tell it," Anza said, covering her ears. "It can't be broked, no, no!"

The Actor reached down, picking up the glass globe, still intact.

"No, it's fine," he said, then he tilted his head. "Huh. The guy with the good penmanship wrote on this wall as well, 'Your mom guzzled it here, too.'"

"What?"

"Glassy globe thing is fine. But I must find this guy's mom before we go," he said and brought it back to the desk. "See? It's all in one piece. I suppose to stick around for more than a century, possibly more with some slippage through time, this thing's gotta be pretty tough."

"Probably that gorilla glass stuff they make smart phones outta," Uncle Jerry said.

The Actor shook his head. "You know, you vacillate from smart to dumb on a whim. Somehow, you got stoned from the police station to here, while being immobile and draped in a shopping cart like a man-baby."

Uncle Jerry's half smile wavered. His lips parted, hanging there for a moment. "I'm not entirely sure if you just asked me a question or not."

Before the Actor could say anything, they heard Raz let out a guttural sound— a half yell, half scream that rattled the broken plate-glass window of the office door. Anza grabbed Uncle Jerry's hand and pulled him out the door, yelling over her shoulder, "Get those pieces together. We have to find the spindle!"

The Actor pulled the metal font and wick manifold from Uncle Jerry's fanny pack and placed them, evenly spaced out, on the metal desk. He stared at them. "It would have helped to see its original box, so I know how they fit tog—"

His words froze midair, the last one dangling from the lower lip of his open mouth. He watched closely, and the lamp parts moved.

The three pieces on the table inched closer to each other in short, uneven bursts.

"Motherfu—"

Thankfully, the throwing star embedded in my shoulder wasn't barbed or laced with some KISS Army-issued poison, and it came out rather easily.

Fapf-fapf-fapf!

"Motherfucker!" Three more metal stars split the skin on my other shoulder and back, but with no time to dig those out, I started running again.

The wounds, after the initial shock, simply felt very, very cold, but not terribly painful. I was surprised by that because I could feel little rivulets of blood streaming down by back.

I caught a quick glimpse of Anza and Uncle Jerry, and they saw me in return. Their expressions told me they could see the metal jutting out of my back. The pilot's fists tightened, and they looked like they wanted to come my way, but I shook them off like a baseball pitcher, rounding a corner to the much darker part of the venue where I could just make out the booths of the dining area.

One of my pursuers saw me, maybe Love Gun, and he shouted— "Feel the burn, demon seed! Those stars are covered in holy *wah-tah*," And then he growled, "*Un-hoo-leeee!*"

He was really making me not like KISS anymore, and I began to hate him for it.

"Should we split up to look?"

Uncle Jerry shrugged. "Maybe, but I got a hunch those nutters are gonna turn on us once they realize we're helping Raz."

"Okay," she said, taking a few steps forward.

In front of them was a compact entertainment area, complete with stage, split into three sections. Near the back, where they were standing, was an area that looked to have been staged with high-top tables and barstools.

The next part was recessed, dropping a foot and a half for what could have been a dance floor or mosh pit, depending on the show. Beyond that was the stage. The old, heavy curtains had been cut to ribbons by vandals; overhead scaffolding hung down like the decaying rib cage of some long-dead creature from the Jurassic era.

"Is such a big place," she whispered, her voice bordering on tears. "How are we going to find? There's so little—"

Jerry tapped her shoulder. When she spun, she saw he was looking up to the ceiling with its odd, dull glitter. He pointed to the twinkling canopy above them, which was at least three stories from the dance floor.

She stared but then quickly said, "What?"

"Up there."

"I can' see... what...? Oh. Oh no."

"Yeah."

The glitter from above wasn't from silver flecks in the popcorn stucco or even residual light from outside. Like a night sky filled with tiny, flickering lights, each little "star" was the tip of a short metal rod.

"One of those is our last piece," Jerry said. "The spindle."

"How do you... how did you even see that?"

"You can see them more clearly if you squint a little bit."

She looked at him. "I thought I saw you doing that, but I thought it was just because you maybe were high on marijuana."

Uncle Jerry looked away from the ceiling and at her, less squinty, as if waiting for something else to be said. When she said nothing, he said, "I get the feeling there may have been a question in there somewhere."

Both of them jumped as the Actor came up behind them. "You guys gotta see this!"

Weaving too quickly through the rundown restaurant, I knew I was risking a busted shin or worse if I slammed into anything in the dark.

The rank smell of rot and sewage was making me gag. I'd spent a number of years working in the bowels of restaurants, as I've said, and I instinctively switched to breathing through only my open mouth. Some of the most revolting depositories of toxic, bubbling goo on earth are about fifty feet from dining areas of the nicest eateries in the world.

Discarded food, broken and dirty dishware, raw meat, congealed animal fat, and at least one uncapped drum of what-the-hell-is-that? can be found in nearly every Michelin-starred restaurant on the planet.

I was reminded of that wee factoid when pushing through a door and finding a broken Dumpster in the loading dock area. It was even darker here and smelled so bad I put my hands to my mouth. My biggest mistake was that I'd let the door go as I came through. It locked as it closed.

Dead end.

All the doors, including the giant rollaway, had been welded shut once the place had closed down.

No way out.

And once the door closed behind me, I knew from experience that, from this side, that door wasn't opening without a key. Or without three homicidal KISS fans bursting through it to kill me.

"Check it out," the Actor said. In one hand, he held the font and wick manifold. In the other, the glass globe.

He tossed the globe in the air, and Anza screamed, "What are you—!"

Falling downward, the globe impossibly arched away from the floor and clamped tight against the wick manifold, which was already mounted on the font. All three parts snapped together automatically.

"Cool, huh?" the Actor said.

"What? Why?" Anza yelled, trembling slightly. "Don' do that anymore." She flicked his ear.

Uncle Jerry's eyes widened. "Why's it do that?"

"I dunno," the Actor said, rubbing his ear. "The pieces are drawn to each other."

Uncle Jerry yelped, then grabbed and hugged the little man, whose feet momentarily dangled in the air. "You're brilliant!"

"Why are you kissing him, with his throwing and smashing important things?" Anza said. She turned to the Actor. "I am not watching your show anymore!"

"We can use these parts of the lamp to find the last piece," Uncle Jerry said.

"What?" the Actor said.

Anza pointed upward.

"Shit, there must be a thousand of them," he said.

"Yeah," Uncle Jerry said. "But as you just showed us, you just get this close enough, and the missing part should—*twang!*—find its way home!"

"But if… wait, you just said 'you,' didn't you? Do you mean the third-person 'you' or 'you' as in *me* 'you.' Because if you meant *me* 'you,' then you're crazy. No way."

Anza looked at Jerry, then back to the Actor. "I not sure, but it sounds like there was a question in there somewhere."

So, I was going to die.

You know that moment where some of the guys go "hey, try this rope swing and swoop into the hayloft" or "do a backflip in the bouncy castle, look, it's easy"?

Then you try the barn rope swing and realize *no way* do you have the grip strength to hold on, and you break your ankle while slamming into the hard dirt. Or you don't know how to do a backflip, and even though it's a bouncy castle full of air, you land on your neck with a fifty-fifty chance of eating all future meals through a straw.

Inside the loading dock, I knew I had to move and found a short set of stairs and climbed up into open loft space above the door I'd just come through. Already I could hear my pursuers clambering down the hallway.

My plan was this: They'd come through the door, and just as it was closing, I was going to go over the loft's metal handrail and swing my body through the open door. It would then slam closed. Them out here, locked away tight. Me back in the restaurant with my friends again, with just minutes left to get the lamp together.

Provided, of course, I wasn't first peppered to death with KISS Army-issued throwing stars. So, basically, it was totally impossible.

Before I could come up with anything better, I saw the flat metal handle turn.

"Wave it around," Anza called up, her voice bouncing around the restaurant's stage area.

"I *am* waving." The Actor was hanging thirty feet in the air from a makeshift harness as Uncle Jerry tugged on a rope that had been thrown over the rickety scaffolding next to the upper balcony.

"Four minutes," Uncle Jerry shouted.

"I fucking hate rope," the Actor muttered. "Hate swinging. Hate swinging on rope." He then yelled, "Pull faster!" and felt a quick tug on the line.

Near the stage, a part of the ancient scaffolding buckled. The Actor had been chosen because he was the lightest of the three. At this point, had anyone else been hanging from the ceiling, the rigging would have certainly come crashing to the floor.

It creaked again.

"Wait!"

Uncle Jerry's eyes were trained on the scaffolding. "Dammit, I'm sorry. This is just too—"

"No, no!" the Actor yelled, his expression excited. "I see it! Holy shit, the damn thing's wiggling. It's moving! Shuffle me over toward the center of the room."

His short arm was outstretched, three quarters of the lamp clutched in his sweaty fingers. Uncle Jerry said he couldn't move him any closer.

"Three minutes," Anza called out, burying her face in her hands.

The Actor looked around and under his breath, whispered. "Dammit." Then, louder: "Loosen the rope."

"Why? What will tha—"

"Do it, do it!"

Uncle Jerry did, and the slack brought the Actor drooping toward the floor. After a few seconds, he said: "Okay, stop."

The Actor then began kicking his feet, swinging from side to side. Anza's expression was a mix of emotions.

Uncle Jerry whispered, "Crazy little bastard's gonna do it."

With each successive swing, the Actor got closer and closer to the wriggling spindle that was trying to free itself and get home.

Another swing, a huge arch... closer.

Somewhere near the stage, a loud clang rang out.

"Stop!" Anza shouted. "Stop, stop! You bring it all down!"

"No stopping!" the Actor shouted to calm his own heaving stomach, the fear churning acid there. Almost... He drew his legs back, and when he was close to the wall, he kicked off as hard as he could, launching toward the final piece.

There was a loud snap. Then another snap, and the rigging began to shudder, the swing now more pronounced. The Actor fought the terror of hanging thirty feet above the concrete floor and kicked his feet to make him arch even further upward.

Above them, in the terrifying few seconds of silence, a tiny flash of light and a *tink* sound.

"Got it!"

Uncle Jerry cheered, and then the entire rigging collapsed, the Actor falling, falling, falling toward the concrete floor below.

After the door opened, I leapt upward and made my swing. Slowly, I saw my feet pass over the tops of their heads. And after one *goddamn* second, I already felt my weak, useless fingers slipping. I just wasn't strong enough.

Once again, the world shook away my brief fever of self-confidence and reminded me that I was just not strong enough.

Baby, you are.

I'm not. And I can't.

You can.

You have too much faith in me. I don't deserve you, Carissa.

I don't. And you do.

Stop. Just... I'm real tired. I tried, baby.

Keep trying. My man is strong.

I ju— I just...

My man is powerful.

Babydoll, please.

My man does not stop when faced with a challenge.

I—

He does not yield.

I just—

My man does not yield. So, whatever he's up against, it will fall.

Okay. Okay, yes.

My husband does not yield.

Yes, okay, baby.

That's my man.

My hands strained. I yelled, willing strength into my fingers.

"I..."

Like tiny birds at the sound of my voice, the three men below me jutted their heads back and forth, searching for me.

"*will not...*"

Then all three faces turned upward and saw me, and I watched as their anger melted into fear in an instant.

"YIELD!"

My hands turned to steel, my grip sure, and I arched over their heads, letting go at the apex of the swing, which launched me through the door and into the dark hall. Landing with a painful thud, flickering starlight briefly filled my vision, I realized I'd hit the floor with the metal still sticking out of my back.

I put that out of my mind and craned my neck back. I momentarily saw the faces of three men before the door slammed closed.

Locked.

"Shit, I did it."

I staggered toward my friends with just seconds until our time was up.

When I came around the corner, my heart fell.

Anza was crying, and Uncle Jerry was shouting at the Actor, who was splayed out on the dirty floor. In his hand, the lamp was complete.

"What's... what happened?"

"He fell. He got the piece, then he fell."

The Actor's eyes were hooded, and through his rib cage, he'd been pierced by the metal leg of a folding chair.

"Jesus, man. We gotta get you to a hospital."

"No," he said, red bubbles forming at his lips. "Your lamp. Go. Save your wife."

"I— Oh, Jesus, man. There—" I couldn't say anything more and began bawling my eyes out.

Uncle Jerry coughed, cleared his throat. "I hate to be the one to say it, but you got less than a minute, Raz."

I looked at them. "What do I do?"

"Go, go," the Actor told me. "That's why we're here, my friend. Go save your wife."

Standing up, I looked to the door. "And since you've got, you know, a lifesaving lamp..." the Actor added, "maybe you can swing back here with it. Unless I'm dead."

"Don't die," I said and bolted for the door.

From the floor, he coughed. "Would it work if I were dead?"

"You don' wan' to be a zombie," Anza said. "If you are dead, stay dead."

"Easy for you to say, you don't have a fucking chair leg sticking out of your chest."

When I hit the door, the sunlight burst in, so bright it felt like I'd been caught doing something illegal.

"There he—"

Not even looking in his direction, I clocked the reporter with my fist, and he went down in a heap. Out of the corner of my eye, I saw the cameraman filming the whole thing. He looked down at the reporter and said something. It sounded like swearing in German, but everything in German to me sounds a little like swearing, so it really could have been anything.

I looked at my watch—fifteen seconds left. "Come on!" I screamed. "Let's go!"

The next moment, the black car pulled up, and I hopped in.

The Advocate looked at me over his reading glasses. This time it was just him and me. His assistant was nowhere to be found.

"You have the item?"

"Yes, all but the fuel, but, yeah, I got the lamp as requested."

"The fue—ah, yes. Of course."

"I did what you asked."

"Well," he said and folded away his reading glasses. "There is the matter of the fuel."

"Screw you. I got your lamp."

"Yes," he said, eyeing it as I rocked it from hand to hand. "You did indeed." His lips were trembling slightly.

I held it out to him, but he threw his hands up like it was on fire.

"No, no. Not for me," he said, then turned. He spoke to the driver behind me, and again, I couldn't understand what words he'd said. Then he turned back to me. "You'll be giving it to him."

"Him?"

The Advocate gave me a terrifying grin and nodded slowly.

I felt the car stop quickly, and he pointed to the door.

As I leaned up, his eyes never left the object in my hands. A moment before I went for the door latch, he reached out but stopped just shy of actually touching me.

"Just… well done, lad. And thank you. After all this time," he said and finally looked directly at me. "Thank you."

"Uh-huh."

Pushing the door open, I can't say I was surprised to see where he had brought me. Back to where it had all begun.

The moment I stepped out, the black car sped away like a nervous whisper, and once again, I stood at the Crossroads.

Chapter Thirty-one

Despite stepping into the car in the early-morning sunshine, here, it was on the far edge of dusk, twilight.

Before me, a relatively young man was sitting on a stump, twirling a cane in his fingers. But not any sort of bobo walking stick with a tennis-ball bumper. This thing glittered gold.

Which made me think it had to be heavy as a mother. Guy must have really strong fingers.

"You got my lamp, boy?"

His face was slightly shadowed, chin to his chest as he bobbed his head slightly, like he was listening to music I couldn't hear. Then I recognized him.

"Holy mother—" I said, then took another step closer. "*Ralph*? Ralph Macchio?"

He looked up and flashed his boyish grin. "That's one of the names I've gone by, sure."

"Wait, wait," I said, scanning the Crossroads, worried there would be some army of demons about to charge at me from all four directions. "What about… the Devil? That dude I made the deal with."

"Ha, that guy?" Ralph said and slowly stood, twirling his glittering cane. "He ain't the Devil, man. You're looking at him."

I held his gaze for a moment, then I said: "Bullshit."

The young star of *The Outsiders* put his hand on my shoulder, and my body flexed into a seizure of pain and heat and such incredible noise, at such an extreme I would have never known it was possible. In a moment, it was over, and I dropped to a knee and dry-heaved.

Ralph "The Devil" Macchio raised his prefect eyebrows. "Any more questions?"

Standing slowly, I drew my hand over my damp mouth and then wiped it on his lapel. Looking at him with double-triple vision, I tried to look strong and unafraid. My best guess: I was looking at him cross-eyed and appeared scared shitless.

"Yeah, one question," I said, trying to clear my vision. "Who the hell was the other guy I met? I thought he—"

"No, that dude works for me. Like a stand-in. I send him out on the occasional gig."

"Oh." I nodded, his features coming back into focus. "Right. Sure. Okay."

"His name's Randall."

"Of course it is."

"I'm only gonna ask one more time," the lead actor from *The Karate Kid* parts *I, II,* and *III* said. "You got my lamp?"

Before I could answer, my wife in her hospital bed materialized next to him right there in the road. Machines beeping and whirring, she had wires leading to her chest with tubes up her nose.

Choking on my grief, I put my hand over my mouth. "Fix her," I cried out. "Just make her okay."

The former teen actor, full-time Prince of Darkness went back to spinning his cane again and grinned a terrible smile. "That's on you, boy."

"What is that supposed to mean?"

"Come on now…" he said, stepping forward and tapping his golden cane on the lamp in my hand. I stepped back, keeping my eyes on my wife. "You give it a good grip, and if you're pure, it will cast a light of *goodness* upon her."

"Me? I don't understand."

"The lamp is fueled by whoever holds it. What's in your heart, Rasputin. If it's pure, it will cast a light to cure her."

Unsure, I held the lamp out, and… nothing.

He laughed. A giant belly laugh that shook the ground all around us.

Again, I held it out. And this time, for a brief moment, it flickered.

The supporting actor of 1992's *My Cousin Vinny* stumbled slightly, and I saw his eyes go a little wide, darting between me and the lamp in my hands.

But as quickly as the ancient artifact had come alive, it was dark and cold once again. Right in front of me, my beautiful wife lay dying in her bed.

I ran over, placed the lamp on the ground, and stroked the thin, damp hair away from her face. "Babydoll," I said. "I love you. Please stay. Stay here with me. I don't—"

My shoulder blade burst into glass shards of pain that sliced their way through my body. I had never imagined a hurt so bad. In a single breath, I coughed all the air from my lungs. I crumpled to the ground. Then, as it had been at the beginning, the rain began to fall.

The next moment, it was a torrent, and I could barely see. The devices around my wife, the ones keeping her alive, began to short and spark, blue tendrils of electricity leaping from machine to machine to machine.

"No!" I screamed and reached up. His golden cane pierced the curtain of rain above me, came down on my arm, and I felt the full force of an earthquake wrack my body.

Rolling back, I tried to get up but instead fell again, face down in the dirty water. I lifted myself, but the Devil struck me down once again. Slowly, I flopped over and looked up through the rain, trying to catch a glimpse of his face.

"You... you said bring the lamp," I shouted, choking on the pouring rain. "I brought it. You promised it would save my wife!"

Again, the cane slammed down upon me, and I felt white-hot fire in every pore, every fiber.

Laughing, he mocked me: "'You said, you said.' Always the same way with you folk. 'You said I'd be rich and famous.' 'You said I'd be president.' 'You said you'd save my wife.' *You said.* Huh!"

Another blow came. I felt my chest constrict and could taste blood in my mouth. But strangely, this time I didn't feel as knocked around as the first blow had left me. Either he was weakening or…

"Thank you so much for that little trinket," he said, twirling the million-dollar walking stick. "You have no idea what a day this is for us. What a day! What a day!"

"I did what you said," I said, slowly getting back to my feet.

"Yeah, and you will do what I say until the end of days, because I own your flabby white ass now!"

"Screw you."

"Now hold on. That's kind of a good thing for you. You're about to be on the winning team," he said, looking as though he were growing taller by the moment. "Oh yeah, it'll be Hell for ya, certainly. But finally… FINALLY… with your help, Rasputin"—he looked around—"I'm gonna run this bitch here now."

As weak as I was, I've always had just one talent, and I was ready with it. Not the smartest, not the strongest, not the quickest. No, never those things.

Man, if I had a super power, it was this: pissing people off.

It just comes naturally.

Drawing in deep breaths, it took nearly all my strength, but I went up on one foot and lifted my arms, curling my hands downward. Satan/Ralph Macchio looked at me, and the sky behind him flickered briefly.

"Motherfucker, you ain't doing a crane at me," he said and seemed to lose a few inches in height. "Tell me you are not doing a *goddamn crane* in front of *me*!"

Yes, I was using the same pose he'd used in the final fight scene of 1984's *The Karate Kid*, starring the venerable Pat Morita as Mr. Miyagi.

Then, it came.

The Devil lifted his own arms and brought his elemental staff down onto my shoulder, and my body felt as though it split down the middle. Screaming, I fell to the ground.

But I stumbled back to my feet and said to the Devil, "I will not—"

Again, he brought his cane down upon me, and the world shook. Something dribbled off my chin, but once again I stood. Out of the corner of my eye was a glow. Not the same blood-red radiance the sky had now become. It was a brilliant, warm, and even loving glow.

I was fueling the lamp.

And it was empowering me.

Holding up my bruised fists, I looked at the Devil through tears and said to the Lord of the Underworld: "I will not yield."

"Then you will die," he said, taking a step toward me.

An earth-shattering force erupted from his fingertips, and I felt my body explode and implode all at once. It was beyond pain. It took me beyond madness. But a moment later, I came back. Splayed out on the ground, I smiled up at him.

The Devil roared and hit me again.

When I'd recovered, I was back on my feet again. I held up my fists once more.

"I will not yield," I said, then spit blood and, I think, a tooth to the dirt crossroads beneath us. "Never to you. Never."

His face actually split, his flesh sloughing off like a snake shedding its skin, and the demon arose on the road in front of me. With his blackened smile, the dark skies above Satan swirled with deep blue and blood red, explosions burst in the clouds above him like a barrage of atomic bombs detonating in the atmosphere, and he gripped his golden staff with clawed fingers and began to bring it down onto me.

But he stopped halfway. Then the expression on his face changed. He wasn't smiling anymore. He turned.

"What, the fu—"

In the darkness, a light began to shine. A beautiful, radiating light like I'd never seen before.

"No!" he shouted, raising his stick. "*What the fuck?*"

Barely able to stand, blood streaming from my eyes and ears, I turned and saw her. Damp hospital clothes hanging off her frail body, she was illuminated by the Lamp of Life clutched in her hands.

My wife said to the Devil: "Get away from my husband."

And with that, a brilliant, pure light burst from the lamp, and in an instant, the dark man with the golden walking stick exploded, the crossroads beneath our feet cracked, and then he was gone.

The rain stopped, and the black skies were traded back for twilight. My lovely wife smiled at me, then collapsed onto the road.

I ran over to Carissa, lifting her head in my arms. "No," I said, tears blurring my vision. "No, don't go. The lamp can save you. I did all this to save you."

I picked up the lamp and held it again, pressing it toward her. Nothing. Gripping it tighter, I squeezed my eyes shut.

Nothing.

Eyes closed and breathing shallow, my wife just smiled weakly.

"It's not fair!"

Slowly she looked at me again. "Thank you, baby. I am so proud to be your babydoll."

"But I can feel you slipping away from me now. This was supposed to *save* you!"

"You did. You did save me."

"I don't understand."

She arched her head back, looking around. "Here, this… this is not all of it. There is more."

I could only nod. "Yes. I don't understand it, but I've seen that."

"And, my lovely Rasputin, to be honest… I haven't always been the angel that you see me as."

"Oh?"

"Yeah. You don't want to know most of it."

"Um, okay."

She took a shallow breath. "Never killed anyone, but there have been times I'm not exactly proud of. Some, um, experimental years. Oh, man, like Carnival in Rio? You ever go?"

"Have you, sweetheart?" I said, trying not to weep, just happy to have a few last moments with my lovely wife.

"Oh, yes. Oh my god, yes."

"Huh, you never mentioned it."

"I won't go into it, but there was this rugby team—"

"Rugby *team*?"

She smiled at me. "A long time ago, doesn't matter. I am yours now. All yours. But before tonight, I wasn't sure that I'd leave here and go to a place of light. You changed all that, Raz." She smiled and put her lovely hand to my face, wiping away my tears. "You did save me. Tonight, you saved me."

"I... How?"

She blinked, her tired eyes rolling back for a moment. Then she said, "Well, I just blasted the Devil to back to Hell. If that don't get me into Heaven, nothing will."

I laughed and pushed damp strands of hair from her face. "Aw, he wasn't the Devil. That's dude's name is Randall."

"Naw."

"Yeah," I said. "Might be."

She smiled at me one more time, and I kissed her lips. That was the last moment in my life I felt pure joy.

With her last breath, she said: "I'm moving to a place of light and love. You'll have to be really, really good. Be incredible, sweetheart. Then we get to see each other again."

"Tall order."

"I know you can do it. I'll wait."

I kissed her gently on the lips, cradling her damp head in my arms. Then she was gone.

A moment later, the black car appeared behind me. I got in, and the Advocate held a strange-shaped, empty box toward me.

"You've screwed this up, Rasputin," he said. "Hell, have you ever! But we can salvage this. Put the lamp in here!"

Shaking my head, I instead pointed the lamp in his direction, gripping it tightly. His eyes went so big they nearly touched in the middle.

"Not yet," I said. "Get me back to New Orleans right now. Then we're done."

Rubbing his jaw, the reporter was again up on his feet.

"There you are! Hand over th—"

I clubbed him one more time and he fell, out cold, back on the ground. Again, the cameraman simply filmed our exchange, but this time he laughed softly.

Inside Angelos, Anza was crying with heaving sobs, and Uncle Jerry was now cradling the Actor's head.

She looked up at me. "Is she… Did you..?"

I smiled. "It's done. It's over. All but one thing."

Standing in front of my fallen friend, I held up the lamp. Again, it only sparked and trembled for a moment, then went dark once more.

Pure. I need purity.

At that moment, I thought only of the love I had for my Carissa. I wrapped my mind, my entire being, in the love I carried for the woman who had pulled me from my own darkness years earlier.

Then, like a drowning man taking his first breath of air, I felt something close to ecstasy, and a brilliant white light burst from the lamp, casting down upon the Actor, who bucked and shook. A moment later, the light extinguished.

Then the lamp exploded in my hands, its four parts bursting in opposite directions, rocketing straight through the walls of the building.

It was gone.

Slowly, the Actor stood and touched the center of his chest where the metal had been. Opening the red robe slightly, we saw all that was left was a crescent-moon scar on his chest the size of a quarter.

Anza hugged him tightly as Uncle Jerry fought tears and lightly patted me on the shoulder. He gave me a strange look.

"Uh, you know you got throwin' stars in your back? Pretty deep."

"Yep. Starting to really feel them right now, actually," I said and realized that my Hell contract had officially ended. I was a free man. A free man with a several throwing stars buried deep in his back. "Yep. Hurts like a mother, actually. Wow, more every second. Real, real bad."

After the Actor was finally released from Anza's embrace, he took a deep breath, looked at the three of us, and smiled.

"So, what do we do next?" he asked.

Epilogue

Alvin Stoddard twisted the ignition in the old truck again, and it slowly *runn-runn-runn-rummed* until it stopped making any noise at all.

He sat quietly with just the sound of a series of numbers warbling out of the speakers and wet flatulence coming out of the old dog in the passenger seat.

It was hot. It was always hot out at the Crossroads. He wiped his brow with his sleeve, popped his door, and slowly climbed out. Under the hood, he saw the problem. Damn near was always the same problem.

Alvin walked slowly to the bed of his truck and coughed as the dust kicked up around him. As he walked past the open door, the dog passed gas once again, then made another disgusting sound from the other end.

"Damn stupid dog."

When he rounded the bed, he stopped and could only stare. His trusty bucket of tar, all blackened on the inside from decades of use, was dry as a bone. He'd used it all up.

"When did I…?"

Then he remembered. And for just a second, he looked around to see if anyone was watching. And for just a moment, he smiled real small. Just to himself.

He then wiped the expression from his face and started walking with his empty bucket, leaving the broken-down truck and the dog behind as he went searching for more tar where the dirt met the blacktop. It was always out here. He just had to walk a ways to find it. Sometimes he'd walk for days, but in the end, it was always there.

Up ahead, he saw that place where he'd gotten it so wrong all those years ago. They both had. As he closed in on the Crossroads, he wondered if maybe she was walking the other way right now.

Alvin was doomed to walk this road for eternity. Sure, he got sent out on an errand every once in a while, but other than that, it was always just this road. Up and down. Down and up. This same damn, dusty, dry road.

She had been put on the other one. Up and down. Down and Up. But they never crossed paths.

Never.

Still, he knew that the old woman, his woman, would be walking somewhere along her road right now. In a way, that meant she was close to him.

Which was all that mattered.

Because if he ever caught sight of his woman, this former lover, even just some shimmy of her form out there in the heat, he'd take a chance and call out to her.

He'd say: "Dammit, woman, will you take back *your goddamn dog*?"

The story continues!
Pick up the sequel to *Hell inc* now on Amazon/

Hell to Pay (Hell inc Series Book 2)

Chapter One

The beer was late. Again.

Whipping through the dark streets of North Dallas, the cargo van's driver earned an impressive collection of middle fingers, horn blasts, at least one "*pendejo!*" and something yelled by a foreign driver that sounded like the Swedish Chef burning his hand on a hot iron skillet.

Delivering beer was, in theory, easy. One day soon, he was sure it would be carried out by drone trucks, but for now, it was at least a way for troubled high school dropouts to keep from stealing purses or peddling drugs. Or worse. But that was only if said beer deliverer could actually deliver said beer at a time that looked very similar to the hour and minute printed out on a clipboard somewhere else in the city.

The driver took the corner way too fast, praying there weren't any cars in the alley behind The Bar. He didn't clear the corner properly, and the van's mirror scraped along the brick, showering sparks onto a wobbly dude peeing on a wall in the dark.

"*Goddamn it*, watch out!"

"Sorry!" the driver yelled out the window for at least the tenth time in the past twenty minutes. He'd gotten lucky. If the peeing guy had been taller, he'd have taken the man's head off.

He risked a quick glance in the now spiderweb-cracked mirror to see if the dude was still upright. "Fuck," he said as he stared at the image. Strangely, the man in the alley looked squished somehow. "Now I've busted the mirror. Great."

He skidded to a stop behind the delivery bay of The Bar and reached for his door. He'd only cracked it open a few inches when it was slammed shut.

"Don't bother getting out," the bouncer said. He wore a black T-shirt with white lettering that simply read THE BAR. However, the way it stretched across the man's barrel chest made it look as if the phrase were yelling at anyone who might read it. "You're late."

The driver's fingers stung. "So was your mother." When the bouncer's beet-red face filled his side window, his indignation vanished. He added, "And look how well that turned out," tacking on a smile at the end like an exclamation point, or just a silent plea not to be beaten to death.

The bouncer didn't have to collect the kegs of beer, but he liked carrying them, one on each shoulder, because he thought it might impress the new waitress. So far, she was the only female employee who hadn't either outright rejected him or threatened police involvement.

"Hey, baby," he said after kicking the rear delivery door closed with his boot and walking deeper into the bar.

The pretty waitress reached up to the kegs and rested her hands on them, sighing. The extra bit of weight drew a soft grunt.

He kept smiling. "I ever tell you that my johnson hooks upward? Family trait. Drives the ladies wild," he said. "Uh, doesn't drive the ladies in our family wild, I mean. I don't sleep with the ladies in my family."

"Uh-huh." She pulled the rubber branded lids off each keg.

His smile fell, and he looked to a big metal door with a latched handle. "Can you at least open the cooler door for me?"

She called back, "Your dick curves upward. Use it to open the door."

Walking the short beer-and-mold-stained hallway toward the kitchen, she glanced up and saw a half dozen customers on barstools. The usual fare—students, sales reps, assorted losers. The odd one out was the strange woman in the cowboy hat.

"Hey, intern," she said, leaning against the door of the cooks' station.

A teenage boy had his arm in the oven up to his shoulder, and her voice made him jump. He dropped the extra-large Italian-style pizza, which sent his wrist banging against the top of the oven. He reflexively pulled his arm down, burning it on the bottom, then lifted it, burning the top again, then the bottom as he pulled his arm out. He dropped the metal clamp on the floor and cradled his hand.

"Poor baby," she said and blew him a kiss.

He frowned, but he thought she was so hot he would keep the memory of those puckered lips for later.

"Can you take these up to the bar?"

"I'm Cook's Assistant Two, *not* an intern. That's not my job," he said, grabbing the rubber lids. "I'll be back in one minute."

The Brazilian cook, the boy's boss, smiled wide, his dark features suddenly glowing. His words slathered with a thick accent, he said, "Make it two. Two minutes."

The waitress slipped past the assistant as he rounded the corner. He peeked back. She was already up on the counter. The cook spread her knees, pulling her tight rump toward his pelvis.

The Cook's Assistant II mumbled, "It's like he brags about the two minutes. Who brags about that?"

He passed the wait station with its double sink and disheveled piles of lazily folded napkins and noticed the dishwasher hadn't come for either of the tubs of plates, glasses, and cutlery. Both were overflowing.

"Not my job either."

A few more feet down the hallway, he stepped up onto the rubber mat and waited at the entryway. He knew better than to go in. Cooks didn't go into the bar area, and bar staff didn't go into the kitchen. Each had their own domain. They were like vampires and werewolves, except hundreds of degrees lamer.

"Cook Ass Two." A husky voice came out of the darkness. "What are you doing in my bar?"

"Not in your bar," he said, pointing at the invisible line. "Outside the bar proper." He held up the two rubber lids.

The bartender tucked his long hair behind his ears, a move the Cook's Assistant II was convinced the guy thought made him look cool. It didn't.

"Why didn't *what's-her-name*, the new waitress, bring them up?"

"She's talking with Cook."

"Talking?"

"Well," the younger man said with a slight Texas drawl, "I expect her tongue is movin'."

A shrug from the bartender. "At least you get a two-minute break out of it."

"I suppose."

"But don't sit in my bar. You stand there. And take that two minutes off your fifteen," the bartender said. "When you get back there, give the counter a Clorox rub before you do anything else."

"Gross."

The bartender nabbed the circular lids from the kid and walked to the beer taps, sliding each into a hard plastic sheath at the front of them. He then grabbed two half pitchers and pulled the taps. First came the sound of air, then hissing and a gurgling noise, then finally foam spurted from one then the other, plopping down in clumps into the rubber mat.

Staring at it made the boy's stomach turn a little.

The bartender turned back to the cook's assistant. "Maybe use two Clorox wipes."

A moment later, beer began to pour from the tap on the left, so he popped a pitcher under it, waited a few seconds, then stopped the flow. After a quick look around the bar, he shrugged and drank the very frothy beer. He stood waiting, with his fingers above the other tap, and wiped the foam from his mouth with his sleeve.

"That one's upside down." The woman's voice sounded like she'd been gargling broken glass.

He looked up. "Huh?"

"You put this one in upside down. Cain't read the name of the brew you got on offer. You gotta turn the little circle bit so it's facing the right way."

The froth turned to beer on tap two, and the bartender pulled it to a stop. Just before downing the brew in the second jug, he smiled, thinking he looked charming. He didn't. "Can you spin it the right way around for me?"

"What do I get out of the deal?"

He eyeballed her.

Ten years earlier, she must have been fine looking. Still a handsome woman, she wore a cowboy hat and western outfit. He didn't know if she was wearing spurs—he couldn't see her feet—but something told him she had a pair. Somewhere. The only makeup she wore were the pistols on either hip.

Welcome to Dallas.

"Do that for me," he said as he drained the small pitcher. "And you'll have my undying gratitude."

Her face was like tanned leather, but when she smiled, she had perfect brilliant-white teeth. "Irony, I suppose some might call that. Your choice to use that word."

"Gratitude?"

"No," she said and sipped at her shot of whiskey. "The other one."

His smile fell. "Are you meeting someone here tonight?"

"Maybe." She nodded and pulled a long knife from the inside of her coat.

He flinched slightly. She then put the tip into the rubber lid and slowly turned it.

"I heard tell he comes in here sometimes."

The barman scanned his rail—broke students, a couple of out-of-town businessmen, but from what he could pick up of their conversation, they were from Japan. No tip there either.

He didn't expect much from the woman in the cowboy hat, but one could never really tell who the big tippers were. Sometimes the weirdos had dough.

He raised his eyebrows, trying to look interested. "Friend or work colleague?"

She finished her drink and tapped her shot glass with a thick fingernail that could hammer in real nails. Impressively, it would be at least the sixth time he'd refilled the tiny glass.

As he poured the shot, he saw she was chuckling.

"What?"

"You talk real pretty, you know that?" she asked. "'Work colleague.' That get you a fair bit of tail, all that fancy speaking?"

"I don't know. I mean, I'm sorry—"

"Ah, don't worry about it now." She took a small sip. "I ain't here for you."

The tone of that sentence convinced him that he knew nothing about the woman and would prefer to know less.

She added, "But yes, he and I, uh, in a manner of speaking… are work colleagues. We both serve the same master." The woman looked at her drink. "Similar, that is."

"I know what that's like." The bartender nodded then looked around the bar, avoiding her eyes. "What's he look like? Maybe I can help you, um, find your fella."

Sip. "Pretty boy. He was on some lame TV show for a while."

"Oh?"

"And if I were a man, which I am not, he could just about blow me without kneeling down," she said and smiled a pearly-white smile.

The bartender was befuddled for a moment then looked toward the door. A man walked in, zipping his fly, stumbling slightly, and the bartender did indeed recognize him but not from TV. The kneeling bit made sense, as the guy stood at the threshold, the door slowly closing behind him.

The dwarf looked toward the bartender and offered a crooked smile.

The bartender called over, nodding toward the woman in the cowboy hat, "I think this lady here's waiting for you, man."

On the doorstep, the man's face went from a very wide, sloppy grin to a straight line. He then spun and fled, the glass in the door exploding behind him.

The Actor ran into the night.

Chapter Two

In the past year, I'd really tried to be good. Or, at least, *do* good.

Those were two very different things. An important distinction. People could be, as my friend Anza once said, "less gooder" and still do good things. Like Hitler.

I mean... ha, I can't even. I just, oh jeez, ha! I should put that on Twitter or something. I could just picture the red-faced, moist-lipped Twitterati, thumbs flapping out their disdain for me on their over-sized, King Kong, carbon foot-printing devices.

Just a bit of fun to remind me I was alive. And I was, despite some compelling evidence to the contrary. I didn't go out much. I was moderately employed. And of course, I didn't date.

My wife, she wasn't alive. She was the opposite of that. However, before she went, she did banish the Devil back to hell, so she was probably now playing beach volleyball with St. Peter.

Of course, it was *me* who found the device that let her do that. Just sayin'. For anyone keeping score. And it was hard, man. I had to travel all over the world. I had help. Uncle Jerry, our pilot, Anza, my best friend's wife—she's still illegal, as far as I know—and of course, the Actor.

Before we went our separate ways, we had one more little adventure together. Didn't go quite as planned, and we all went back to our own lives. That seemed like a lifetime ago.

I looked over at a picture of my wife and me sitting on my bed stand. Um, we weren't sitting on a bed stand in the picture, you know, the photo. That's where I had the photo.

"I'm moving to a place of light and love. You'll have to be really, really good. Be incredible, sweetheart. Then we get to see each other again."

That, it turned out, was harder than it seemed.

Sure, I could look around for lost cats—I did, didn't find any. Strangely, I lost one in the process—or give my time at the library. I was asked to leave after rearranging their fiction section so all the blue-covered books were with the other blue-covered ones, red with red, etc. It looked *amazing*. Librarians, as hot they were with their tight little bun hairdos and pencil skirts, they no likey.

For a while, I'd even volunteered at a Puerto Rican hospital after I'd stumbled across an online ad from some Christian group. That was a weird experience.

That said, despite what I'd seen, I wasn't religious. I knew there was a heaven and hell—and of course Hell inc., a takeover faction down below that was trying to dethrone the Devil—but I preferred to stay unaffiliated.

My goal in life, now of course, was to do as much good as possible so, one day, I could join my wife and we could spend eternity just hanging out. That was all I wanted, but my twenties had been some rough years. I would have to do a lot to get my ledger back in the black. To hang with Cassie, I needed my remaining years to be opal, for Chrissakes.

But that meant, of course, I had to stay on this side of the topsoil.

Going back to Atlanta, at least for a while, was out of the question.

I mentioned that my friends and I had bounced all over the globe searching for pieces of the lamp, as instructed by the Devil. I'd made a stupid pact with the fucker at the crossroads, which despite all my efforts, turned out all right.

Atlanta could no longer be my home, which I learned about ten seconds too late some months ago. When I'd landed, instead of heading back to the old house, I'd been aggressively diverted—read: kidnapped—to face a former benefactor.

The drug dealer we'd blackmailed to lend us his private jet wasn't happy about how it had been returned. He'd also been not so happy that some of his product that had been hidden on board had gone missing.

"I think that was Uncle Jerry. It helped him stay awake," I'd said, "for a few days."

In the leafy atrium of Enrique's Peachtree Battle home, he dropped theatrically into a chaise lounge. On either side of him, two large men stood looking for an excuse to hurt someone.

When I went to sit, he said, "*Aa, aa, aa!* Only I will sit during an admonishing."

"Whatever, man," I said, shifting from foot to foot. "If you're mad about the blow, talk to Uncle Jerry."

"Uncle Jerry is dead."

That was a gut punch. A moment later, I found I was sitting down despite his protestations. I'd lost track of my friend, thinking the guy was invincible. Always time to catch up. That wouldn't be the case now. "What? Dead?"

Enrique seemed to take some pleasure in my dismay. What a prick.

"He was stupid. Got into some trouble in Baja."

"*Where?*"

"Baja California. But I think Baja California Sur, not the northern part."

I couldn't believe my friend was dead. Couldn't process it.

"What happened?"

"Well," the drug dealer said, stroking his chin. "I think the people of southern Baja were tired of being governed by those in the north. Two entirely different areas, and the governor, he didn't—"

"No, man! What happened to Uncle Jerry?"

He stopped stroking. "He did what Uncle Jerry do. He made the wrong people mad."

"Jesus."

"Which is what you've done. With me."

"You are my wrong people?"

"That's correct," he said, his robe flapping open, and I was treated to an image that I would take a lot of drinking to delete from my memory. "And it's not like you made your neighbor in the next trailer angry because your dog was barking at the moon all night. No. They might call the *policia* or maybe poop in your Walmart barbecue grill."

"Right."

"Me," Enrique said, standing over me. I kept my eyes off the robe flap. "I kill the dog."

I was still shaken, the world spinning around me. "Wait," I said. "You're going to kill my dog?"

"No, that is not—"

"I don't have a dog. There was a squirrel that would come by sometimes and eat out of the bird feeder. It was for the birds, but he would hop up there. Birds stopped coming around, so we just made it a squirrel feeder."

"Fine, fine! I kill the squirrel."

"You're going to kill a squirrel?"

"NO! You're not listening," he said, spun around, and plopped back into his chair. He grabbed his drink, pushed the tiny umbrella aside, and took a long draw from his straw. "According to my accountant, you owe me one hundred seventy-four thousand two hundred and seventeen dollars."

"Would you take a check?"

"No!" he said then thought a moment. "Nobody uses checks anymore, *pendejo*! You have twenty-four hours to get me my money. If you don't, I'll have you killed."

I swallowed hard. "Is that before or after you kill the dog and squirrel?"

He then shouted a long string of Spanish at me—despite being, as I knew, from Bakersfield—and I got the hell out of there.

That had been about eight months ago. And of course, that was significantly longer than the twenty-four hours I'd been given.

Since returning to the US, my "to-do" list had grown.

1. Pay Enrique $174, 217.

2. Do many good things so that when I die, I can join Cassie.

If I didn't do number one quickly, I would have no time to do the second one. And that was the one that mattered to me. However, that kind of cash wasn't easy to come up with.

I pulled out my phone and thumbed my bank account app. It read, *$243.17.*

I had a ways to go.

As I sat there in my North Dallas duplex, feeling sorry for myself, it took me a moment to finally hear the knocking. Slowly, I eased out of bed and went to the door, but then I froze for a moment. Knocks at my door weren't uncommon after a recent entrepreneurial enterprise of mine had just started to take off. But mulling over my debt to the "wrong people," I was suddenly spooked.

I looked down at my hand on the door handle.

What if Enrique found me?

I looked out the peephole and saw nobody there. Someone was messing with me.

Then, another knock. This time louder, more forceful.

Again, I looked out the peephole. No one. I tried to see left then right through the tiny fish-eye lens. Then slowly, rising into view, I saw a hand with the middle finger raised.

Cracking open the door, I looked down.

"Hey, Raz," the Actor said.

* * *

I had been living in the unfinished duplex that I'd rented cheaply because the previous tenants had been methheads who'd left the place a mess. Tiny holes speckled the walls where they'd put incense to cover the smell. They'd probably been cooking the stuff.

"Nice place," he said and sauntered in, plopping down on my couch.

My mouth hung open for a moment.

He stared at me with a weak smile. "Nice to see you too."

"What?" I asked, stammering slightly. "H-how?"

The Actor swiveled his head around and took in the room. "You've done well for yourself, I see. No TV, no chairs. Is that a bloodstain on the carpet?"

"Uh," I said, closing the door and locking it. I sat on the other end of the couch. "Dog vomit, I think."

"You got a dog?" he asked then muttered, "That might be handy."

"Huh? No, no dog," I said dreamily. "I sort of had a squirrel for a while."

"What?"

"But there's a good chance it's been assassinated."

The Actor pulled his eyebrows together, frowning. "What are…?" he started then shook his head. "Don't care. Do you have anything to eat? I'm starving."

I started to get up then turned back toward him. "How did you know I was here?"

He smiled at me. "'Bring Back the King.'"

Ah.

After the Actor's show had been canceled, one night, when I was drunk, I'd created a Kickstarter campaign to bring his character back with his own show. I'd raised just over twelve hundred bucks. Not enough to pay for a pilot, so I'd put that very small nest egg into starting my little businesses in North Dallas.

"Sorry you got killed off," I said, walking toward the kitchen.

"I *wasn't* killed off," he said. "I killed everyone else. Bloodbath." He shrugged and laid his head back on the armrest of the couch. "Show over."

Cracking the fridge open, I tried to find something to eat amongst the litany of brown bottles.

"I see you ditched the little pink robe," I said.

"*Red* robe," he said. "I had it enshrined. To remind me of my bravery and valor."

"Uh-huh," I said. Giving up on the food, I grabbed two brown bottles and returned to the couch. "You still didn't explain how you found me."

He pointed at the bottles in my hand. "Do I get one of those, or are you drinking both?"

I handed him one.

He said, "You shot your little fund-raising video outside a construction site." He dropped his chin to his chest and quoted me. "'This is where we'll film the series, but I need your money, my lords and ladies, to finish the project.' Pathetic."

"Whatever."

"You can even see in the video the placard in the background where it says it's the ground-breaking for a day care."

I shrugged. "It... I mean, it was initially all in good faith."

"How initially?"

I popped open the home brew. "When I first turned on the library's computer to make the Kickstarter account." I took a sip and frowned. "After that it... well, I sorta needed the money."

"Uh-huh." He tried to twist the cap. "Ow!"

I grabbed it from him, opened it, and handed it back. I pointed at the bottle. "Started my own label. Ready to make my fortune."

He took a sip and smacked his lips. "This is horrible. You won't be able to do that."

"It's fourteen percent alcohol and infused with THC."

He shrugged. "You might be able to do that."

"Maybe. Just keep it away from open flames." I sipped the horrible brew. "So, I assume this isn't a pleasure visit."

He took another long swig then rolled the bottle in his tiny fingers. "I kind of fucked up, Rasputin."

"Figured that."

"Actually, it's kind of your fault. So, I was hoping, you know, maybe since I helped you out before..."

"*My* fault?" I asked, then a glimmer of realization hit me. "Oh Jesus. What did you do?"

He stood again, pacing the room. He kept his voice even, but I caught him glancing out the window once or twice.

"Listen, it's not easy for a guy like me to get work in this industry."

"Because you can't act?"

"Fuck you."

I laughed. "No, man, I'm kidding. Actually, I thought you were really good in the one with the train."

He sighed. "Everyone likes the train one."

"Fine. Get another train movie."

"Actually." His eyes went distant for a moment. "I did get offered a sort of train movie."

"Cool. Do that one."

"Except a different, um, kind of train. An adult feature."

"Right."

"And I would be somewhere between the diner car and the caboose."

"Christ, don't ever tell me about that again, 'kay?"

He glanced at the door then quickly sat down. "Listen, I'm in real trouble, man."

"We all got problems." Mine was a deranged drug dealer with a pedantic accountant and a homicidal dislike of nut-addled tree rodents.

He looked at his finger and put the slight cut from the bottle cap into his mouth for a moment. "My contract was supposed to make me king. King of Hollywood. Like the next, I dunno, Brad Pitt or Tom Cruise."

"How's that working out for you?"

"Not so good."

I shrugged, took another sip, and shivered from it. "Then get a better agent."

Slowly, he shook his head.

"What?"

"Not that kind of contract."

Oh shit. "What did you do?"

He stood and paced again. "Well, it worked for you. Kinda."

"What did you do, man?"

He stopped and turned to me, his eyes wide, red rimmed. "I went to the crossroads."

"Oh, fuck no."

"Oh, fuck yes."

"Why?"

"After the show ended, I thought I'd have loads of offers! But it was drier than Justin Bieber's panties at an art gallery."

Gross.

"So I made a deal."

"What did you do?"

He came over and kneeled in front of me. "You've got to help me."

"How?"

"I've got an ironclad contract with the Devil. It didn't work out."

"They never really do."

"I know that now," he said. "You've got to help me!"

"Jesus, man," I said, my eyes moving toward the door. "Holy shit, man. Can you, I dunno, get out of it?"

He took my hands in his. They were shaking. "There's no way to get out of it. I've checked. Had a half dozen lawyers look at it."

"They can read hell contracts?"

"Not a problem, most work for hell already."

"Figures," I said and started to take a sip of my beer, but he reached up and pulled the bottle back down.

He looked me in the eyes. "You've got to help me steal my contract back from the Devil."

Chapter Three

I felt sick.

But in truth, that could have been blamed, in part, on my shitty beer.

For the next few minutes, I told the Actor about the Sword of Damocles swinging over my head. Except it was a Honduran drug dealer instead of that Damocles guy, and the sword was more likely a large-caliber semiauto.

I had a massive pile of cash to raise before he found me, or I was dead, and I had no idea how I was going to come up with that kind of money.

"Maybe," the Actor said, rubbing his three-day-old beard, "we can do this so both of our problems are solved."

"What?" I sat up, interested for the first time. "How?"

"Well, all we need to do is somehow find out where hell keeps its records. You said you dealt with his chief council, the advocate… it could be that that guy has them. Or at least knows where they might be."

"Okay."

"So we find out, bust in, find my contract, and hightail it out, burn the contract in a fire and roast marshmallows over it, man!" He punched the air, excited.

I stared at him. "How does that help me raise a hundred seventy thousand bucks to stop Enrique from killing me?"

The Actor froze midair-punch. "I dunno. I was just kinda focused on my part. That other stuff doesn't worry me so much."

"Thanks."

"You know what I mean," he said. "Come on. I helped you on a deadly moronic quest that was none of my business. I'm just asking you to do the same."

"You were *compelled* to help. You had to!"

"Same diff," he said. "Except it's more important this time."

"Why?"

"Because now it's about me."

I couldn't help but like the guy, but it never took long to remember why he made me want to repeatedly punch him in the face. Still, on the surface, he always played a hard-out, selfish prick. I knew that deep beneath, he had a heart. I'd seen it. And I owed him. He was right about that.

"Okay."

He stared at me for a moment, like I'd told a joke but was waiting to whip out the punch line. After a moment, he asked, "'Okay' what?"

"Okay," I said and stood. I finished my beer, fought off a brief wave of vomit, then threw the bottle into the corner. It bounced and landed next to the couch. "I'll help you."

"Really?"

"Yes, really," I said then sat back down. "But we need a plan. A good plan."

For the first time since he'd walked through my door, he gave me a real smile. He nodded and took another sip of his beer. "Good. Good."

He then threw his beer bottle where I had, and it shattered, spewing the brew all down the wall and across the stained carpet. I heard sizzling as the fibers began to curl. I would have to work a bit on the formula.

"That's actually not bad," he said. "Mind if I have another?"

"You didn't finish the first one, man," I said, pointing at the carpet, which appeared to be smoking slightly.

"New thing," he said and crossed behind the couch to the fridge.

I heard clinking behind me.

"I'm trying to cut down on my drinking, so I never finish a whole one." He handed me a bottle over my shoulder and sat back down. "Not quite on the wagon, not quite off. So, I call it 'half wagon.'"

"You should write a self-help book," I said and opened my beer.

"Yeah?" he asked, eyes unfocused again.

I grabbed his bottle, opened it, and handed it back.

One more time, I saw his eyes flit to the door. "Well, I was drunk when I made my deal, so I guess this is me trying to do better."

That gave me a thought. "Isn't that a factor in getting out of your contract? You know, impaired or something so you were in no condition to make a deal?"

"If that were the case," he said, slugging his beer, "Hollywood would go dark."

"Okay," I said and sighed. "We need a plan, but—" I sipped from my own bottle. "Plans are hard."

"Check," he said, drinking deeply again.

"But I have an idea."

He burped and said, "I'm all ears," and again threw his bottle to the wall, but that time it bounced and flew back toward him fast.

Two things happened. First, despite the brown bottle rocketing back directly, *impressively*, toward his melon, it missed. Second, it missed because it exploded in midair, sending brown glass and shitty beer raining down onto us. I supposed I could accept that it was really only one thing that happened.

The thick glass of the bottle had apparently been made virtually wallproof, however it seemed to be susceptible to, *what, dust mites?*

"What the hell just happened?" I started to laugh, but as the Actor dove behind the couch, that vocalization died somewhere behind my teeth. Looking up at the window, I saw a woman there.

She was dressed like she'd just stepped out of a saloon from a hundred fifty years ago. Her two were pistols raised, and with the Actor no longer in her sights, she turned them toward me.

I rolled and went over the back of the couch, landing on the Actor.

"Fuck!"

"Sorry, man. There was no—"

"No, *her*!" he said and slipped from beneath me. On all fours, I watched as he crept toward the side of the couch. "Shit, shit, shit!"

"What is going on?"

The Actor peeked around the corner of the single piece of furniture in the room, snapping his head back as two more shots rang out.

One embedded into the couch, the other the drywall behind us, spitting out white chalky grit.

"She found me," he whispered, eyes bouncing around the room. "She's relentless. Like the terminator. Except she can't be killed and she never sleeps!"

"Dude, that's actually exactly like the terminator." I flattened my back against the sofa. "Who is she?"

His eyes wild, he let his mouth hang open for a moment before the word rolled out. "Sally."

I paused. "I'm going to need a bit more to go on."

Above us, one of the recessed lights became an ex-light, raining more glass upon us.

The Actor said, "She's a sort of, um, contract negotiator."

"What does th… wait, she works for the Devil?"

He nodded like he was having a seizure.

"What does she want?"

Three more lights above us exploded, and we covered our heads. We were surrounded by a white-sand beach of glittering glass.

"My contract was supposed to make me 'king of Hollywood,' right? Well, stupid, I was made king but in the storyline of my *show*. The Devil's part is done, so," he said, getting back on his hands and knees, "collection time."

"She kills you, and you go work for the Old Man?"

"Yes, something like that. I think."

"Why doesn't he just wait? The way you live, you'll be dead in ten years."

"Because there is a prophecy that says I am the one," the Actor said. "The one who will one day kill the Prince of Darkness."

I stared at him for a long moment.

"Bullshit."

Two more lights above us exploded.

He said, "Of course that's bullshit." He began to pull off his shirt. "He wants me dead, so I join the ranks—to be a slave and tortured or maybe do community theater, which would be a bit of both."

"We've got to get out of here," I said, eyeballing the kitchen. It would be a tough crawl, and we would likely be exposed for a second or two. Plenty of time for Sally, the shooter, to put slugs in both of us. "If we can crawl to the kitchen, it's about five steps to the back door, maybe seven for you."

"Fuck you."

"No, fuck *you*, man." I watched him put his shirt under his knees and reluctantly pulled mine off as well. "You could have warned me you were bringing some nineteenth-century gunslinger to my door!"

He frowned. "I think she's eighteenth century."

I peeked between a couple of dirty cushions.

Cowboy hat, dirty-blond hair twisted into a braid that draped over her shoulder. She wore a brown vest over dark denim jeans and a pair of black leather chaps.

"No, man, she doesn't look, I dunno, all colonial times or anything. Definitely mid- or late-eighteen hundreds."

"Right, *eighteenth* century!"

"That's nineteenth. It gets confusing because seventeen hundreds is actually eighteenth, eighteen hundreds is nineteenth," I said in a low, panicked whisper. "But you have to count the first century, which is actually zero through one hundred."

"Ugh, confusing."

"Right?"

Both of us sat bare-chested on our shirts. I nodded for him to grab the couch at the bottom. Slowly, we scooted our knees and pulled the massive piece of ancient furniture backward, toward the kitchen door.

As we did, another couple of rounds hit the cushions. Feathers filled the air, which was a concern because it was a foam couch.

Sally had laid glass all around us, but with the shirts beneath our knees, we could slowly scoot back, using the couch as a shield, without getting cut.

"Jesus, I think she's in the house," the Actor hissed.

"I locked the door," I said. "That should give us an extra minute."

The Actor looked over at me and scowled. "You have man titties, man."

"Shut up."

"And you look like you're wearing a sweater," he said. "A sad brown sweater full of sad little holes."

"Really? That's what you want to talk about *now*?" I looked at him. "Christ, do you shave your chest?"

"No, of course not," he said. "I have other people do that."

"Ugh," I said. "Maybe you already work for Satan."

The Actor looked at me and smiled slowly. "You missed me, didn't you?"

I raised my elbow and looked back. We were nearly at the door to the kitchen and home free. Safe.

That's when I heard a click, and the front door handle turn. She was coming inside.

"New plan," I said, jumping up. "Let's run!"

"I thought you said you locked it!"

"Run, man!"

To avoid the remaining glass, we both jumped, landing in the kitchen, rolling end over end and banging into each other.

Sally came through the door, both pistols held high. She pointed at us, and I put my hand out and flung the refrigerator door wide open.

Thwack, thwack!

I definitely wasn't getting my deposit back.

Seconds later, we were out the door, running through the backyard.

Continue reading by picking up Hell to Pay on Amazon

Made in the USA
Monee, IL
05 February 2024

52962291R00256